Readers love CONNIE BAILEY

Song and Key

"*Song and Key* is a mash-up of the contemporary and paranormal, with romance and a dash of mystery to please every fan."

—The Skiffy and Fanty Show

Finding Family

"If you are looking for a captivating sweet romance with a touch of mystery, and like stories where the kids have a good part I recommend this."

—TTC Books and More

"…it was an adorably sweet, men with children plotline that I enjoyed. Everything was practically perfect in every way, but it wasn't annoyingly so."

—The Novel Approach

By CONNIE BAILEY

The Bastard's Pearl
A Case of Mistaken Virginity
Catman's Reward
Frozen Fire
Golden
Human After All
Initiation
Insert Here
Kaji Sukoshi & The Shining One
Miles to Go
Moonlight, Tiger, and Smoke
Ragged Dick
The Raw Prawn
Return of the Sun
Revenant
Rusty American Dream
Serendipity Kit
Smoky
Something for Nothing
Suspension of Disbelief
Table for One
Thoroughbred
Three Wise Men
True Blue
Until It's Time to Go

DREAMSPUN BEYOND
With Alix Bekins: Song and Key

DREAMSPUN DESIRES
Finding Family

Published by DREAMSPINNER PRESS
www.dreamspinnerpress.com

Connie Bailey

FROZEN FIRE

Published by

DREAMSPINNER PRESS

5032 Capital Circle SW, Suite 2, PMB# 279, Tallahassee, FL 32305-7886 USA
www.dreamspinnerpress.com

Frozen Fire
© 2022 Connie Bailey

Cover Art
© 2022 Jenny Eickbush
http://www.jennyeickbush.com
Cover content is for illustrative purposes only and any person depicted on the cover is a model.

Trade Paperback ISBN: 978-1-64405-981-4
Digital ISBN: 978-1-64405-980-7
Trade Paperback published March 2022
v. 1.0

Printed in the United States of America
∞
This paper meets the requirements of
ANSI/NISO Z39.48-1992 (Permanence of Paper).

Chapter One

JULIAN PARRY waved as his parents drove away from Heathrow Airport in their elderly Jaguar. Though they often made him feel nine rather than nineteen, he would miss them while he was in America. However, no amount of incipient homesickness could dull the excitement of his first trip across the Atlantic. He turned to say something to his dance instructor, but Kelly Holloway was engrossed in a conversation with his partner, Alexandru "Sasha" Vasile.

As always, though they'd known each other for a decade, Jule was struck by what an odd pair his coach and his coach's partner were. Sasha's warm personality, compact build, ruddy coloring, high, square cheekbones, and mane of dark hair were a sharp contrast to Kelly's cool composure, clean-cut blondness, and angular Scandinavian features. But good looks were the least of their good qualities. They had been his teachers, friends, and surrogate uncles, supporting him every step of the way in his mission to become a premier danseur. Without them, he might still be a good dancer, but he doubted he'd be about to board a jet bound for the US and the New York City Ballet. Filled with a pleasant sense of anticipation, Jule stayed awake for the entire eight-hour flight across the Atlantic. He was a little nervous, but he'd had a lot of practice in calming himself before a performance. He'd learned to enjoy the stirring feeling, to let it energize him and sharpen his focus instead of paralyzing him. When they landed in New York, he didn't feel tired at all, just eager for whatever came next.

Next was a sensory-overload cab ride from LaGuardia International to a suite at Manhattan's Marriot Marquis hotel. Suitcases were unpacked, the view marveled at, the adjoining rooms explored, and the room service menu found.

"It's still hard to believe we're actually in New York," Jule said about twenty minutes later. "But here I am eating a cheeseburger with a view of Times Square."

"Don't get used to it," Sasha said darkly. "The calories, I mean, not the view."

"I know," Jule said as he continued to gaze out the window.

It was night now, but there was no darkness in Times Square. Every building pulsed with light, displaying words and images both moving and static. Jule focused on the advertisements for Broadway plays. He didn't see anything promoting an upcoming ballet, but he was going to change that. There was no reason a dance production couldn't be as popular as a play or film. People just needed more exposure to it, and he was going to—The ringing of the room phone jarred him from his thoughts.

Kelly answered. "Holloway," he said tersely. His face went still as he listened to the caller. After a few moments, he said, "Sure. Why not?"

Sasha frowned at Kelly's tone. "Who was that?"

"Downes. Mr. 3-D himself."

Jule turned to stare at Kelly. He knew that name, but it was insane to think David Dulac Downes, director of The Downtown Ballet—the company Jule secretly wanted to join—was on the phone.

"What did *he* want?" Sasha asked, his tone making it clear it couldn't be anything good.

"Would you believe he wants to talk to Jule about joining The Downtown Ballet Company?"

"What?" Jule exclaimed. This couldn't really be happening. He had to be dreaming.

Sasha frowned. "Why didn't you just tell him Jule is going to join the New York City Ballet?"

"He's in the hotel. Wants to take us out for drinks or whatever," Kelly said without answering Sasha's question.

"To which you said, 'Sure, why not?'" Sasha shook his head.

"We'll run into him eventually. Might as well get it over with."

Sasha noticed Jule paying rapt attention to the conversation. He gave Kelly a significant look.

Kelly glanced at Jule. "Do you want to change into something fresh?"

Jule bolted into the adjoining room. As he quickly dressed, he tried to keep his thoughts in line, but he wasn't as successful as he usually was. The notion that he'd be face-to-face with the man he'd recently come to admire was as exciting as visiting a new country. He was devoted to ballet and revered the classics, but he was drawn to the innovation and passion that were evident in videos of Mr. Downes' original ballets. If anyone was going to make ballet accessible, it was David Downes.

"YOU SURE about this?" Sasha asked Kelly.

He knew what was bothering Kelly. He knew the courage it had taken to leave their English haven and return to New York. He also knew the strength of Kelly's belief in Jule's talent and his determination to see the lad succeed, a determination he shared.

Sasha knew neither he nor Kelly would falter, because they were doing this for Jule. For the boy who had become a son to them—a couple who'd never dared hope for children. Only for Jule or Kelly would Sasha be willing to come back to this world of contrasts so sharp they could leave scars on your soul. It was a world of beauty and cruelty, where the effortless grace of a dancer's leap was bolstered by hours of brutal practice, where refined manners hid cutthroat politics, and smiles were a baring of teeth. Sasha had been happy to leave it behind, but not once did he consider letting his beloved or the child of his heart come here without him.

"Yep. Like you said, *I* left this world. I'm back on my own terms, and I can walk away again whenever I want. And I really do think it's better to get this over with and get on with what we came here to do."

Sasha snorted. "We've been working toward this since Jule was ten. I think we're ready."

"I think *he's* ready." Kelly met Sasha's gaze. "What if *I'm* not? He depends on me."

"And *you* can depend on me, but don't worry, you're ready." Sasha crossed the short space that separated them and put his arms around Kelly. "I came with you to remind you of that."

"I hope you're right. I really do."

"It's been ten years, my heart. And it's not as if you're *crawling* back. You left that world. It didn't leave you." Sasha held him tighter before letting him go. "You can handle it."

"God, I'm glad you're with us."

"You think for a minute I'd let you walk into this snake pit alone?"

"Whoa." Kelly grinned. "Harsh."

"I made you smile, though."

"Well, you have a gift, lover." Kelly leaned in to kiss Sasha.

Sasha smiled. "Good. Would you mind if I stay here for a while? I'd like to have a nap on something that isn't moving."

Kelly cocked his head to the side. "You sure?"

"Yes. I didn't think I had caught the jet lag, but it's catching me. I'll try to join you later. Someone has to keep an eye on our boy while David has you distracted."

"Should I say hi to David for you?"

"I would never allow you to speak for me," Sasha said in mock-outrage.

Kelly laughed and then turned as Jule came back in.

Sasha approached Jule. "You should take your coat in case you leave the hotel."

"I don't want to carry it. If we leave, I'll come back up for it."

"As you wish." Sasha ran his hands over the shoulders of Jule's sports coat, smoothing the material. "You look very handsome, by the way."

Jule rolled his eyes.

"Come on, let's go so Sasha can get his beauty sleep," Kelly said.

"You're not coming?"

Sasha smiled at Jule. "I'm a little tired. Go meet David. It will be an experience, I promise you." He winked.

"You know him?" Jule looked from Sasha to Kelly.

"From a long time ago," Kelly said dismissively. "Let's go."

THEY TOOK the elevator to the eighth floor and stepped out into the aptly named Broadway Lounge. Through the big windows, Jule could see the neon lights of the theater marquees near Times Square. Next to the hostess station, a man rose from a lobby chair, pulling Jule's attention away from the scenery. He watched the stranger fix his large, dark eyes on Kelly, push his fingers through a thick, wavy mop of salt-and-pepper hair, and adjust the cashmere topcoat that hung from his shoulders like a cape. With the famous New York night sky as his backdrop, he looked as glamorous to Jule as a movie star from the silver screen's Golden Age.

"Kelly Holloway. Mr. Perfect," he called out. "Can it really be you?"

Kelly moved toward him. "David," he murmured coolly as he took the hand David held out.

"*Je n'y crois pas!*" David took a step back and looked Kelly up and down. "You haven't changed. You still look like Prince Charming on Christmas break from Harvard."

"You grew a beard."

"Isn't it dashing?" David stroked the silky goatee and mustache combination. "When you're still getting carded at thirty, it's time to do something about it. *Très élégant,* no?"

"Satanic is the word that comes to mind," Kelly said. "And you're forty-two."

"Thank you." David looked more pleased than insulted. He turned his potent gaze on Jule. "You must be Julian Parry."

"Yes, sir, but no one calls me Julian. It's just Jule." Jule offered his hand, though he was a little confused by Kelly's stiffness toward David.

"I'm very glad to meet you," David said, maintaining eye contact. "I've heard good things from my friends in London."

Jule was sure his shock showed clearly on his face.

"What? You don't think word gets around?" David smiled as he relinquished Jule's hand. "You've been noticed!"

"I hope that's a good thing," Jule said. He was a little overwhelmed, not only by David's words, but by the man's sheer magnitude of presence. He was larger than life, in constant motion, exuding energy like a small sun, the opposite of Kelly's rock-solid composure.

David chuckled. "It's a *very* good thing. Now, let's go talk over a drink."

"I'll get a table," Kelly said.

"Already taken care of," David replied. He made a sweeping bow that should have looked ridiculous but didn't, at all. "This way."

David led them to a curved banquette with a view of the Square. As he approached the table, a young man and woman stood up to greet him.

Jule tried not to stare, but both were astonishingly attractive. She was petite with an hourglass figure shown to advantage in an ice-blue, strapless cocktail dress. Her waves of red-gold hair framed a heart-shaped face with ivory skin and jade-green eyes. Her companion was as tall as Kelly's six feet and two inches, and he had short chestnut hair and warm brown eyes. The dark umber designer suit he wore was sharply tailored to accent his broad shoulders and long legs. Either one of these glamorous strangers would have looked right at home in an ad for an expensive cologne. New York was turning out to be as stylish and cool as Jule had imagined.

"Since you showed me yours, it's only fair I show you mine," David said drolly. "Charlotte Navarre and Lucas Madding, my *prima* and *primo*, my stars."

Charlotte and Lucas said hello, handshakes all around, and sat back down. A member of the waitstaff arrived and took orders.

"Water?" Charlotte remarked on Jule's request. "Come on. Live a little."

"It's *sparkling* water," Jule said.

Charlotte laughed. "You're cute. Here, try my Cosmo."

Ever polite, Jule sipped the pink drink. "That's actually very nice," he said as he handed it back. "But I'm not twenty-one."

"The rules don't apply to this table," David said. "I've declared it a sovereign territory."

"You haven't changed a bit either," Kelly said.

"Thank you." David managed to bow from a sitting position. "Want to change your order?" he asked Jule.

"Well… I do fancy a beer. Eighteen is legal in the UK, you know."

David hailed a waiter and ordered a local brew. "It's your first night in New York," he said. "You have to celebrate."

"So far, I've seen the airport, the streets from a taxi window, and this hotel, which was all impressive." Jule said. "I can't wait to see more."

"It's only the greatest city in the world," David said. "I hope you like it enough to make it your home."

"That's the plan," Kelly interjected. "Jule has an audition for the NYCB tomorrow."

"Does he now? Classy," David said knowingly. "I wish you the best of luck with that."

"Do you now?" Kelly said in the same tone David had used.

Before David could respond, the waiter returned with Jule's beer. As Jule was raising the bottle to his lips, it was plucked from his hand. He looked up and saw Sasha standing over him.

Sasha addressed the waiter. "Please bring us vodka and grapefruit juice," he said.

"Sasha!" David exclaimed as he stood to shake Sasha's hand. "It's good to see you."

"If you say so." Sasha's expression was wary as he sat on the banquette in the space Kelly made for him. He took a long swallow of the beer before setting the bottle down. "Very tasty," he said. "You would like this brew, Jule."

"Mate," Jule said reproachfully.

"No beer for you," Sasha said firmly. "I let you out of my sight for five minutes and you're breaking the rules already."

"One beer," Jule said plaintively.

"Too many calories. You will have vodka with grapefruit juice. Case is closed," Sasha said. He glanced around the table. "Who are these two charming young people?" he asked.

Lucas and Charlotte introduced themselves.

"It's a pleasure to meet you," Charlotte told Sasha. "I had a huge crush on you when I was twelve. When you left the Romanian National Ballet, I cut a photo of you out of *People* magazine and taped it to my bedroom wall."

"I'm flattered, obviously," Sasha said.

"My mom started taking me to dance lessons when I was six, but you made me *want* to be a ballerina. I was devastated when you retired."

Sasha raised expressive eyebrows.

"Because it shattered my dream of partnering you some day," Charlotte explained.

"So very flattered." Sasha put a hand on his heart and smiled warmly at her.

"My dreams were crushed too," Lucas said. "If anyone cares."

Jule chuckled, and Lucas turned to smile at him. Jule felt a sweet spasm at his core that released a warm tide into his bloodstream, sped up his heartbeat, and brought a blush to his cheeks. He was surprised by Lucas's interest and then anxious about his response to it. What an inconvenient time to start feeling those mysterious things people sang about in love songs. He looked quickly away from Lucas and instantly felt foolish. He took a big swallow of his drink to cover his unaccustomed nervousness.

Kelly turned to David. "What did you want to talk about?" he asked.

David glanced at Charlotte before he answered. "Just some boring business."

"Ugh, business talk," Charlotte said loudly.

Lucas stood. "If you bosses are going to talk business, us young'uns are going next door to the club." He offered his arm to Charlotte. "You too," he said when Jule remained seated.

Jule looked to Kelly.

"Let the kids have some fun," David said. "The club is right in the hotel."

Sasha nudged Kelly.

"Go ahead," Kelly said to Jule. "This shouldn't take long. We'll come get you when we're done here."

Charlotte smiled at Jule over her shoulder. "Come on. It'll be fun. I promise."

Having been given permission, Jule saw no reason not to enjoy himself.

As THEY walked into the club, Charlotte declared that the song playing was her favorite and pulled Jule onto the dance floor. She was pleasantly surprised when it quickly became evident that Jule could dance to something other than classical music. When the song ended, Charlotte fanned her face and pretended to be out of breath.

"Would you get me a glass of water, please?" she asked.

"Of course."

While Jule went to the bar, Charlotte joined Lucas at the table. "Hey, boy."

"What's the story, girl?"

She leaned toward Lucas. "You're up, killer," she said over the music.

Lucas glanced over at Jule, who was still waiting at the bar. "Nothing?"

"Not a single spark. That boy is either gay or a robot."

"If he can resist you, I have to concur. You showed him the sights, right?"

"I gave him the guided tour," Charlotte said. "If he could have seen any farther down my dress, he'd know I waxed for the occasion." She smiled. "He's a dreamy dancer but a complete gentleman, therefore gay."

"Maybe I can get him to forget his manners."

"Give it your best shot."

"Girl, I got this."

"Here he comes," she said as Jule approached the table.

"HERE YOU are," Jule said as he set a glass of ice water in front of Charlotte.

Lucas stood as another song started. "Ready for another dance?" he asked Jule.

"You and me? Are you serious?"

"Absolutely. No one will care. This is New York." Lucas paused. "You're not a homophobe, are you?"

"No!"

"Go on," Charlotte said. "I'm going to catch my breath."

Jule followed Lucas back to the dance floor. He was hesitant at first, but Lucas was clearly having such a good time that Jule forgot to be self-conscious. He was actually having fun by the time the song ended. A slow song came on next and Jule started to walk off the dance floor, but Lucas grabbed his hand and pulled him back. Before Jule could react, he was in Lucas's arms, chest-to-chest with him.

The rush of heat that threatened to melt Jule's bones made him feel dizzy. Automatically, he followed Lucas through a few steps of a slow waltz as the effect of Lucas's touch grew on him. He'd felt attracted to a few of the men and boys he'd known—including a brief, embarrassing infatuation with Sasha—but that vague heat was nothing like the lava currently running through his veins. The notion that he might actually catch fire didn't seem at all ridiculous.

"Everything okay?" Lucas asked.

Startled by the question, Jule stammered a little. "What? Yes. Fine. Lovely. Why?"

"You have such a weird look on your face. It's cute and all, but I have to wonder what you're thinking."

Jule swallowed, unsure what to do or say. He'd had sudden erections before, but never while he was dancing with someone. Then again, he'd only danced with girls before. He was afraid Lucas would realize he was turned on and be disgusted with him. "Maybe it's jet lag?"

When Lucas slid a hand down to Jule's lower back and pulled him closer, Jule was sure Lucas could feel the hard evidence that he was aroused. He was right.

"Oh my," Lucas purred. "Does dancing always get you this excited?"

"This is so embarrassing," Jule said.

"Not for me it isn't." Lucas grinned. "I take it as a compliment."

Jule stared at him in surprise.

"If this is too uncomfortable for you, we can stop," Lucas said.

"I just—I don't want to offend you."

"We already covered that." Lucas looked into Jule's eyes. "Has this never happened to you?"

"Well, yeah, but not, you know...." Jule's voice trailed off.

"No, I don't know, but I'm getting the feeling you don't have a lot of experience, you know, sexwise." Lucas smiled. "Have you ever been on a date?"

Jule shook his head. "I don't have time for that."

"Well, that is a disgrace, and I won't stand for it. One way or another, I'm taking you out while you're in New York."

"I don't think—"

"Hush." Lucas put a finger to Jule's lips. "You don't have to think. I'll take care of everything."

Jule's lips tingled, and he could still feel the warmth of Lucas's finger after it was gone. For some reason, Lucas's touch scrambled his thoughts. "I want to sit down," he said.

"What's the matter?"

"It's too embarrassing, really."

"Jule, just stop. I don't care that you're turned on. In fact, I'm *thrilled* you're turned on."

"Why?"

"Because you turn me on."

"What?"

"Why so surprised?" Lucas stopped dancing. "Tell me the truth. Have you ever even kissed anyone?"

Jule shook his head. "And now I'm more embarrassed than I've ever been in my life."

"Don't be. I'm betting you've dedicated every waking hour to ballet since you could walk."

"Close." Jule smiled. "I had schoolwork as well."

"And we're smiling again. Excellent. So, you haven't had time for a love life, but you do want one, right?"

"Well, sure, someday."

"How about today?"

Jule looked up at Lucas in confusion.

"Am I moving too fast?" Lucas asked.

"I have no idea. I don't really know what you're on about, so I can't tell if you're fast or slow."

"I am *never* slow," Lucas said.

"I'm not trying to be rude."

"Okay," Lucas said as the song ended. "I can see you're confused, and why not? Clearly, this is all new to you. So why don't you put yourself in my hands, and I'll guide you through it."

"Through what?"

"Sex, of course. Isn't that what we've been discussing?"

"Oh. Then yes, you're too fast."

The next song started playing and Lucas chuckled. "We should either start dancing again or get off the floor. People are starting to stare."

Unsure what to do, Jule went default mode. "I think I should go find Kelly."

"If you want, but I think we're getting along just fine without him." Lucas gave Jule a warm smile.

Jule made a conscious effort to compose himself. He'd had a lot of practice and was pretty good at it, so he was surprised how hard it was to ignore his reaction to Lucas.

"Come on." Lucas took Jule's hand and led him off the dance floor.

Charlotte smiled at Jule and Lucas as they returned to the table. "You looked so cute dancing together! I'm totally jealous."

"Take it easy on the rookie," Lucas said.

Charlotte pouted a little. "Do you want me to stop teasing you, Jule?"

"I didn't know you were."

Lucas and Charlotte laughed.

"I'm so glad we met," Charlotte said. "You're really cute. You have that cute accent, and you're just… you're not like anyone else I know in New York." She leaned to kiss Jule's cheek and almost overbalanced.

Lucas grabbed her arm and pulled her upright in her seat. "No more Cosmos for you," he said.

"Shall I fetch more water?" Jule asked.

"That would be great," Lucas answered.

LUCAS WAITED until Jule walked away to speak to Charlotte. "Girl, how messed up are you?"

Charlotte pulled herself together and sat up straight in her chair. She patted her hair, smoothing some wisps back from her face. "You don't have to worry about me, boy."

"Good. It would appear you were right about Mr. Parry's orientation, but he's beyond naïve. He fucking blushed when I brought up casual sex."

"He turned you down?"

"I'm not sure he knew exactly what I was offering, but yeah, he couldn't back away fast enough. Pretty sure we're dealing with what I like to call—"

"A cloistered virgin," Charlotte finished for him.

He nodded. "Or CV if I'm sexting."

Charlotte knew the type all too well. People raised from birth to follow a demanding discipline in a rigorous program that allowed no time for anything but their art. All their lives were in service to dance, until the thing they'd served so faithfully left them too broken to continue. Cold creatures in whom the spark of creation only flared to life when they performed. Frozen fire, David called them.

It was a price Charlotte wasn't willing to pay. What she lacked in technical brilliance, she made up for in personality, and in Lucas, she had a dance partner who matched her flair for radiating an earthy magnetism. Together, they had set audiences ablaze. So what if her figure was too curvy to fit the teen-boy body type of the typical prima ballerina? She was a popular dancer and planned on being a star, a legend even.

"You'll thaw him out," she said confidently. "I can tell he's already smitten, and why not? You *are* the hottest thing going."

"True, but I'm not sure it's a good idea."

Charlotte laughed. "Give me a break." She glanced at Jule at the bar. "You can't tell me you don't want to hit that, you big sex addict."

"No, I can't tell you that, but believe it or don't, I'm not a *complete* dirtbag. He's a *kid*."

"You're just showing him a good time, not turning him out."

"If by *good time* you mean getting into his pants." Lucas paused. "You know what I mean."

"Look, no one's *making* you do anything… and it's not like we haven't done this before. Besides, you aren't tricking him into it. He wants you. I can tell."

Lucas finished his drink and set the glass down. His expression was enigmatic when he spoke again. "Your words have the ring of truth."

"So, what's the problem, boy?"

"No problem, girl." Lucas winked. "Like I said, I got this."

JULE RETURNED with Charlotte's water. "Are you feeling better?"

"I'm fine," she said breezily. "Skipped lunch today and got a little light-headed."

Jule nodded his understanding. Skipping meals in favor of practice was standard operating procedure in his world. "Would you like something to eat?"

"Eventually. Sit, please."

Jule sat. He felt very much out of his depth with these two glamorous, gorgeous people, but he was having a good time despite the constant small culture shocks. Just because it was different didn't mean it was wrong or dangerous, and good lord, wasn't Lucas bloody beautiful? Everything about him beckoned Jule closer, and it wasn't just physical. Jule already loved Lucas's sense of humor and the way Lucas made him feel like an equal.

"Are you sure you're all right?" he asked Charlotte.

"I'm sure. Don't worry about me."

Jule turned to Lucas. "Would you like to dance, then?" he asked, feeling very sophisticated.

"Yes, very much so."

Jule was having such a good time dancing with Lucas that he was actually disappointed when he spotted Kelly, Sasha, and David entering the club. He was a little unsettled by how easily Lucas had distracted him from his mission, but it was only temporary, after all.

Lucas sighted them as well as they walked to the table where Charlotte sat. "Uh-oh, Mom and Dad are home," he said to Jule.

Jule laughed. "Woof, what a mental image."

Lucas grinned. "Horrifying. It's too bad, though. I don't want you to go yet."

"Me either, but I'd have to go soon anyway. I have an audition tomorrow."

"The NYCB, right? Impressive."

"Yeah."

"You should come by the studio while you're in town," Lucas said, as though Jule visited New York all the time. "I think you'd like it. We're a lot less traditional than the NYCB. Fewer sticks up our ass, you might say."

Jule laughed again. Lucas made him feel… accepted, as though he was one of the guys. He liked this feeling a lot. "I would say bum not ass," he replied as casually as he could.

"Shit," Lucas said. "I made eye contact with David. He's making the face that indicates our asses are required thence."

"I like the way you talk. And the way you dance." Jule paused. "I like you a lot."

Lucas shook his head in wonder at Jule's candor. "You don't have any friends at all, do you?"

"I have Kelly and Sasha."

"Right. Just as I thought. You spend too much time with the grown-ups. Tell you what, I'm not that much older than you. I'll be your friend in New York."

"Excellent." Jule smiled at Lucas as they reached the table.

"Having a good time?" David asked.

"Yes, very," Jule answered.

"Good, good. Kelly and I had a talk *très intéressant*, but I'll let him tell you about it. Meanwhile, I want you to know the door of The Downtown Ballet is open to you."

Jule glanced at Kelly before he replied. "Thank you, Mr. Downes."

"We should probably go," Kelly said.

"We don't want to keep you up past your bedtime," David said. He winked at Jule. "The best of luck to you. I mean it."

Kelly, Sasha, and Jule walked to the bank of elevators and waited a few seconds for one to arrive.

"Did you have a good time?" Sasha asked.

"I did. Charlotte and Lucas were very gracious."

"Gracious, huh?" Kelly said as they stepped into the elevator.

"They made me feel welcome."

"I'm sure they did."

"Why would you say it like that?"

"You mean my sarcasm?"

"It doesn't sound like you."

Kelly frowned. "I guess New York brings out the worst in me."

"Then why did we come here?"

Kelly didn't answer until they got off on their floor. "We didn't come to New York for me. We came here for you."

"But if you're not happy—"

"You worry about your audition tomorrow, and let Sasha worry about me, okay?"

"Are you going to tell me what you and Mr. Downes talked about?"

"Not tonight," Kelly said as Sasha keyed open the door to the suite. "Now go to sleep. Another big day tomorrow."

"Sleep well," Sasha said.

Jule went to the adjoining room and got ready for bed. His nerves were still humming pleasantly with all new things he'd seen and done. He'd met Mr. Downes and been invited to join his company! It was beyond thrilling, and yet, Lucas overshadowed all of it. He could still feel the warmth of Lucas's hands everywhere he'd touched him, and he wanted to feel that touch again. Even more than that, he wanted Lucas to smile at him in that way that made him feel like they were the only two people in the world.

Jule halted that train of thought as he got into bed. There was no point getting stressed about something he had no control over. And there was absolutely no point in wasting time on something that had nothing to do with his goal. Out of long habit, he cleared his mind and drifted into sleep.

Chapter Two

JULE WAS having breakfast alone in the hotel's concierge lounge when his phone rang. The only people who ever called him were Kelly, Sasha, and his family. He didn't recognize the number on the screen and answered out of curiosity. "Hello?"

"Hey," Lucas said. "It's Lucas. Remember me?"

"Of course, but how do you know my number?"

"David worked some magic. Probably because he couldn't stand the sight of me begging."

"I don't understand."

"There's nothing to understand. I like you, and you said you like me, so I want to see you again. When do you think that could happen?"

"I… don't know."

"Come have breakfast with me. I know a great place."

"I have to talk to Kelly first."

"Of course, you do." Lucas sighed. "Call me back, okay?"

"Give me five minutes."

"Tick tock," Lucas said before he hung up.

Jule left the concierge lounge and knocked on the door of Kelly and Sasha's room. Meeting Lucas for breakfast in no way furthered his plans, yet here he was about to take the unprecedented step of altering his schedule.

Sasha let Jule in. "I thought you went to get some breakfast," he said.

"I did." Jule moved farther into the suite and saw Kelly at the desk. "Hey, don't we have a couple of hours before the audition?"

Kelly swiveled the chair to face Jule. "Three to be exact. Why?"

"I thought I'd go down to Times Square and look around a little."

Kelly raised no objections. "Be sure you're back in time for your warmup."

"Of course, I will. Thanks."

"Do you want company?" Sasha asked.

"I need you here," Kelly said to Jule's relief.

"Don't forget your coat," Sasha told Jule.

"I won't." Jule went into his room to fetch his parka and hat. "Bye," he called out as he left. He felt a little guilty for not being completely honest with Kelly and Sasha, but he had the impression that Kelly didn't like Lucas. At any rate, the guilt didn't dampen the excitement he felt at the thought of seeing Lucas.

As Jule walked to the elevator, he called Lucas. "I can meet you," he said.

"Where are you now?"

"Getting into an elevator."

"Okay, go out through the Starbucks on the ground floor. I'll meet you there."

Lucas was indeed waiting just inside the crowded coffee shop. He looked as appealing as an autumn day with his leaf-brown hair, dark amber eyes, and burnt-orange scarf. When he saw Jule, he gave him a big smile.

"Happy you could make it," Lucas said. "Hungry?"

Jule, who'd just eaten a bowl of fruit with yogurt, nodded. "I'm always hungry, according to Mum."

"This way," Lucas held the door and they stepped out in the cold.

Lucas took Jule's arm to guide him through the press of people to the curb. He hailed a cab and gave the driver an address. It was a short ride to Tenth Avenue and a restaurant called 44 ½.

"You'll love this place," Lucas said.

"How do you know?"

"What?"

"We don't know each other, so how would you know what I like?"

"Allow me to rephrase? I *want* you to love it. Is that better?" Lucas asked as they walked in.

A superbly muscled waiter in a tight T-shirt showed them to a table. Lucas asked for a Bloody Mary and Jule a glass of grapefruit juice.

"They could put some vodka in there for you," Lucas said when the waiter had gone.

"For breakfast? Anyway, I'm not legal to drink in the US."

"True, but they probably won't card you here."

"It's just after ten o'clock."

"True again, but this is New York. Normal rules don't apply."

"Still, I don't think it's a good idea to drink before an audition."

"Audition shmaudition." Lucas flapped a hand dismissively. "David says the NYCB would be criminally stupid to turn you down."

"How can he say that when he's never seen me dance?"

The waiter returned and took their orders for the recommended house eggs Artur.

"How do you know David's never seen you dance?" Lucas said.

"I don't." Jule thought for a couple of seconds. "It's possible he was in the audience at one of my public performances. There haven't been that many, though."

"Did you know there's a video of you performing in the *Nutcracker* when you were fourteen?"

"Bloody hell, I'd forgotten. It was a Christmas pageant." Jule paused. "I was dreadful."

"Hardly." Lucas smiled warmly, and Jule's heart gave a little skip before resuming a normal rhythm. "I mean, you weren't exactly elegant, but as David said, you hadn't grown into your legs yet. He's dying to get you to dance for him." He leaned back as the food arrived.

Jule was quiet for a few minutes. After taking a few bites, he put his fork down. "I'd love to dance for Mr. Downes, but Kelly—Mr. Holloway is dead set on getting me into the NYCB."

"Surely that's up to you."

"He's been my teacher and my guide since I was nine. I trust him."

"It's your decision." Lucas shrugged. "I just think you might be happier with us."

"What's happiness got to do with ballet?"

"Are you quoting someone?"

Jule smiled. "Kelly may have said that a few times."

"He's wrong. It's possible to be a good dancer without torturing yourself 24-7."

"I don't think of it as torture."

"Of course you don't. You've been conditioned to accept pain as the price of excellence."

"Are *you* quoting someone?"

Lucas chuckled. "Sadly, that came directly from me."

"But it's true that you can't progress without stretching yourself to your limits and then going beyond them. Don't you agree?"

"I do, but it doesn't have to consume your entire life. You should make time for something besides practice and sitting around with an ice pack for company."

"I'm doing that right now."

"Good boy."

"I think Kelly would call you a bad influence."

"As long as he doesn't call me a bad dancer, I'm okay with that."

Jule smiled at Lucas. "I've seen you dance," he said. "You're definitely not bad."

"Let me guess. You saw that taping of *Rite of Spring* with me and Charlotte."

Jule nodded as picked up his glass of juice. "There's a clip of it on Downtown's website."

Lucas rolled his eyes. "A few critics called it *combustible*, as I recall, also *robust*. They seemed to like words with *bust* in them. Probably because they were impressed with Charlotte's rack. They went on to say that such blatant eroticism had no place in a hallowed work blah blah blah. The audience seemed to like it."

"Sasha called it sensuous. Kelly said it's *meant* to be sensuous, so your critics were wrong."

"Sensuous," Lucas repeated. "I like that. How about we walk back to the hotel and work off some of this food?"

"Good idea," Jule answered.

Jule enjoyed striding along next to Lucas through the streams of people flowing in all directions along the crowded streets. "I haven't seen much of it, but I think I like New York."

"Good. I'd really like it if you stayed a while. For purely selfish reasons."

"You keep saying things like that. I don't know what to think."

"Come here." Lucas took Jule's arm and steered him to an area with a few trees and some benches. The benches were full of people holding shopping bags or eating street food. Lucas drew Jule over to one of a pair of pillars supporting a wrought-iron gate. There was relative privacy in the niche formed by the column and the hedge wall. "What are you confused about?"

"Are you chatting me up, or is this just how you are with everyone?"

"I thought I was pretty up-front about it. I like you. I want to know you. I want to dance with you. Eventually, I want to make love to you. I'd actually like to do that now, but—"

Jule took a couple of deep breaths that did nothing to slow down his racing heart. "I have no idea what I'm doing, but I'd like to know you better too."

"I really want to kiss you right now."

Jule took a half-step back.

"Relax," Lucas said. "This is a little too public, even for me."

"It's funny."

"What?"

"I just thought, if I were a girl, you wouldn't think twice about kissing me in public."

"That's the sad truth of our society." Lucas put his hands in his coat pockets. "So, what do you say? Can I keep chatting you up?"

"Do just as you like."

"That would get us arrested for lewd behavior."

"We can't have that." Jule smiled. "I have an audition in an hour."

"I should get you back to the hotel."

Lucas walked with Jule to the portico of the Marriott. "Thanks for coming out with me. Call me when you have free time?"

"I will." Jule paused as he took a moment to register just how much he wanted to see Lucas again. He reminded himself that this was *not* why he'd come to New York.

"Good." Lucas studied Jule's face for a long moment. "Soon," he said. "I'm going to get that kiss."

Jule's face felt suddenly hot, and he was horribly sure he was blushing.

Lucas put a hand on Jule's shoulder so that his thumb rested on the bare skin of Jule's neck for a second before he pulled it back. "Good luck at the audition," he said.

"Th-thanks," Jule stammered before he walked into the hotel. His entire body tingled from the delicate brush of Lucas's touch. He'd felt attracted to other boys before, but nothing like this. He was going to have to exercise some willpower, or he'd be walking around with a stiffie most of the time. That wouldn't help his chances with the NYCB.

Jule went straight to his room and changed into workout clothes before he knocked on the adjoining door. He walked in carrying a bag with some hand towels and a change of clothes.

Kelly looked up from his laptop as Jule came in. "Sasha, would you call for a car?" He gave Jule a long look. "You look good," he said. "You look ready."

"I feel ready." Jule set the bag on the bed. "I thought I'd be more nervous."

"You've always had nerves of steel," Sasha said as he put down the phone. "And ice water in your veins… like your teacher."

Kelly looked up at Sasha. "You almost managed to make that sound like a compliment."

Sasha ignored the comment and went to the closet for his coat.

Jule hesitated a moment before asking, "What if I don't, you know, pass the audition?"

"We'll talk about that if it happens," Kelly answered. "But it won't. Maybe I've been too sparing with praise, but any company would be lucky to get you. Your technique is flawless, every move immaculate, but your performance is never mechanical. You project your joy in dancing. In other words, you're not just a virtuoso. People genuinely like you, and that's a real gift."

"Oh… kay."

"I guess I didn't answer your question."

"I was talking about more practical issues. Like, would we go directly home?"

"I honestly can't conceive that they'd turn you down."

"But if they did?"

"Have you been keeping up your French language lessons?"

"*Est-ce que le ciel bleu?*" Jule smiled. "So, Paris Opera Ballet is still your second choice?"

"It's Sasha's *first* choice for you."

"I'm glad he's here. He makes any place feel like home to me."

"He'd be happy to know that. Anything else?"

"*Non, rien, monsieur.*" Jule shook his head. "You plan. I dance."

"It's worked well so far. Why mess with it?"

"The car will be waiting," Sasha prompted as he shrugged into his coat.

THE DRIVER of the town car dropped Kelly, Sasha, and Jule off at Lincoln Center. They didn't need directions to the School of American Ballet. Kelly could still find the school and the Koch Theater blindfolded. He'd performed there for a much shorter time than he'd planned, but every detail was still etched in his memory. Each landmark reminded him of the career he'd once dreamed of.

Kelly looked over as Sasha's hand brushed his. "I'm fine," he said, though Sasha hadn't asked. They'd never needed a lot of words to communicate.

They were greeted in the lobby and shown to one of the smaller studios where Jule could warm up. Precisely forty-five minutes after their arrival, they were joined by the artistic director, Dominic Jacobs. He shook hands with Kelly and Sasha and then turned to watch Jule finish a series of *assemblé* jumps.

"Thank you for coming in person," Dom said. "There's only so much you can determine about a dancer by watching an audition tape."

"I couldn't agree more," Kelly said.

"Very well. Whenever you're ready, then."

"We aren't going to wait for Mr. Halvorsen?"

"The director was called away suddenly to accept an award at the San Francisco Ballet gala."

"I see." Kelly hid his disappointment. He gestured to Jule, and Jule came to stand in front of him. "Julian Parry, this is Mr. Dominic Jacobs."

"Good to meet you," Dom said. "I've heard very good things about you."

"I hope to prove they're true, sir," Jule said.

"I like your attitude," Dom said. "Of course, I'd expect no less from a dancer trained by Kelly Holloway. I find it somewhat strange the ballet world hasn't heard of you before."

"That was intentional, sir." Jule looked to Kelly.

"I didn't want Jule to be distracted by applause until I felt he could handle it," Kelly said.

Dom nodded. "By applause, I'm sure you don't mean the sound of palms meeting with force. In fact, I'm sure you mean the regrettable lionization of talented young dancers."

Kelly nodded. "We've both seen it happen."

Dom nodded again as his expression turned sober. "At close range. Such a pity when a talented young person's focus is distracted by adulation." He cleared his throat and addressed Jule. "If you're ready to show me what you've got, I'm ready to watch."

Jule's gaze went to Kelly again, and he nodded. Without further preparation or accompaniment, Jule launched into his show piece. For four minutes, he performed *pirouettes*, *grand jetés*, *tour jetés*, *jetés tournant*, and every other step that showcased his technique.

"Well… I'm impressed," Dom said when Jule ended with a *fouetté* and a deep *cambré*. "Amazing aplomb for someone so young and his *ballon*—" He chuckled. "I wasn't sure he was going to come back down."

"He's very accomplished," Kelly agreed. "But does he deserve a place in your company?"

"If he doesn't, I don't know who does." Dom paused. "However...."

"However?" Kelly prompted.

"Mr. Halvorsen mentioned he had some reservations about your expectations." Dom smiled. "But I think we can agree we'd be foolish not to admit Jule to the corps."

"The corps?" Kelly repeated.

"Well, yes, we'd expect Jule to spend a year in the *corps de ballet* learning the Balanchine technique."

"He dances Balanchine," Kelly said through clenched teeth. "Were you watching?"

"I meant that he needs time to fit in with our—"

"He doesn't need any—" Kelly paused. "No wonder Halvorsen scrambled and left you with this detail. He never could do his own dirty work."

Dom cleared his throat again. "I don't know about that, but our offer stands. We're willing to take Jule on, provide a room in the dorm, and instruction as well as a stipend."

"Thanks, but I'd rather—" Kelly broke off when Sasha touched his arm. "Thanks for your time," he said. "Jule, let's go."

"I can see you're disappointed," Dom said. "But as Mr. Halvorsen says we can't bend the rules for one unless we bend them for all."

"Yeah, I might have heard that from him once or twice in the past." Kelly would have said more, but Sasha gave his arm a squeeze.

Dom reacted to the acid in Kelly's voice. "I hope you understand this isn't personal."

"Of course not," Kelly said. "It never is." He walked away, and Sasha and Jule followed.

WHEN THEY returned to the hotel, they found a gift basket had been delivered to their rooms. Enveloped in iridescent cellophane, the basket dwarfed the table it sat on.

Sasha plucked the card from its holder and read aloud. "With the sincerest compliments of The Downtown Ballet Company, you are cordially invited to attend a gathering." He smiled. "There's an address and a phone number to RSVP."

"I don't feel much like a party," Kelly said.

"I don't understand why you're so upset," Jule said. "I was accepted. That's what we wanted, isn't it?"

"Their offer was an insult," Kelly growled.

Jule was stunned by the bitterness in Kelly's voice.

Sasha put a hand on Jule's shoulder. "It's not a good time for a talk, I think." He looked at the card again. "The party is right here in Manhattan. Would you like to go?"

Jule glanced at Kelly before he answered. "I'd like to, but should I?"

Kelly glanced up at his favorite student, and his heart rose up as it always did when he saw Jule. If there was a better boy on earth, he'd be surprised. A better *man*, Kelly amended. Jule was nineteen as of November 2, but that was barely a week ago, and Kelly had a hard time thinking of him as grown-up. Partly, it was the fact that at five feet eight inches, Jule stood almost half a foot shorter than Kelly's six feet two, and he had an open, guileless face with big brown eyes and a saddle of freckles across his nose. Kelly smiled.

"Go have some fun," he said. "While I sort myself out."

"Why don't you go change while I make a call?" Sasha said to Jule.

Jule looked to Kelly once more, but Kelly was looking out of the window. Feeling oddly set adrift, Jule went to his room.

SASHA USED the room phone to make his call.

"You've reached the phone of David Dulac Downes. Please leave your message after the chime."

Sasha waited for the tone. "This is Alexandru Vasile calling. We'd be pleased to accept—" He stopped speaking when someone picked up.

"Hey, this is David. I'm thrilled to hear you'll be attending my little soirée. There's no set time, so drop by whenever you feel like it. We never close."

"Thanks. I don't know if Kelly or I will be there, but Jule would probably enjoy attending a real New York City party."

David laughed. "I'm not sure I can promise actual debauchery, but we can get pretty wild." He paused. "Just kidding. We've never had the cops show up."

Sasha cleared his throat. "Still, I would appreciate it if you kept an eye on Jule. Can I trust you at least that far?"

"Say no more," David said. "I can see you've kept him sheltered. I won't let him be sold to human traffickers."

"Thank you." Sasha broke the connection and went into Jule's room. "You're expected."

Jule turned from his inventory of his suitcase. "What?"

"I accepted the party invitation for you. What are you going to wear?"

"I've no idea how to dress for a party in Manhattan. I'm not sure there's anything in my case that would—"

"I'm betting there will be a few flashy types at this party, but no need for you to outshine anyone with your clothing. You have bearing."

"I have what?" Jule looked up from a stack of shirts.

"The way you carry yourself is enough. You could wear anything and still look like a prince."

"What?"

"Never mind." Sasha picked out a mint-green button-down shirt and a pair of dark gray trousers. "Wear this with your navy jacket and your boots." He pulled out a narrow dark green tie. "And this for a touch of class."

"Thanks. What time is the party?"

"Mr. Downes says you may arrive whenever you are ready."

"I'll have a shower and change, then."

Sasha went back to his room and sat next to Kelly on the bed. "It's not the end of the world, my heart," he said softly.

"Isn't it?"

"How could it be?" Sasha put his arm around Kelly. "I'm here. You're here. We're together. That's world enough for me."

Kelly turned to take Sasha in his arms. "You're right," he said in a tight voice. "I just—" His words ended on a choked sob.

Sasha stroked Kelly's back soothingly. "You did everything right. Jule did everything right. It's not your fault Mr. Halvorsen holds a grudge." He kissed Kelly's forehead. "There are other ballet companies. It's not over."

Kelly sat up from his slump. "I'll get it together."

"I know you will. Meanwhile, we have this suite all to ourselves while Jule is at the party."

Kelly leaped on the distraction. "Are you sure we should let him go?"

"It's only a party."

"At David's house."

"David may be a devil, but he won't get our boy's soul. Believe me."

"Wow, do I really sound that bad?"

Sasha nodded. "I love you anyway."

Jule cleared his throat as he came through the door that connected the rooms. "How do I look?" he asked.

"Like a dreamboat," Sasha said as he stood.

"No one says dreamboat," Kelly informed him.

"Then what did I just say?"

"Don't be daft," Jule said as Sasha came over to fuss with his tie.

"You look very handsome," Kelly said. "I'm not going to issue any warnings. I trust you to behave yourself."

"Thanks." Jule paused. "Is everything okay?"

"Just go enjoy the party. We can talk later."

"I want to go, but I feel a little guilty for enjoying myself after this afternoon."

"That was not your fault. You were perfect. Believe me."

"You're sure?"

"We are sure," Sasha said. "Go, but give a call before you come back."

"And not too late," Kelly added. He paused. "Though, it's not like we have big plans for tomorrow."

"Go," Sasha repeated. "So I can cheer him up."

"Are you sure you don't want me to stay?" Jule looked at Kelly in concern.

"I'm sure. In fact, it's essential to the cheering up that you leave."

Jule blushed. "Well… bye then." He hurried out the door.

Chapter Three

A CAB dropped Jule at a brownstone on the Upper East Side. The lower façade and the stairs to the street were festooned with tiny white lights. Behind the glass of the front door, a young dancer in a long white wig and snowy petal-like layers of diaphanous organdy held up a candle as thick as her wrist. Silently, she beckoned, and Jule stepped inside the evergreen-scented warmth. The girl silently pointed down the hall and then resumed impersonating an angel.

"Posh," Jule said under his breath as he glanced around at the elegant furnishings. His parents were well-off, and he lived in a very nice house, but it was nothing like this. He particularly liked the natural seasonal decorations of evergreen boughs, pinecones, and branches of holly with centerpieces of dried pears, pomegranates, and cinnamon sticks. It smelled pleasantly like a pastry shop.

"Jule!" David appeared at the end of the foyer. He came forward to hang Jule's coat on a rack. "Come, come, come," he said excitedly, taking Jule's hand. He didn't seem offended when Jule pulled his hand free but continued to walk briskly toward the rectangle of light at the end of the broad entrance hall.

Jule followed David into an explosion of color and sound. He stopped on the threshold to accustom himself to the scene and spotted Lucas right away.

"Jule!" Lucas waved from one of the throne-like chairs at the end of the antique refectory table doing duty as a buffet. He got up and made his way through the other twenty or thirty guests.

David smiled at Lucas. "I'll leave Jule in your capable hands," he said before he went to join a group of people by a grand piano.

"I'm so glad you could make it," Lucas said.

"Me too." Jule looked around. "This place is gorgeous."

"Right? David's grandparents left it to him. It's the only way you can get a place in this neighborhood. Someone has to die." Lucas reacted to Jule's dubious expression. "It's just my sick sense of humor showing."

"But it's true, isn't it?"

"Well… yeah." Lucas found his smile again. "Why don't I introduce you to a few people?"

"Sure."

Lucas pointed out a young man and woman near the marble-faced fireplace. "Our fellow dancers at Downtown, Samira and Danilo. Adopted by the Sutherlands as babies. They're both from Bosnia, but they're not related, though they grew up as brother and sister and dance partners. Weird, right?"

"It's certainly… unusual, I guess."

"So diplomatic." Lucas chuckled. "Okay, let's see, you already know Charlotte. The tweedy gentleman she's talking to is Jamison Hayward, Downtown's musical director, pretty brilliant guy. Next to him is Artur Avocado—just kidding, it's Artur Avakian. He's a patron of the arts, as they say. They're both Brits like you. Also, I think they might be playing hide the salami in private."

"You're not so much introducing me as gossiping."

"I could stop."

"No, it's fine. I like listening to you talk."

"Yeah, me too." Lucas smacked his forehead dramatically. "You've been here over five minutes, and you don't have a drink in your hand. This shall not stand!"

Jule laughed for the first time since the audition, but not for the last time that night. He met more of the dancers of David's company, as well as some patrons and a few artists of other stripes. He managed to finish a martini in just over an hour. Everyone he met was warm and friendly toward him, taking him instantly into whatever group Lucas led him to. Everyone appeared to be wildly happy that he was in their midst. It was his first experience with popularity, and it made his head spin faster than the drink in his hand.

"You look happy," Lucas said in Jule's ear as they watched Jamison playing the piano.

Jule was already giddy, and the effect of Lucas's warm breath on his skin was instant and almost overwhelming. His pulse pounded in his ears, his heart raced, and he felt as though the temperature had gone up about twenty degrees. Abruptly, he needed to be somewhere else. He slipped between two people and headed away from the crowd.

Lucas caught up with Jule in three steps. "Everything okay?"

"I just need some air."

"No problem. This way."

Lucas led Jule up a couple of flights of stairs and out onto a rooftop terrace. They walked to the edge and looked down at the traffic before turning their backs on it.

"It's beautiful up here," Jule said.

"Yeah, about thirteen million dollars' worth of beautiful. You feeling better? You looked like you had a touch of social anxiety."

"No, that's not it." Jule paused. He wanted to take back his words, because Lucas had given him the perfect excuse, but he also wanted to be honest. "I mean, it was a bit overwhelming, sure, but I was enjoying myself. Everyone is being so nice to me."

"Why wouldn't they be?"

Jule shrugged. "You were right when you guessed I don't have a lot of friends. I have Kelly and Sasha, but Kelly is my coach, and Sasha is my homeschool teacher, so it's a bit—"

"Complicated?"

"Yeah." Jule smiled. "It's nice to talk with someone who understands."

"You've got my number. Call me anytime. I love to talk."

"Thanks."

"How'd it go with the audition? Are we celebrating?"

Jule's brows drew together in a slight frown. "I passed, but I didn't. I mean, I was accepted, but we didn't accept their terms. At least, I think that's what happened."

"So... you're not a member of the NYCB yet?"

Jule shook his head and was startled when Lucas swept him up in a hug. He was used to occasional hugs from Kelly and daily hugs from Sasha and Mum, but those embraces had nothing in common with this one. Heat like a desert wind blasted through him, and the world melted like candle wax. He put his arms around Lucas and held on tight.

"I'll take that kiss now," Lucas said. "If it's convenient."

Jule looked up at Lucas in clear invitation. This would be his first real kiss, and he was ready for it. Or so he thought.

Lucas leaned in and covered Jule's mouth with his. His lips moved gently on Jule's for a few moments before he lifted his head.

Though the kiss was almost chaste, it had an immediate and powerful effect on Jule. Eager for more, he put an arm around Lucas's neck and pulled him into a kiss that almost bloodied his lip.

Lucas took a step back. "Wow."

"Shite. I did it wrong, didn't I?"

"No," Lucas said swiftly. "You didn't do anything wrong. It's just… I think we should probably go back in before people start gossiping about us."

This was a novel notion to Jule, the idea that he could be the subject of gossip. "I suppose you're right," he said. "But…."

"But?" Lucas smiled. "Listen, if you're as turned on as I am right now, we have two choices."

"Go on."

"We can stay here, make out like crazy, and shoot off in our tighty-whiteys, or we can be classy, go back to the party, and, at some future point, make out like crazy somewhere we can take our time and shoot off in our tighty-whiteys. Either works for me."

Jule very much wanted to keep kissing Lucas, but his training kicked in. "You're right. We should go back to the party."

"Come here." Lucas pulled Jule into another hug before letting him go. "Okay. Just checking. Now I'm ready."

"Checking for what?" Jule asked as he followed Lucas.

"To see if you really felt that good."

"And what did you decide?"

"That I'm a lucky guy."

David spotted Lucas and Jule as they reached the bottom of stairs and came over to them. "Just the person I wanted to see," he said expansively. "Jule, can we talk for a minute?"

"Of course, sir."

"I'll get right to it. I'm creating a new ballet. Or rather, I've created a ballet. It's complete in my head. I just have to get the steps diagrammed so Jamison can write a score. Of course, it will probably change in practice, but I'm confident enough to offer it to you now."

"What?"

"He's trying to say he's created a ballet just for you," Lucas informed Jule.

"That's… incredible," Jule said. Already high from the vodka and the kisses, he was starting to feel like he might float away.

"I hope so," David said. "And I very much hope you'll perform it someday, because you were the inspiration. It's not the first ballet with pas de deux for two men, but I think it will be the best."

Jule was reeling now. It was just too much to take in all at once. "I'm… gobsmacked."

David chuckled. "In a good way or a bad way?"

"I meant that I'm honored. Sorry, but I was literally stunned like a rabbit in headlights."

"So… that's good?" David smiled at Jule.

"Yes. I'm absolutely thrilled. It's just that so many good things are happening at the same time. It makes me a little nervous."

"Fuck that noise." Lucas put his arm around Jule's shoulders. "The good things are happening because you deserve them, am I right? Or am I right?"

"*À cent pour cent*," David said. "Jule, I wouldn't invite you into my company unless I thought you were star material. I mean, yeah, sure, your technique is the cleanest I've ever seen, but I see more in you. If you join my company, I promise you, I'll take you to the next level."

"I'd have to discuss it with Kelly, and he'd have to be part of any contract I make with you."

David and Lucas exchanged a glance. "Of course," David said. "If that's what he wants."

"Why wouldn't he want to continue coaching me?"

"He'd have to be crazy," Lucas said.

"Well, that's all I wanted to say," David said. "You kids go have a good time. Shoo!"

"I should probably call a cab," Jule said. "I'm not used to staying up late."

"Christ, you're right!" Lucas exclaimed. "Why, it's nearly ten! *P.M.!*"

David chuckled. "If you have to leave, there's a black town car out front. Tell the driver where you want to go. And please sleep on my proposal."

"Thank you, sir. I will."

Lucas and Jule put on coats in the foyer and walked outside. David's driver got out of the car idling at the curb, pocketed his phone, and waved at Lucas.

"I'll ride along," Lucas said as the driver moved around the car to open the back door.

Lucas got in, and Jule followed him.

"Mr. Downes said to take you to the Marquis?" the driver said as he got behind the wheel.

"That's right," Lucas answered. "Take your time." He turned sideways to face Jule. "It's a short ride."

"I suppose it is."

"Have you ever been kissed in the back seat of a car?"

"Never."

Lucas smiled. "You have much to learn, young padawan."

Jule laughed, delighted to find a fellow Star Wars fan. "I find your lack of faith disturbing," he retorted.

"Oh, so you want to play. I love it." Lucas leaned closer to Jule. "The Force is strong with this one."

"The Force *can* have a strong influence on the weak-minded."

"That gives me such a boner." Lucas's lips were an inch from Jule's.

Jule wasn't nearly as nervous as he had been before that first kiss. He smiled at Lucas. "Scruffy-looking nerf herder," he whispered.

Lucas closed the gap between them, cupping the back of Jule's head as he claimed Jule's mouth in a hungry kiss that didn't end until the car slowed. He let go of Jule, and Jule's arms slid slowly from around his neck as the car eased past a line of taxis.

"I can't sit here too long," the driver said.

Lucas looked into Jule's eyes. "I'll call you tomorrow."

Jule shook his head. "I'll call *you*," he said. He got out of the car and then ducked his head back inside. "Thank you. I had a good time."

As the car drove away, Jule paused to look up at the falling snow. Since he was little, the sight of falling snow had been mesmerizing to him. If he stared long enough, he became disoriented. He felt as though the flakes were hanging suspended, and he was falling up into the sky. It wasn't frightening at all. It was, in fact, very peaceful to imagine floating up to the stars in slow motion. No noise. No heat. No pressure.

JULE SAW the Do Not Disturb sign on Kelly and Sasha's door and remembered he should have called. He took extra care to be quiet as he let himself into his room. He brushed his teeth, stripped to his underwear, did his exercise routine, and got into bed. For the first time in his life, he had trouble falling asleep. He kept remembering the feel of Lucas's lips on his, Lucas's hands on his body, Lucas's tongue....

He put his hand on his hard cock and shivered at the sensation even through the layer of cotton. It wasn't enough. He reached into his briefs and took hold of his shaft. He imagined Lucas's hand moving on him, and it wasn't long before he came. The intense orgasm left him breathless and sleep came quickly after.

Chapter Four

JULE'S PHONE woke him the next morning. "Hi, Sasha," he said. "I'll be right there."

He pulled on a long-sleeved T-shirt and a pair of sweatpants before he joined Kelly and Sasha.

"We ordered breakfast from room service," Sasha said. "Sit and eat."

Jule tucked into the plate of steak and eggs.

"Did you have a good time last night?" Sasha asked.

Jule swallowed, drank some orange juice, and then answered. "You should see Mr. Downes's house," he said. "It's fantastic. Lucas said it's worth thirteen million. *Dollars*."

"I've seen it," Kelly said. "You're right. It's fantastic."

"Did you meet anyone interesting?" Sasha asked.

"*Every*one was interesting." Jule picked up a triangle of wheat toast. "And they all liked me."

"Of course they did." Sasha refilled his coffee cup from the carafe.

"Okay," Kelly said. "We've got some caffeine and food in us. Let's discuss NYCB's offer."

"What is there to talk about?" Jule asked as he set down his fork. "I thought—"

"So did I, but—Look, I can't take this away from you just because I didn't get what I wanted. Mr. Jacobs made a more than fair offer. The company rarely takes on a dancer who didn't attend the School of American Ballet."

"Are you saying you want me to accept the offer?"

"It's less than I wanted for you, but it's a very good offer."

"No, it isn't."

Kelly's face reflected his surprise when Jule disagreed with him. "Excuse me?"

"I mean, it might be a good offer, but it isn't good enough for me," Jule said.

"I see," Kelly said. "What would be good enough?"

Jule gathered his courage and spoke. "Mr. Downes offered me a place in his company."

"And?"

"Just hear him out," Sasha said.

"What would be the point? He's *nineteen*. He can't make this decision, Sasha, and I won't let him ruin his career before it starts."

Jule looked from Kelly to Sasha. "Forget it. It's not worth it."

Sasha frowned. "That's not true. You care deeply about this, and Kelly is going to do you the simple courtesy of listening without interrupting."

Kelly crossed his arms over his chest as he stared at Sasha. "So, you know about this and I don't?"

"Of course, I do," Sasha said. "And it's not me you're mad at. Now, listen to Jule, please."

"All right. I'm listening."

Jule cleared his throat. "I didn't prepare a speech."

"Just tell him what you want," Sasha said.

"I want to dance for The Downtown Ballet."

"Why?"

"Well, first because, at the NYCB, I'll be one of five danseurs competing for parts, and that's after serving time in the corps. At Downtown, I'll be second only to Mr. Madding. But the biggest thing is how comfortable I feel with the company."

"Comfortable?" Kelly snorted. "When has ballet ever been about comfort?"

"Kelly," Sasha said in a soft admonishment. He turned to Jule. "Tell him why."

"After talking to some other dancers, it's clear to me that some things aren't tolerated at the NYCB."

"Go on."

Jule took a deep, calming breath. "Apparently, it's all right to be gay, as long as you keep it hidden."

Kelly blinked. "Are you telling me you're gay?"

"Are you telling me you didn't know?" Jule replied. "I just assumed you did and didn't care to talk about it."

Sasha put a hand on Kelly's shoulder. "Think before you speak, my heart."

Kelly nodded. "I should have cared enough to bring it up, is that your point? If so, it's a good one." He smiled at Jule. "I didn't know for sure you were gay, but I had a pretty good idea."

"That's what I thought," Jule said. "And honestly, I would probably have been embarrassed to death if you tried to talk to me about sex."

"Yep, me too." Kelly glanced at Sasha. "Anything to add to that?" Sasha shook his head.

"Why did you change your mind?" Jule asked Kelly.

Kelly glanced at Sasha before he answered. "You deserve to know this, Jule." He sighed. "I had this plan where I trained a dancer who would be the best ever seen, and the director of NYCB who tossed me out would have to grovel in front of me. How sad is that?"

Jule frowned. "I don't believe that's the only reason you coached me."

"No, of course not. I loved you the first time I saw you, when you let go of your mom's hand to shake mine, no fear in you. You've never done anything to shake that love. I'm proud of you, both for passing the audition and for having the courage to stand up for yourself."

Jule threw his arms around Kelly in a warm hug before letting go. "Thank you."

"If you think about it," Sasha said, "letting the director have Jule within his grasp and then taking him away is even better than the original plan. Once Jule becomes a star, Halvorsen will eat his own seared heart on a bed of arugula."

Kelly chuckled. "For a hopeless romantic, you have a wicked mind."

"You have no idea," Sasha said in sinister tones.

"Okay," Kelly said. "I'll call David. Jule, this is no reason for you to skip your morning routine."

Jule nodded and left to use the hotel's exercise room.

KELLY CALLED David and was answered on the second ring.

"Kelly!" David sounded surprised. "To what do I owe the pleasure?"

"Don't play dumb. You know why I'm calling."

"I don't, though. *Et c'est la vérité.*"

"So, you're going to make me say it?"

"Is there any chance you're calling to tell me Jule wants to dance for me?"

"You know I am. Your sleazy charm strikes again."

"Harsh."

"Not harsh enough by half. Let's get this over with. Do you have any free time today?"

"For this, I'll make time." David paused. "Two o'clock. At the Downtown building. I'll send a car at one thirty. Suit you?"

"We'll be there." Kelly hung up.

"Well?" Sasha raised his eyebrows at Kelly.

"We're meeting David at two at his studio. You can tell Jule if you want."

"I think you should do it."

"Why?"

"Why?" Sasha echoed. "Because I'm smarter than you."

Kelly nodded as he stood up. "Thanks for reminding me." He smiled at Sasha and then went to knock on Jule's door.

"Come in," Jule called out. He tossed away the towel he was using on his wet hair and sat down on the foot of the bed.

Kelly looked at him for a moment before he spoke. "I don't say this often enough. I'm so proud of the way you've grown up."

"Stop it."

"Okay." Kelly got back to business. "Be ready to leave in half an hour. We're going to meet with Mr. Downes."

"Seriously?"

"Very seriously. He's sending a car at one thirty."

Kelly watched the smile spread over Jule's face and felt a warm glow in his chest. As usual, Sasha was right. He'd been working toward a goal for so long, he'd lost sight of what was really important. He'd had his shot and he'd blown it, but for all the right reasons, and he had no reason for regrets. A little justice would be nice, though.

A LITTLE before two in the afternoon, Lucas and Charlotte arrived at the smaller Downtown studio as per Mr. Downes's request. Lucas plugged his phone into the speakers and selected his dance playlist. He and Charlotte practiced a few steps and lifts, but it was clear to Lucas she had as little enthusiasm as he did. He went to turn off the music and then walked back over to Charlotte.

"Looks like David's going to get what he wants... as usual."

"If you're talking about Julian Parry, you're right." Charlotte unclipped her thick strawberry-blond hair and shook it out to fall to her waist. "The only obstacle there was his coach."

"So, what's *his* story?" Lucas asked as he sank down to the floor, leaning back against the wall of mirrors. "Holloway looks like a brooding Viking prince."

Charlotte pulled up her leg warmers and took a drink from a water bottle before she answered. "You don't know this one?"

"Obviously not, or I wouldn't have asked."

"That's right. You're such a New Yorker now that I forget you came from some tiny town in the armpit of the Midwest."

"No, I'm from upstate. Tuxedo Park."

"I like my story better. Anyway, Kelly Holloway is a bona fide legend. He turned his back on fame and fortune for the man he loved."

"Spill the tea, girl."

"Well, the way I heard it, he was the hot new premier danseur of the NYCB when he fell for this dancer who left the Romanian National Ballet in disgrace. The director of the company gave him an ultimatum. He had to choose between dancing and his lover. He told Director Halvorsen to get bent, *jeté*-ed into the sunset, and started a dance school far, far away."

"Wow. That's both tragic and cliché, and I'd never do that."

"No kidding. What a chump, right?"

"Yeah, I like to think I'd have found a way to have both."

"Different times, boy," Charlotte said. "A lot has changed since then."

"Thank God."

"Hey, you're lucky. You're a switch-hitter."

"You know, princess, sometimes you can be—"

"What? Crass? Callous? Another C-word?" Charlotte shrugged. "No apologies."

"No, of course not. None expected." Lucas glanced over as David, Kelly, and Jule came into the studio. "Righteous," he said under his breath.

"Yummy," Charlotte agreed.

Jule in a suit and Jule in a practice leotard were two different animals. Every well-defined muscle of his sleek frame was on display in the thin knitted silk of the old-school sleeveless leotard and tights combination. Each step he took was innately graceful and completely unself-conscious. He was clearly confident and focused on the task before him.

For several minutes, Jule performed every basic step and then moved on to more difficult ones, with no evidence of effort. Each attitude he struck was marked by an elegant length of line and perfect form. Each motion was informed by strength and grace. He made it look easy and finished the audition with a deep bow to David and Kelly.

Lucas stood up and began applauding. Charlotte joined him.

David smiled at Jule. "You couldn't ask for a greater compliment," he said. "Welcome to The Downtown Ballet." He glanced at Kelly. "If that's what you want."

"It's what *we* want," Kelly said.

"Outstanding," David said. "We'll talk about details later, but—" He broke off as the door opened.

Jule frankly stared at the tall woman in the leopard coat who strode into the room like an *haute couture* model on a runway. She was beautiful in the bloodless fashion of someone who dwells in the rarified air of the top stratum of society, pale features pared down to the elegant bones. Perfectly straight flaxen-blond hair framed her face like a parted veil, and her eyes were the silver-gray of rain. The only color was provided by her red, shantung sheath dress and a slash of poppy on her mouth.

"Cath!" David said brightly as he came forward to take her gloved hand and kiss it.

"Did I miss the audition?" she asked.

David didn't meet her eyes. He turned to the others. "Kelly Holloway, Julian Parry, I'd like you to meet Catherine Dahlman, my partner in The Downtown Ballet."

"Nice to see you," Kelly said. "Your family has been a real friend to ballet."

"We all do what we can," she said airily before turning her cool gaze on Jule.

"Ma'am," Jule said. "A pleasure to meet you."

Catherine studied him for a few seconds and then turned to David. "I need a few moments of your time." She smiled at the others. "If you could spare David?"

David and Catherine walked to the far end of the long room.

"HOW DARE you?" Catherine said when they were out of earshot.

David discreetly rolled his eyes. "What outrage have I committed this time?"

"You're holding auditions without informing me?"

"I knew you'd be as excited as I am to acquire him. I didn't need to ask you."

"You should have anyway. As a courtesy, if nothing else."

David rolled his eyes. "Oh, give me a break. You're only mad because I bagged him first."

"How dare you."

"You're repeating yourself, *Doudou*."

"We can't have that," she said stiffly. "You might become bored with me."

David heard the implicit threat that *she* might become bored with *him*, so he mollified her because this was the long-established pattern of their relationship. He knew the steps of this dance by heart.

"Cath, you're my oldest friend, and without your help I wouldn't have this ballet company. So, yes, I should probably have let you know what I was up to, but it would have been such a great surprise to present it to you as a done deal."

"You seem so certain of yourself," she said in a neutral tone.

"I'm certain about Julian Parry. You watched the video with me."

Catherine sighed. "Ad nauseam."

"And?"

At last, she gave him a smile. "And you're right, of course. Julian Parry is the best young dancer I've seen since, well, you know, *you*."

"Then you agree he's an asset to the company."

"How could I disagree and not look like a fool?"

"And you're certainly no fool." David batted his eyelashes at her.

"Stop it." She smiled a genuine smile. "I try so hard to be mad at you."

"Don't be absurd. Everyone loves me. Now, come and talk to Jule and reassure him you're not about to eat him alive."

"Don't be naughty."

"I wasn't, but now that you mention it, he *is* quite *délicieux*, isn't he?"

Catherine sniffed. "He's a child."

"Not in those tights," David retorted.

"I forbid you to conceive a grand, doomed passion for that admittedly attractive infant."

"You *forbid* me?" David said with a gleam in his eye.

"Common sense forbids you," she said over her shoulder as she walked away from him. She gave Kelly a cordial smile as she approached. "I wonder if you remember that we've met before," she said.

"Of course. It was at one of Mr. Halvorsen's New Year's Eve parties."

"It was a… *memorable* evening," she replied. "As I recall, it was one of the German troupe who fell into the Christmas tree on the second-floor landing."

"And rode it all the way down to the foyer." Kelly smiled.

"What *was* his name?"

"His first name was Ivo. I remember because one of the German girls shouted as he went down."

"Gruenwald," Catherine said. "Ivo Gruenwald. Everyone was frantic thinking he'd break a leg."

"But he didn't have a scratch on him." Kelly chuckled. "He bounced up and demanded a beer."

Catherine smiled. "I thought Director Halvorsen was going to have an aneurysm."

"A few people might have been hoping for it," David said.

"Really, David," Catherine chided. "Rickard Halvorsen is a family friend."

"Not my family," David quipped.

"But it could have been," Catherine retorted. "If you hadn't chickened out of the engagement."

"This is great," Jule said. "I'm not sure what you're talking about now, but I'd love to hear some more stories."

"Hey, it was a long time ago," Kelly said. He glanced at Jule. "And we weren't that wild."

"Kelly is right," David said. "We weren't that wild. However… I might know a few more stories with *him* in them, and I'll tell them to you when the moment is right. I'm sure there'll be plenty of opportunities now that you've joined us."

"I would like that very much."

"No, you wouldn't," Kelly said. He glared at David.

"*You* were wild, though," Catherine said to David. "Maybe Jule would like to hear stories about you."

Jule smiled at her.

"You have a nice smile," Catherine said. "You should learn to use it." She turned back to Kelly. "It was good to see you."

"Same here," Kelly replied.

"David, I'll see you this evening?"

"Dinner at eight," he answered breezily. "Don't be late."

Catherine kissed his cheek before she left.

Chapter Five

AFTER CATHERINE had gone, David called Lucas and Charlotte over. "We've established that Jule shapes up to be a stellar soloist, but what kind of partner is he?" He turned to Jule.

"It's not my forte," Jule said, before Kelly could speak. "But I've had the training."

"Jule can do the lifts," Kelly added. "He's great at loading and suspension, but he needs some smoothing out on the unloading. It's just a matter of practice, but we haven't had a lot of luck finding the right partner."

"Well then, let's get smoothing." David grinned. "Unless you have somewhere else to be?"

Kelly raised his eyebrows at Jule.

"I'm game," Jule said.

"I'll let Sasha know we'll be a bit longer," Kelly said as he took out his phone.

David put his arm around Charlotte's shoulders and rested a hand on Lucas's forearm as he spoke to them. "Let's show Jule how we do it Downtown style. Nothing *too* fancy, but lay it all out for him." He turned to Jule as Charlotte and Lucas moved to the middle of the studio. "I know what you're thinking. Lucas is six foot two and Charlotte's five foot nothing. He won't have any problem lifting her over his head, but you—" He paused. "I imagine your size has been a worry for you."

"I did worry quite a lot when we first realized I'd stopped growing at five foot eight, but I don't think about it anymore." Jule shrugged. "We do the best we can with what we have, and anyway, I'm the same size Nureyev was. I'm actually taller than Baryshnikov."

"Kelly taught you well." David glanced toward Kelly, who was still on the phone.

"It's a bit surreal seeing how people react to him here," Jule said. "I've known him half my life, and he's always been this modest, no-nonsense guy dedicated to teaching children to dance. I mean, I knew he was a big deal a long time ago, but he's like a *legend* here."

"That he is. He's a pretty special guy, your coach, though he'd never admit it. Ballet lost a real talent when he retired so young. He had a lot of good years left. Hell, Nureyev danced well into his fifties. Kelly could have had that kind of career."

"He doesn't talk about it."

"Then I won't either. Looks like Lucas and Charlotte are ready."

Lucas and Charlotte had finished discussing the series of steps they were going to perform and assumed positions. Charlotte rose *en pointe* with the working leg extended behind her. Lucas stood beside her, with one arm around her waist and one hand supporting her upraised arm. In a few gestures, they became a prince and a princess.

"Lovely," Jule said softly.

"They do make an attractive pair," David agreed. He put a hand casually on Jule's shoulder. "You'll look just as good, I promise, and you'll be able to lift Charlotte as smoothly as Lucas is about to do. You already know the mechanics. You just need practice."

Jule watched the subtle movements as Lucas prepared to lift Charlotte. She leaped into an arabesque, and Lucas was there, using her momentum and his strength to raise her to a shoulder sit. He took hold of her waist and elevated her over his head. She extended her arms and legs and appeared to fly as he paced forward. With no sign of strain, Lucas handed her down, and she spun away in a series of pirouettes as he pursued.

"Good enough," David called out. "Thanks, kids."

Kelly walked over to join them. "They're wonderful," he told David. "So expressive."

"Lucas and Charlotte excel at emoting," David said proudly. "I know it's considered a little vulgar by some to show too much genuine emotion in classical ballet, like it's kabuki or something, but I don't give a shit."

Kelly smiled. "Did you ever?"

"You got me." David smiled. "Man, I miss those days sometimes."

"I don't." Kelly's phone rang. He answered and looked to Jule. "Sasha is making reservations and wants to know if we have any preferences for dinner."

"You *have* to let me take you to dinner," David exclaimed. "I in*sist*. I'm going to make a reservation right now."

"Nowhere noisy, please," Kelly requested.

"I know just the place." David paused. "Damn. I forgot about—" He paused. "It's not a problem. I'll call her." He took out his phone and walked a few feet away.

"So, what's the verdict?" Lucas asked as he and Charlotte approached.

"Are you all ours?" Charlotte winked at Jule.

Jule looked at Kelly.

"It does appear that way," Kelly said. "We have to work out some details, of course."

"That's brilliant!" Jule beamed at Kelly.

"It's not what I wanted for you, but if it's what you want, I'm behind you all the way."

"Lucky Jule," Charlotte purred to Lucas.

"And lucky us," Lucas said. "Jule, welcome to the Downtown."

THE MEMBERS of David's dinner party met outside the Public Theater.

"I thought we were eating, not seeing a play," Sasha said quietly to Kelly.

Not quietly enough. "There's a restaurant on the mezzanine called the Library," David said. "You'll love it. It's from the Astor era." He looked at the time on his phone. "Come on, Cath," he said under his breath. "This place won't bend the rules, even for me."

"What's wrong?" Kelly asked.

"We can't be seated until our party is complete," David said distractedly as he texted. "And she knows it, so she's power-checking me."

"She's what?"

"Oh, you know, just reminding me who calls the shots. You understand balance of power; you're in a relationship."

Kelly exchanged a glance with Sasha. Clearly, David and Catherine's relationship was not like theirs. Kelly's gaze went past Sasha to settle on Jule, who was talking with Lucas and Charlotte.

Sasha touched Kelly's hand. "What are you thinking, my heart?" he asked softly.

"Just borrowing trouble, as usual."

Sasha glanced at the trio of young dancers. "You're worried about Jule being swept off his feet by the big city and falling in with the wrong people?"

"Why do you bother asking when you can read my mind?"

"Because I respect you, of course." Sasha smiled. "And I'd bet you can tell me what I'll say next."

"That you tried to warn me, and I should let Jule make his own mistakes?"

"Trust him. Trust your own teaching."

Kelly sighed and then smiled fondly at Sasha. "Do you ever get tired of being right?"

"Of course, it becomes tedious." Sasha sighed, "But it's my job to balance you."

"Hey," David said as he put his phone away. "No PDA, please."

Kelly and Sasha turned to look at him. "What?" Kelly said.

"Are you kidding?" David said. "You looked like you were just about to kiss."

"I know the meaning of propriety," Sasha said.

"Oh good, then maybe you can teach me." David grinned. He glanced over at Lucas, Charlotte, and Jule. "That's a pretty sight," he said. "Remember how it felt to be that young and strong, standing on the threshold of the rest of your life?"

"Eh." Sasha shrugged. "I was never that pretty."

"*They* are going to light up the stage," David declared. "And the NYCB is going to be *sick* that they let Jule get away. I should buy stock in antacids."

"You think so?" Sasha said. "The NYCB has many talented young dancers, I hear."

"They don't have anyone like Jule," David said. "It goes beyond technique or aplomb, which he has, by the way, for days. The way he lights up when he dances isn't something you can teach. He just… *glows*. And he's not even twenty yet. Can you imagine the dancer he'll be in five years?"

David wasn't saying anything Kelly didn't already know, but it warmed his heart to hear it said aloud by someone who knew what they were talking about.

"You're only right," Sasha said.

David chuckled, his eyes going to the three dancers again. "I envy them… a little. So much has changed since we were performing."

"And yet, so much has stayed the same," Kelly replied.

"If you're referring to the 'don't ask/don't tell' policy, it really is a shame," David said.

Before he could say more, he was interrupted.

"DAVID," LUCAS called out. "What's the word?"

"Just a few more minutes," David called back.

Lucas rolled his eyes. "Waiting on the queen once again," he said to Charlotte and Jule. "It's just her way of letting the peons know she's so much more important than us."

"I thought she was nice," Jule said.

"You met her for a minute," Lucas said. "And of course, she was nice to *you*."

"Give it a rest, boy," Charlotte said. "Being bitter ages you, and you want to keep that handsome face for as long as you can."

"Girl, if you would just agree with me, I could stop."

Jule looked from Lucas to Charlotte and back again, confused by the sudden sharpness of tone.

"Okay. She's a woman-shaped glacier just barreling along, freezing and grinding down everything in her path," Charlotte replied. "Good enough?"

"Fucking perfect analogy for that frostbitten bitch." Lucas drew breath to speak again, but the shocked expression on Jule's face stopped the hateful words in his throat.

"Sorry, but you're going to hear a lot of trash talk," Charlotte told Jule. "Pay no attention, unless you hear your own name. It's always good to know what people are saying about you."

"Is it?" Jule said uncertainly.

"There's always going to be someone who wants to tear you down so they can get ahead. Sad but true. The more successful you are, the worse it gets."

"That's awful," Jule said. "But those are just a few people. Most people aren't like that."

"You don't know a lot of people," Lucas said.

"No, he's right," Charlotte said. "But a few is all it takes if the poison spreads." She smiled. "I'm a slut. I slept my way to *prima ballerina*. My bedroom has a revolving door. My favorite dish is David's tube steak smothered in underwear."

Jule gasped audibly.

"That's what people say, though." Charlotte laughed. "And so what? Let them talk. I refuse to act like a nun. I'm not some porcelain princess you can keep on a shelf."

"True that," Lucas said.

"What do they say about you?" Jule asked Lucas.

"Same," he answered with a straight face. "Tube steak. Yum."

Jule stared at him for a few seconds. "Are you taking the piss with me?"

Lucas grinned. "I'm exaggerating a little." He stopped smiling. "But just a little."

Jule laughed. "I think I'm starting to get your sense of humor."

"Don't take anything he says seriously, and you'll be fine." Charlotte reached out to adjust the knot of Jule's tie. "Don't you worry about a thing, baby boy, because Uncle Luc and Auntie Char are going to be here to make sure you're fine. You already know how to dress like an adult, so you're way ahead of some people."

"Thank you. I appreciate that. I've danced a few ballets as a guest artist, but I'm used to working solo, so I imagine I'll be feeling overwhelmed for a bit."

"Just don't let the competitiveness throw you," Lucas said. "Stay focused. That's key."

"You sound like Kelly," Jule said. "I mean it as a compliment."

"You're adorable." Charlotte patted Jule's cheek. "Are you looking forward to hoisting me?"

"Excuse me?"

"She means lifts," Lucas said. "I think she was being vaguely vulgar to embarrass you. Frankly, a weak effort from our girl."

"Just having a little fun with the rookie." Charlotte pouted alluringly.

"Eyes front." Lucas said. "The queen has arrived." As everyone turned toward the street, he leaned over to whisper in Jule's ear. "I can't wait to be alone with you again."

Jule, who'd begun to wonder if Lucas even remembered kissing him, smiled warmly. He watched David greet Catherine with a kiss on each cheek as he hugged to himself the knowledge that Lucas liked him. He hadn't imagined it.

"Let's eat," David said as he took Catherine's arm.

Kelly and Sasha followed them into the building with Lucas, Charlotte, and Jule trailing them.

"Are they dating?" Jule asked.

Charlotte laughed. "Sorry, but that struck me so funny."

"Why?"

"David and Miss Dahlman are business partners," Lucas said. "Rumor is they were an item back in the day, even got engaged, but I've never seen any evidence that a woman could turn David's motor over. I suppose it's possible."

"They act like a couple," Jule said.

"I'm sure she'd like that," Lucas said. "You could almost feel sorry for her. Almost."

Jule reacted to the bitterness in Lucas's voice. "You really don't like her, do you?"

"I don't like anything that can spit venom."

"Hush," Charlotte said. "What if she hears you?"

"Then it's off with my head, I guess."

"What a waste that would be," Charlotte said.

"You're both awful," Jule said, but he smiled to show he was teasing.

At the table, Jule ended up between Lucas and Charlotte and directly across from David, who immediately ordered champagne.

"I have an announcement," David said, once glasses were filled. "Jule and Lucas already know a bit about it, but you'll all hear it first in its entirety."

It was clear from Catherine's face that this was a surprise to her, and she didn't like it much. However, she raised her glass with the others.

"I've written a ballet... almost." David winked. "I call it *Fireheart*. Not too original, I know, but the story will be. It will chronicle years of the oppression gay people have endured. It will celebrate courage and the triumph of love. I'm pretty proud of it." He drained his glass.

Everyone drank except for Catherine, who discreetly set her glass aside.

"That's very... bold," Kelly said to David. "You *should* be proud."

"It won't be the first ballet with an LGBT theme." David shrugged. "But I'm excited about it. I think it's really good."

"It's time," Sasha said. "It's past time for a ballet like that."

"Agreed," David said. "And in Lucas and Jule, I have the right dancers to embody my vision." He filled everyone's glass again.

CATHERINE DIDN'T speak to David again until they reached her penthouse apartment where he held chronic roommate status. She tossed her clutch onto the foyer table and shrugged out of her sable coat. Without pausing, she left the fur on the floor and stalked into the kitchen area.

David picked up the coat and hung it on a rack near the door before he followed her. "Cath," he said warmly as he walked up to her. "I know I ambushed you, but—"

"What are you thinking?" she asked sharply as she turned toward him.

"I'm thinking you want to talk to me about something."

Catherine closed her eyes for a moment, as though feeling the twinge of a headache. "Why didn't you discuss this with me?"

"I knew you wouldn't be interested, so I didn't bother you with it."

"You wrote a new ballet, and you didn't want to *bother* me with it?" Catherine was incredulous. "*Bordel de merde.*"

David shrugged and walked out to the living room.

Catherine followed carrying two fingers of vodka in a tumbler. "The truth is you were afraid to tell me, weren't you?"

"Afraid?" David turned from the view of city lights. "Is that what you think?"

"You knew I wouldn't approve."

"Actually, I was certain you'd be thrilled to give your support to a work of art that highlights a social injustice that—"

"I don't want to hear your bullshit. I want to have a discussion."

"It's almost midnight."

"Neither of us is going to turn into a pumpkin." Catherine swallowed half the vodka.

"One of us might become pickled, though."

"Don't be cute. It doesn't work on me anymore."

"Then say whatever it is you feel compelled to say… or whatever the booze compels you to say."

Catherine's pale face lost all color. "I'm not drunk, and I won't back a queer ballet," she said flatly.

"Then you won't. Anything else before I go?"

"Don't be absurd."

"*Bébé*, I was born this way."

"I meant there's no reason for you to go all the way home."

David stared at her. "You don't think I'd stay here, do you?"

"Why not? Just because we have a disagreement is no reason to be uncivil."

"Actually, it is. And we're not having *le différend, Doudou*. You made a pronouncement."

"I made a business decision. I won't put money into a project that won't earn it back."

"So, the whole 'supporting the arts' thing is just window-dressing?"

"A dance about gay sex is not art."

David was silent for several long moments before he spoke again. "I see. Well, you're wrong about that, but this isn't about my ballet, is it?"

"Don't try to make this about something it's not."

"But it's always about the same thing. Why do you do this to yourself? Why can't you leave the past in the past?"

"How can you ask me that if you truly care about me?"

"It's pointless to talk to you when you've been drinking." David sighed. "I'll see you for lunch tomorrow?" He dodged the glass Catherine threw at him. "Waste of the Goose," he said calmly before he turned toward the door.

"David," Catherine said as he reached for the doorknob.

David paused.

"When you think about it, you'll see I'm right," she said.

He left without replying.

Chapter Six

THE NEXT morning, Lucas met Jule at the entrance to The Downtown Ballet's complex of buildings. "Hi," he said. "Ready for the guided tour?"

Jule smiled. "What do you think?" he asked cheekily.

"I think this is the beginning of a new era for The Downtown Ballet and my love life, and I'm very excited about it."

Jule chuckled. "You're outrageous."

"You love it."

"Yeah, I do, but should I?"

"Yes, you should." Lucas led Jule down a broad hallway. "The doors on either side lead to the smaller studios. Directly ahead, those double doors lead to the main studio."

They walked through the doors at the end of the hall and were briefly outdoors before entering another building. Lucas turned right, and they stopped at the second door on the left. "This is your room."

Jule opened the door and stepped in. It looked just like a college dorm room from American movies, except the furniture was nicer. There were two twin beds, a closet, a long counter/desk with two chairs, and a half bath.

"Showers are downstairs in the locker room. You don't have a roommate, but I could probably be persuaded to sleep over," Lucas said.

Jule was looking out one of the two tall windows. "I can see Lincoln Center from here."

"Yeah, this is a choice location for sure. All hail Queen Catherine and her influential family."

"I just meant... I always thought I'd be dancing there someday."

Lucas grimaced. "Yeah, the NYCB pretty much owns it." He brightened. "But it's not the only venue in the ballet world." He came up behind Jule and, after a moment, put his arms around him. He smiled when Jule relaxed into his embrace. "You're going to be a star. Never doubt that. The NYCB will come begging."

"That's not what I want."

"Then I guess I don't understand what you're saying."

"I want to be a great dancer."

"Done."

"But I would never make anyone beg. I feel horrible just thinking about it."

When Lucas turned Jule in his arms and bent his head to kiss him, Jule didn't protest, but pressed closer.

"So that's how it is," someone said from the doorway.

Jule recoiled, but Lucas kept an arm around his waist.

"Hey, Bram," Lucas said coolly. "What's shakin'?"

"Bupkes. I was just passing by and looked in the door."

Lucas snorted. "Unlikely."

As Jule composed himself, he studied the visitor. Bram was Lucas's size and just as flagrantly handsome with thick dark hair, crystal-blue eyes, and a bright white smile. His memory provided the name of one of the San Francisco Ballet's principal male dancers. "You're Abraham Silber," he blurted out.

"Yes, I am." Bram smiled indulgently. "But you can call me Bram."

Jule's ingrained manners prompted him to reply. "I'm Julian Parry. You can call me Jule."

"I thought that was you. Catherine mentioned you." Bram's gaze went to Lucas. "You moved even faster than usual, Madding."

"Shut your stupid mouth," Lucas suggested.

"Rude," Jule said automatically. "I mean… It's nice to meet you, Bram."

"What are you doing here, Bram?" Lucas asked loudly.

Bram addressed Jule. "I'm looking forward to seeing you dance," he said. "I hear you're something special."

"I can confirm that," Lucas said. "We're in the middle of a tour, so if you wouldn't mind?"

"A tour, huh? Is that what they're calling it now?"

"Is there something you want to say to me?"

"So many things." Bram grinned. "But you're busy right now. Catch you later." He turned his megawatt grin on Jule. "Nice to meet you too." He waved before walking away.

"What an ass," Lucas said while Bram was likely still within earshot.

"He's not the one who left the door open," Jule pointed out.

"If you're going to be logical, we can just stop right now."

"What?"

"I'm kidding. If you don't like my teasing, I can stop."

"I want you to do as you like."

"I'd *like* to kiss you again, but you have a lunch meeting with David, so we'll have to postpone any fooling around for now."

As they walked more halls, Jule's brain ignored the upcoming meeting in favor of thinking about fooling around with Lucas later. It was absurd, but he fancied he could feel the heat of Lucas's body next to his. He was so distracted that he wouldn't have been able to find his way back to the dorm room without a map.

At five minutes until twelve, Lucas brought Jule to David's office. This was a sixty-by-forty space with fourteen-foot ceilings and a wall of mirrors opposite a wall of glass. All but a twenty-by-twenty carpeted area was floored in maple. David was standing at a portable barre, wearing sweatpants and a T-shirt. As Lucas and Jule entered, David patted his face with the bright red scarf around his neck and came forward to greet them.

"I like this." Jule took another look around the room.

"It's a good space," David said. "I designed it myself."

"It's perfect."

David smiled. "I thought I'd have lunch delivered if it suits you."

"You're the boss," Jule said.

"I've got a thing," Lucas said. "Call me later."

"Me or Jule?"

"Why not both?" Lucas left.

"FOOD SHOULD be here any minute," David said. "Do you like Indian cuisine?"

"I'm from London. Curry is our default fast food."

"Good. Good. While we wait, can I show you a couple of things?" David grinned. "I'm just so excited about *Fireheart*. I can't wait to get started."

"I'd love that," Jule said.

David walked to the middle of the wood floor and Jule followed.

"Tell me what you think of this." David stood with feet in fourth position, arms curved softly in front of him as though hugging a fragile ghost. He took three gliding steps before launching into a cabriole leap. He turned in midair to land on one foot and perform a revolution. He stopped with one leg extended behind and the forward knee bent, arms upraised, and head thrown back.

"That was lovely," Jule said.

"Especially for a man staring fifty in the face?"

"I have no idea how old you are, and it doesn't matter. You're sort of… ageless."

"That's probably the nicest thing anyone's ever said to me." David smiled. "Now, let's see your version."

Jule left his shoes and socks on the carpet and assumed the first attitude David had shown him. He ran through the same steps and came to a halt in front of David.

"I like your energy," David said. "But this needs to be softer, not so crisp. You know?"

Jule nodded. "Again?"

"I should think so, *monsieur*," David said haughtily, making a pompous face.

Jule smiled at David before he performed the steps again and then a third time.

"Beautiful," David said. "There's just one thing." He came to stand behind Jule. "Give me the *en haut* again, left foot *tendu*."

Jule obediently raised his arms above his head, palms turned inward, in a series of graceful curved lines that gave the illusion of extending past his fingertips.

David let his gaze linger on the perfect hemispheres of Jule's butt. "*C'est un joli cul*," he said.

"*Merci*," Jule said. "Yours is quite nice, as well."

"I shouldn't be surprised you speak French, should I?"

"You can be surprised, but I'd rather you complimented me for my form and not just my arse."

"I'll try to show a bit more class. Can you hold that position for another few seconds?"

"Of course."

David ran his hands up Jule's arms, gently but firmly realigning them to a shape more pleasing to him, one that more accurately illustrated the emotion he was trying to convey. With subtle pressure, he altered the tilt of Jule's head.

"I'm sorry. I didn't realize class was in session," Catherine said as she came into the room.

David didn't look up. "I wasn't expecting you after the way we left things last night."

"I dropped by on the off-chance you still wanted to go to lunch."

"Obviously not. I'm working."

"Are you now?"

David heard the insinuation in her tone and finally made eye contact. "Do you have business here?" he asked.

Catherine's posture stiffened as she turned her attention to Jule. "It looks as though you've already settled in."

"It's different here, but I'm getting used to it, ma'am. Everyone has been so helpful and nice to me."

"Yes, I would imagine people *are* nice to you." Catherine smiled. "Why wouldn't they be when you're so nice?"

"I try to be," Jule said. "Mr. Holloway—Kelly taught me that comportment is more than just physical. First, I'm a dancer. Second, I'm an ambassador for dance. How I behave reflects on more than just me. It reflects on my teachers and my art."

"Are you real?" Catherine blurted out.

"God, I hope so," David said under his breath.

The speaker on the desk phone chimed. "DoorDash is here," said the receptionist.

"Thanks," David called out. "I can't believe you," he said to Catherine as he walked to the office area.

Catherine followed him the few steps to the desk. "*You* can't believe *me*?"

David glanced at Jule, who was putting his socks and shoes back on. "Don't make a fool of yourself."

"I'm not the fool here."

David met her gaze. He raised an eyebrow.

"Well, what would you call a man your age drooling over a teenager?"

"I'm not—So that's what this is about." David turned toward the knock at the door. "Jule, would you get that?" He focused on Catherine again. "Too bad you can't stay for lunch."

"We need to talk, David."

"*You* need to talk, you mean. Tell you what, give me a call and make an appointment, but I warn you, I'm about to be mega-busy. Bye now."

"Let me know when you've finished pouting." Catherine walked away from him. She nodded coolly to Jule on her way to the door.

Jule brought the takeaway bags over to the desk. "She always looks so smart," he said.

"She was a model… briefly."

"Did she ever dance?"

David shook his head as he pulled items from the bags. "She took lessons until she was thirteen. She had a growth spurt and was five ten by the end of the year. Some idiot told her she was too tall to be a ballerina, and she believed it."

"She'd have been a lovely Giselle."

"Wouldn't she though?"

"It's too bad someone put her off dancing."

"I agree. I think she would have been happier."

David handed Jule plastic utensils. "It's not very posh," he said, affecting a British accent a la Monty Python. "But go ahead and tuck in."

"Thanks," Jule said. He wasted no time digging into the food. "I really like the flow of those steps you showed me," he said when he stopped for a breath. "They're so… romantic is the feeling I get, but also sadness, like, you know, *Romeo and Juliet*."

"Your words please me." David grinned. "That's exactly how I want the audience to feel. I want people to leave the theater feeling they've seen a story of great love and courage."

"Does it have to be a tragedy?"

"You mean… can the lovers be alive the end?"

"Yes, and together."

"You don't ask for much."

"Sorry." Jule put down his fork. "I get carried away sometimes."

"Don't be sorry. Your fire is one of the things I love about you." David paused, as though he'd said too much, and then went on. "You should let it shine out more often."

Jule smiled. "It's easy to lose myself in the story of a ballet and to become the character for a while. It's harder in real life."

"Guess what? That's pretty much what life is."

"I suppose. In a way…." Jule met David's gaze. "Are you saying we're all playing parts? Like Hamlet?"

"Right. Shakespeare did say something like that, didn't he?" David deployed one of his most charming smiles. "Don't listen to me. I'm an old cynic."

"Would a cynic write a ballet like *Fireheart*?"

David was genuinely touched and couldn't respond for a moment.

"I didn't mean to be rude," Jule said.

"You weren't." David cleared his throat. "It was exactly what I needed to hear. Now, while we let lunch settle, let's talk about any ideas you might have, and then we'll run through a few more steps. Sound good?"

"There's nothing I'd rather be doing, sir."

"Are you trying to make me feel old? Everyone here calls me David."

"If you say so…. David."

"Good. Now, watch and learn."

Chapter Seven

KELLY CAME out of the bathroom and found Sasha dressed for the day. He was surprised, as he'd expected his partner to be in the king-size bed, enjoying a rare opportunity to sleep in.

"I miss the school," Sasha said before Kelly could speak.

"Me too." Kelly gave Sasha a hug. "Thanks again for coming with me. I know how much you hate New York."

"I don't hate New York. I hate what happened here, but...." Sasha sighed. "It was a long time ago."

Kelly picked up the shirt Sasha had laid out and put it on. "I'm still a little worried about leaving Jule here."

"He seems happy to me."

"Yeah, but—Never mind."

"Don't never mind me. What's bothering you? Is it David? I can understand if you have concerns, but Jule is—"

"Lucas Madding bothers me."

"Ah."

"I know that tone. You think I'm being foolish."

"It had to happen eventually. Jule is dedicated, but you can't expect him to be a monk."

"I know, but.... This just isn't what I wanted for him. I don't care that he has a boyfriend. I'd just rather see him with someone who's not...."

"Someone who's not Lucas?"

"Well, yes, but someone closer to his age would be nice. Lucas must be ten years older than Jule."

"He's twenty-seven. I looked it up."

"Of course you did," Kelly said fondly.

"Jule may be naïve, but he's not a child. He's an intelligent, focused young man with a clear goal. Okay? Now, what other objections do you have?"

"I just wish he didn't have to sneak around. It's... sleazy."

Sasha looked wounded. "How can you say that? We did the same."

"It's not the same," Kelly said.

"How is it not?"

"You and I were in love."

"Who are you to say Jule is not in love?"

"He probably is, dammit." Kelly sighed. "I wish I could say the same for Lucas."

"What *are* you saying?"

"I'm saying Lucas is romancing Jule on David's behalf."

"But they already have Jule."

"Yeah, mission accomplished, but it must be nice to have someone like Jule head over heels for you."

Sasha nodded. "But as long as Jule is happy, I see no reason to be upset."

"I'd like to talk to him about this, but I know I'd screw it up, and he'd just end up mad at me."

"You're right. You'd only make it worse."

"Thanks."

Sasha put his arms around Kelly. "We prepared Jule as best we could, my heart. Now, we must let him make his own way."

Kelly kissed Sasha's nose. "Then I guess it's time we got back to work," he said.

Sasha nodded as he let Kelly go. "We can't expect Mrs. Johnston to run the school by herself, after all."

JULE CAME in from the next room just in time to hear Sasha's statement. "What are you talking about?" he asked.

"Sasha's giant ego," Kelly joked.

Jule rolled his eyes at Kelly. "No, you said something about Mrs. Johnston as I came in."

"Oh, right. Well, we can't leave her alone with hordes of dance students for much longer."

"You're going back to England?"

"That was always the plan," Kelly said. "We train you. You win a place with the… with *a* ballet company. We go home and run the school, and maybe even train another great dancer."

"I know, but—" Jule paused. "I thought perhaps you'd stay here a bit longer. As my coaches. David would be happy to give you a salary, I'm sure." He reacted to Kelly's change of expression. "What?"

Sasha answered. "I don't think Kelly would be happy working for David."

"Why not?"

"We have history," Kelly said. "I don't want to go into it." He sighed. "We're not leaving today, but I'd like to be back at least a week before Christmas."

"The pageant," Jule said.

"Yeah, the Christmas pageant is a lot of work, as you know. The school will need us there."

"I need you *here*!" Jule said with more force than he'd intended. He saw a clear message pass between Kelly and Sasha as their gazes met.

"You're ready," Kelly told Jule. "You can do this without me or Sasha. I don't think it. I *know* it. Sasha knows it. David knows it. The only one who doesn't know it is you."

"Maybe I *can* do it alone, but I don't want to."

Kelly smiled. "The truth is that I have nothing else to teach you. You've surpassed me already, and you're just nineteen. It's time for you to find another teacher, one who'll take you farther."

"*Fiu*," Sasha said softly to Jule. "I call you son because you're the child of my heart, and I've always been proud of you. You're honest and kind and you work hard without complaint."

"Sasha's trifecta of human perfection," Kelly interjected.

"Shush," Sasha said before addressing Jule again. "It's time for you to change. I won't use any examples like cocoons and butterflies, but you know what I'm trying to say."

"Yes, but I still don't like it," Jule answered.

"What has *liking it* got to do with ballet?" Kelly said.

Finally, Jule smiled. "I can't stop you from going," he said. "But I'd keep you here if I could. It's hard to remember when you weren't in my life."

"We're not leaving your life," Kelly said. "We'll always be there for you."

"And we will be expecting free tickets to performances," Sasha added.

Jule laughed in spite of his heavy heart. "I really don't know what I'll do without you."

"You'll do your own laundry, that's one thing," Sasha said.

Jule hugged Sasha. "Thank you," he said in a choked voice.

"Hey," Kelly said. "No dramatics. We're not leaving for at least a couple of days." He put a hand on Jule's nape. "And after we're gone, you'll be so busy that you won't have time to miss us."

Sasha let go of Jule and smiled at him. "Now go. You don't want to be late on your official first day with a ballet company."

"Not exactly my first." Jule returned Sasha's smile. "I was already a member of the illustrious Holloway Academy of Dance."

Kelly rolled his eyes, but he looked pleased. "You'll be fine."

Jule nodded. "I won't let you down."

"The thought never even occurred to me. Now, get to work."

JULE LEFT with his duffel bag over his shoulder. Sometime tomorrow, he'd move the rest of his clothes from the hotel to the dorm, but he wanted one more night with his unofficial uncles. He took a cab to the school and hurried inside to the big studio.

"Jule! Join us," David called out as Jule entered the large light-filled room. He was facing a half circle of dancers in practice clothes, all sitting on the hardwood floor. They turned to look at Jule as he crossed to them.

Charlotte gave Jule a big, welcoming smile. "Hey, kid," she said. "Welcome to the show."

Lucas gestured for Jule to sit next to him.

"I'm sorry if I'm late," Jule said.

"Class hasn't officially started yet," David said. He paused. "And now it has. Today, I want to talk about our Christmas season ballet. I realize I've done my usual procrastinating and now we're entering crunch time, but I also realize you're the kind of company that can pull it off." David stood and moved about as he continued speaking. "As we all know, the NYCB puts on the sacred *Nutcracker* every year. We're too young to have a Christmas tradition, and frankly, I don't want one. I'm not a fan of being locked into something, and neither are you or you wouldn't be here." David indicated the surroundings with a sweep of his arm.

"You're damn skippy," Lucas said.

David chuckled. "Well put." He looked around the crescent of dancers. "I hope you'll all be pleased to hear that I've chosen *The Sleeping Beauty*. I'll be happy to explain why." He paused, but no one spoke up. "You're probably thinking that it's a very traditional ballet, but hear me out. It actually has a lot of room for innovation." He pointed at Jule. "You have the look of a man who wants to say something."

"The fairy tale characters," Jule said.

"*Exactement!*" David smiled. "The king, queen, prince, and princess have very well-defined and beloved dances associated with them. Ditto the Lilac Fairy and the evil Carabosse, but… all those other characters such as Puss'n'Boots, the Bluebird, the Big Bad Wolf, and so on, well…. We can do just about anything we want with them. I've talked to Marilee, and she's very excited about getting started on costumes."

"Have you decided who's dancing which role?" Charlotte asked.

"You, my kitten, will be dancing Princess Aurora. I've called Catriona Costain, and she's agreed to return for the season to be our queen. I'll be taking the role of King Florestan." David took a bow and waited for the noise to die down. "Thank you. Thank you. Prince Desiré will be danced by Lucas, naturally, and Jule will be our Lilac Fairy."

There was silence for a moment before Lucas said, "I love it." He grinned at Jule. "It's brilliant."

"Brilliant? You really think so?" David preened.

"I love it too," Charlotte said. "And I can't wait to see your costume, Jule."

"Moving along," David said. "Samira, you'll be the Crystal Fountain Fairy. Sophie will take the part of the villainous Carabosse. Now that's the costume I'm looking forward to."

"I'm hoping it will have a Maleficent kind of vibe," Sophie said.

"Dani," David called out. "You're our Puss'n'Boots. Dylan and Astra you'll be the Woodland Fairy and Garden Fairy. Other roles will be assigned to members of the corps." He looked up as the door opened and the musical director entered. "Jamison, right on time."

Jamison nodded to David and the dancers and continued on his way to the piano. He sat, propped his music, and raised the cover to reveal the keys. As Jamison warmed up his fingers, David gave instructions to his troupe.

"For the next two weeks, every waking moment will be spent mounting this ballet. Over the coming days, you will come to hate me as a slave driver. Go right ahead. Hate me all you like as long as you get the job done. No one here, with the possible exception of Jule, hasn't danced *Sleeping Beauty* at least once."

"Mr. Holloway—" Jule coughed. "*Kelly* made sure I knew quite a few of the classical solos for a premier danseur, so I know parts of the prince's role."

"Mr. Holloway certainly is thorough," David said. "How do you feel about the role I gave you?"

"It's an interesting choice, sir…. David."

"Sir David. I like the sound of that." David waited for the chuckles to die down. "Interesting is good. I do hope audiences find our little ballet interesting. So, let's have some fun with it."

Let's have some fun with it. Never, in all the years Jule had studied with Kelly had his instructor ever uttered those words in connection with dance practice. He wasn't sure how he felt about it until Lucas offered a hand to pull him to his feet.

Lucas's warm touch and subtle wink turned Jule's thoughts in another direction. He understood ballet and didn't doubt he could perform whatever steps David devised for him, but whatever this thing with Lucas was, it was unknown territory. He wasn't afraid anymore, but he *was* flailing a little. When he was confused, it was his habit to seek guidance from those older and presumably wiser. He looked at David and realized just how much he was going to miss Kelly and Sasha.

Chapter Eight

Two DAYS later, when Kelly and Sasha checked out of the Marquis, Jule was there to see them off.

"You really don't have to go to the airport with us," Kelly told Jule.

"You've said that a million times. I'm going," Jule insisted.

"They don't even let you come in anymore. All that security."

Sasha joined the conversation. "Jule, you'd just have two long, expensive cab rides. Listen to Kelly. He's actually right."

Jule sighed. "I know. I just want to spend every possible second with you."

"I understand," Kelly said. "I'm going to miss you."

"You can call us anytime," Sasha assured Jule. "Anytime. Don't bother trying to figure out what time it is in London. Just call."

"I will."

There was a knock at the door. "Bellman," someone called out.

Kelly opened the door, and a young man in a hotel uniform pulled a luggage cart into the room. "Everything against the wall is going," Kelly said. He handed the man a twenty. "If you could take this down to the valet, there should be a car waiting under Holloway."

"A pleasure, sir." The bellman loaded the four pieces of luggage and left.

"This is it." Kelly held out his arms for a hug.

Jule threw his arms around Kelly and held him tightly. "I can never thank you enough for everything you've done for me."

"Just don't embarrass me." Kelly ran a hand over Jule's hair.

"My turn," Sasha prompted. He wrapped his arms around Jule and held him close for several seconds. "You make me proud, child of my heart," he murmured.

"I'm going to cry like a baby," Jule said in a small voice.

"No, you won't." Sasha let him go. "You'll cry like a man."

Jule smiled through his tears.

"Let's go before we all start crying like a bunch of old queens," Kelly said.

Sasha led the way to the elevator and across the lobby. Kelly said a few more words to Jule, random advice about New York, places he should see when he had time, and the like. And then they were outside in the cold, approaching the queued taxis, airport shuttles, and limousines, and the groups of people waiting for transportation.

Kelly approached the valet stand, more money changed hands, and one of the attendants opened the back door of a big car idling just out of the flow of traffic. Sasha kissed Jule's cheek and got into the vehicle beside Kelly. The car pulled away, exhaust pluming from the tailpipe like dragon's breath. In moments, it was lost to Jule's sight, and he turned, heart sinking, to find a cab to take him to the dorm.

"Jule!"

Jule looked to his left and saw Lucas just outside the Starbucks.

"Do you want coffee?" Lucas shouted.

Jule walked over to him. "Yes, thank you. A mocha latte, no whipped cream."

Lucas opened the door and Jule followed him into the crowded coffee shop. In slightly more than ten minutes, they were back outside with large cups of flavored coffee.

"What are you doing here?" Jule asked as they started walking through Times Square.

"I remembered you said Kelly and Sasha were leaving this morning and I figured this is where you'd be."

"And?"

"And?" Lucas shook his head. "I came to see you, of course. I thought you'd be bummed and maybe I could cheer you up. What would you like to do?"

"That's very kind of you." Jule sipped his latte. "To be honest, I don't know what I want to do. I'm just feeling a bit blah, you know?"

"If you were at home and feeling blah, what would you do?"

"Go to the studio and practice."

"Then let's go dancing." Lucas's eyes gleamed. "Have you ever been to a gay bar?"

"It's just past eight in the morning."

"You're right. My favorite place doesn't open till five. What are we going to do until then?"

"I'm going to the school and practice my part."

"As your David-appointed coach it behooves me keep you company."

"I'm glad to have you," Jule said as they started walking.

Lucas cleared his throat. "By the way, it's okay if you want to, you know, touch me, or anything."

"Anything?"

"Yeah, no." Lucas grinned. "I'm going to have to watch what I say around you, aren't I?"

"Kelly says it's a good idea in general to be careful what comes out of your mouth." Jule smiled back at Lucas. "And then, Sasha always says it's good to watch what goes into your mouth also." He laughed, and Lucas laughed with him.

"Seriously, though, if you wanted to hug me or something, I give you blanket permission in perpetuity."

"Thank you," Jule said gravely. "It's a real honor."

"So," Lucas said after a few moments. "Is it okay if I touch you?"

"What did you have in mind?"

"Yeesh, I'm talking about holding hands, not a sixty-nine on the sidewalk."

Jule chuckled. "I actually like hugs, so, you may hug me whenever it's appropriate."

"You're a test, kid, but I love it. Have I mentioned I'm crazy about you?"

"Not in those words."

"And you like *me*, right? I mean, you wouldn't let me get so close if you didn't, right? That must mean you like me, right? Right?" Lucas paused. "Jesus, I'm babbling."

"I like you, and yes, and yes." Jule answered Lucas's questions in order.

Lucas took Jule's free hand and pulled him into the windbreak of a bank on the corner. "Sorry to inject so much drama into your day, but I need some reassurance. I find myself wondering if you feel the same way about me as I feel about you. Weird, huh?"

"I don't know. How do you feel about me?"

"Are you kidding?" Lucas glanced over at a woman using the automated teller and lowered his voice. "I just told you I'm crazy about you."

A small crease appeared between Jule's eyebrows. "You only met me a week ago."

"I know it's insane, but I swear I have very strong feelings for you. Or about you. Which is it?"

"I don't believe you. You couldn't possibly love me. You haven't known me long e—"

"I love everything about you," Lucas insisted. "I love the way you look and talk and walk. I love watching you dance. I love the way you eat, the way you drink, the way you take a little breath just before you start talking. I love your kindness and your dedication, and I hope I get to see more of that sense of humor you flash once in a while." He shrugged. "I could go on like this all day, but you get the idea."

Jule blinked.

"Is there anything you want to say?" Lucas asked.

"Same," Jule said.

"That's it?"

Jule nodded. "You're saying you're fascinated, and I'm saying, so am I."

"Fascinated?"

"Pretty sure that's the right word, though I'm no genius."

"But that's good, right? Fascination is good."

"I don't think it's either good *or* bad. It just means I can't take my eyes off you."

"Same." Lucas smiled. "I can't get you out of my head."

"Good, that's settled then. Can we go now?"

"Not just yet." Lucas put his arms around Jule and pulled him close.

After a brief moment of stiffness, Jule relaxed and returned the hug. "This is nice, but I really need the practice."

"We can practice hugging anytime you want."

"Wanker." Jule laughed as he pushed away from Lucas. "You know what I meant."

Lucas grinned. "After you."

Jule kept his thoughts to himself as they continued their walk. He missed Kelly and Sasha fiercely already and wished he could talk to them about what had just happened. He liked how it felt when he was with Lucas, but it was a little worrisome as well. He had the sense that things could get out of control quickly, but on the other hand, it excited him. And those were just the physical reactions. He couldn't begin to get a grip on his emotions when Lucas was nearby. He felt pulled in two directions with equal force, and he would have to find a way to balance it... if he could. And if he couldn't? Jule shied away from the thought, and the very avoidance of it made him uneasy.

JULE AND Lucas went to the small studio David had set aside for them. There was a lot to learn in a short time, but Lucas already knew Prince Desiré's part. He had partnered Charlotte as the Princess Aurora three years ago during The Downtown Ballet's first season. He'd been twenty-four and she twenty; it was his first starring role for Downtown and her first for anyone.

Lucas was concentrating so hard on the steps that he missed a few cues that Jule wasn't his usual committed self. It wasn't until Jule swore loudly at a misstep that Lucas caught on to Jule's mood. He turned off the music and faced his partner.

"You okay?"

"I'm fine," Jule said curtly.

"You don't seem fine."

"You'll just have to take my word for it."

Lucas frowned. "Why the attitude?" He paused. "Is it me?"

"No," Jule said more sharply than he'd intended. "Sorry, I didn't mean to bark."

"Are you having trouble with the new steps?"

"No."

"I didn't think so, but I had to ask."

"I'm sorry if I'm being a prat." Jule sighed.

"I'm not sure what that means exactly."

"It means I'm letting my problems affect our practice time like a selfish git—"

"You have problems?"

"I'm just... confused about some things, and I'm not used to being confused. I've always known exactly what I was going to do next, but now...."

Lucas moved closer. "Tell me what's bothering you."

Jule didn't back away, though he wanted to. Having Lucas this close did nothing for his nerves, but he wasn't going to retreat. "It *is* you, all right?"

"No. That is very much *not* all right. Tell me what I did, and I'll fix it."

Jule almost smiled. "You can't. When I said it was you, I was fibbing a little. It's really me."

"What's wrong with you? Because, God as my witness, I can't see anything."

"Look, I'm perfectly confident in my dancing ability, but this thing with you... I can't seem to get a handle on it." Jule paused and then spoke in a calmer tone. "My life has been all about control, but I can't control my reactions to you. I'm a little shaken up."

"That's actually pretty normal when you *like* someone, and I do believe you recently declared your extreme like for me."

"I said I was fascinated." Jule finally smiled. "It's really messing with me, though."

"It's supposed to." Lucas returned the smile. "Just go with it."

"I wish I could be sure. How do I know if I'm falling in love?"

Lucas's face showed his surprise at these words, but he answered quickly. "That's easy. Love is just feelings, Jule. How do you feel when you see me?"

"It makes me happy."

Lucas ran his fingers lightly up Jule's arm and curled them around his nape. "How do you feel when I touch you?"

"Like I might explode because it feels so good."

"Well, there you are."

"But is it love or just... you know?"

"Sex?"

Jule nodded.

"Okay, I get it. You're a late bloomer and—Scratch that." Lucas met Jule's eyes. "Why don't you tell me what you're thinking?"

"I've never felt like this before, and it scares me a little."

Lucas smiled. "It's okay if you're nervous. It's perfectly normal."

"For a guy?"

"Yep, even for a guy." Lucas cocked his head to the side. "You know, I'd think being around Holloway and Vasile all the time, you'd be used to seeing, you know, examples of...."

Jule smiled. "I've never seen more than a pretty hot kiss."

"Get your mind out of the gutter, Parry. I wasn't suggesting they gave you hands-on instruction in the art of man on man."

"*Bloody hell.*" Jule shook his head. "I'm going to pretend you didn't say that."

"I retract it." Lucas smiled. "We don't have to talk about it if you don't want to."

"It's not that I don't *want* to take it further. I just get so overwhelmed. When you kiss me, I feel like I'm drowning. Drowning in honey."

Lucas cocked his head to the side. "Drowning in honey, huh?"

"Warm honey," Jule amended.

"Yeah. I see where you're coming from. Okay. I can cool it."

"What?"

"I don't have to come on so strong. I can control myself."

"Wait." Jule hesitated, but the habit of honesty was too strong. "I don't want you to stop."

Lucas grinned. "Yay. That makes me happy, but we can take it slower if you want."

"That should work." Jule rolled his eyes. "I can't believe I'm being such a twit."

"Do I look like I care?"

Jule smiled. "I don't know what made you like me, but I'm glad."

"Oh, are you now?" Lucas said slyly.

"Of course, I am. You're gorgeous and sexy and an amazing dancer. And you're funny, and you love Star Wars. I like everything about you, and the really amazing thing is that you like me too."

"I do like you." Lucas leaned closer. "A lot." He covered Jule's lips with his in a gentle kiss. "All better now?"

Jule nodded. "Better," he said. He took a deep breath. "Now let's see if I can manage to not embarrass myself again."

Lucas shook his head. "Kid, you're working at a level most people can't even see without a telescope. You've got nothing to be embarrassed about on a dance floor."

"I used to think that, until David threw these acrobatic moves into my solo."

"Seriously, I can't fault your steps. I don't know what you're talking about."

"I just don't feel confident in them yet. I've never had to perform a front walkover in a ballet."

"I have to say, it makes for a very splashy entrance."

"Then let's get back to it."

Lucas put the music back on, and for another forty-five minutes, Jule worked on his entrance as the Lilac Fairy. The steps were a progression of fluttering *battements*, airy jetés and single pirouettes linked by acrobatic flips. By the end of the session, with Lucas's help, he was performing the passage without a fraction of hesitation. Ballet positions and gymnastic moves flowed together in a seamless progression that made it seem as though Jule was barely touching the ground.

Neither heard the practice room door open. "That's looking good," Bram said.

Jule and Lucas turned toward him.

Bram smiled disarmingly. "You work well together."

"Thanks," Lucas said. "I didn't know you were still in town."

"I was persuaded to extend my stay. I'm taking a small role in the Christmas ballet."

"Won't your company miss you?" Lucas asked.

"No doubt, but their loss is New York's gain."

Jule smiled. "I look forward to working with you."

"Now, see," Bram said to Lucas. "That's how a civilized human communicates."

"Yeah, well, he's British," Lucas retorted.

"Wow, you haven't changed at all. Still a smug smartass."

"Thanks, I guess."

"How long have you known each other?" Jule asked.

"I saw him dance once when I was a small child," Lucas facetiously. "So, Bram, is there something we can do for you?"

"Oh, I'm sure there are any number of things you could do for me, but I just stopped by to check you out, and by you, I mean Jule."

"Isn't he dreamy?" Lucas fluttered long lashes.

Jule smacked Lucas's upper arm. "Watch it, mate."

"I'm used to what passes for Luc's sense of humor," Bram said. "You're a surprise, though. Not his usual type at all."

"What's his usual type?"

Bram grinned. "Me."

"Oh." Jule paused. "So, basically, tall, dark, and handsome?"

"Don't forget the baby blues," Bram said, fluttering his own extravagant eyelashes.

"Who could?" Lucas said coyly.

"You managed somehow." Bram shook his head. "But I'm not here to talk about the past. Who cares, right? This is a progressive dance company."

"Interesting." Lucas cleared his throat. "Well, we've got a lot of work to do, so…."

"I hear you. See you around," Bram said as he left.

"Maybe we should start locking the door," Lucas said.

"Why are you acting like that?"

"Like what?"

"Like you're angry about something."

Lucas sighed. "Bram does not bring out the best in me."

"Why?"

"Let's not talk about him." Lucas put his arms around Jule from behind and bent his neck to whisper in Jule's ear. "Why don't I lock the door?" He slid his hands down Jule's abs to his lower belly, stopping just short of his crotch. "Sound good?"

Jule's breathing had grown shallow, and every inch of him ached for Lucas's touch. He nodded.

Lucas locked the door and turned the music back on. He approached Jule in a half-comical, half-serious dance made up of slinky, sliding *glissades*. He beckoned to Jule and pulled him into his arms when he was close enough.

"Work with me," Lucas murmured. "Up you go."

Lucas put an arm around Jule's waist and one just under his knee and prepared to lift. Jule went en pointe adding his energy to the maneuver. Lucas raised Jule overhead but didn't hold the position for long.

As Lucas eased him down, Jule wrapped his legs around Lucas's waist and lowered his head for a kiss. The kiss went on for some time as Jule slid slowly down Lucas's body.

"Wow," Lucas said when he drew back. "That was the sexiest kiss ever."

"Don't be so quick to rush to judgment. We're just getting started."

"I love it when you're sassy." Lucas tightened his embrace. "Damn, you feel amazing."

"How long do I have to wait for another kiss?"

Lucas laughed softly before he took Jule's mouth in a kiss that should have set off the fire sprinklers. He was not slow getting his hands under Jule's tunic so he could run his fingers over bare skin.

Jule broke the kiss when Lucas slid a hand down the back of his tights. "Bloody hell," he gasped.

"Too fast?"

"No. No, it's fine. It just—" Jule smiled up at Lucas. "It just feels *so* bloody good."

Lucas grinned. "We're just getting started," he quoted back to Jule.

"When you touch me, I just get so excited, I can't think."

"Remember when I promised to guide you through things?"

"Yeah."

"I meant that shit." Lucas met Jule's gaze, and he stopped moving his hands. "You miss Holloway, huh?"

Jule was confused by the change of subject. "Of course, I do, but why bring it up now?"

"You're used to having a mentor. There's nothing wrong with that. I'm just offering to be whatever you need."

"That's beautiful." Jule put his arms around Lucas's neck and pulled him down into a kiss.

Lucas cupped Jule's asscheeks, kneading the resilient muscles, grinding against him, as the kiss continued. He broke the kiss, pulling his hands free to turn Jule around so he could push them down the front of Jule's tights and under the dance belt.

"Fuck," Jule gasped, when he felt Lucas's fingers on his bare cock.

"Okay?" Lucas asked.

"Yes." Jule nodded vehemently. "Very much okay."

Lucas kissed and nibbled his way from Jule's ear down his neck as he stroked Jule within the limited confines of the tights and dance belt.

Jule held his breath as the incredibly good feeling growing at his core merged with his intense need to be close to Lucas. His desire for the man outpaced the physical sensations until his feelings became too big to contain. More excited than he'd ever been in his life, he gave a suppressed cry of release as he coated Lucas's fingers with come. "Bloody hell." He took a deep breath to try to slow his racing heart.

"You like that?" Lucas turned Jule again so he could see his face. "There's a lot more where that came from, but only the first one is free."

Jule groaned. "I sense some sort of joke."

"Would I joke at a time like this?"

"Probably." Jule rested his head on Lucas's shoulder. He sighed deeply. "That was nice."

"Nice?"

Jule laughed softly. "*Exceedingly* nice."

"I can see I'll have to step up my game."

"It's not a game."

Lucas's smile slipped. "Yeah, I know," he said quickly. "That's not what I meant."

"Good. I care for you, you know."

"Of course, I know that." Lucas gave Jule's shoulders a squeeze.

Jule yawned. "Sorry. I feel so tired all of a sudden."

Lucas smiled as he kissed the top of Jule's head. "Time for a nap."

"Wait. What about you?"

"That's what the nap is for." Lucas gave him a devilish wink.

JULE WALKED into Lucas's apartment and descended two shallow steps to a large open area. The loft wasn't huge but had been ingeniously designed to make maximum use of the space. The room was open to the pitched roof fourteen feet overhead. Sectional furniture and an enormous television screen marked off a living room. In the opposite corner, rice paper screens offered privacy to the bedroom.

Abruptly, Jule dashed to the other side of the room. "You have your own practice studio! I'm so jealous," he said from the thirty-by-thirty platform of hardwood boards. He glanced to the left. "And a Jacuzzi! Mate, that's luxe!"

"I dated a contractor for a while. He wasn't what you'd call pretty, but boy, was he good with his hands."

Jule chuckled. Emboldened by his newly semi-sexually experienced status, he replied cheekily. "You're not so bad yourself when you aren't slacking off."

"Oh, is that right?"

Lucas lunged at Jule. Jule pivoted and jumped to his right. Lucas made a grab for him, but Jule spun away again. After a few minutes of horsing around, they faced one another, panting with laughter, across Lucas's bed.

"It doesn't seem like you want a nap," Jule said.

"Oh, I do. I really do, but first… have you ever tried a sixty-nine?"

"I'm game," Jule said feeling very adult. He was startled into laughter when Lucas lunged across the bed, but it was hard to keep laughing with someone else's tongue in your mouth.

Eventually, they napped, falling asleep in a welter of half-removed clothing.

Chapter Nine

JULE WOKE and opened his eyes. He blinked at the unfamiliar ceiling for a few moments before he remembered. He was in Lucas's bed. Lucas's arm rested across his chest. Lucas himself was asleep facedown on his pillow. Jule wondered how the man was breathing before he let his gaze travel down the long slopes of Lucas's back to the perfect twin curves of his ass. A little shiver of desire shimmered up Jule's spine, and the breath caught in his throat. If he had any doubts left that he was attracted to men, they were irrefutably laid to rest. The warmth in his heart assured him it was more than just a physical pull that led him to Lucas's bed.

Jule gingerly moved Lucas's arm so he could slide out of bed. He found his phone and saw that it was almost seven o'clock. He didn't want to disturb Lucas, but he knew Lucas would want to be woken up. His life was full of these little quandaries now that he was on his own. After a few more minutes of gazing at Lucas's sleeping face, Jule leaned over and kissed him.

Lucas woke and pulled Jule back onto the bed. He rolled over and pinned Jule beneath him. "Hey there," he said as he looked down into Jule's eyes.

"It's nearly seven."

"Irrelevant." Lucas bent his head and claimed Jule's mouth in a deep, slow kiss. "How about a rematch?" he drawled.

"Mate, I'm a wet noodle," Jule said. "I couldn't get it up right now if you—" He broke off with a gasp when Lucas reached through the fly of his boxer-briefs and took hold of his cock.

"Oh, I think you can."

"You… might… be right." Jule closed his eyes for a moment. "But I'm famished."

"I really want to make a joke about man gravy… but I won't." Lucas kissed Jule again and then let him up. "I promised you dinner and dancing, as I recall."

"At your favorite bar." Jule found his trousers and pulled them on. He looked at his discarded shirt, decided it wasn't too wrinkled, and put it on.

"Heads-up," Lucas called out.

Jule looked up in time to catch the shoe Lucas threw at him. "Thanks, I was wondering where it wandered off to."

Lucas finished buttoning his shirt. "So… how do you feel?"

"Fine." Jule looked over at Lucas. "Why?"

"Isn't this another big step into adulting for you? Sleeping at your boyfriend's place?"

"It was a nap."

"Oh, well, excuse me." Lucas threw a purple tie at Jule. "We'll have to arrange a sleepover."

"I'll have to get permission to be away from the dorm overnight."

"As your coach, I might be able to swing that."

"Favoritism, Madding? Really?"

Lucas laughed and came over to stand behind Jule. He took the ends of the tie hanging around Jule's neck and knotted them. He spun Jule around and fussed with the collar of his shirt for a minute, reminding Jule of Sasha.

"Will I do?" Jule asked, after the wave of homesickness passed.

"And then some." Lucas loosened the knot of the tie. "Perfect. Let's go."

They took a cab to the Monster bar on Grove. Jule liked it right away; it reminded him of pubs he'd been to with his parents. He realized he hadn't called his mother in a while and made a mental note to do that.

They were shown to a table for two and given menus. Jule ordered the cheeseburger and Lucas the french dip. Lucas asked for a Harp beer and Jule had sparkling water. The cheerful server left them in peace after making sure they had what they needed.

"Sasha would kill me if he knew how many calories I'm about to put away," Jule said.

"You'll burn them off. Don't worry so much."

Jule looked around the restaurant. "It's really… cozy here."

"Yeah, I like it here. There's music after nine." Lucas nodded toward a piano. "And dancing."

"Excellent." Jule wiped his mouth and dropped his napkin on his empty plate. "I could use some exercise."

"What about the workout I gave you?"

Jule blushed. "That was before the burger." He took a drink of his water.

"Maybe we should have that sleepover tonight."

"Are you always this greedy?"

"No!" Lucas sounded wounded.

Jule grinned. "Mate, you should see your face." He paused. "Sorry. I couldn't resist."

"It's fine for you to tease me. I like being teased. I just wasn't expecting it." Lucas put a hand on his chest. "I took you seriously for a second there."

"I'd advise you to get used to it."

"I'm all aquiver." Lucas looked over as a lanky man with a mop of dark curls sat down at the piano. "Excellent." He turned back to Jule. "This guy's good. He plays a lot of old, swingy kinds of stuff like Sinatra. I love the way he does 'Summer Wind.'"

The piano player tapped his microphone and launched into a wittily upbeat, instrumental version of "Cry Me a River." A few couples, all male, took to the dance floor. Jule and Lucas's server came back and Lucas ordered another beer. Jule asked for more water. The song ended, and the piano man played the opening notes of another. The performer began to sing in a smoky baritone.

"Come on." Lucas stood up and held out a hand to Jule. "I love this song."

On the dance floor, Lucas took Jule's left hand in his right and wrapped his other arm around Jule's trim waist. He led Jule through some swaying, pseudo-swing dance steps to the midtempo beat.

"This is fun," Jule said.

"Right?" Lucas grinned.

"I've never heard this song before. It's great."

"You're great." Lucas kissed Jule's nose.

"And you're a bit soft."

"Oh, I assure you, that can change quickly."

Jule laughed. "You're absolutely mad."

"You know you love it."

The music changed to a slow instrumental version of "Stormy Weather." Lucas pulled Jule into his arms. "You still okay with me leading?" he asked.

"It's fine." Jule looked up into Lucas's eyes. "I like it."

"Man, I wish I could put this moment in Tupperware." Lucas sighed.

Jule slipped his hand from Lucas's so he could put his arms around Lucas's neck. It felt so good moving languidly to the music, his cheek on Lucas's shoulder, Lucas's hand on the small of his back. The world was warm and soft and full of the promise of more good things to come. Maybe he wasn't so bad at being an autonomous adult.

Jule and Lucas danced to every song until the piano player went on break. Each dropped some money in the man's tip jar before they returned to their table.

"You want anything?" Lucas asked when he spotted their server headed their way.

"No, mate. I'm happy."

"Well, I've got a hard-on with your name on it."

"Actually, that does sound good."

"Thanks, man," Lucas said to the server. "I just need the bill, please." He settled the tab, added a tip, and turned to Jule. "Ready?"

Jule stood up and shrugged into his jacket before following Lucas out to the street. It was just after ten, and the sidewalks were still teeming with people. "I'm not sure if I'll get used to how crowded it is here," he said.

"It's not crowded in London?"

"I suppose parts of it are, but not where I live."

"I got used to it. I don't even notice anymore." Lucas held up a hand for taxi. "So… are you coming back to my place?"

"Curfew in less than an hour, so no."

"I'll see you home, then."

"Great. We can snog until curfew."

"Sounds like a plan."

A cab pulled over and they got in. In the semidarkness of the back seat, Lucas rested his hand on Jule's thigh for a moment before moving higher. Jule bit his lip when Lucas's fingers made their way to his crotch and stroked it through the fabric.

"God, I thought I was going to break my zipper," Jule said as the cab drove away. "You're an evil man."

"Yeah, yeah. Let's get inside. Curfew in twenty minutes." Lucas swatted Jule on the ass as they went through the double doors.

Jule opened the door to his room, and Lucas shoved him inside. When Jule turned to face him, Lucas took him by the shoulders and pushed him back against the door. Jule raised his chin and Lucas leaned in to kiss him, resting his hands on the door on either side of Jule's head.

Jule moaned his approval when Lucas ran his hands down to slip into his back pockets.

"Zipper-busting time again," Jule said as he pulled back to take a deep breath.

"We should let that puppy out."

"I like what we're doing right now."

"Roger that." Lucas took Jule's mouth again as he kneaded Jule's firm buttcheeks, fingers creeping deep into the crack.

Jule got his hands between them and unbuckled Lucas's belt. He unbuttoned Lucas's trousers and pulled the zipper down. Working determinedly, he got a hand through the fly of Lucas's boxers. He took hold of Lucas's cock and squeezed.

"Fuck yeah," Lucas sighed into Jule's mouth. He found Jule's hole and rubbed the sensitive skin with the tip of his forefinger as Jule stroked his cock.

Jule was surprised when Lucas broke the kiss and turned him to face the door, and then he was gasping for breath with Lucas's strong fingers wrapped around his aching cock.

Lucas stroked Jule with one hand and wrapped his other arm around Jule's waist. He pressed his crotch to Jule's ass and pulsed his hips.

"I can't—" Jule's breath hissed in through his clenched teeth. "Can't hold it."

"Don't even try," Lucas said, his breath warm on Jule's nape as he stroked faster.

"Fuck." Jule gasped and filled Lucas's hand with come.

Lucas was a little surprised that he was capable of getting off dry-humping up against a door through two sets of clothing. "Jee-*zuss*!" He leaned heavily on Jule, panting for breath. It was a few moments before he shifted his weight. "Sorry."

Jule turned and leaned against the door. Slowly, he slid down until he was sitting on the carpet. "For what?"

"Squishing you."

"It was amazing."

Lucas smiled. "That *was* pretty amazing. I can't wait to get you in a bed completely naked with several hours of free time. The nap doesn't count. I never got you out of your boxers."

Jule's heart rate doubled. "That does sound like fun," he said as calmly as he could manage.

"Yeah, it does, doesn't it?" Lucas paused. "Then again, it might just kill me."

Jule held out a hand, and Lucas pulled him up into a hug.

"I should go," Lucas said.

Jule rose on his toes to kiss Lucas. "You can go. Honestly. You've sexed me up proper."

"So, my work here is done?"

"For now." Jule bit his lip. "But it'll be nice when it doesn't have to be such a wham-bam sort of thing. I want more than sex from you, you know?"

"You want another hug?"

"Ugh, am I being a massive wanker?"

"No, you're not," Lucas said. "And I'm not making fun of you." He put a hand on Jule's cheek. "We should probably talk about this."

"Probably, but not now." Jule opened the door. "Good night."

"Yeah, okay." Lucas leaned back in for one more kiss, and then he was gone.

Jule closed the door and leaned his forehead against it. He loved being with Lucas. He loved feeling the way Lucas made him feel, like he belonged to something without burdens or expectations, but he couldn't help wondering what Kelly would say about his extracurricular activities. On the other hand, if being with Lucas didn't interfere with dancing, what harm could there be in it? Now, if he could only be sure that Lucas felt the same way.

Chapter Ten

JULE HAD just finished warming up when Lucas entered the studio. He flashed Lucas a smile before continuing the steps he was practicing.

Lucas couldn't take his eyes off Jule, while vacillating between delight and doubt. He'd never met a better person, and he wanted to be with him, but what if he was making a fool of himself? His dedication to his career allowed for affairs, but not for a serious relationship. He couldn't allow his life to be complicated by the needs and desires of a significant other. And yet, here he was with his heart in his hand ready to have that conversation with someone he'd known less than a month.

Lucas was also pretty sure starting a relationship with a teenager was a terrible idea, but then again, Jule wasn't an average teen. And dammit, being with him felt *so good*. He'd almost forgotten how this affair had started, and he didn't care to remember. Maybe it was time he got serious about someone, and he couldn't think of anyone better than Jule to be serious about.

His thoughts were interrupted as Jule performed one of the showier runs of steps.

"That looked great!" Lucas called out. "Honestly, I think you've got your solo down."

"I haven't tried it in costume yet." Jule came over for a bottle of water. He gave Lucas a pat on the butt as he passed by.

"Aren't we getting bold?" Lucas teased.

"It's my new dance teacher," Jule said. "He's really randy."

"Lucky you."

Jule smiled. "Seriously, I can't believe how lucky I am. I'm in New York. I'm in the company I wanted to be in. I have a super-fit, talented boyfriend, and Mr. Downes is writing a ballet for us. I don't know how it could get any better."

"Boyfriend? Really?" Lucas met Jule's gaze.

"If you aren't my boyfriend, what are you?"

"Your lover?"

Jule thought for a second. "That's a really grown-up word," he said.

"Are you ready for it?"

"I don't think so, but thinking has never been my best quality. Man, I miss Kelly and Sasha a lot sometimes."

"Allow me to restate my willingness to be whatever you need me to be."

Jule put his arms around Lucas. "That's lovely, but you can't be Kelly or Sasha. Nor would I want you to. That would be very weird." He looked up into Lucas's eyes. "I like you just as you are."

Lucas swallowed the lump in his throat. "Not surprising since I'm practically perfect."

"What? Like Mary Poppins?"

Lucas smiled as he leaned in for a kiss. "Would Mary Poppins do this?" He cupped Jule's crotch and gave it a gentle squeeze as he slid his tongue into Jule's mouth. He loved Jule's reaction to his caress. The lightest touch was enough to put Jule in a state of arousal, and his instinctive, unfettered responses had led to the best sex of Lucas's near-legendary love life. It was even more remarkable when he considered they'd barely begun exploring. "Just keeps getting better and better," he murmured as he broke the kiss.

"It's amazing," Jule said and then added something he'd never said before. "I wish we could ditch practice and go to your place."

Lucas groaned. "Stop. That kiss gave me half a hard-on. If you keep talking, I won't be able to walk, much less dance."

"Only half?" Jule asked innocently.

Lucas smiled. "I get hard so much around you that I'm going to ask David to write a sword fight into *Fireheart*."

"Was that a joke?"

"Well… yeah. I guess it wasn't funny."

Jule smiled impishly and feigned ignorance. "It might be, but I didn't get it."

"A sword fight. You know." Lucas leered.

"Yeah, I know what a sword fight is, but what's that got to do with chubbies?"

"First of all… *chubbies*." Lucas chuckled as he repeated the word. "Second, in America, we have many fine slang terms for penis. One of them is pork sword."

Jule stared at him for a moment, almost overdoing the innocent act. "Is that true?"

Lucas raised his hand in a Boy Scout salute. "I swear."

Jule laughed. "Now I have this insane mental image."

"Right?"

Jule assumed a heroic stance, arms in third position, and thrust his pelvis forward. "Speak again, varlet, and I shall cross pork swords with you!"

Lucas cracked up. He grabbed his crotch. "Have at me, scoundrel," he managed to say. His eyes went to the door as it opened, and Jule turned in the same direction.

"ON A break?" David asked as he came in. "Good. I want to talk to both of you for a few minutes."

"It's not really a good time," Lucas said.

"No, it's fine," Jule contradicted. "I feel like I've made progress already today." He glanced at Lucas and smiled.

David cleared his throat. "Good. Good. I've made progress too. *Fireheart* is almost mapped out. Maybe I should stop tinkering with it, but the truth is, we can't get serious about it until after New Year's." He paused. "However, there's no harm in plowing ahead as if everything is going to come together, right?"

"Absolutely," Lucas said.

"To that end, I'd like to set up a studio meeting for the three of us so I can show you a few things. Then you can try them out and see if they work. If you have suggestions for improvement, I'll want to hear and see them."

"Time is really tight right now," Lucas said.

"Obviously," David said. "I don't want you take time away from *Sleeping Beauty*, but if you find you have a few minutes, please let me know."

"I'm dying to see more of the steps," Jule said. "Why don't you show us now?"

"I'm free," David said. "If you're sure I'm not eating into your practice time."

"We were nearly finished," Jule said. "I was thinking about food, actually. I had this sudden craving for sausage."

Lucas smirked. "Let's get going, then. Jule's in the mood for a foot long."

David rolled his eyes. "That was childish yet vulgar. Well done." He walked to the middle of the floor and beckoned to Jule. "Watch closely, Luc," he said unnecessarily.

"Where do you want me?" Jule asked.

David smiled. "Remember the steps I showed you in my office?"

"Of course."

"Good. You're going to jeté into an arabesque. Hold it while I get in position. I'll be as ready as I can, but it's been a while since I did a lift. I'm going to bring you up to shoulder height and then lower you into a fish dive."

"Just that?"

"Yes, Jule, just that." David smiled at Lucas. "Do you believe this kid?"

"Not for a minute," Lucas replied. "Let's see it, then."

Jule launched himself in a graceful leap. He landed on his right foot and extended his left leg behind him at ninety degrees. His arms were raised above his head in a soft oval.

David lifted Jule with an arm around his waist and one around his thigh. He held the position for a second before lowering Jule into a perfect fish dive.

"Nice!" Lucas called out.

"Help me out, Jule," David said. "I'm not sure I can swing you all the way back up."

Jule lowered his elevated leg and took his weight on one foot until David handed him into an upright position. It happened quickly, but Lucas noticed.

"He weighs a little more than a ballerina, huh?"

"And I'm getting too old for this *merde*," David replied. "Get over here."

Lucas walked over and took David's place.

Jule paced off three steps and turned. He was so tuned in to Lucas's body now that he didn't even think about the preparation. He leaped and Lucas caught him on the landing and elevated him, held him suspended for a three-count, and then swung him down into the fish dive. Jule felt Lucas telegraph an added move with his hands, and he was ready when Lucas flung him onto his feet. He smiled as he landed lightly and spun back to face Lucas.

David applauded when they came to a stop. "I knew you'd be a great team," he said. "Work on that, and I'll get you some diagrams soon. Play with it. Have fun."

"I don't think I've ever had this much fun," Jule said.

"Good." David tousled Jule's hair. "Hey, why don't you two come to my cocktail party tonight. It's going to be small, and there'll be a couple of people you know."

"I would love to," Jule said. He looked to Lucas. "What about you?"

"Free booze? I'm in," Lucas said.

"Good. See you at seven, okay?" David left.

"Promise we won't stay long?" Lucas said to Jule.

"At the party? Why?"

"You'll have to forgive me if I'm not thrilled by the idea of watching David drool over you for hours."

"What?" Jule looked up from removing his practice shoes.

"You didn't know the boss man was crushing on you? He wrote a ballet for you. That could be a clue."

"Rubbish."

"If he hasn't come on to you already, he will." Lucas frowned. "I'm not wrong about this."

"Even if you're right, it doesn't matter. I like *you*."

"Don't underestimate him. He wants to be your Svengali."

"I don't know what that means."

"He wants to control you, to shape you, and turn you into his creation."

"Like Frankenstein?"

"Actually, Svengali is a better analogy."

"Why would you say that?"

"Because David didn't build you. That would be Kelly."

"No, I meant why would you say that about David?"

"Because I care about you?" Lucas paused. "He did the same thing with me and Charlotte."

"Tell me."

"Charlotte and I knew each other before we joined the company. She was in the corps of the New York Theater Ballet. I was dancing for American Ballet Theater. We met at a party in Manhattan and hit it off. The first time we danced together, we both knew we were a perfect match. Sleeping together was a mistake, but we fixed it."

"I wondered. I mean… the way you dance together is, you know, *hot*."

"She said the same thing about us. So did David. He carefully orchestrated an image for us by choosing roles very deliberately. Not that we complained. He made us into names in New York, which was what we wanted. I'm just not sure it's what *you* want."

"Don't worry about me." Jule smiled. "I'm still hungry. Let's have something to eat. Then I'd like a nap and a swim before we get ready for David's party."

"A chance to see you in a Speedo?" Lucas pretended to ponder.

Jule laughed. "You see me in tights every bloody day."

"When am I going to see you completely naked?"

"You could join me for a nap." Jule grinned at Lucas's surprised expression. "I'm starting to enjoy that look on your face," he said, surprised at his boldness but loving it.

Lucas laughed. "Payback is a bitch, don't forget."

"I'm not scared."

"Good. Now, let's go. And how about a shower instead of a swim after the nap?"

"Taking a shower doesn't replace the exercise I'd get from swimming."

"Don't worry. You'll get plenty of exercise before the shower."

"Why are we still standing here?"

"WELCOME TO mi casa… again," Lucas said grandly as he unlocked his apartment door. He gestured to Jule to go in first. Avidly, he watched Jule walk around, stoking the heat at his core, growing more aroused by the second. Boys were not his thing, nor girls; he preferred an older sexual partner, someone with depth and experience, so he was still surprised by the strength of the attraction flowing between him and this naïve kid. This was enough to convince Lucas that what he felt was more than physical attraction. However, he couldn't deny that the physical attraction was strong.

"I want to fuck you so bad right now," he growled.

Jule answered as Lucas joined him in the living room area. "You want to put your willie in my bum?"

"Uh… yeah. Pretty much what it boils down to."

"I'll have a go, then," Jule said, before he could think twice.

"What?"

"What are we waiting for?"

"Are you serious?" Lucas peered into Jule's face. "There's no rush."

"Yeah, mate. I'm game."

"It's not a test or anything. You don't have to do this to be cool."

"I know. Why are you arguing?"

"I'm not arguing." Lucas paused. "It's just that you were *so* naïve when we met. Inexperienced, I mean."

"I really was." Jule smiled. "I didn't know what I was missing. Can you deal with the fact that I'm excited about sex?"

Lucas swallowed. "I, uh, sure."

"You don't sound excited about it anymore."

"No, I am. Extremely. You just surprised me."

"I want to try everything. Now seems like a good time to try this."

"Yikes." Lucas held out his hand. "I'm shaking."

"So, you *are* excited." Jule smiled. "Me too." He started unbuttoning his shirt.

"Have I created a monster?"

"What are you talking about? I'm a teenage boy. Aren't I supposed to be excited about sex?"

"Yeah, but I just want to stress that you don't have to do anything you don't want to."

"I know that."

"I know you know that, but you're such a good… student."

Jule stopped in the act of sliding his trousers off. "Mate, I'm doing this because I want to do it… with you."

"Well then, carry on."

Lucas went into the bathroom and opened a drawer. He took out a couple of items and returned to the bed. He swallowed hard when he saw Jule sprawled on his sheets completely naked. "Righteous," he said under his breath and then raised his voice. "Forgive me if I take a moment to appreciate the view."

"Why are *you* still wearing clothes? That's not fair."

"Christ on crackers!" Lucas dropped the small squeeze bottle and box of condoms he carried. In record time, he shed his shoes, socks, pants, and shirt. He held out his arms at shoulder height and faced the bed. "Happy?"

Jule smiled "You're only the most beautiful man I've ever seen," he said sincerely. He rose to his knees on the bed. "Come over here, please."

Lucas sat on the side of the bed and pulled Jule onto his lap facing him. "Give me some sugar," he said, raising his face for a kiss.

As Jule leaned in to kiss him, Lucas pulled him so close their cocks were touching. Lucas was surprised when Jule spurted all over his abs.

"Hey, did you just come?" Lucas asked unnecessarily.

Jule nodded.

Lucas held Jule close, his breath stirring Jule's hair as he spoke. "That's cool. I was looking forward to going down on you, but there'll be plenty of time for blow jobs."

"I got too excited. This is what you do to me."

"No harm, no foul, rookie." Lucas kissed Jule's ear. "Fuck, you smell good."

Jule licked Lucas's neck. "You're delicious."

"I don't want to rush you or anything, but my dick's so hard it would make a diamond jealous."

"Yeah, so I feel." Jule shifted his weight.

"Brat."

Jule laughed softly. "So, what's next? Guide me through it like you promised."

"If you're sure…."

"No, forget it, I've changed my mind." Jule laughed again. "Your face!"

"Well, that does it." Lucas folded his arms. "No fucking for you, mister."

"I'm sorry."

"Nope."

Jule backed away from Lucas and settled on the pillows. "All right, then. Sleep well."

"You're better at this than I am," Lucas admitted. "I want you even more now."

Jule smiled at Lucas. "Same here."

"So, we're going to do this."

"Yes, but seriously though, you will have to tell me what to do. I mean, I'm not completely ignorant, I know what goes where, but you know…."

"Relax. I'm going to make this so good for you."

"That sounds promising. So… am I okay on my back or should I…?"

"Yeah, on your back is fine. So fine." Lucas held up a square foil packet. "I swear to you I have no diseases, but you'd be smart to insist I wear this."

"I trust you."

"You shouldn't." Lucas rolled the condom on. "Just to be safe."

"You're the guide."

"Look, we don't have to do everything right away. Some things we don't ever have to do at all, if you don't want to."

"Why are you stalling?"

"For reasons already mentioned, plus I don't want this to be something you built up in your head like it's the Holy Grail of sex or something."

"It's more like a new kind of food. How do I know if I like it if I don't try it?"

"How can I argue with that?" Lucas picked up the lube. "You know what this is for?"

"I can guess."

"Ready?" Lucas waited for Jule's nod. "Try to stay relaxed, right?"

Jule jumped when Lucas ran a finger up his crack. "Bloody hell!"

"You call that relaxed?"

"Your hands are cold, you evil man." Jule piled up several pillows and leaned back against them.

"My bad." Lucas rubbed his hands together.

"Get on with it, then."

Lucas got on with it but slowly. He smiled when Jule reacted to his intimate caresses with groans of pleasure. He continued until Jule's legs were trembling and he was gasping for breath.

"Ready?" Lucas took his hard length in hand.

"Do it," Jule said breathlessly.

Lucas pulled Jule's ass onto his thighs, settled Jule's calves on his shoulders, and nuzzled the head of his cock against Jule's lube-shiny port. He worked it through the tight ring of muscle and felt Jule tense up. After taking a few moments to soothe him with light caresses, Lucas eased forward by millimeters until half his length was sheathed.

Jule let out a long breath and shifted restlessly.

"Everything okay?"

Jule blinked away tears. "It bloody *hurts*, mate."

"I know. You want to stop?"

"Of course not." Jule sounded indignant now. "I've been hurt worse learning a new step."

"All right, then."

As gently as possible, Lucas drew back and pushed in again.

Jule let out a grunt, and his toes curled tightly. "When does it start feeling good?"

Lucas got a rhythm going and wrapped his fingers around Jule's wilted cock. He shifted his weight and entered Jule at a new angle as he stroked him. He was pleased when this evoked a strong reaction.

Jule moaned each time Lucas thrust, and Lucas's excitement climbed another notch at Jule's enthusiastic response. It took some willpower and a lot of talent to maintain a steady stroke with Jule counterthrusting enthusiastically, but Lucas managed while shuttling his fist to the same beat.

Lust, pride, and exhilaration rose rampant in Lucas as his lover came undone at his touch. He let go of Jule's sated shaft and took hold of his hips. Holding Jule firmly in place, Lucas thrust powerfully for a few strokes until his orgasm ignited. His fingers sank into resilient muscles as his seed reeled out inside Jule.

Lucas caught his breath before gingerly disengaging. He moved to lie on his side beside Jule and put a hand on Jule's cheek.

Jule opened his eyes and turned his head to look at Lucas. "So that's what it's like," he said hoarsely.

"You okay?"

Jule nodded, and Lucas moved to kiss his forehead. "I wasn't sure at first," Jule said. "It hurt quite a lot, but then… *wow*."

"I'm glad I could make it good for you." Lucas traced Jule's abs with a finger as he spoke.

Jule giggled. "That tickles actually."

Lucas flattened his hand against Jule's taut belly and let his fingers creep downward.

"Seriously?" Jule groaned. "I'm done in."

Lucas laughed softly before he leaned in and gave Jule a sweet kiss.

Jule threw an arm over Lucas's chest and a leg over Lucas's thigh. He nestled his cheek in the hollow of Lucas's neck and sighed contentedly.

"You want to cuddle?" Lucas asked hesitantly.

"Why? Is it too gay for you?"

"No," Lucas said quickly. "You got me all wrong. This is my jam." He wrapped both arms around Jule and held him close. "We should probably have an actual nap before the party."

"Brilliant." Jule's eyelids were already at half-mast. In another moment, he was asleep.

After a few minutes, Lucas got up and disposed of the condom. He then wet a washcloth and tenderly cleaned up the traces of their lovemaking. With a deeply contented sigh, he spooned up to Jule and fell asleep.

Chapter Eleven

JULE WOKE, immediately realized Lucas was gone, and then relaxed when he heard him in the bathroom. He eased back down onto the pillow and took stock. There was a burning sort of soreness in his bum, but nothing to concern him. He didn't think bottoming, as Lucas called it, was something he'd want to do every day, but it was definitely a roller-coaster ride he'd take again when the time was right. He hoped it wouldn't be too disappointing for Lucas, but honestly, he thought he'd be happy with snogging and hand jobs for the rest of his life.

It was really the closeness that he craved. He loved just being next to Lucas, and he absolutely adored cuddling with him. The physical proximity and the touching fed his hunger for this man's presence in his life. In a very short time, Lucas had somehow become indispensable, and his absence caused an ache behind Jule's sternum. He still wasn't sure if it was a good idea to fall in love, but it was happening whether he wanted it or not.

Jule heard the water cut off and got out of bed to corral his discarded clothing. After his shower, he pulled on his jeans and his T-shirt and sweater.

"Is that what you're wearing?" Lucas asked when Jule came out of the bathroom.

"I don't have much choice. My clothes are in my dorm room."

"The black jeans will pass, but that sweater…."

"This is my favorite jumper."

"Then wear it at home. That green does you no favors." Lucas went to the clothes rack to the right of his bed. "Here." He tossed a garment at Jule.

Jule caught the soft fabric and held it up. "It's pink."

"It'll look great on you. Trust me." Lucas came over and pulled Jule's Kelly-green sweater over his head. After Jule put on the rose-pink sweater, Lucas turned the sleeves up into cuffs. "There. Perfect."

"It's a bit… long." Jule pointed to the bottom of the sweater that hung to midthigh.

"Everyone's wearing tunic-length now."

"You aren't."

"I can't pull it off, but you sure can."

"Why do I feel like you're playing a trick on me?"

Lucas pulled Jule into his arms. "You want the truth?"

"Always."

Lucas ran his hands down Jule's back. "I love the feel of cashmere, and that's the only reason I want you to wear this sweater."

Jule pressed closer. "That feels nice," he said. "I'm a little turned on."

Lucas chuckled. "You're still technically a teenage boy."

"And?"

"You're basically a boner factory."

"It's not like I can deny it."

"After the party, I'll walk you to your dorm," Lucas said in Jule's ear. "And we can make out till curfew."

"And now I'm pitching another tent."

"But no one will ever know, thanks to my genius idea."

Jule looked down. "In terms of concealment, it works a treat."

"Ready to make a dent in David's liquor cabinet?"

"I've never actually been drunk."

"You're fucking kidding me."

Jule shrugged. "There are a lot of things I haven't done."

"You should drink too much at least once so you'll know better next time."

"That's a very good point."

"Come on. I'll guide you through it."

Lucas took Jule's hand and held it during the elevator ride.

Jule hadn't been joking about still being aroused. He could hardly believe he'd spent the past couple of hours having sex with his super-fit boyfriend in a Manhattan loft and was now on his way to a glamorous cocktail party on the Upper East Side. His life kept getting better every day. If only Kelly and Sasha and Mum and Dad could be there, it would be perfect.

Lucas flagged a taxi, and they held hands surreptitiously throughout the ride. Once in the door of David's brownstone, there was no need to hide. They were greeted warmly by David's usual choice of close friends: Jamison, Artur, Marilee, Charlotte, and Catherine. Bram was there as well with a beautiful young woman who was introduced simply as Amani.

"Finally, someone my age," Amani joked as she held out her hand to Jule.

"I'm guessing you're a dancer," he replied.

She laughed as she looked down at her long, muscular legs. "Can't hide it."

"Amani is one of San Francisco Ballet's baby ballerinas," Bram interjected.

"You know I hate that name," she said.

"It's cute," Bram said.

"It's patronizing," Charlotte said.

"It is a bit," Jule said. "I wouldn't want to be called a baby danseur."

"No danger of that," Charlotte drawled. "You should wear pink more often. It's definitely your color. Sexy."

Lucas rested his arm on Jule's shoulder. "Told you," he said under his breath.

"Amani's looking to make the jump from San Fran to the Big Apple," Bram said.

"I'm here to meet with David," Amani said. "Keeping my fingers crossed."

"I'm going to get you a drink," Lucas said in Jule's ear. "Meet me by the Christmas tree."

Jule looked up at him and smiled. He excused himself from the group to look at the Christmas tree in David's front window. With him, he took the glow engendered by Lucas's attention.

"You and Lucas still seem quite chummy," Catherine said at Jule's elbow.

Startled, Jule turned from the twinkling lights to face her. "Hi. I didn't notice you were standing there."

"Who could blame you?" She nodded at Lucas's departing figure. "That's a much better view."

"He's been very good to me," Jule said. He smiled as he thought about what they'd been doing that afternoon. "I can't thank him enough for helping me get settled here."

"I'm sure you manage to show your gratitude, in your own unique way."

Though there was nothing objectionable in Catherine's words, Jule felt as though she was subtly mocking him. "I hope so," he said.

"I'm sure you're succeeding, or he wouldn't still be hanging around."

"I'm not exactly sure what you're saying, ma'am." Jule deliberately used a formal tone.

"Ma'am?" Catherine gave a brittle laugh. "I'm simply surprised you lasted this long. Lucas usually moves on quickly. You really haven't figured it out yet?"

"Figured what out?"

"You're a child, but you can't possibly be *that* naïve. You have to know David sent Lucas to *recruit* you." Catherine paused. "To be accurate, I should say he sent Charlotte first, but clearly, she wasn't what you were looking for."

"I wasn't looking for anything. Not like that."

"Oh dear." Catherine feigned astonishment. "You really didn't know?"

"What I don't know is why you'd say such an awful thing to me."

"It never occurred to me that you were still under the impression Lucas had fallen for you. What a faux pas on my part."

"I can't understand why you'd tell me that, even if it was true." Jule met her gaze. "Unless you just wanted to hurt me."

"If you're going to be uncivil, I'll find someone else to talk to." Catherine walked away from him.

Jule went around the room until he found David talking with Marilee. He stopped beside them and waited for a break in the conversation.

"Hey, here's our new star." David said. "I was just hearing all about how good you look in purple, Mr. Lilac Fairy."

Marilee smiled at Jule. "Wait till you see what I did with the wings. I had an inspiration just as I was about to leave the sewing loft."

"Then I guess I'll see you tomorrow." Jule didn't return her smile. "Would you mind terribly if I had a word with David?"

"No, of course not. I need a fresh drink anyway."

"You don't look happy," David said when Marilee had gone. He hooked an arm through Jule's and guided him to a quiet corner. "What's wrong?"

Jule pulled his arm away and blurted out. "Did you set Lucas on me?"

"What does that mean?"

"Did you tell Lucas to pretend to be interested in me so I'd join your company?"

David's face went still. "Why would you ask such a question?"

"Kelly says if someone answers your question with a question, they're about to lie to you."

"Someone should collect his sayings and publish the *Wisdom of Jesus Kelly*."

"Just answer my question, please."

David shrugged. "I asked Lucas and Charlotte to make you feel welcome."

"How welcome?"

"This looks intense," Lucas said as he walked up with a martini glass in each hand. "What are you talking about?"

Jule looked at Lucas and then turned back to David. Whatever he saw in David's eyes convinced him he'd been played for a fool. The pain was immediate and immense, squeezing the air out of him. "What a couple of bastards," he said before he hurried away from them.

"WHAT THE hell?" Lucas turned to David. "What did you say to him?"

"It's not what *I* said to him. Someone told Jule that your interest in him might not be all that pure, if you know what I mean. He came to me for confirmation."

"And you told him it was a lie, of course."

"I didn't have a chance to deny it. I tried a little soft soap first, but he wasn't having it."

"Shit." Lucas handed both glasses to David.

"Let him go," David said. "Talk to him after he cools down."

Lucas ignored him and went after Jule. He came out the front entrance in time to see Jule reach the other side of the street. "Jule, wait!" he called out. "Shit," he repeated when Jule kept walking. Lucas used the crosswalk, moving as quickly as he dared on the icy surface.

When Jule glanced back, Lucas called out to him, and this time, he stopped.

"Please," Lucas said. "Wait for me. We need to talk."

"I don't want to talk to you."

"Stop!" Lucas shouted when Jule starting walking again. He broke into a jog as he watched Jule cross another street.

JULE TURNED and watched in horror as Lucas's foot skidded across a patch of ice. His heart seized when Lucas ended up on his back with his ankle bent over. The "walk" signal changed and a cab blared its horn as it blew by inches from Lucas's head. Jule ran to the group of pedestrians gathering around Lucas.

"Lucas!" Jule shouted as he pushed through the crowd. He went down on one knee beside Lucas.

"I'm an idiot. Call me an ambulance if no one has yet."

Jule looked stricken as he called 911. "How bad does it hurt?" he asked Lucas.

"Bent it over about ninety degrees. Hurts like a son-of-a-bitch."

"Shite."

"Yeah, I think it's fully fucked."

"This cannot be happening." Jule took Lucas's hand. "You're going to be fine. You have to be."

"Look, I know you're—" Lucas broke off with a gasp of pain. "I know you're pissed at me, but promise you'll reserve judgment till we talk?"

"I promise I'll try."

"Fair enough." Lucas grimaced. "This is really painful. On several levels."

"Don't be such a big baby."

Lucas managed a smile. "That's my boy," he said. "Whatever you decide about me, don't let this thing knock you back, you hear me? You just go on and be fabulous as God intended."

"If you insist."

"You kill me, you know that?"

"I nearly did. What if you'd been hit by a car?"

"On the sidewalk?"

"Shut up."

"Thanks for coming to my rescue despite hating my guts right now."

"Shut up," Jule repeated.

"I know it looks bad, but—"

"No buts, here's the ambulance. I'll let David know what happened. Call me when you're patched up." Jule waited for Lucas's nod and then made way for the EMTs. As he left the scene, he took out his phone and called David. After hanging up, he made another call.

SASHA WOKE from a dream of fire alarms and a burning studio. He realized his phone was ringing and grabbed it off the nightstand. He looked at the number. Quickly, he accepted the call.

"Jule, *esti bine*?" Sasha glanced at Kelly, but his partner slept on. "Are you okay?"

"Not really. I know it's early there, but can you talk?"

"Of course." Sasha got up and walked naked to the bedroom door. "Tell me what's wrong," he said when he was in the hall.

"Lucas got hurt. His ankle. I don't know how badly, but I don't think he'll be able to dance for a long time."

"Bloody hell!" Sasha entered the kitchen and turned on the light over the stove. Leaning back against the counter, he spoke again. "And you? You're all right?"

"I'm not hurt, but I feel awful."

"Of course, you do. Someone you care about is hurt. Just be as helpful as you can. That will make you feel better." Sasha paused when he heard what sounded like a sob. "Jule?"

"I don't—I don't know if I can be around him right now."

"Please, tell me what happened."

"Lucas was only pretending to like me so I'd join the company."

"Dammit! Kelly was right," Sasha said. "I will come there and bury Lucas Madding."

Sasha's threat thawed Jule's shock a little. "Wouldn't you have to kill him first?"

"He would die, *eventually.* If you want, Kelly and I will be on next plane to New York."

"In the middle of getting ready for the Christmas pageant?" Jule sighed. "I'm all right. I just wanted to talk to someone, and I didn't want to wake Mum."

"Are you certain he did this thing?" Sasha hesitated and then plunged ahead. "Because to me, he had the look of a man falling in love."

"He didn't deny it."

"What made you suspect him?"

"It was something Miss Dahlman said. When I asked David, he as much as admitted he put Lucas up to it to get me in his company."

"If only he'd known you *wanted* to join Downtown Ballet." Sasha took down the coffee canister. He'd not be getting any more sleep tonight. "What are you going to do?"

"I don't know. He says he can explain."

"Then don't you think you should listen?"

"I wish I knew. I really like him, but if he betray—" Jule's voice broke on the word, and it was a minute before he spoke again. "If he could treat me like that, like I'm not human, if he can deceive me like that, how can I be with him?"

"I don't have an answer, but if you care for him, hear him out. Listen with an open heart."

"I'll do my best."

"When have you ever done anything else?"

"I feel better. Thanks. It must be 3:00 a.m. there. I should let you go back to bed."

"It's two and it doesn't matter. You can call anytime."

"I love you, Sasha. Give my love to Kelly also."

"I will, and never doubt that we love you."

JULE BROKE the connection and looked up at the snowflakes materializing as they fell from the night sky into the lights of New York. He felt the familiar sense of disorientation… of falling upward. It was mesmerizing, but he needed to be grounded now. He had come here for a purpose, and he needed to stop letting himself get distracted, no matter how appealing it was to imagine letting go of everything. He needed to focus on what was most important—his dance career—but he was reeling from the double punch of Lucas's deception and Lucas's injury.

Jule dropped his gaze to the sidewalk and composed himself. He needed to get to the dorm before curfew, but he kept walking instead of getting a cab. The cold was soothing somehow, and the barrage of traffic noise helped block out his thoughts. But only for so long. He couldn't escape the fact that Lucas was hurt because of him. Because he'd run out into the night like a willful child. He was glad he hadn't told Sasha about that.

Jule made it back to his room just before curfew and got ready for bed. Though it was late and he was tired, he had trouble falling asleep. As soon as he woke the next morning, he reached for his phone.

Chapter Twelve

LUCAS ANSWERED on the first ring. "Jule!"

"Hi. How are you? Are you home?"

"Just got here."

"Is it all right if I come by?"

"I would love that. You still have your key, right?"

"Of course. See you soon, then." Jule hung up and went out to catch a cab. On the ride, he renewed his resolve. He was hurt, but he was going to be fair. He was going to keep his emotions on a leash and deal with whatever he needed to deal with. It had always worked in the past, and he had no reason to think it wouldn't work now... until he saw Lucas.

Lucas was on the couch with his casted foot propped on the coffee table when Jule came in. "I'm really glad to see you. Come on in and have a seat."

Jule avoided looking at Lucas's leg. "Are you all right? Can I get you anything before I sit?"

"I'm good. Grab whatever you want from the kitchen."

"Seriously, how bad is it?"

"It's not good, but let's talk after you get comfortable."

Jule hung his coat up and sat on a chair facing Lucas. "Are you ready to explain?"

"It's going to hurt a lot more than my ankle does." Lucas peered at Jule with a concerned look on his face. "Are *you* okay?"

"I can't go through another night like the last one. I was so worried about you."

"Hey," Lucas said softly. "I'm sorry."

"That's a good start. I'm sorry too."

"Jesus, this is so hard," Lucas said. "You know what? I'm on pain meds, but I'd like a shot of something. Surprise me."

Jule went to the kitchen and poured a water glass half full of vodka.

"Damn!" Lucas said when Jule handed him the glass. "Is this your idea of a shot?" He took a swallow. "If I could manage to bleed a little, would you feel sorry for me?"

Jule continued to look at him silently, giving no indication of the turmoil within.

"Okay, I confess. David did ask me and Charlotte to show you a good time. It's also true that he hoped we could lure you over to Downtown. Maybe I'm a dirtbag for agreeing to it, but it's also true that I fell in love with you. You have to believe that."

"I do believe it. I don't *know* it to be true, but I *want* it to be true. And that makes it hurt even more." Jule frowned. "You're right, this is hard."

"I'd take it back, if I could."

"I just can't get past the fact that you were willing to—What was it you were willing to do?"

"You mean, would I have slept with you as a favor to David? Yeah, I would have. It wouldn't have been the first time I've fucked for an advantage, and it's not like you aren't attractive to me."

"But don't you think it's dishonest? And insulting to me?"

"Yeah." Lucas shifted position and grimaced. "It was a shitty thing to do. I've thought about it a lot, and I owe you an apology."

"How could you do it?"

"Because once I met you, I wanted to do it. I wanted to seduce you, I mean. My attraction to you wasn't faked."

"Nor was mine."

"I really wish I could hold you right now, but I'm assuming that's off the table."

"I don't know," Jule said candidly. "I should be angry at you. I *am* angry at you. And David."

"And Charlotte?"

"Her as well. Maybe I don't belong here."

Lucas reached out, but Jule stayed where he was. "Don't start thinking like that," he said. "If you don't like the way the world is, you don't run away. You try to change it."

Jule looked away from him and blinked back tears. "You're right." He cleared his throat. "If you need anything, please call me. I'm angry and hurt, but I care about you. If there's anything at all I can do to help…."

Lucas swallowed audibly. "Understood. So… is there any hope at all for me?"

Jule stood up. He hurt so badly that he couldn't stand to stay another minute. Every cell in his body cried out for Lucas's body, and the strain of resisting the pull was enormous. He just wanted to hold Lucas and be held by him, but those feelings were tainted now. He couldn't trust them. "If you don't need anything right now, I'll go. Cast meeting."

"Right. I wonder who's going to replace me."

Jule saw the pain in Lucas's eyes. "As if anyone could," he said.

"Thanks," Lucas said in a choked voice.

Jule shrugged into his coat and wrapped his scarf around his neck. He could tell Lucas was putting up a brave front, and so he was careful not to let Lucas see the wetness on his cheeks. "Take care, all right?"

"I don't know how."

As Jule waited for the elevator, he was sure that even if he lived to be one thousand years old, he'd never forget how awful he felt at this moment.

WHEN HE was back on the street, Jule took out his phone and called home.

Julia Parry answered. Instead of hello, she said, "Are you all right?"

Hearing his mother's voice undid Jule. He put a hand over his mouth as his eyes filled with tears again.

"Jule? Jule? Are you there? Jule! Answer me."

Jule swallowed the lump in him throat. "Yeah, Mum," he said hoarsely. "I'm here."

"Sasha told me what happened. Are you okay?"

"I feel just awful."

"Do you want to come home? Because it's all right if you do."

"I don't know what I want."

"Well, that's not like you." Julia's voice was calm and soothing. "You've always known exactly what you wanted since you were a tiny thing."

Jule sniffled. "It's horrible. I actually do know what I want, but…." His voice trailed off.

"I'm assuming we're talking about this Lucas Madding fellow that Sasha mentioned?"

Jule nodded, remembered he was on the phone, and said, "This isn't how I wanted to come out to you."

"Darling, you know that doesn't matter, no matter what your father might say."

"Thanks, Mum," Jule said, because he couldn't think of the words to express how much he loved her.

"I love you, too. Now tell me how I can make this better."

"I don't know what to do. I want to be with him, but I can't. It hurts too—" His voice choked off.

"I can be in New York in a few hours, darling," Julia said.

"No." Jule took a deep breath. "No, I can handle this. I just needed to talk to you."

"My son, you can handle anything. You have to believe that. I just wish—" Julia paused. "You know it doesn't matter to me who you love as long as you're loved in return. I wish fate had been kinder to you, but I think the best thing to do is what your heart tells you."

"That's what Sasha always says."

"Well, you have to listen to your head too. Try to maintain a healthy balance."

"That's what you always say."

"Am I wrong?"

"No."

"I really wish I was there," Julia said. "I can hear the pain in your voice, and I want to make it go away. Sasha said he wanted to punch Lucas's pretty face."

"Then it's probably a good thing you two aren't here. You'd be booked for murder in no time." Jule took another deep breath. "Thanks," he said. "Talking to you helped."

"I'm glad. I love you more than I could ever say." Julia took a snuffling breath. "My advice is to stay busy."

"Rehearsals for our Christmas ballet are intense right now, and with Lucas out…." Jule sighed. "I'm on my way to a rehearsal now. I'll have enough to do, believe me."

"Jule? Listen, you'll be fine, you hear me? Remember who raised you and who trained you, hold your head high, and blow them away with your mad skills."

Jule chuckled at her phrasing. "I will."

"Good boy. We're going to have a long talk soon, but for now, remember I love you, my Jule, and always will."

"I love you too. I'm going to hang up now before I start crying again."

"You should never be ashamed to cry."

"Yeah, but it's crazy cold, and having wet cheeks is no fun."

"For God's sake, son!" Julia exclaimed. "Get indoors this minute and take a hot shower."

"I will, Mum. I love you," he said before he disconnected.

Feeling a bit better, Jule hailed a cab.

DAVID JOINED the *Sleeping Beauty* cast in the big studio. Everyone had heard about Lucas's injury and the atmosphere was subdued. Jule was conspicuous by his absence.

"You've probably all heard the bad news by now," David said, pacing as he talked. "Our male lead—" He cleared his throat. "Lucas had an accident yesterday, a slip and fall, as the insurance commercials say. Nothing's broken, but he hyperextended a ligament, the anterior talofibular to be exact. Needless to say, our boy won't be doing any fancy dancing anytime soon."

David waited for the round of groans to subside. In the silence, Catherine entered and stood by the door, waiting for David's attention. He saw her but went on with his speech.

"I was up most of the night thinking about it. Obviously, we'll have to replace Lucas for at least a couple of weeks, maybe a month, and with the Christmas season upon us, it's a real problem."

"Maybe Jule could take Lucas's role and someone else can dance the Lilac Fairy," Charlotte said.

David pursed his lips. "I thought about that," he said. "We could go with that plan, but I think we can come up with something better."

"David?"

David turned toward Catherine. "Can it wait?"

"Of course. I wonder if you'd mind a suggestion, though?"

"Of course," he said in the same cool tone.

"Has it occurred to you that Bram is still in New York?"

It was a moment before David answered. "Yes, it has, mostly because he has a part in the ballet already."

"Well, I'm certain he already knows the part of the prince, and surely it would be easier to replace a secondary role."

"I'll think about it and discuss it with him… or not."

"I could speak with him if you like," Catherine said.

"I said I'd have to think about it first."

"So you did, but you're rapidly running out of time." She paused. "When do you think you might be able to meet with me?"

"I'll call you." David softened his tone. "Soon, okay? *Bonne journée.*"

Catherine nodded to David but didn't glance at the dancers as she left.

"So." David turned to face the group again. "Bram, anyone?"

Charlotte shrugged. "It wouldn't be a problem for me. He's about Lucas's size, so we wouldn't have to adjust any of the lift prep. And he's not hard on the eyes."

"I saw him in *Sleeping Beauty* in LA," Dani said. "He crushed it."

"He does look like a prince," Samira added.

The door opened again, and Jule came in. "Sorry I'm late. Lucas was released from hospital a couple of hours ago, and I wanted to make sure he was comfortable."

"How is he?" Charlotte asked.

"Miserable," Jule answered.

"Think it'd be okay if we dropped in after?"

"I think it'd be good for him," Jule said as he finished shedding his outerwear.

"Are you okay?" David asked.

"I'm fine. Let's get on with it."

"Are we ready to work?" David asked the room and received a unanimous affirmative. "Okay, then. Everyone has the blocking for the big ballroom scene memorized, right? Good. Let's try a run-through." He pressed play and music marched out of the speakers.

After practice, David asked Jule to stay after everyone else had gone to change into street clothes. "Before you showed up, we were talking about Lucas's replacement," he said. "No one likes it, but we don't have any choice."

"I know. Lucas knows it too. He doesn't like it, but he understands."

"Bullshit."

"Do you have someone in mind?"

"Cath suggested Bram Silber. Thoughts?"

"He's certainly capable, according to Lucas. From the videos I've seen, I have to agree."

"Good. Good. Anything else?"

"Well, he *does* look like a prince."

"That's what Samira said. Okay. I'll talk to Bram." David put a hand on Jule's shoulder and looked into his eyes. "How are you really doing?"

Jule shook David's hand off. "I'm fine. I'm not the one who ran across an icy street and bunged up my foot after my boyfriend found out I was a lying hound."

"Am I sensing a little resentment here?"

"I wouldn't doubt it."

David frowned. "I think it would be a good idea for you to say what's on your mind. I promise I won't freak out and blow up."

"I'm very angry with both of you, you and Lucas. Charlotte as well, but... not as much."

"Jule—" David paused to rethink his words. "I guess it would be odd if you weren't angry," he said wearily.

"Right. So... you'll let me know if Bram says yes?"

"You'll be the first to know."

"Really? Somehow, it thought it might be Miss Dahlman."

"You're probably right." David sighed. "You know, my life was a lot less complicated before I saw that video of you."

"I suppose mine was less complicated before I heard of The Downtown Ballet. We had a plan and it was on track, and then I saw the publicity photos for your production of *Rite of Spring*. As soon as I saw them, I knew I wanted to work with you. I also knew Kelly wouldn't hear of me joining any company but the NYCB."

"I know he wasn't thrilled by the idea of you joining my company. Kelly and I have history."

"I thought you must. I used to ask him about his days with the NYCB, but he never wanted to talk about it beyond describing the ballets he'd danced in."

"It's not my story to tell, but you probably already know that Kelly was forced out of the company by the director... because Kelly refused to follow the code."

"The code that says you can be gay, but you'd better not act gay?"

"That's the one. Kelly couldn't bear to treat Sasha like a dirty secret."

"Of course he couldn't."

"It was a shock, though. Kelly was the most by-the-book dancer I've ever known. He followed every rule, and tradition was sacred to him. I thought he was kind of dull and annoying."

"So, he was the opposite of you, you mean. Except for the annoying part."

"Ouch." David shook his head. "You sounded a lot like Lucas just then."

"I shouldn't be surprised. He makes an impression."

David cleared his throat. "Well, I did think it was a dirty deal that someone turned Kelly in." He saw he'd caught Jule's interest again and kept talking. "He was letting Sasha stay in his rooms at the men's dorm, and someone told Director Halvorsen."

"Someone?"

"I don't know who it was, but it had to be someone with a grudge. Kelly was nice enough, but a lot of people thought he thought he was superior to everyone else."

"He probably was."

"Ha." David smiled ruefully. "Probably true. And now I've told you the story I shouldn't I have told you."

"I won't tell Kelly you told me."

"Good. Good. So… are we good here?"

"I should join the others," Jule said.

"Right. Go. Tell Luc I'll drop by soon."

"Tell him yourself. I recommend texting," Jule said as he left.

David watched Jule walk away, feeling the now-familiar blend of desire and regret. He found Jule irresistible, but he knew this boy would never be his, for so many reasons, among them Jule's age and the fact that Kelly had more or less left Jule in his care. Even a rogue like him had to admit there were some lines you just didn't cross, no matter what his ego was telling him to do. He shook off the mood that was trying to drag him down and took out his phone. He had arrangements to make.

Chapter Thirteen

JULE WAS working at the barre when David and Bram entered the studio. He turned from the wall of mirrors and let his upraised arms fall to his sides.

"Hey," Bram said as he came forward to shake Jule's hand. "No one likes to get a role this way, but I'll do my best for the production."

"I'm glad you were able to help us out," Jule replied.

"I doubt Luc feels the same way."

"He's disappointed," Jule said. "If that's what you mean."

"Of course, it is," David said. "What else would he mean?" He gave Bram a warning look. "I know you and Luc aren't besties, but leave it outside, okay?"

"Sorry," Bram said sheepishly. "It's a habit."

"Are you taking over coaching me as well as the part of the prince?" Jule asked.

"Uh, no, he's not," David said. "I'll be working with you on *Sleeping Beauty*. Today, I want to spend a couple of hours working out some steps for *Fireheart*." He reacted to Jule's look of shock. "I know. I know. It's yours and Lucas's, but I need to move forward. By the time it's finished, Lucas will be ready to dance again."

Jule's jaw had a stubborn set, but obedience was his habit, and it was a strong one. "If you think it's the right thing to do," he said.

Bram and Jule ran through the steps Jule already knew until Bram assimilated them. David paced them, offering criticism and occasional praise, stopping them to adjust the curve of an arm or the angle of a leg. Jule found Bram easy to work with, quick on the uptake, and all business until it was time for a break.

"You're limber," Bram told Jule. "Even for a dancer." He caught the bottle of water David tossed. "And your breathing is clearly better than mine."

Jule shrugged. "Kelly insisted I learn several disciplines to make me a better dancer."

"Oh yeah?" Bram looked up from removing his practice shoes. "Like what?"

"Acrobatics. Swimming. Yoga."

"Interesting," David commented. "I'm off to do the minimal amount of deskwork to keep Catherine happy. See you tomorrow."

"Yoga is all about breath control," Jule said after David was gone.

"I think I may have heard that somewhere." Bram grinned. "I *am* from NoCal, after all."

Jule smiled. "So, I should assume you surf and eat sushi?"

"You should assume I'm vegan." Bram paused. "I'm not."

Jule's smile broadened. "Mum says I'll eat anything that doesn't eat me first."

"I'd definitely eat you first."

"What?"

"Just a little sexual innuendo."

"Oh. Right."

"I assumed you were queer, but only because I saw Madding giving your tonsils a tongue swabbing the day I met you."

"I don't try to hide it."

"You're not exactly swishy either, though you *are* a ballet dancer." Bram grinned again.

"Can we talk about something else?"

"You embarrassed?"

"No, I'm just not interested."

"Are you hungry? I'm starving. Want to get a bite somewhere?"

Jule only hesitated for a few seconds. "Yeah, I'm famished."

Bram took Jule to Junior's and recommended the egg salad. Jule declined after reading the description and ordered a chef's salad.

"So...." Bram wiped his mouth and put his napkin back in his lap. "Why Downtown?"

"What?"

"Word is you had a spot at the NYCB, but you turned it down to dance for David."

"That's what happened." Jule took a drink of his coffee.

"Why?"

"You make it sound like I was offered a Ferrari and chose a Ford Fiesta."

Bram chuckled. "Well, it *is* kind of like that, isn't it?"

"Not to me. In fact, it's the other way round." Jule paused. "A year ago, NYCB would have been perfect for me, but now I want something else. Something less... traditional, I guess."

"Then Downtown is the place for you. David is allergic to tradition."

"Good. I love the classics, but I don't want to see ballet become stagnant."

Bram sipped his iced tea. "Go on."

"What I really want is for everyone to like ballet. I don't want dancing to be seen as some aristocratic thing. I want it to be, um, accessible, I guess is the word."

"I like that. That's definitely a worthy goal."

"I think David's new ballet is exactly the kind of thing the dance world needs."

"You could be right. So, when did you decide this was your mission?"

"I think I was ten."

Bram laughed. "So, you want to make ballet fun, huh?"

"I want it to be less posh. I don't want people to think of it as boring. Too many people think opera, museums, and ballet are only for snooty types."

"Well, you're certainly not wrong." Bram studied Jule's face long enough to make Jule uncomfortable.

"What?"

"Just looking at you. You've got the kind of face people like. You're not intimidatingly handsome, but you're good-looking in an approachable way."

"Um, thanks?"

"I'm saying you have audience appeal, and I do believe you have a better than even chance of making ballet... warmer."

Jule smiled. "This is going to sound awful, but you're much nicer than I expected."

"I don't look like a nice guy?"

"It's not that."

"It's Lucas, right? He doesn't like me. And you like him, so...."

"Exactly." Jule rolled his eyes. "Silly, isn't it?"

"Maybe, but it's normal for a human. Anyway, Lucas has his reasons for keeping me at a distance. I was pretty cocky when I was your age, and so was he. Neither of us has changed much. You want the whole sordid story?"

Jule nodded, afraid of what he might hear but too curious to say no.

"You asked for it. When Lucas was in the corps at American Ballet Theater, they did a tour of the West Coast. While they were in San Fran, he and I and some of the other dancers went out on the town. I put the moves on one of the guests, and we had a private party in a bathroom stall, if you know what I mean."

"I can guess."

"What I didn't know—and he didn't tell me—was that he was with Lucas. Then when he got caught, he totally misrepresented what happened, so I came off looking like a predator at best. Lucas wanted to kick my ass, and rightly so, if it was true, which it wasn't. In fact, it was his idea, the boyfriend's, not Lucas's. You know, I don't blame Lucas for believing him over me, but dammit—" Bram sighed. "Anyway, it was a long time ago."

"I've only known Lucas a few weeks, but I already know he's stubborn. He's not stupid, though. If you wanted to bury this thing, I think we could make that happen."

"I don't know." Bram made a comical face. "He scares me."

Jule rolled his eyes again. "I should go," he said. "I have a costume rehearsal in an hour."

"I could come with. I haven't seen your costume yet."

"It's everything you ever imagined a Lilac Fairy should be."

"Now I *have* to see it. If you don't mind."

"Why would I?" Jule sounded genuinely mystified.

"I guess I just assumed your boyfriend wouldn't want you spending a lot of time with me."

Jule struggled for a moment with his sense of privacy and his innate honesty. "I'm not sure what to call it right now, but we're… I'm not… I'm not happy with him right now."

"I'm sorry to hear that." Bram sounded less than sincere to Jule.

"I just have a lot to think about before I can—"

"Forgive him?"

Jule nodded.

"Okay. This is clearly none of my business," Bram said as he picked up the check. "But if you need to talk about it, I'm here."

"Thanks. I usually talk to Sasha, but the time difference makes it awkward." Jule stood. "Thank you for lunch also."

"Sharing a meal is the best way to get to know someone a little better, or so sayeth the collective wisdom of my people." Bram followed Jule outside. "Hang on," he said when his phone rang.

Bram spoke for a moment and then made a sour face at Jule. "I've been summoned," he said. "I'll have to see that costume at rehearsal tomorrow."

"See you then." Jule turned away and walked to the corner to look for a cab.

CHARLOTTE CAME early to rehearsal so she could talk to David alone. She found him in his office and made herself comfortable while he finished a phone call.

David put down his phone and looked across his desk at Charlotte. "I see you almost every day," he said. "But I never get used to how beautiful you are."

"Please. I'm in my warmups with my hair in a scrunchy."

"You're drop-dead gorgeous. Deal with it." David smiled. "What can I do for you, *bijou*?"

"We haven't talked for a while." She returned his smile. "You've been so busy with Jule."

"Have I neglected you?"

"I'm teasing you. I know how you are when you have a new toy."

"Easy," he said with a note of warning in his voice.

"Meow." Charlotte made her kitten-face at him. "Okay, so the rookie is off-limits. Let's talk about me. We haven't discussed my future recently."

"Your near future is dancing the part of the Princess Aurora in *Sleeping Beauty*."

"Once upon a time, we discussed mounting one of the classics as a showpiece for me. Is that still on a back burner at least? I mean, I know I'm Princess Aurora, but *Sleeping Beauty* is a seasonal ballet. I want one especially for me."

"There's no reason for you to be feeling insecure. You're still my number one ballerina. That's why you're my Princess Aurora."

"True." Charlotte changed tacks. "I guess with Lucas out of the picture for now, you won't be working so much on the gay ballet," she said casually.

"Why would you think that?" David raised an eyebrow.

"Well, you know, you were pretty clear that you wanted Lucas and Jule in the leads, and Lucas is laid up for a while."

"It's a minor setback. As soon as the curtain goes down on the last performance of *Sleeping Beauty*, we're going to go at *Fireheart* hard-core."

"Does that mean you wrote in a part for your number one ballerina?"

"It hasn't called for a beautiful young woman character yet."

"Speaking of that, I was talking with Jule, and he liked my idea of updating *Giselle*. Supernatural stuff is really popular right now."

"With whom?"

Charlotte heard the subtle derision in his voice. "With literally everybody."

"I'm not interested in staging the most-performed ballet of all time, especially one with a *ballet blanc* second act."

"Oh, come on. You're just being a buzzkill. The second act is beautiful with everyone dressed in pure white."

"It's boring."

"Hardly. Why won't you let me have this?"

"The truth? You're just not right for the part."

Charlotte stared at David in shock. "Why?"

"Giselle is a ghost. You look less like a ghost than anyone I've ever met, except maybe that ginger kid in the beginner class, you know.... Brendan." David stood. "We should get to the studio so Marilee can get you into your costume. You'll just have time for a warmup."

"Can we talk about this later?"

"Of course, but do yourself a favor and pick a different ballet. Something less... ethereal."

Charlotte let it rest for the moment, but she was determined to dance the lead in *Giselle*. She was certain it was the vehicle to bring her to prominence. Lucas as Albrecht would be the perfect foil, but if his injury diminished his dancing, she could probably convince Bram to partner her as a guest star.

Charlotte preceded David into the large studio, greeting the others as she crossed to the far side of the hardwood floor. She went into the curtained-off area where the wardrobe mistress was working.

"Hey, Marilee," she called out.

"You can come on back," Marilee answered. "We're all decent in here."

Charlotte pulled back a curtain and stopped in her tracks. "Wow," she said.

Jule looked at her over his shoulder as Marilee fussed at his costume. "I think we're almost done."

"I don't see how it could get any better," Charlotte said. "Great job, Marilee."

"Thanks. Much appreciated." Marilee grinned. "You can get down now, Jule, and give me a spin, please."

Jule stepped off the shallow platform and did a couple of pirouettes in the limited space. The diaphanous layers of his tunic in various shades of pale purple chiffon floated out like wings of mist and swirled gracefully to rest when he stopped.

"Damn!" Charlotte said succinctly. She shook her head as she watched Jule go through a few more steps. "You've outdone yourself, Marilee. That costume is pure magic. I can't wait to see the final version of mine."

"I'll join the others and let you get back to work," Jule said to Marilee. He left without speaking to Charlotte.

"*Brrrr*," Charlotte said when Jule had gone. "Am I the only one who felt a chill?"

"I guess so." Marilee gestured. "Onto your pedestal, my princess."

DAVID CAME over when Jule walked out of the dressing room. "Beautiful, *mon tresor*," he said. "Let's see what it looks like when you move."

Jule paced off about fifteen feet and ran through a series of steps. The floating layers of translucent, tattered silk-chiffon combined with interleaved layers of sturdier tulle made Jule appear to glide through a jeté. It looked as though he might stay airborne rather than come back to earth. The illusion of a winged fairy alighting was quite convincing.

"Excellent," David said. "And now, the rest of us have something to live up to." He turned to the rest of the cast. "Let's see some hustle, kids. Get those superb buns moving."

About two hours later, David called a halt. "All right, people, looking good. I think it's time we got out of these costumes so Marilee can make whatever adjustments are needed before tomorrow's rehearsal. Everyone should be here by one. Those of you who need to be here earlier should have received a text from me. Miss Costain will be with us tomorrow as well, so we'll have close to a full cast rehearsal. Need I remind you to bring your A game? I didn't think so. *Bon nuit, mes enfants*. Sleep well."

After costumes were returned to the wardrobe mistress, some of the younger members of the company hung around for a few minutes. Jule was last out and would have passed by the group in the hall if someone hadn't called out to him.

"Hey, stuck-up," Amani said.

Jule turned to her. "Excuse me?"

"Are you too good for us?" Her words were sharp, but her eyes twinkled mischievously.

"No."

"Then come hang out with us."

"Really?"

"Sure, why not? We don't have cooties."

"I didn't think you'd want me." Jule walked over to stand next to Amani.

She laughed. "And we thought you were stuck-up."

"Yeah," Dani said. "You're always with Lucas and Charlotte or with David. So, we thought you thought you were something special."

"Were you watching him?" Amani turned to Dani. "He *is* something special."

"He can dance," Dani said with a shrug.

"That's a real compliment coming from him," Samira said. "So, who wants to join us?"

"For what?" Jule asked.

"Before you came out, we were talking about clubbing since we don't have to be back here until one tomorrow," Samira said. "Come with us."

Amani put a hand on Jule's arm. "Yeah, come out and dance with us. It'll be stellar."

"Well, if it's going to be *stellar*," Jule joked.

"You'll love this place," Dani said. "It's kind of a ballet bar."

"What does that mean?"

Charlotte turned from her conversation with Dylan and Astra. "A lot of dancers hang out there," she said.

"It's even called The Barre, like b-a-r-r-e," Dani said.

"I get it," Jule said. "So, I assume they're used to people showing up in warmup clothes."

"Very," Charlotte said. "Let's go. We're going to need a couple of cabs."

"Take the car," David said from the studio doorway. "And be home by midnight. I need you well rested tomorrow."

Chapter Fourteen

THE BIG car dropped the group a street over from the club. The gaggle of dancers drifted in, shed their outwear at the coat-check station, and looked around to gauge the evening's atmosphere. The dance floor was only half-full, and there was plenty of room at the bar.

"I'll grab those two tables on the right," Dani said. "We can push them together."

"Just a sec. We're being paged," Charlotte said. She spotted Bram waving from the bar and gestured to him. "You guys don't mind if he joins us, right?"

"Now that you ask…." Dani said drily.

Charlotte smacked his shoulder. "Don't be a dick."

"I'm not, I just don't need the competition," Dani said.

Charlotte laughed and waved Bram over. "Hello, handsome," she said as Bram kissed her cheek.

Bram also kissed Amani and Samira on the cheek and shook hands with the boys. "So, big night out for the future stars of ballet?"

"Just chillin'," Amani said. "You know we have a full rehearsal tomorrow afternoon."

"I'm ready," Bram said. "Why don't you guys sit, and I'll get a server over here."

"Already taking over," Amani said under her breath as he moved away. She smiled at Jule. "Oops, did I say that out loud?"

"He didn't hear you," Jule said. "And you're right. He likes being in charge." He pulled out a chair for her.

"Why thank you, kind sir," she said archly as she sat.

"Jule's a gentleman," Charlotte said. "The real deal."

"Jule is gay," Dani blurted out. "Sorry, but I mean, it's not like it's a secret."

"Really?" Amani gave Jule an assessing stare. "Too bad for me. I was starting to develop a serious crush."

"On me?" Jule looked surprised.

"Yeah, you." She poked his chest. "You sexy thing."

"Rubbish." Jule looked away from her.

"No, Amani's right," Charlotte said.

"What's our baby ballerina right about?" Bram asked as he returned. Amani repeated her comment.

"That sounds right to me," Bram said. He sat next to Charlotte, across from Jule.

"You're all mad," Jule said as the server arrived. He ordered a shot of vodka with lime as per Sasha's list of approved substances. It was low-calorie and so strong and tart that he was forced to sip it. He could make a shot of vodka last for hours.

Dani and Samira got up to dance. After a few moments, Charlotte joined them, and then Dylan and Astra.

"You feel like dancing?" Bram asked.

"Me or him?" Amani pointed a thumb at Jule.

"Either or both."

"You're so naughty, Bram-Bram," she said.

Jule smiled. If the words had come from Charlotte, they would have sounded like a flirty invitation. From Amani, they were somewhere between a clinical observation and disapproval. He grinned when she got up and went to dance with Charlotte.

"Am I high or was I just dusted?" Bram asked.

"I don't know what that means."

"Dusted? It's like when you're in a race, and you think your car is unbeatable, but some other player blows right by you. They leave you eating their dust. Get it?"

Jule sipped his drink. It was cold and sharp, and he could feel it all the way down to his stomach. In an odd way, it made him feel more dialed in as he focused on Bram. "I get it."

"How was rehearsal?"

"It was rehearsal."

"Okay." Bram took a drink of his beer.

"You did get dusted, by the way."

"She's a firecracker, isn't she?" Bram glanced at Amani. "And she's got the moves."

"I like her. She's everything I love about ballet now. She's like a visible sign that things are changing."

"Just because she's not white."

"Well… yes, but no. There have been great ballerinas who weren't white, but she—" Jule looked over at the dance floor. "It's not about color. I feel like she'll break some different stereotypes." He sighed. "I'm not saying this very well."

"That's certainly true." Bram grinned. "I agree Amani's no delicate flower, but neither is Charlotte, no matter how they look." He reacted to Jule's change of expression. "What? I meant it as a compliment."

"I know."

"So why the no-fun face?"

"It's personal, all right?"

"Oy, don't tell me! You and her?"

Jule shook his head.

"Okay, good, because that would have surprised me, and I don't like surprises."

"I'll make a note."

After a few moments of silence, Bram spoke. "Remember when I said you could talk to me? The offer is still open."

"I liked her, and now I can't, and it's a weird feeling. I don't like it."

"Why can't you like her?"

Jule sighed. "She lied to me, all right?"

"People lie all the time, Jule."

"I don't."

"Well, you're definitely not the norm."

Jule sipped more vodka. "Look, I know people tell lies or exaggerate or whatever, but this was a big lie, and it hurt me."

"I understand. You don't have to tell me anymore if you don't want to."

"She pretended to be my friend."

"Ouch."

"And Lucas as well."

Bram didn't speak for several seconds. "Um, are you saying Lucas *pretended* to be interested in you?"

"That's what happened. David told them to be nice to me, which was code for something else."

"Are you sure?"

"I asked David, and he didn't deny it." Jule looked up as the others returned to the table.

"We'll talk later," Bram said. "Okay?"

Jule nodded and then turned his attention to Amani. "I'd love to partner you someday," he said.

"Ooo, Mr. Parry," Amani cooed while fluttering her lashes. "I'd love that too. How about right now?"

"Sure." Jule stood, and she took his hand to lead him to the dance floor.

Jule's phone rang while he was dancing, and he waited until they were back at the table to return the call. "Hi, Lucas. How are you?"

"Better, but I miss you."

Jule steeled himself against a flood of emotion and managed to keep his voice steady. "I'll see you as soon as I can."

"Hey, Jule, want to dance again?" Amani called out.

"Who was that?" Lucas asked.

"One of the ballerinas," Jule said into the phone. He waved to Amani to go ahead. "I'm at a lounge called The Barre."

"Yeah, I know it well." Lucas swallowed. "Well… have fun."

"I am."

"Don't worry about me. I'm fine."

Lucas's tone was light, which meant he was hurt; Jule swallowed and made himself answer in the same tone. "I know."

"Well. Bye then."

"Good night. Sleep well." Jule hung up. He smiled at Amani as he joined her on the floor again. Talking to Lucas was painful, but he was getting better at hiding it.

An hour or so later, Jule decided it was time to go. He brushed aside the chorus of boos and stood up. Samira and Dani got up as well and said goodbye. Dylan and Astra had already gone to catch a train. Bram followed the others onto the sidewalk, leaving Charlotte and Amani at the table. Samira and Dani hailed a cab, and Bram followed Jule down the sidewalk.

"Wait up," Bram said as Jule started across a side street.

Jule slowed his steps until Bram caught up.

"Headed to the dorm?" Bram asked.

"Yeah. Don't want to break curfew."

"Are you going to walk all the way?"

"Until I get there, yeah."

"Mind if I walk with you? I'm staying with Catherine, and she keeps odd hours. She won't care if I come in late."

"If that's what you want to do."

"It *is* what I want to do. I like you, Jule. You couldn't tell?"

"What? Like you like me, or you *like* me?"

"I don't know yet," Bram said honestly.

"Well, that's as clear as everything else in my life right now."

"Hey, ease up on yourself. You're what? Fifteen?"

Jule stopped walking.

"It was a joke," Bram said.

"I know." Jule sighed. "I'm just not good company right now. I'd rather not inflict myself on anyone."

"Look, I consider myself your friend, or at least a colleague, and I'd rather not let you walk off in this mood. What do you say we talk for a minute?"

"I'm not sure who my friends are anymore, but I appreciate your concern."

"So, what's up? You looked happy when you were dancing."

"I always look happy when I'm dancing. Ask anyone."

"You're way too young to sound that bitter."

"I'm not. Bitter, I mean. Why do people always think I'm being cynical when I state facts?"

Bram laughed softly. "That's actually a very good question."

"Do you have a very good answer?"

"Not to that one." Bram looked around. "You want a coffee or something? We're not far from an all-night diner."

"Curfew?"

"Right. I forgot. Come on, then. Let's plow."

Snow started falling as they walked. Jule once again experienced the odd vertigo of watching the flakes spin into sight as they entered the field of light. An infinity of bright and dark. No curfews. No obligations.

"It's so beautiful," he said.

"What's that?"

"Just the way the snow falls into the light. It's beautiful. I've always thought so. It's just so peaceful."

"It is indeed. Have you ever landed at an airport after dark when there's snow on the ground?"

"No."

"The lights along the runway are sapphire blue, and the way they look against the snow is really something."

"I imagine it is."

After a few moments of silence, Bram spoke again. "Hey, I'm really sorry David pulled that shit on you. I know how I'd feel if that happened to me."

"I don't want to talk about it right now."

"Okay, but just so you know, I don't feel sorry for you. I feel sorry for them."

"Thanks." Jule glanced over at Bram as though seeing him for the first time. "Seriously. That means a lot."

"Yeah, the very worst feeling is when you look like a fool in your own eyes."

Jule didn't answer, and they walked in silence until they reached the school.

"Can I come up?" Bram asked.

"Against the rules, but you know that."

"Yeah, I guess I do. Well, I should say good night, then."

"Me too. I still have my routine to do before bed."

"Okay, then." Bram leaned in but stopped a centimeter from Jule's lips.

For a moment, Jule's mood and the vodka urged him to close the gap and feel the warmth of Bram's mouth. But Bram was not Lucas, and the impulse passed quickly. "Please don't," he said, whether to Bram or himself was hard to say.

Bram moved back. "I didn't mean anything by it. I kiss everyone."

Without another word, Jule went through the doors and down the hall. What the hell was happening to him? Had he really almost kissed someone just because he was…. Jule stepped into his room and closed the door but stood there for a moment with his hand still on the wood. Lonely. He was lonely. Not for his family or Kelly and Sasha but for Lucas.

Chapter Fifteen

AT EIGHT the next morning, Jule presented himself at David's office as requested. The door stood open, so he knocked on the frame.

David gestured grandly for Jule to enter. "Please come in. I'm glad you had time this morning."

"I'll always have time for you."

"What a lovely thing to say."

"Not really. After all, you're the director of the company."

"I see. Care for a cronut?"

"I'm not familiar."

"It's a cross between a croissant and a donut."

"Yes, please!"

"Help yourself to coffee or tea at the caddy there and then have a seat."

"Thanks." Jule's tone turned wistful. "I probably shouldn't have pastry, though."

"I order you to eat at least half this cronut." David pushed the plate closer to Jule. He watched as Jule took a bite of the flaky pastry. "Good, right?"

Jule nodded.

David cleared his throat. "How angry are you with me?" He frowned at Jule's blank look. "On a scale of one to Three Mile Island."

Jule swallowed, put the pastry aside, and took a drink of his coffee. "I don't know what Three Mile Island is. I'm upset, but I'm not angry, though I don't feel very, um, kindly toward you. This cronut, though— It's really helping your case."

"So, you don't hate me?"

"No, I don't. I don't like what you did, but I don't hate you."

"Whew." David smiled. "You've just been, you know, distant."

"I can't believe I'm saying this, especially to you, but I have personal problems."

"Can I help?"

Jule stared at him. "You're part of the personal problem."

"Well, then, I have an insider's perspective."

"That shouldn't make sense." Jule took a moment to think about what he wanted to say.

"Just tell me in your own words what's going on with you. I'm asking as the ballet's artistic director and as your friend... I hope."

"It's hard to think of you as a friend. I've admired you for a while."

"I'm flattered."

"Also, a friend wouldn't do what you did to me and Lucas." Jule paused. "I would never do that to anyone. Why would you think it's okay to play with people like that?"

David was silent for several seconds. "I just want what's best for the company," he said.

Jule didn't reply.

David cleared his throat. "I can't imagine what you must think of me."

"I think you should apply some of the compassion you put into your ballet to the people in your life."

David looked taken aback. "That's a very grown-up observation. Is that how you really feel about me? I'm heartless?"

"You—" Jule swallowed the first words that came to his lips. "You treat people like dolls or maybe chess pieces."

"This is actually *not* the first time I've been told that."

"I don't mean to be disrespectful, and it's not my place to tell you how to act, but I don't have to put up with it either."

"No, you don't, and I realize that. I know my company is lucky to have you. No one else knows it yet, but when they get a look at my—our *Sleeping Beauty*, they'll know it. I hope you're prepared for the attention you'll receive."

"I suppose we'll see. Meanwhile, please don't screw me around again or—"

"I won't. I promise."

"Or I'll walk away," Jule finished.

"You signed a contract."

"I know, but I don't care. I'll leave the company."

"It would kill your career."

"No, it wouldn't." Jule stood up. "I might never be a star, but I'd still be a dancer. Thank you for breakfast."

"Let's not end the meeting like this." David came around his desk. "I can see now that I can't manipulate you, so let's wipe that slate clean. What do you say? Can you accept my apology and move on?"

"I think we should at least try if we're to continue working together."

"Good. Good." David sighed in relief. "I don't have to tell you how disastrous it would be to lose you now. Opening night is two days away."

"I'm aware, and I'm off to practice now. I don't want the others to wait on me."

"And yet, they will gladly wait for you."

"What does that mean?"

"Nothing bad. When you're exceptional, people will make allowances, you know?"

Jule frowned. "Maybe they shouldn't."

"Maybe, but they will. That's the way the world is." David opened the door for Jule. "I'll see you all at four," he said as Jule walked away.

JULE'S PHONE rang as he was leaving the studio for a break. "Hi, Lucas."

"I'm in the area. Want to get a bite?"

"I'm not sure I could eat right now."

"Where are you?"

"Walking down the hall to the loo."

"Meet me out front in a few minutes?"

Jule sighed. "Sure."

"Hey, curb your enthusiasm," Lucas joked.

"See you in five."

When Jule walked out of the bathroom, he could see Lucas outlined against the glass front door. Lucas leaned on an elegant cane and held a takeout cup in the other hand. Jule pushed down the surge of emotion, waved casually, and went to join him.

Lucas handed Jule the large cup. "It's a smoothie," he said. "In lieu of solid food. The lady who made it said it would keep you going till dinner."

Jule sipped from the straw. "It's good. Thanks." Honestly, it tasted too much of banana, but he didn't want to sound ungrateful.

"Walk with me to Dante Park? We can sit and talk. If you don't want to talk yet, I understand."

"No, it's fine." Jule followed Lucas out of the building.

"At the risk of making you uncomfortable, it kills me that I can't give you a hug."

"I'd like a hug, but I can't take the chance." Jule coughed. "When you touch me, whatever good sense I have goes out the window."

They walked in silence until they reached the triangle of Dante Park at Lincoln Plaza. No one else was sitting at the café tables. They chose seats near the edge of the area and sat, breathing clouds into the cold air.

"I'm not going to say anything you don't know already," Lucas began. "But I have to restate it. I will do anything to get back to the way it was between us."

"It can't be the same ever again. You know that."

"Maybe not exactly, but we could try." Lucas waited for a reply that didn't come and then went on. "How would you feel about that?"

"I just—" Jule's voice choked off for a second. "I can't stand the way I feel. I'm trying so hard to be mature and stay on track."

Lucas held out a hand.

"Don't."

"It hurts to see you like this."

"It hurts to care about you."

"Well, at least you care. That's something."

Instead of replying, Jule took another drink of the smoothie.

Lucas leaned forward in his seat. "If you loved me once, you can love me again. I believe that. Just tell me what I have to do to get a second chance with you." He took a breath. "It's been a couple days since we've spoken. I get worried."

"I didn't realize it had been that long. I've been so caught up in the production." Jule looked up and caught the expression on Lucas's face. "I'm sorry. It must be killing you to sit this one out."

"Well, I'm not dead yet. And I'm getting stronger every day. The physical therapist is confident I'll make a full recovery."

"But that ankle will always be a little weaker now."

"Fuck you, you fucking realist."

Jule almost smiled. "You'll just have to be more careful, that's all."

"I'll be back and better than ever," Lucas said firmly. "No one's dancing *Fireheart* with you but me."

Jule sipped the smoothie, hoping to get rid of the lump in his throat.

"Jule, look," Lucas said. "I know it hurts sometimes, but not all the time. Sometimes it was really good. Remember?"

"It's not a fair trade."

"Fair? What's fair about any of this?" Lucas shook his head. "What if I'd just met you in a normal way? If David hadn't felt compelled to scheme?"

Jule felt as though his heart was in a blender, but he managed to say what he had to say. He told the truth. "There's no point talking about it."

"Of course, there is. You loved me. I know you did. I could feel it."

"I felt it too."

"I'm asking for a chance to make it right. I believe that what I feel for you is love, and I believe you love me too. That's worth a second chance."

Jule met Lucas's eyes. "I can't give you an answer right now. Let me get through the season, and I'll be able to think about something other than dancing."

"All right." Lucas moved the conversation to a slightly safer subject. "I should warn you I'll be around a little more often, so you might run into me. Just because I can't jump around doesn't mean I can't practice arms."

"You're one of the most expressive dancers I've ever seen," Jule said, feeling as though he'd made it through a minefield to safe ground.

"I appreciate you saying that. We'd better get you back now. Opening night is tomorrow, so I'm sure you've got a gazillion last-minute things to do."

"Not really, but there's a dress rehearsal at four in the big studio."

"Mind if I watch?"

Jule almost said no but changed his mind. "Please do. You can give me notes afterward." He tried to ignore the warmth that spread through his chest when Lucas gave him a grateful smile, but it felt so good that he had to smile back. If he'd had any lingering doubts that this man was his kryptonite, they died then and there. He had no natural defenses against Lucas. Even if he didn't take him back, he'd always love him, and Lucas would be the yardstick every man in his future would be measured against. If only he could trust him the way he trusted Kelly.

"Come on." Lucas stood and took hold of his cane. "I'm looking forward to seeing all the costumes."

"They're amazing. Marilee did an incredible job." Jule looked over at Lucas and was struck once again by how handsome he was, but that was just window-dressing. It was the soul blazing behind those warm amber eyes that he loved.

"What's that look? What are you thinking?" Lucas asked.

"Thinking is for people who can't dance."

Lucas laughed, and the strain between them eased a little further. During the walk back, the tension went away almost completely. They were trading lame Star Wars puns when they reached the studio.

"Jule," David called out as they entered the hall. "Marilee's looking for you. Hi, Lucas. How are you?" he said as he walked briskly toward them.

"I'm much better." Lucas twirled the ebony walking stick like a baton. "I'll be back in the saddle before you know it."

"You are missed," David said sincerely. "And you're still my number one."

"That's nice to hear. God, I miss this awful place."

"Well, come on in. I know everyone will be thrilled to see you." David flung open the door to the big studio.

Jule took Lucas's free hand and pulled him into the room.

Charlotte spotted them first. "Luc!" She hurried across the floor, the diaphanous layers of her white-and-gold costume streaming behind her like ethereal wings.

"You look like a dream I had once," Lucas greeted her. "You're a goddess!"

"You look good enough to eat with a spoon, boy. Does this mean you're back?"

"Partially. We'll talk later. You get back to work now, girl."

Charlotte went back to her place next to Bram. Bram waved at Lucas and mouthed *welcome back*. Everyone who wasn't actively busy came up to shake Lucas's hand or give him a hug.

"You want to say something before I call this melee to order?" David asked.

"Thanks, everyone," Lucas said loudly. "I had no idea I was this well-liked. If I had one wish, my ankle would be one hundred percent right now, but since I can't have that, my wish is that you go on that stage tomorrow night and dance a kick-ass *Sleeping Beauty*."

"Done," Jule said. He held up his fist for Lucas to bump.

Lucas bumped Jule's knuckles. "Go kick some ass, then," he said.

JULE FINISHED practice and was surprised to find himself alone in the studio. Everyone else had departed without his notice. He felt a twinge of disappointment that Lucas wasn't there, but he shrugged it off quickly. Opening night was imminent, and he couldn't afford to be distracted.

He gathered his things and went to the locker room for a shower. After changing into street clothes, he headed down the main hall. To his right, the door to one of the smaller studios stood open. Inside, he could see a group of boys and girls who looked to be under twelve. The children faced a wall of mirrors and raised their arms into fifth position.

Jule took a couple of steps until he could see the back half of the studio. His gaze found Lucas, and he couldn't look away from the tall, athletic form as Lucas moved to the front of the class. He watched Lucas lift his arms into fourth position as an example to the students. He remembered how good it felt to be held in those arms.

For several minutes, Jule stood just out of sight and watched Lucas teach. He didn't see a hint of impatience in Lucas's manner. Lucas was gentle and easygoing, making light of mistakes, even pretending he couldn't tell his left arm from his right to save a student from embarrassment. It was nothing like Kelly's precise, professional technique, yet there was something about Lucas's demeanor that reminded Jule of his mentor. Not until now did he see the same air of solid commitment, the intangible quality that made you feel as though he'd stand by you to the end.

Abruptly, Jule realized the class was breaking up, and he hurried away. For some reason, he didn't want Lucas to know he'd been watching him. It would be like admitting a weakness.

As Jule stepped out the front doors into the cold, he wondered why he felt that way. Why would it be so bad to let Lucas know that he missed him? Was he *that* afraid of getting hurt again? What would Sasha say to that? What would Mum say?

Jule put his hand on his phone to call Sasha or Mum, but he didn't take it out of his pocket. Instead, he thought about it some more as he walked to the dormitory. Maybe it wasn't so black and white. Maybe Lucas deserved a second chance. Why did he believe he had no option but to give Lucas up? Maybe he was being too harsh. It had all happened so fast. One minute, he was full of joy with a dream job and a dreamy lover, and the next, he was reeling from the gut-punch of betrayal. Ever since, he'd been dealing with the pain using the tried-and-true method of staying in motion until he was too tired to do anything but sleep.

Would it really be weak of him to take Lucas back? Though it had been brief, he couldn't forget how happy he'd been when they were together. Lucas was a perfect fit for him in so many ways. And if he gave him a second chance, and it turned out that Lucas really was a bastard, he could always walk away again. Maybe it would show more strength to try to make it work.

Jule sighed again. He didn't believe Lucas was a bastard, not really. The man he knew in private was simply too sweet to be that shady. In his heart, he believed Lucas when Lucas said he felt badly about what he'd done. He also believed Lucas when said he'd fallen in love. He still didn't know why someone as gorgeous and sophisticated as Lucas would fall for him, but stranger things happened all the time, he supposed.

For now, Jule decided, he would concentrate on performing his part in *Sleeping Beauty* to the best of his abilities. He would let go of the lingering shock and pain. When the production was over, and they started work on *Fireheart*, he knew he'd have to decide one way or the other about Lucas. There was no way he could dance with him, be that close to him, without something breaking. Whether it was his pride or his heart remained to be seen.

ON OPENING night, the backstage area of the theater was a hive of activity. Jule and Charlotte were finished in wardrobe at the same time and went to have a peek at the stage. After a quick look, they stood together out of the way of the stagehands and watched the coordinated chaos around them. David buzzed through the scene occasionally like a bee seeking out flowers.

"Did I mention you look stunning?" Jule asked. He ran his gaze over Charlotte from her upswept red-gold hair glittering with ornaments down the bodice crusted with pearls, the filmy, floating layers of the calf-length skirts, the iridescent shimmer of her tights, and the glinting gold embroidery of her toe shoes. "Like a fairy prin—" Jule broke off midword.

"What?" Charlotte said.

"I just thought of the perfect ballet for you."

"Well tell me, rookie."

"*A Midsummer Night's Dream*. You would be a perfect Titania."

"Yes, she would."

Jule and Charlotte turned to see that David had come up behind them.

"I'll give it some serious thought," David said.

"Fantastic!" Charlotte beamed.

"I want to be Puck," Jule said.

"I don't think you have a choice," David said drolly. "Lucas will make a great Oberon. Can't you just see him with a pair of horns?"

"He does well enough with the one," Jule said.

David looked at him in surprise. "Was that sexual innuendo, Mr. Parry?"

"Damn right it was," Charlotte said. "Good one, Jule."

"I take it from your idleness that the two of you are ready," David said. "You certainly look ready." He touched one of Jule's prosthetic pointed ears. "These look so real." He put his fingers under Charlotte's chin and tilted her face to the light so the dusting of gold powder shimmered. "Exquisite."

"Heigh-ho," Bram said as he joined them. His costume was the most traditional of the production, and it suited him perfectly: cobalt-blue velvet tunic over black tights and boots with silver embellishments. He also wore a jeweled dagger and a short cape of black velvet with the same ornamentation as the boots.

"My prince has come," Charlotte said. "Oh God, did I really just say that?"

"I'm afraid so," David said.

"You shan't recover," Jule predicted.

Bram shook his head "No point in adding to that."

"Break a leg, everyone," Catherine said as she joined them. She carried a large bouquet of pale pink roses. "These were just delivered."

"For me?" Charlotte said.

"Actually, they're for all of you. I'll put them somewhere safe until after the performance," Catherine said. "But here's the card if you'd like to read it now."

Jule took off his supple lavender gloves and opened the small card. "It's from Lucas," he said. "He wishes he could be on stage with us, but he'll be here in the audience." He smiled. "If we fuck it up, he's going to kick our asses."

"He'll have to get in line behind me," David said. "I gotta go get into my costume. See you just before the curtain goes up."

"Wait for me," Catherine said. She turned back to Charlotte, Jule, and Bram. "I want you to know that I have the utmost confidence in your ability to dazzle that crowd out there." She walked away before anyone thought to thank her.

Bram glanced at the digital clock over the backstage entrance. "It won't be long now," he said.

"I can't wait." Charlotte glanced at Jule.

Jule, still coasting on endorphins from his warmup routine, smiled at her. "Me either. I have to say, I'm really excited to be performing with you."

"I'm looking forward to the audience reaction to your entrance," Bram told Jule.

"I'm actually jealous. That's how spectacular your entrance is," Charlotte added.

"But you're the star of the piece," Jule reminded her. "I'm basically a cameo. All right, that's an exaggeration, but you know what I mean."

"Yeah, I think I do." Charlotte smiled and then leaned close to kiss his cheek and say something only he could hear. "Sorry for being such a cunt to you. Thanks for not holding it against me."

Jule's eyes widened in surprise, but before he could reply, they heard the orchestra tuning up in the pit.

"It's getting close," Bram said unnecessarily.

The three stood together as the corps gathered onstage. David walked by with Catriona on his arm, both in costumes worthy of a Renaissance court. A hush fell over the theater, and then the curtain went up.

Chapter Sixteen

AFTER THE final curtain came down, Lucas went to David's brownstone to make sure the caterers had everything in hand. He found Catherine there ahead of him and let her give him the task of handing out champagne flutes. He watched a fortune in Moët being opened as he greeted arriving guests.

"You," Lucas said when Jule appeared in the hallway. "Come here."

Jule came over and let Lucas give him a one-armed hug.

"You were spectacular," Lucas said.

"Thanks. I feel great."

"Yes, you do." Lucas lifted an eyebrow. "Now, go and receive your accolades graciously."

"Jule!" Amani called from the other room. "Come here! You *have* to see this Swan Lake cake!"

Jule looked at her over his shoulder.

"Go on," Lucas said. "Be a kid for a while." He watched Jule walk away, his expression wistful.

Catherine offered Lucas a flute of champagne.

"No, thanks," he said. "Why have sham pain when I already have real pain?"

"Clever," Catherine said. She watched Jule join Amani and laugh at something she said. "That girl is going to shake up a few institutions."

"Good for her," Lucas said flatly.

"Do you think she'll shake him up?"

"I'm not worried about Jule."

"Liar." Catherine smiled. "What can I get you to drink?"

"I've always been a vodka man, but I'll get my own drink, thanks." Lucas walked away before he could slip and say something snide. He knew it was smarter to be civil, but he'd not forgotten how shabbily she'd treated him when he was the temporary apple of David's eye.

About half an hour later, Jule found Lucas in the kitchen. "Hey, I just came for some water."

Lucas pointed to the smaller refrigerator.

Jule took out a bottle, opened it, and leaned back against the counter to take several long swallows.

"If you could stop being sexy for five minutes, that would be great," Lucas said.

Jule laughed and spit water down the front of his shirt.

"That'll work." Lucas tossed him a hand towel.

"Yeah, not so sexy now." Jule giggled.

Lucas stared at him. "Are you drunk?"

"I don't know. I feel pretty good, though."

"How much have you had to drink?"

"I did some shots with Char and Amani. Does that count as drunk?"

"Depends. How many shots and how much time between them?"

"Um." Jule looked as though he was thinking hard. "We were trying to see who could drink the most shots in ten seconds."

"Good grief! How are you standing?"

"I'm fine." Jule grinned. "I'm fantastic." He drank more water. "I won!"

"I can't argue with that. You were really good tonight, you know. You've got an amazing future ahead of you."

"I'm having an amazing present right now."

"Good."

"Hey, Amani showed me some hip-hop steps."

Jule pushed away from the counter to demonstrate and immediately overbalanced.

Lucas caught Jule and held him upright until he was relatively steady.

Jule put his arms around Lucas. "This feels so good," he said, his voice muffled against Lucas's shirt.

"That it does," Lucas agreed. "But we probably shouldn't be doing this."

"Why not?"

"Because you are what is officially known as shit-faced."

"I'm drunk?"

"You're inebriated, pickled, bombed, smashed, hammered, wasted, etcetera."

Jule giggled.

"You just giggled. I rest my case."

"Rubbish." Jule giggled again. He looked up into Lucas's gaze, his dark eyes liquid and longing.

"Give me strength." Lucas shook his head. What was he going to do with a drunk, amorous armful of Jule? "Come on, man. Let's get some more water into you."

"I don't want water."

"Okay."

"I wanna kiss."

"Yeah, me too, but no can do."

"Why not?"

"Because you aren't thinking clearly right now." Lucas put his hands on Jule's shoulders and took a half step back. "Suppose we kiss, and it leads to more? Suppose you wake up in the morning, sober, and regret having sex with me? It happens."

Jule was quiet for a few seconds. "You're right," he said. "I can't snog you." He turned away from Lucas and walked unsteadily to the door.

"Wait."

"Nope. Need a drink."

"You need to hydrate and go to bed."

"I need—*Bram*!"

Bram stopped in his tracks and turned toward Jule. "Bram I am," he said drolly.

"You have two drinks."

"I do. Would you like one?"

Jule nodded.

"Come on, then." Bram glanced at Lucas, meeting his eyes for a long moment before he returned his attention to Jule. "This way to Liquorland."

Jule wandered away with Bram. Seeing no point in staying around to have his heart cut out sans anesthetic, Lucas found his coat and went home.

BRAM PICKED a bottle up from the liquor cart. "I believe vodka is your poison." He poured a double shot and handed it to Jule.

"Is there lime?" Jule asked.

Bram found a bottle and squirted juice into Jule's glass. "Best I can do," he said. "We appear to be out of fresh limes."

Jule gulped down a third of the drink. "Sfine," he said.

Bram chuckled. "You're cute when you're hammered."

"He's cute all day long," Amani said as she stopped beside the liquor cart. "Pass me that bottle of Jack?"

Bram opened the bottle and poured until she said stop.

"You're pretty," Jule said.

"Me or Bram?"

Jule laughed. "You're both pretty."

"True," Bram said. "So, are we going to stand around guzzling David's booze and blowing sunshine up each other's asses, or are we going to have some fun?"

"What sort of fun?" Jule asked.

"Yeah, what sort of fun?" Amani echoed warily.

"Party game?"

Amani curled her lip. "Sounds like a lame excuse to cop a feel."

"Well, to be fair, that describes most party games," Bram said.

"The only one I know is Spin the Bottle," Jule said. "I've never played it, though."

Amani shook her head. "What are we going to do with this boy?" she said to Bram.

"I can think of one or two things," Bram replied. "But we'd need more privacy."

"You had to go there." Amani took Jule's hand. "I'm going to get you away from this bad influence."

Jule let her lead him away, but he looked back at Bram over his shoulder. He smiled when Bram followed. In a few minutes, they were part of a group that also included Charlotte, Jamison, Marilee, and David.

"Bram," Charlotte called out. "Be a guy and fetch me a drinkie, please."

Bram obligingly inquired if anyone else wanted alcohol and then went back to the cart. He made a drink for Charlotte, turned around, and almost bumped into Jule. "Whoa!"

"Sorry," Jule said. "I need a drink too."

"Okay. I'll wait for you."

Jule splashed more vodka into his glass and followed Bram back to the group.

Bram watched Jule down half a double shot. "Hey, you might want to take it a little slower there, tiger," he said softly.

"Mokay," Jule said solemnly.

"You're okay, huh? That's cool. Just let me know if you start to feel dizzy."

Jule snapped off a pirouette, flinging alcohol everywhere. "See? I'm fine." He looked at his empty glass. "I need a drink, though."

Bram took the glass from Jule's hand.

Jules blinked at Bram. "Mate, I feel a bit off."

"I thought you might. Come with me." Bram put an arm around Jule and walked him down the hall to the guest bathroom. "You go on in and get rid of a few gallons of ego."

"I could do with a wee." Jule walked into the bathroom with exaggerated care. As he unzipped, Bram closed the door.

"Ugh," Jule said as he came out several minutes later. "Thank God for mouthwash."

"Better?"

"Yeah. Thanks for whisking me away before I made a massive fool of myself."

"Actually, I whisked you just *after* you made a fool of yourself."

Jule grimaced. "Thanks anyway."

"No problem. I sort of told Lucas I'd look out for you."

"What? When?"

"He didn't ask me to or anything, and I didn't literally say that to him, we just, you know…. There was a Look."

"No, I don't know."

"He looked at me. I looked at him. We didn't need to say anything."

"You're mad."

"We should get back before Amani comes looking for us."

Before Jule could answer, Charlotte called Bram's name. They were pulled back into the group, and Jule found himself sitting between Charlotte and David. Amani was now in David's chair. She winked at Jule.

"I won this chair in a party game," she said.

Jule laughed.

Charlotte shared her martini with Jule. David shared his brandy. At some point, Jule became aware David was gone because he missed the warmth of David's thigh pressed against his. It was his last coherent thought for some time.

Around three in the morning, Jule passed out and Bram put him on a couch in the front room. Jule slept soundly as Bram followed the last of the guests out of David's house and closed the door behind him.

Chapter Seventeen

AFTER THE third time his phone rang, David glanced at it, saw it was just after noon, and answered this one. "I'm trying to sleep," he said.

"David!" Catherine spoke sharply to get his attention. "Be quiet and listen. You definitely have to hear this. Have you seen the *Times*?"

"The paper?"

"Yes, the *New York Times*."

"Did I mention I was asleep?"

"Go look at it right now. I'll wait."

"I'll call you back."

"No! David! Don't you dare hang—" Catherine's voice was cut off as David disconnected.

He got out of bed, wrapped a robe around his naked body, and walked downstairs. Halfway down, he stopped at the sight of Jule sprawled on his couch, sound asleep. Silently, David continued down the stairs and across the floor. He paused to pull a fake fur throw over Jule and then went to the front door. As he returned with the paper, he saw that Jule was now awake.

"Good morning," David said. "I hope I didn't wake you."

"I'm sorry," Jule said.

"For what?"

"I think I must have had too much to drink last night."

"It certainly *was* a lot. Come on. I'm going to make coffee."

"Fantastic. I need the toilet first, though."

"Help yourself." David tucked the paper under his arm as he walked to the kitchen.

When Jule came in a few minutes later, the smell of brewing coffee permeated the kitchen. David handed him a mug. "Thanks."

"You didn't have to sleep on the couch. You could have taken one of the spare bedrooms."

"You had already gone to bed, and I don't like to presume."

"No, you sure don't. That's one of your salient characteristics, I'd say." David sat down at the small kitchen table.

"What does that mean?"

David took the lid off a cut-crystal cake-saver and revealed a stash of assorted danish. "It means that your manners are one of the first things people notice about you. It's not a bad thing. Pastry?"

Jule took a cheese danish and bit into it. "I didn't mean to drink so much," he said after he swallowed the bite.

David waved his hand dismissively. "You're not the first young dancer to sit at my kitchen table with a hangover, though I feel I should at least make a pretense at warning you about drinking too much."

"I don't think I have a hangover."

David peered at Jule, who looked absurdly fresh for someone who'd absorbed a vat of Russia's finest and slept in his clothes. "No headache? How's your stomach?"

"I feel fine. Just a little embarrassed. Honestly, I don't remember much from last night."

"It was a night to forget all right." David finished his apple danish and reached for a cherry-filled pastry. "You didn't see this," he told Jule.

"See what?"

"Good boy." David let his gaze linger on Jule's face.

Jule wiped his mouth and chin. "Did I get it?"

"What?" David paused. "No, there's nothing on your face. I was just looking at you."

"Oh. Okay."

"Since it's just the two of us, you mind if I get something off my chest?"

"Of course."

"Of course, you mind? Or you don't?"

"I don't."

"You know I'm a little obsessed with you, right?"

Jule looked up to meet David's gaze. He shook his head.

"I've been enthralled since I saw the first few seconds of that somewhat crappy film of you putting everyone around you in the shade."

"That's a bit much."

"No. No, it isn't. You have no idea of yourself. You *think* you do, but you don't. Not even Kelly really sees it. *Me*." David pointed to himself. "I know what you can be. I promised I'd take you to the next level, and I will. But—" He sipped his coffee.

"But?"

"Look, I don't doubt your commitment to the art, and I *know* you've got the chops, but lately you've shown a regrettable tendency to get tangled up, romantically I mean."

"I see." Jule set his cup down. "Before you say anything else, there's something you should know. I want to dance my best for you, but I won't let you tell me how to live."

"Fine." David's mercurial temper sparked. "Do as you please. Fuck 'em all. Just don't bring it into the studio or onto the stage."

Jule sat up a little straighter. "Are you not feeling well?"

The non sequitur jolted David from his pique. "What?"

"If you were hungover, for instance, I could probably understand why you'd speak so rudely."

"Oh, excuse me, was I vulgar?" David asked mockingly.

"You know you were, and you did it on purpose to bully me. Though I can't imagine why."

After a short silence, David spoke. "Fuck me." He sat back in his chair. "I forgot that you can see through me. You and Cath. Bites in the ass, both of you." David startled a chuckle from Jule, and he laughed too. "She calls it keeping me honest."

Jule replied with obvious reluctance. "Well, I have to say, you're better than this."

"You really think so?" David was half-amused and half-intrigued. "Please go on."

"I know so, because I admire you. And if you really were as shady as you sometimes appear, I wouldn't be able to admire you."

"Well, case closed, then. Now what?"

"Now we understand each other better, I hope we won't have any more misunderstandings."

"I see," David said. "Are you proposing we keep a professional relationship. Colleagues?"

"I think of you as a mentor."

"Thank you. That's very… flattering."

"So, since I think of you as a mentor, you can understand why I'd appreciate it if you'd step up your game, as Lucas likes to say."

"I'll get right on that." David smiled. "This isn't the conversation I expected to have, but it's a good one. I'll remember not to try running any games on you."

"Or anyone." Jule shook his head. "I can't understand why you think you need to use dirty tricks to get what you want. You're smart and talented and charming. You don't need to fool people."

David met Jule's gaze. "You know, you…." His voice trailed off. "Let me ask you a question."

"Of course."

"Are you cool with the whole obsession thing?"

"Excuse me?"

"What if I wanted to be closer to you?" David said bluntly.

Jule blinked. "Closer than a mentor? You want to be best mates?"

"Suppose my admiration for you extended to the physical."

"Just so there's no misunderstanding," Jule said. "Are you saying you want me to be tangled up with you? Romantically?"

"*Touché*." David winced as his words came back to bite him. "You aren't going to let me get away with anything, are you?"

"I learned my lesson the first time you fooled me."

"You haven't forgiven me." David sighed. "Nor should you. I promise to do better, if you'll consider continuing to work with a man whose ego makes a fool of him more often than not."

"I do think you're better than you behave."

"I'd almost have to be, wouldn't I? I promise to restrict my obsession to you as a dancer. To your career. Are my terms acceptable?"

"Was that some kind of test?" Jule asked.

David didn't answer; his downcast gaze had fallen on the paper beside his plate, open to the entertainment section. His eyes widened as he focused on the large color photo at the top of the page. "*Ça alors*," he said under his breath. "I'll be damned." He took his phone from the pocket of his robe and called Catherine as Jule stared at him.

"You saw it," she said.

"It's fantastic!"

"It is indeed. I've spoken with the *Times* dance critic since I spoke to you. She'll be in the audience again tonight and would like to speak to you before or after the performance. I comped her ticket, of course."

"After. Or—" David stared into space for a moment. "Just set it up and I'll be there."

"Will do." Her voice was gleeful. "I can almost hear the wheels turning in your head."

"So, I guess I was right to scoop Jule up while I had the chance, then?"

"Yes, you're a very clever boy. Mummy is ever so proud of you. I'm sorry I don't have more time to stroke your ego, but I have calls to make. *Tiens moi au courant!*"

"Yes, of course, I'll keep you posted." David put the phone down. "I haven't heard the girl that excited in years." He grinned at Jule's blank expression. "You have no idea what I'm talking about." Still grinning, he held up the paper.

Jule stared at the arresting image of him in the Lilac Fairy costume frozen at the zenith of a grand jeté above the bowed heads of the corps. "Bloody hell," he said under his breath.

"Isn't it fabulous?" David beamed. "Listen to this, and I quote the esteemed dance critic of the *New York Times*: Mr. Downes's reimagining of the beloved classic *Sleeping Beauty* cannot be faulted. The exquisite set design and costumes embellish magical passages that convince you that you've been transported to Fairyland. The players are perfectly cast and dance their roles to perfection, but I must single out one performer, a supernova among the shining stars.

"Newcomer Julian Parry literally bursts onto the scene as the Lilac Fairy, another bit of clever casting from Mr. Downes. Rather than emerging daintily from behind the corps, this Lilac Fairy flies from the wings, over the heads of the corps, to make his entrance in a series of acrobatic figures that left this balletomane giddy.

"I strongly advise all lovers of dance to see Mr. Downes's witty, enchanting production while it's still on offer."

David handed the paper to Jule. "You look amazing. That costume looks amazing. The corps looks amazing. The set looks amazing." He came around the table to look at the photo over Jule's shoulder, leaning on him a bit. "God, your form is *flawless*." He tousled Jule's hair.

Jule looked up at David. "If you say so. I should probably get to the dorm and have a shower."

"I have spare bathrooms."

"Hm, but I doubt your clothes would fit me."

"You're going home for warmups, right? I have spares of those too. And they should fit just fine."

Jule sighed. "I can't think of any more arguments, and I don't really want to go outside yet."

"Then it's settled. You'll shower, grab some tights, maybe have a little lunch, and then head to the theater. You can ride with me."

"That's my day planned, then." Jule glanced at the photo again.

"Catherine is ordering extra copies," David said. "We'll get a good print of the original and have it framed for the studio."

"Why?" Jule sounded horrified.

"Why not?"

"Sorry, that was a gut reaction. I'd be honored, of course." Jule blushed. "It just seems so… I don't know. Conceited?"

"Stop it. You're constantly on display. This is no big deal." David paused. "Speaking of that, I have an interview tomorrow with the dance critic from the *New York Times*."

"That's great! Isn't it?"

"It's free publicity, *chouchou*. Maybe you should be there with me."

"I'd rather just dance, thank you."

"Ah, but you're an ambassador of dance, remember?" David wagged a finger at Jule.

"Which bathroom should I use?"

"Okay, new subject." David chuckled. "Top of the stairs, turn left, second door on the right. Towels are in the hall closet."

David watched Jule climb the stairs before he skipped back to the kitchen. He called Catherine again, and they talked for fifteen minutes about maximizing the exposure. After he hung up, David took a shower and dressed. When he came downstairs, Jule was waiting in the living room. David tossed him a gym bag.

"Ready to slam some protein?" David asked. He beckoned to Jule to follow him to the kitchen. He opened the fridge. "You didn't think I'd let you go to work with nothing but sugar and caffeine in your system, did you?"

"I'd rather not predict what you might do."

David laughed as though Jule had made a joke. "Sit. I make a mean omelet, but I hate having anyone moving around while I cook. If you want something to drink, get it now."

David watched Jule pour a glass of milk and then went to the stove. He moved around the kitchen with a brisk efficiency that had little in common with his usual languid flourishes. It wasn't long before he set a plate in front of Jule.

Jule looked at the vegetable omelet and sausages. "This looks lovely. Thank you."

David brought over a jug of orange juice and poured two glasses. "Eat up, champ," he said. "You need to be on your toes tonight."

Jule groaned. "That joke was awful."

"Get used to it, *mon tresor*."

"No thank you." Jule tucked into his omelet.

DAVID'S CAR dropped them at the venue near the backstage entrance. Catherine was waiting when they reached the dressing room area.

"You have the look of someone bursting with news," David said.

"The *Times* called back."

"Great. I hope you let them know I'll be happy to talk to them."

"I'm going to go warm up," Jule said, eager to be away from Catherine.

"Wait just a moment. Let's have a look at you."

Jule froze and stood still while Catherine gave him a thorough visual appraisal. He endured her inspection and hoped she wouldn't say anything mean. He was sure he could keep from answering in kind, but getting upset before he had to perform was the last thing he wanted.

"You need a haircut," Catherine said.

"No," David said firmly. "No hairs will be cut."

"Why not? You have to agree that his head looks like a home for birds at the moment."

"I want it long for *Fireheart,* and I don't like the look of wigs."

"No haircut, then," Catherine capitulated emotionlessly. "What about a stylist? If he's going to be in the public eye representing the company, I'd prefer that he be presentable."

"Go crazy," David said and then grinned at the look of dismay on Jule's guileless face.

"I don't want to look foolish," Jule said.

"Don't worry," Catherine said. "David is foolish enough for both of you."

Jule saw Lucas come in with Charlotte. "Excuse me," he said. "I need to talk to Lucas."

"Go on," David said, and Jule walked away.

"Hi," he said as he stopped next to Lucas and Charlotte.

"Hey." Lucas smiled. "How you feeling?"

"I'm supposed to ask you that."

"I'm much better, thanks. You going to warm up?"

"Yeah, want to come?"

Lucas smiled. "I won't be much help, but I make a great spectator."

Charlotte rolled her eyes. "Have fun, boys. See you on stage."

DAVID SOUGHT Jule out before the performance and found him in one of the dressing rooms.

"I'm sorry to bother you now, but we both know you can't be rattled," David said.

"That's a myth, actually." Jule leaned into a lunge, stretching his muscles.

David licked his lips. "I need your help," he said. "I've planned a small exhibition of a passage from *Fireheart* for a very limited audience. I need you and Bram to perform it."

"I'd rather not." Jule worked the opposite leg as he spoke. "But I want to be helpful."

"Good. Good. It will only take a few minutes, and it could create a lot of good will for The Downtown Ballet. I don't have to tell you we'll need it, do I? Even coming off a win like *Sleeping Beauty*, we're going to encounter resistance."

"I said I'd do it."

"No, you didn't, but thank you." David turned to leave but paused. "Lucas said your rehearsal today was exciting. That's not a word he uses lightly."

"I'll do my best to bring that excitement to the stage, sir."

David sighed. "Call me David," he said for the hundredth time. He received no answer and left Jule to finish stretching.

Chapter Eighteen

AT ALMOST exactly ten thirty the next morning, the phone on David's desk rang.

"We're ready for you," Catherine said.

"On the way," David answered. He looked over at Jule. "Are you sure you don't want to come with?"

Jule nodded. "So sure."

"It's nothing to be afraid of," David remarked as he tugged at the gold-fringed scarf he was wearing in lieu of a necktie. "Just an interview."

With his thick unruly curls, burgundy velvet jacket, and gold earring, Jule thought David looked every inch an artist. "I'm sure you'll be enough drama for one dance critic."

"I try," David said drolly.

Jule waved him off and was glad when David left. He finished practice and was improvising some steps in front of the mirrors when David returned.

"If you care, the interview went wonderfully."

Jule turned from his reflection to look at David.

"Allow me to once again quote the dance critic of the *New York Times*. 'I want you to know that I believe Julian Parry is going to be a legend.'"

"That's really going out on a limb," Jule said.

David chuckled. "Here's another quote. 'My father and grandfather breed thoroughbreds for racing. I can look at a colt and tell if he's a winner. It's in my genes. I look forward to watching Mr. Parry's career.'"

"Wow. That's quite an endorsement."

"I think it's a sound prediction. Not only are you a superb dancer and a charmer as well, you have me on your side. How could you not succeed?"

Jule immediately thought of Kelly and how Kelly had been forced to retire, but he didn't bring it up. Times changed, and why spoil this moment that David was so clearly enjoying to the hilt?

"The article will be in the Sunday entertainment edition," David said gleefully. "Copies will be delivered here."

"So, it went well."

"Could you be just a little bit enthused?"

"I just want to dance."

"Okay, I get it," David said. "But I have to say that she walked in prepared to love us." He patted Jule on the head. "Thanks to you, my Lilac Fairy Godmother."

Jule rolled his eyes. "Rubbish."

"The important thing is that she's an important critic, and she likes us," David said. "Downtown Ballet can get a lot of mileage out of publicity like this."

Catherine opened the door and put her head in. "Are congratulations in order?"

"*Oui*, madame." David grinned. "Maybe us East Coasters need to clue in to some Hollywood style. Make a splash and all that."

"I'm not sure we need to go quite that far," Catherine said drily.

David kissed her cheek. "Thanks for setting it up."

"It was a pleasure. I have other business to attend to now. Will I see you at dinner?"

"I'll call if I can't make it," David said. He put a hand on Jule's shoulder as she walked away. "I feel very optimistic about the future."

Lucas came in but stopped just inside the door. "What's shakin'?"

"We're feeling optimistic," Jule said.

"That's good, right?"

"It depends on how you look at it."

"Devious," David said.

"I learned from the best," Jule replied.

"Ouch. Score a direct hit," Lucas said.

"You're included in my statement," Jule told him.

"Before this devolves any further," David said. "I suggest you two go someplace else until it's time to get into costume. Go on. Go away." He made shooing gestures. "*Allez, allez.*"

"Hey, guys." Bram joined them in the hall. "What are you going to do with your free time?"

"I thought I'd practice a bit longer," Jule said.

"Stop making the rest of us look bad," Lucas said. "Let's go do something fun."

"Sorry, but I can't forget my responsibility to everyone else in the production."

"Do you hate him as much as I do?" Bram asked Lucas.

"All the time," Lucas replied.

"Wankers," Jule said.

"Yeah, I could really go for a wank right now," Bram said.

"I'm a New York Wankee fan," Lucas said.

"Wanks for the memories," Bram retorted.

"I can't wait for Wanksgiving," Lucas topped him.

"Stop it," Jule said. "You're not funny."

"Why are you laughing?" Lucas asked.

"I'm laughing at your foolish faces."

"We may be foolish, but we're you're fools," Bram said. "Correct me if I'm wrong, but you two are broken up, right?"

"I'm certainly broken up," Lucas answered.

Jule walked faster.

"Hey." Lucas caught up with Jule. "Sorry. I didn't mean to be a dick."

"You weren't. I just feel awful about the whole thing, and I don't want to talk about it, especially in front of Bram."

"Why don't you come over when you have some free time, and we'll talk in private? You clearly aren't putting this behind you."

"No, I'm not." Jule glanced over at Lucas. A wave of tenderness put him off-balance, and he blurted out one of Lucas's lines just to be saying something. "Could you stop being outrageously attractive for five seconds?"

Lucas made a goofy face.

Jule laughed just as Bram came up beside them.

"What's so funny?" Bram asked.

"Lucas's face."

"Accurate."

"Hey!" Lucas said, pretending to be hurt.

"Don't try it on," Jule said. "Self-pity isn't your forte."

"And compassion isn't yours," Bram said. "How about easing up on my boy Luc?"

Jule looked at Bram in surprise. "How is it your business?"

"You're speaking right in front of me. I can only assume you meant to include me."

"Fair enough," Jule said. "I'll not do it again." He walked away.

Chapter Nineteen

AFTER THE sold-out Christmas Eve and Christmas Day performances, David hosted a "Midnight Christmas" at his house for those few who couldn't go home. A buffet was set out and the liquor cabinet opened. The guests sat around the lovely tree in the front bay window. After the performance adrenaline had worn off, David lit the fire laid ready, and the small group moved to the living room. Catherine sat next to David on the couch, and he put an arm around her shoulders as they gazed into the flames.

Jule was idly wondering what Lucas was doing with his family when Bram nudged him.

"Want to go dancing?"

"Yes, please. Maybe it will snap me out of this self-pity."

"Have fun, kids," David said as they left. "Don't forget the exhibition tomorrow."

Bram flagged a cab and gave the driver an address. In a short time, they got out in front of a bar called Therapy on West Fifty-Second. It was brightly lit, and Jule could hear the music from the sidewalk.

The only seats were at the end of the bar, but neither one cared. Jule let the loud music, bright lights, and constant motion fill his senses, relieving the hollowness he felt.

"I'll be right back," Bram said after they ordered drinks.

Jule sipped his vodka and lime and looked at the pretty bottles behind the bar. He was surprised when someone spoke close to his ear.

"Is this seat taken?"

Jule looked up at the man pointing to the empty seat. "I'm sorry, but yes, it is."

The man cupped his hand over his ear indicating he couldn't hear Jule. He leaned closer. "You're hot. Want to mingle?" he said in Jule's ear.

Jule edged away. He shook his head.

The man put a hand on Jule's shoulder and leaned in again.

Jule shook him off. "I'm not interested," he said loudly.

The hand came back. "Hey, I'm just—"

Bram grabbed the stranger's wrist and moved his hand off Jule's shoulder. "Is there a problem?" he asked.

"Who the fuck are you?"

"And now we have a problem," Bram said.

The stranger looked into Bram's eyes. "No, no problem, man." He backed away.

Jule quietly stood and moved quickly away. He found a rear exit near the restrooms and risked setting off an alarm by opening the door. No alarms went off as he slipped out. He'd reached the sidewalk before he heard Bram call his name.

"Jule! Wait."

Jule stopped and waited for Bram to catch up.

"Why'd you ditch me?" Bram asked.

"Mate, you were being an ass."

"No, that guy was being an ass."

"And then you out-arsed him."

"I'm confused here."

"I'm being an arse too."

"Wait. What just happened?"

"I was dealing with some unwanted attention, and you went full caveman."

"I thought I was—" Bram paused. "Okay, I admit it. I saw a guy hitting on my—"

"I'm listening," Jule prompted.

"Not sure what to call you."

"Your friend?" Jule suggested. "Or at least a colleague?"

"Right. I saw some drunk rando hitting on my friend, and I got all alpha and shit. BFD."

"You sound like Lucas right now."

"I can't tell if that's a compliment or not."

"It's an observation." Jule raised his face to the sky and watched the falling flakes for a moment, but the comforting sense of oblivion was absent. "I don't think I've ever felt this alone."

Bram put a hand on Jule's arm. "You're not alone."

"I feel like I am." Jule started walking again and Bram kept pace.

"Well, I imagine you miss your family. I know I miss mine. I'm almost thirty, but I still love being at my parents' house during Hannukah."

"I didn't know you were Jewish."

"Are you kidding? My name is Abraham Silber."

"Anyone can be named Abraham."

"Yes, but would just anyone know it's the fourth day of Hannukah?" Jule smiled.

"So, you didn't like the club," Bram said.

"It's all right."

"It's a twink palace," Bram scoffed. "I shouldn't have taken you there. Where are we going, by the way?"

Jule stopped. "I've no idea where I'm going."

"I'd invite you to my place, but…."

"No, this is perfect. Depressed at Christmas wandering the streets of New York in the snow." Jule paused. "I assume I'm depressed anyway. I should be, shouldn't I?"

"Why don't we just walk, and you can talk? Tell me everything. It'll make you feel better, like throwing up when you eat something bad."

"Where to start?" Jule put up the hood of his parka. "Okay, I do miss my family. My mum, Kelly and Sasha, Mrs. Johnston, even the kids."

"That's understandable."

"And I feel torn. I want to take Lucas back, but I don't want to be a fool."

"To be fair, it was a pretty shitty thing for him to do."

"He's not a bad guy, though."

"No, he's not."

"I miss him."

"Be weird if you didn't."

Jule glanced over at Bram. "What would you do if you were me?"

"If I'm you, who's me?"

"What?" Jule paused. "Oh, I see. I'm you, then. We've switched places."

"In that case, I'd go home with you and let you make me forget all about Lucas Madding."

Jule frowned. "That's not helpful."

"It could be."

"Please tell me how sleeping with you would help my situation."

"It would make you feel better."

"Why did I even ask?" Jule wondered aloud. "You're right, though. Sex *does* make me feel better. At least with Lucas it does. But he's the only person I've ever had sex with, so I can't really say for sure."

Bram took a breath to speak, but Jule continued.

"It's true, I haven't had a lot of sex, but I do know that no matter how much I like it, it won't fix anything for very long."

"I wish I'd known that when *I* was nineteen."

"I should go to bed."

"Nonsense. Come on. I know a quiet place where we can have a couple of drinks and be miserable together. Sound like a good idea?"

Abruptly, the idea of a few drinks was very attractive. "No, but let's do it anyway."

Chapter Twenty

THE NEXT morning, before the exhibition, David asked to speak with Jule alone.

"You're ready for this, right?" David said, his voice echoing slightly in the locker room.

"Yes and no."

"Look, I know you aren't particularly happy about it, but—"

"No, I'm not. I honestly can't believe you're doing this."

"Why not?"

"You don't feel disloyal?" Jule blurted out.

"Stop acting like I killed your dog. We're just going to put on a little showcase for a couple of people who could be very helpful."

"Without Lucas."

"If he was up to it, he'd be here. *Tu comprends?*"

"*Oui, je t'entends*, but we should wait for him."

"Why are you being so obstinate? You've practiced these steps with Bram."

"I know, and he's good. He's as good as Lucas, technically, but he's *not* Lucas."

"Well obviously."

"Bram and I dance well together, but it isn't the same."

"It will do for a demonstration," David said firmly.

"It will do," Jule repeated without inflection. "And that's good enough for you, is it?"

David snapped. "Look, if you can't perform, tell me now, but don't subject me to your sulking. Grow up."

Jule blinked in surprise at how much David's words hurt him. It was a couple of seconds before he answered tonelessly. "I can perform."

"Then finish getting changed. I'll see you in the studio in half an hour."

"Was there anything else, sir?"

David glared at Jule, but when he spoke, his voice was softer. "Yes. In addition to the heavy hitters I invited, a photojournalist from *Vanity Fair* will be in attendance… at his request."

"Should that mean something to me?"

"VF is a *tres* classy, glossy magazine. Priceless publicity for us. So, you should be extra charming." David reached out to pat Jule's shoulder.

Jule recoiled. "I'm going to warm up," he said. He turned on his heel and left.

Bram was waiting when Jule came into the studio. "Ready to razzle-dazzle 'em?" he asked cheerfully.

"I don't think I've ever felt less like dancing."

"Whoa. We need a quick change of mood here. David's counting on us to knock the socks off these people."

"What's it about, anyway?"

"I thought he was pretty clear that we were raising money."

"But doesn't Miss Dahlman fund the productions?"

"I don't think she's keen on this one, so I imagine he's looking to supplement whatever she's willing to donate." Bram shook his head. "I don't get her objections. It's a great ballet."

"It's brilliant."

"It certainly is. Ready to rehearse?"

"No, but I need to, so let's do it."

Jule and Bram ran through the entire passage they were going to perform, finishing just before David showed up. He was accompanied by two men and one woman, all of them in suits. With a nod to Bram and Jule, David escorted his guests to comfortable chairs along the wall. As they settled in, the double doors opened, and a man strode in. He paused briefly as though expecting applause and then continued across the floor, his bootheels click-clocking on the hardwood.

Jule stared at the stranger in fascination. Tall and slim with the lean muscles of a greyhound, he wore boots and black jeans with a purple shirt and a long brocade jacket lined and trimmed with sheepskin. His shoulder-length mane was swept back from his starkly handsome face and fell in ringlets against his collar. Though he didn't resemble David, it was clear to Jule that he was from the same tribe.

"I'm Jeremy Belanger from *Vanity Fair*, but everyone calls me Jezza," he said in a BBC-British accent as he unslung a large leather bag from over his shoulder. He set the bag on a chair and held out his hand to David. "*You* are David Dulac Downes, Mr. 3-D, genius choreographer and artistic director of The Downtown Ballet Company. Thank you for accommodating me."

David shook Jezza's hand. "Not at all. We're happy to have you. Do you need any help with anything? Any equipment?"

Jezza grinned, showing strong white teeth. "I've brought everything I need with me." He patted the satchel. "Please don't let me disrupt anything." He opened the bag and took out a camera.

David moved to stand in front of the semicircle of chairs. "Ms. Devereux, Mr. Greene, Mr. Walters, and Mr. Belanger, I'm so pleased you could be here today, and I believe you'll find it worth your while." He turned to Bram and Jule. "Lady and gentlemen, I'd like to introduce Abraham Silber and Julian Parry. Today, they'll be dancing a pas de deux for your consideration. As I informed you in my invitation, the ballet is called *Fireheart*."

BRAM AND Jule performed the dramatic dance from the second act oblivious to Jezza moving around them taking photos. It was very athletic and set to a stirring piano theme that turned sorrowful at the end. The dancers bowed to the small audience, and David nodded to them—the signal that they were dismissed. Bram and Jule bowed again and left for the locker room.

"Now that you've seen what I have to offer," David said. "I'd like to hear your thoughts."

Ms. Devereux cleared her throat. "You know I had reservations about attending, which I expressed in my email to you. As I expected, given your history, you've shown me that you haven't matured at all. You're still more interested in spectacle than art. Those are my thoughts."

"Mr. Walters?" David moved on swiftly.

"While I like to think of myself as progressive, I must agree with Ms. Devereux. I can't fault the steps or the dancers, but the subject… well, let's just say it's a bit too unconventional and leave it at that."

Mr. Greene didn't wait to be called on. "It's a magnificent pas de deux, David, but we both know it won't fly."

"Of course it won't," Ms. Devereux added. "This is highly reminiscent of your so-called *Woodstock* debacle. I would have thought you'd have learned something from a failed production, a production that cost your investors a goodly sum, yet here we are."

David sniffed. "Well—"

"Excuse me," Jezza said. "I'd like to give my thoughts as well."

"Of course," David said. "So sorry."

"First of all." Jezza eyed the other three guests. "You three are everything wrong with ballet. Second, it's a brilliant pas de deux, and if the rest of the production measures up to it, it will be a classic for the ages. Third, this is a ballet whose time has come."

"Thank you," David said. "That's what I was hoping to hear."

Devereux, Greene, and Walters stood.

"I'm not finished," Jezza said. "I want you know that I'm appalled you can call yourself patrons of dance while disparaging a flawless example of all that's best about ballet. Open your minds for heaven's sake. This isn't the Dark Ages."

"We'll be going now," Greene said. "David, I hope you come to your senses and abandon this project. You're a very talented man who has much to offer to ballet."

"*If* I stay inside the lines" David added.

"Yes, exactly," Devereux said. "What makes you think you're so exceptional that codes of normal conduct don't apply to you?"

"I'll tell you exactly what makes him—" Jezza said before David cut him off.

"It's useless," he told Jezza. "These are just lame excuses. Their minds were made up before they walked in. I hoped seeing Bram and Jule dance the steps would sway them, but clearly they've lost sight of why we dance in the first place."

"Goodbye, Mr. Downes." Ms. Devereux marched to the door with Greene and Walters in her wake.

"Well, that could have gone better," David said when the doors closed behind them.

"Mmm, yes," Jezza agreed. "The lady seemed particularly keen on letting you know what an utter disgrace you are."

"Well... she was one of the investors in my ill-fated balletic homage to the Summer of Love."

"That's... surprising."

"Apparently, she had no idea what her money was being used for." David rolled his eyes. "Catherine takes care of the financial side of things, so who knows?"

"I hesitate to ask in this moment of disappointment, but do you suppose I might speak with Mr. Parry for a bit? I'm keen to do an article on him."

"Are you now?" David perked up. "Very discerning of you."

"He's the future of dance, darling, but you know that already."

"Wow. Okay. I do feel the same way, but hearing someone say it out loud is very gratifying."

"He's why I'm here today. Forget those dinosaurs. They're the past."

"I like what I'm hearing. It's very refreshing." David took out his phone. "Hang on a mo, and I'll set you up." He called Jule, who sounded resistant but agreed to meet Jezza. "So, what you want to do," he said when he hung up, "is take the hall to the right and—"

"David!" Catherine said angrily as she entered the studio. "What the hell are you doing?"

"Oops," David said. "Looks like I've got a situation here. Go out the doors and down the hall to the right. Look for the locker room sign. Talk later. Bye."

Jezza grabbed his bag and made his exit under Catherine's baleful gaze.

"Why do you insist on constantly going behind my back?" Catherine said when Jezza was gone.

"This meeting had nothing to do with you."

"Am I not part of this company anymore?"

"You've made it clear that you want nothing to do with *Fireheart*."

"God give me strength! Please don't tell me you brought Tobia Devereux, Daniel Greene, and Clarence Walters here to talk about your queer ballet."

"Why else?"

"I had faint hopes that you were trying to get in their good graces."

"I had faint hopes they'd recognize art when they saw it and actually approve of something new for a change."

"David, your ballet might be fine for some avant-garde troupe in a converted warehouse in Hell's Kitchen, but you're playing in the big leagues. You're right next door to Lincoln Center. To keep the cachet you currently enjoy, you'll have to learn to play ball."

"I've never been good at sports. You know that, *Doudou*."

"What are you going to do, then?"

"I'm going to continue working on my production. I had hoped for a limited debut on New Year's Day, but without Lucas—"

"Listen to me," she interrupted. "I'm not bluffing. I will withdraw all financial support if you insist on cutting the company's throat for your obsession." She lowered her voice. "Honestly, David, all this trouble to get a teenager into your bed?"

David recoiled as though she'd slapped him. "Go ahead, then, if that's what you think my motive is. Do what you have to do. I'm not giving up my dream."

"You need me."

"Has it escaped your notice that I'm the director of a famous company now? I'll find investors and raise the money I need."

"You can certainly try."

"What does that mean?"

"It means most of the deep pockets are friends of mine who wouldn't care to cross me. The rest are people you've pissed off or pissed on at one time or another. It means I don't like your chances."

"We'll see."

"I daresay we will."

"Are we at the point where I ask for your keys to the building?" he asked.

"Since I pay the rent, I believe it should be the other way around." Catherine smiled at him. "But I'll give you two weeks to vacate."

"What about the school? The kids?"

"Is now the time to be thinking of that? Or was it before you made your decision?"

"You won't do it," he said. "I know you."

"Perhaps not as well as you think." She gathered the folds of her fur around her and swept from the room. As she exited, she nearly ran into someone entering.

"Pardon me," Jule said politely.

"No, I don't think I will," she replied as she walked away.

Jule gazed after her with a puzzled look on his face and then opened the door. "David," he said. "Jezza wants to talk to me over lunch. Is there any reason I shouldn't go?"

"None I can think of."

Jule started to leave, but something in David's voice stopped him. "Are you all right?"

"Not at all, but don't worry about it now. Go charm the pants off Mr. Belanger."

"I don't do that kind of thing."

"*Fait chier*!" David dug his fingers into his hair and tugged in a gesture of frustration. "Just go and do whatever it is you do that causes otherwise reasonable people to treat you like the original Kid Jesus."

"What?"

"Forget it. Just go. I have a lot to brood on."

"If you're sure," Jule said doubtfully.

"I want you to leave," David said heavily.

Jule eased the door closed and walked away.

Chapter Twenty-One

BRAM AND Jezza were waiting near the entrance when Jule came down the hall.

"Did you decide where we're going?" Jule asked without enthusiasm.

"We've narrowed it down," Jezza said.

"Do you want to go somewhere like *Five Guys* or somewhere quieter?" Bram asked.

"As long as I can get a drink," Jezza said. "I'm desperate for one after that scene."

"Care to elaborate?" Bram asked.

"Once I have some alcohol in me, I'll most likely reveal everything." Jezza buttoned his merino-lined coat and wound a colorful scarf around his neck. "Shall we?"

They caught a cab, and Bram asked the driver to take them to Ascent on Broadway. It was a few minutes after four and the cocktail lounge had just opened. They were the only customers, and the hostess let them choose a booth that overlooked Central Park.

Jezza immediately ordered a Moscow mule and the first five appetizers on the menu, explaining they were for the table. Jule dutifully ordered sparkling water with lime and Bram asked for a beer. After a few moments spent admiring the view, Jezza leaned back and cocked his head at Jule.

"London boy, are you?"

"That's right."

"You sound well educated."

"Um… thanks. So do you."

"I'm a product of the boys' school system. Tutors on the family estate, then Eton and on to Oxford. And yet here I am with my big, posh accent, following pop stars around with a camera."

"I'm not a pop star," Jule said.

"Not quite yet, my darling." Jezza smiled. "But soon enough, I promise you. You will be a pop culture icon." He looked up as their server returned with drinks and the assurance that the appetizers would be out soon. Jezza ordered another drink and the waiter left.

Bram took a drink of his beer. "You going to make Jule a star?" he asked lightly.

"Me?" Jezza chuckled. "Not bloody likely. I'm simply going to chronicle the process." He turned to Jule. "With your permission and Mr. Downes's, of course."

"What does that mean?" Jule sipped his water.

"It means I'd be around a lot, talking to you, taking photos, shooting video, etcetera."

"Et cetera?" Bram watched Jezza finish his drink.

Jezza smiled at Bram. "It's a little Latin phrase that means anything excluded will be deemed included. Get it?"

Bram mirrored Jezza's lupine grin. "Yeah, I get it. You're not here to talk to me. You're only interested in him, but you're British *and* well educated, so you're polite about it."

Jezza looked over at Jule. "Is it me, or is there a weird energy here?"

Jule looked at Bram and then back at Jezza. "Bram can be a bit of an alpha male stereotype sometimes," he said.

"Ah, that would explain it." Jezza took the drink the server handed him. "I should have told him to keep them coming," he joked.

"Is that how it's going to be?" Bram asked. "Me getting double-teamed by two Brits?"

"Only if you're very lucky," Jezza replied.

Jule laughed despite his morose mood, and before anyone could speak again, the food arrived. After finishing plates of shrimp skewers, fish tacos, lobster egg rolls, and crab salad, Jezza insisted on another round of drinks. Jule ate sparingly, asked for sparkling water again, and then excused himself to the bathroom.

Jule returned a few minutes later. "You want that last egg roll?" he asked Bram.

"Go for it."

Jule crunched into the egg roll. "I didn't know I missed hearing an English accent," he said to Jezza, before turning to Bram. "It's weird to think that I sound like that to you."

Bram raised an eyebrow. "Not exactly."

Jule raised both eyebrows as he chewed another bite.

"You're not sleazy," Bram explained. "Or full of yourself."

Jule shook his head. "So judgmental."

"Whereas Jezza is simply mental."

Jezza cleared his throat. "Thank you, Bram," he said. "Now let's talk about Jule. And by let's talk, I mean, I talk, and you listen, okay?" He waited for Jule to nod. "I've been a photojournalist for fourteen years. I've seen thousands of trends come and go. I've also seen the rise of personalities who became legends. I've seen the famous and the infamous. You, my darling, could be another Nureyev, a Baryshnikov. All you have to do is want it." Jezza smiled. "Even if you don't want it, fame will find you, I'd bet my own money on it."

"I don't want it."

"I don't think you can avoid it. Would I be here if I hadn't heard about you? Word is already getting around, thanks to your friend at the *New York Times*. She's an absolute *maven!*" Jezza leaned toward Jule. "It's inevitable, darling, but if you're as smart as I think you are, you'll let me be your guide."

Jule met Jezza's gaze, as Lucas's voice echoed in his head, telling him, "I'll guide you through it." It was several seconds before he answered. "If that happened, if I got famous, I'd be grateful for any advice."

"Or." Jezza leaned even closer. "You could get out in front of it and take control. That way you can dictate your image."

"My image?"

"You can craft how you want the public to perceive you."

Bram snorted.

"I'm fine with my image as it is," Jule said.

"So am I," Jezza said. "You're a natural, but consider this. You're about to appear in an LGBTQ-themed ballet. Suppose part of your image is that you're quite tastefully gay?"

"I'm… not sure."

"You're sure you like kissing boys, though, right?" Jezza smiled. "They say gaydar is a myth, but I'm never wrong about this."

"Why would anyone else need to know?"

"I read the interview with David in the *Times*," Jezza said. "He said you want to take ballet off the pedestal and make it fun for everyone. Well, there's a large ballet-loving LGBTQ community that needs an openly gay icon. It could be you."

Jule looked at the ice in his glass. "I'm not sure," he said again. "I need to think about it."

Jezza cleared his throat. "Let me give you my phone number," he said. "You can let me know when you've made a decision."

"I don't want you to waste your time waiting."

"Don't worry, my darling. There's a Korean boy band playing Madison Square Garden tomorrow night, and I've got a backstage pass."

"I hope you have fun," Jule said. "I'll talk to some people and see what they think, and I'll call you."

"Wonderful." Jezza finished his drink. "Do you still want to know what happened at the meeting of bigwigs?"

"To judge by your face, the answer is no," Bram said.

"It's pretty grim," Jezza said. "Three of the most influential people in the world of American ballet pissed all over David's dream."

"As expected," Bram said.

"I told him to wait," Jule added.

"Your David doesn't seem the sort to let others dictate to him."

Bram snorted again.

"So, they won't endorse him," Jule said.

Jezza shook his head. "They were quite harsh, I thought. It was more of a denouncement than a simple refusal. I know he's ruffled some feathers in the past, but he clearly wasn't expecting such a blunt response."

"That's why he sounded a bit off," Jule murmured.

"I'm sorry it went that way," Jezza said. "But you're about to make ballet cool again, like it was the year Rudi defected from Russia."

"You aren't old enough to remember that," Bram said.

"No, but I often wish I was. I would've been right at home in the sixties."

"Now *that* I believe." Bram cast a significant glance at Jezza's clothing.

"At any rate, I've consumed five alcoholic beverages in about two hours. Who wants to pour me in a cab and point me toward the Gramercy Park Hotel?"

Jule waved as the cab pulled away. "I like him," he said.

"Most hustlers are likable until they get what they want from you."

"Well, you'd know, wouldn't you?"

"Ouch," Bram said. "That sounded more like Madding than you."

"Sorry. I didn't mean that. I just have a lot on my mind."

Bram nodded. "Sure, I understand. See you tomorrow."

Jule walked away from Bram, wishing he could call Lucas. Of course, he *could* call Lucas, but things would get complicated, and he'd start feeling bad. No matter how much he missed Lucas, he had enough to deal with right now. Aside from the break-up, the pressure David was putting on him was almost unbearable. Dancing the pas de deux from *Fireheart* with Bram shouldn't be such a big deal, but… it was. The fact that he wasn't dancing with Lucas ruined it for him. He didn't see how he could perform the ballet with the passion it deserved. And now this Jezza person wanted to focus more attention on him.

Jule looked up, but it wasn't snowing tonight. Clouds obscured the moon and stars, making the night sky a perfect metaphor for the dark emptiness in his chest. Everything had been going so well, and now, the shining future was tarnished. The weight of all he was responsible for fell on him at once. Abruptly, he couldn't bear his thoughts any longer.

DAVID ANSWERED his phone with none of his usual upbeat greetings. "What do you need, Lucas?" he said.

"Is Jule there?"

"Not to my knowledge, but he's a clever boy. He might have sneaked in while—"

"David, I'm not in the mood for your sarcasm."

"What *are* you in the mood for?"

"Jule isn't answering his phone. Would you try calling and see if he'll pick up?"

"Sure, give me a minute."

David hung up and rang Jule's phone. When he got no answer, he called Lucas. "No luck."

"Okay, now I'm officially worried. I've been trying to reach him since ten o'clock, but no one knows where he is."

"Well, he isn't exactly happy with any of us right now. Maybe he just wants some time alone."

"You know what he's like. He wouldn't disappear without letting someone know where he was going."

David sighed. "True. Jule is nothing if not considerate. Now you've got me worried."

"I'm probably overreacting."

"Because you care."

"I love him, David."

"Go find him, then. And keep me posted."

"Will do."

"*Bon nuit.*"

"Good night." Lucas hung up.

LUCAS CONTINUED searching for Jule by phone and on foot. Around 1:30 a.m., he had been to the places he'd visited with Jule. Abruptly, he remembered the one place in New York that Jule had mentioned wanting to visit. Though he had no reason to believe Jule was there now, he was suddenly certain he'd find him there. He hailed a cab and reached the Empire State Building a little after 2:00 a.m. where he was stopped by a security guard.

"We're closed, sir."

"I think my friend is up on the platform," Lucas said.

"I said we're closed, sir."

"And I said—"

"You can leave the same way you came in… sir."

"Just tell me if he's up there or not, okay? I'm worried about him."

"Why?"

"Well… he's been depressed, you know?"

"There's nobody up there."

"Come on, man. I'm really worried."

"Maybe I should call the cops."

Lucas took out his wallet. "Or you could just let me go up and have a look." He held out several twenties.

The guard sighed. "Okay, go on up, but nobody finds out, you get me?" He tucked the money inside his tunic.

"Don't worry about it. I just want to take him home."

"Get out of my face before I change my mind. Yeesh." The guard deliberately turned his back as Lucas got into the elevator.

Lucas spotted Jule quickly. His heart soared and then plummeted again when Jule moved closer to the edge. Lucas hurried over to him. The fact that Jule's outerwear consisted of nothing more than a fleece hoodie put a cold knot in Lucas's stomach. However, he didn't immediately try to warm Jule up. He stood silently next to him and looked out over the city. Dusk was surrendering to darkness, shadows collecting in the glass and steel canyons, rising like smoke to meet the evening sky. The few clouds were torn to rags by the blasts of cold wind. Lucas reached the end of his patience and touched Jule's cold hand where it rested on the railing.

Jule recoiled.

"Whoa!" Lucas exclaimed. "Are you okay?"

"I don't know what's happening," Jule said in a voice that shook. The tracks of tears glistened on his face.

"You're having an anxiety attack."

"I am?"

"That's what it looks like, and I have some experience with them."

"I don't panic."

"You do now." Lucas softened his tone. "It's nothing to be ashamed of. I had several the year my father died. Severe stress and emotional overload will do that."

"I can control myself."

Lucas raised an eyebrow in an expression that clearly said at this point Jule's sense of control was a dubious prospect at best.

"Look, I don't know why I'm being like this." Jule's voice was tight with frustration. "I'm sorry."

"Don't apologize. I know you aren't fucking up on purpose."

Jule faced Lucas. "Thank you."

"For what, exactly?"

"For calling it what it is. If you were Kelly or Sasha or Mum, you'd excuse my behavior and tell me everything would be fine."

"Well, I think everything will be as good as it can be, but you definitely fucked up." Lucas smiled encouragingly. "Want to tell me why?"

"I don't know really. Just suddenly—"

"What?" Lucas reached out but stopped short of touching Jule again.

"I was thinking about *Fireheart* and how much it depends on me. And then I started thinking about the publicity campaign Jezza wants. And the money we don't have. I'm still mad at myself for running from you and getting you hurt. And I thought I could trust David but now I'm not sure... I'm not sure about anything anymore."

"You've got a lot of pressure on you." Lucas sighed. "Jule, I know you hate being treated like a child, but dammit, you are a teenager. Not for much longer, sure, but still.... Look, I don't know many people of any age who could carry the weight you carry and not crack."

"I don't crack."

"Then what's happening right now?"

Jule drew breath to speak, but nothing came out of his mouth.

"You disappeared without letting anyone know where you were going," Lucas said calmly. "And you were actually rude to a couple of people, if Bram's telling the truth. Believe me, you're cracking. You're not nuclear, but for you, this is practically the equivalent of a meltdown." He put a hand on Jule's shoulder. "It's nothing to be ashamed of, you hear me? Like I said, it's amazing that you maintained for as long as you did."

"I just don't think of myself as the sort of person who has a breakdown."

"No one does. Hey, listen, it's not only okay, it's beneficial to lose control every now and then. I'm not saying you should make it a habit, but you need to cut loose occasionally."

"That's not what I was taught."

"I know. You're as disciplined as a US Marine fresh out of boot camp."

"Well, I *was*."

"I'm a bad influence, huh?" Lucas moved his hand to cup the back of Jule's neck.

Jule gazed up into Lucas's eyes. The confidence that had once shone so brightly was dimmed by shadows of doubt, fear, and something less easily defined.

"Come on," Lucas said. "Let's sit down, and then you let it all out. You'll feel a lot better. Trust me on this."

"I've been up here letting it out for a while."

"Yeah, but now someone's listening." Lucas put his arm around Jule's shoulders.

Jule fought against accepting the support, but after a few moments, he yielded to the temptation to lean on someone else. He reminded himself that this wasn't just anyone. This was Lucas, whom he loved, or believed he loved, and wasn't that the same thing?

"Let's get out of the wind," Jule said softly.

They sat together with their backs against the retaining wall.

"Thanks for... for coming to find me," Jule said.

"Hey, I love you, stupid."

Jule almost smiled. "You're the stupid one," he retorted lamely.

"That wouldn't surprise anyone," Lucas said. "But it's not because I love you."

"Maybe someday, I'll figure out why." Jule shivered. "I wish I hadn't come up here without my coat and gloves. Or my hat. Or my dignity. I wish a lot of things."

Lucas put his arms around Jule. "Tell me," he invited. "Start at the beginning."

Jule shoved his hands deeper in his pockets. "When I came to America, I had a plan—*we* had a plan. My future had been mapped out, and I'd been training for it since I was nine. I knew exactly where I was going and what I was going to do when I got there.

"And then I got to New York and everything changed. I didn't join the NYCB. I didn't step into a career path that would make me a premier danseur in a couple of years. I didn't impress the people at the top with my classical perfection and my passion for my art. And Kelly and Sasha left me on my own. And David wants me to dance *Fireheart* with Bram."

"I think you did pretty well anyway," Lucas said.

"The point is that the plan fell apart. If I'm honest, it was doomed as soon as I learned about David Downes, and then I met you, and we had sex. And then I lost you, and I felt like you got what you wanted from me and I was a fool."

"Cue ominous music?"

"You're the most wonderful thing that has ever happened to me and the scariest."

"Oh... well... that's good. I guess."

"You're a big part of the reason I'm falling apart. I should be fully committed to dancing, but sometimes, all I want to do is snog you. I don't know how to make you understand how scary this is for me. For my whole life, I've known who I am and what I want. I've always known what comes next, but now—" Jule's voice choked off.

"It's okay," Lucas said soothingly. "And I do understand how scary it is. When my dad died...." He took a deep breath. "Dad was my dad, but he was also my coach, my confidant, my best bud. He kept all my secrets, got me out of scrapes, and guided me by example. Him not being there was like losing a limb. I had no idea how I was going to live without him. But I did. And I was scared every day for about two years."

Jule took a long, snuffling breath. "Two years?"

"Give or take a few months. I drowned myself in dance practice and booze for a while. Convinced myself that best way to honor him would be to get married and be a father. I did a lot of things that seem insane to me now."

"How'd you get over it?"

"I didn't. You never really get over a loss like that. You just somehow learn to live with it. After a while, it doesn't hurt every minute of every day. One day, you realize that you went for hours without thinking about it."

"But when you think about it, it still hurts."

"Yeah, it does, but the pain isn't the main thing anymore. You remember all the good things, all the good times, and you're, you know, grateful that you had them. At some point, you realize you're basically feeling sorry for yourself."

Jule was quiet for a moment before he spoke again. "You're right."

"That sounded more like you."

"I'm fine."

"No, you aren't, but you will be." Lucas squeezed Jule's shoulders. "I believe that."

"So do I."

Lucas stood and pulled Jule to his feet. "I'm just glad you're okay. When I was on my way here, I was having the worst thoughts."

"You didn't think I was going to jump off!" Jule exclaimed.

"It crossed my mind."

"Making a big, ugly emotional scene isn't enough for you? I have to attempt suicide?"

"Cut it out." Lucas pulled Jule into a hug. "Just let me be glad you're all right."

"If it helps, I'd *never* kill myself."

"I'll hold you to that, mister."

"As long as you hold me." Jule returned the hug.

"I will never let you go." Lucas swallowed. "How about I take you home and put you in a tub of very hot water?"

"I'm not sure I should, but I'm sure I need to. That'll have to do for now." Jule looked up. "It's starting to snow." He took a ragged breath. "I've always liked watching the snow at night. It makes me feel, I don't know, free, I guess."

"Free?"

"I like to imagine that I'm floating in space."

"That sounds really cold and empty."

"No, it's nice. Just floating with no schedule or responsibilities."

"Okay, now it makes sense." Lucas hugged Jule tighter.

"You make me feel the same way. Like everything is—"

"Hey, assholes!" The security guard stopped a few feet away from Lucas and Jule. "This ain't a no-tell hotel."

"Sorry." Lucas grinned at Jule. "I found what I was looking for. We'll get out of your hair now."

"Damn right, you will. Let's go." The guard gestured toward the exit.

"THIS IS the best bath ever," Jule said about an hour later.

Lucas trickled more hot water over Jule's head and down his back. "I think you're thawed out now."

"I wasn't quite frozen."

"Believe me, you were very much frozen."

"I feel like there's a deeper meaning in there somewhere."

"Ask David to explain 'frozen fire' to you."

"I'll think about it." Jule sighed.

"You're also very pink," Lucas said.

Jule chuckled. "As opposed to what?"

"You were turning blue a short time ago."

"Then I'd have been purple at the halfway point."

"You mean lilac, fairy."

"Oh, that was awful," Jule said.

"Just trying to stay on your level."

"Thank you for rescuing me."

"What else would I do?"

"I don't know." Jule twisted his neck to look back at Lucas. "I guess it took me a while to realize just how good a person you are."

Lucas brushed sweat-damp hair off his forehead. "Yeah, I know I don't give the best impression. Mom told me."

"I've always been able to count on the people in my life, you know? My Mum and Dad, Kelly and Sasha. I'm just saying that it's nice to know you're one of those people." Jule's eyes opened wide. "You won't tell them about this."

"Not unless you want me to. I did call David, by the way, just to let him know you're not in the river."

"Thank you." Jule yawned.

"And that's the signal that it's time for bed." Lucas helped a limp-noodle-Jule out of the tub, dried him thoroughly, and guided him to bed. After removing his soggy clothing, he stretched out next to Jule and breathed him in until sleep took them both.

Chapter Twenty-Two

DAVID CONTACTED key members of his company and asked them to meet at his townhouse the next day. He looked around the room meeting the gaze of each person in turn: Jule, Lucas, Charlotte, Jamison, Marilee, and Bram.

"I've got some bad news," he said. "Catherine has withdrawn her support of The Downtown Ballet. As you know, she was responsible for three-quarters of our funding, so this is—"

"Dire?" Jule suggested.

"Yes." David nodded to Jule. "But it isn't the end of the world. We're still breathing and able to dance. I have some ideas for raising money, but I'd be glad to hear more."

"Showcases," Charlotte said immediately.

"On my list," David replied. "A program of splashy variations and romantic pas de deux always puts butts in seats."

"I can make costumes for pennies," Marilee said. "They won't last, but...."

"You could do a GoFundMe online," Bram said.

David considered for a moment. "Nope, I'm not too proud to beg for money. Anyone know how to set it up?"

"I know someone," Lucas said.

"So, you'll handle it? The money thing?" David arched an eyebrow.

"I've got this."

"Good. Good." David sighed. "I'm doing my best to keep up a brave face, but I don't mind telling you I'm a wreck. *Ma vie est un bordel en ébullition.*"

Charlotte came over to sit next to David and take his hand. "I can't believe she'd yank the rug out from under us like this, but we'll get through it."

"If a bunch of hustlers like us can't raise the money, then there isn't any money to be raised." Lucas turned to Jule. "Excepting you, of course."

"What? You think I can't hustle?" Jule retorted.

"You lack a certain moral flexibility," Lucas told him.

"Lucas is right," Bram said. "Let us worry about the money. You just dance."

"Sure, they're jerks," Charlotte said. "But to be fair, they're right. Let us handle the money-grubbing."

"I said *I'll* handle it," Lucas said.

Charlotte opened her mouth to reply and then turned her head at a knock on the door.

"Who the hell?" David said as he stood up. He went to the door and returned with Jezza Belanger. "Look what was left on the doorstep."

"Hello, darlings," Jezza said. "Sorry to crash the party. I was hoping for a few minutes with David, but obviously, I can return later."

"You're here now," David said. "Too late to get away. Take a seat, Limey."

Jezza sat next to Bram. "Please go on," he said.

"We were just discussing ways of raising money," David said.

"Were you?" Jezza looked delighted. "That's exactly what I wanted to talk about. I'm sure you've already thought of showcases and calling on donors." He waved a hand as though dissipating smoke. "But as I was looking at your website, I couldn't help noticing that you have no merchandise beyond those uber-cliché silk-screened tote bags."

David pursed his lips. "Merchandising requires start-up capital, if I'm not mistaken."

"True, but I can help with that. I'm not rich, but I have some substantial savings."

"You'd be willing to put money into this company?" David asked. "Why?"

"You know why." Jezza met David's eyes. "I believe in you. I believe in your ballet. And most of all, I believe in Jule." He turned to Jule. "I promised myself I'd never do this again, but—Let me make you a star, and you can stand back and watch the money pour in."

"I have to hear this," David said.

"I expect to be laughed at," Jezza said. "But I have a plan, and it will work. I know it will, because it's worked many times before. All I need is cooperation." He smiled at Jule. "You'd have to put up with all sorts of nonsense, I warn you, my darling."

"Okay, we'll talk about that later," David said. "Anyone else have an idea we haven't heard yet?"

"*The Full Monty*," Jule said.

David blinked. "Did you say *The Full Monty*?"

"It's a movie."

"I know it's a *movie*," David said. "Are you suggesting a Chippendale-style revue with my dancers?"

"I'd buy a ticket to that," Charlotte said.

"I'd be in line behind you," Jezza added.

"I was joking," Jule said.

"You know what would work?" Jezza said excitedly. "A calendar. I could take some portraits of the dancers in their costumes, workout clothes, whatever. No nudity, naturally, but *so* much implied sensuality."

"I don't know," David said. "I'm a rebel and all, but isn't a calendar a bit, I don't know, cheesecakey?"

"Why don't you let me take some photos, and you can choose which go in the calendar?"

"*If* there's a calendar," David said. "It would *have* to be *tasteful*. Understood?"

"Naturally." Jezza looked around. "Perhaps I can attend your next rehearsal and take some shots there."

David was a little taken aback at how quickly Jezza was moving. "I can't think of any reason why not. Anyone? No? Okay, everyone, remember to comb your hair tomorrow for your class pictures." He turned to Jezza. "So how long does this take?"

"Don't you worry about that, my darling. I'm going to fast-track it with some friends in publishing."

"Why am I not surprised you have a plan?"

"I'm excited about this," Jezza said. "I've actually wanted to do this for some time, though to be completely honest, I was hoping to publish a book of ballet photography."

"Hey, you're not dead yet," Lucas said.

"Profound," Bram commented.

Jezza stood. "What time should I arrive?"

"Four o'clock would be good," David said. "But this brings me to another issue. As of this morning, we no longer have access to the school, the equipment, or wardrobe. I've secured space to practice in, but we've got a lot of work ahead of us." He smiled at Jezza. "I'll text you the address. See you around four."

"Teatime, it is." Jezza let himself out.

"Brass tacks time," David said. He looked at Lucas. "You're almost there." He held up his thumb and forefinger a centimeter apart. "Another week, maybe two, and I'll let you perform." He turned to Bram. "Until then, you're still my Philip, and obviously, Jule, you're still my Alex." He smiled at Charlotte and missed the look of disappointment on Jule's face. "And I have a part for you. You will be my Aphrodite, my angel, my spirit of love."

"Yes!" Charlotte's eyes sparkled.

"See. It's not all bad," David said. "What you all have to decide is whether you want to remain associated with me. It's highly possible that Catherine is poisoning all the wells we hope to drink from. It's also possible your reputations could be tainted by association."

"Fuck you, David," Lucas said. "Fuck you for even saying something like that to us. We're family." He broke into a grin. "I'd stick with you if only to chap Catherine's ass, but there's also the matter of you taking a chance on a *difficult* danseur a few years back. If it wasn't for you, I might not even have a career."

"I'm along for the ride," Bram said. He smiled. "I kind of like the idea of being a pinup boy."

"Hey," David said. "Let's avoid that kind of talk. We're already going to catch hell for being sacrilegious, as it is."

"Catching hell is my jam," Lucas said. He turned to look at Jule. "What about you?"

"You could always reapply to the NYCB," David said.

Jule resolutely shoved aside his doubts and fears and answered as he imagined Lucas would. "Don't be daft. You'll never make it without me."

David waited for the laughter to die down. "All right, then. We have a crude plan."

"What do we do first?" Charlotte asked.

"We work our butts off getting *Fireheart* ready."

DAVID'S TOWN car having been a perk of his former position, he, Lucas, and Jule took a cab to meet the rest of the cast at the new studio. The space was above a business in Hell's Kitchen and was normally occupied by students of modern dance. It was large and had a barre and a wall of mirrors. Those were the pluses. Sadly, it also had a dingy drop ceiling and poor lighting. When Jezza arrived with his equipment, it was clear he wasn't happy with the place.

"Do what you can," David told him. "If it doesn't work out, we'll find another place, but right now, this is what we've got to work with." He went back to watching Bram and Jule.

Jezza chose a corner where a blank wall met the wall of mirrors. He set up some lights, some diffusers, and a folding screen. After several minutes of readjustments, he had the light bouncing off the mirrors and softened by the diffuser panels. Within a three-sided booth, he created a misty radiance that seemed to come from nowhere and everywhere.

One at a time, Jezza photographed the dancers present. Charlotte, Lucas, Bram, Jule, Dylan, Dani, and Amani posed while Jezza moved around them with various cameras before taking a final photo with a large camera on a tripod. When he'd finished with the cast, he beckoned to David.

David gave Jezza a *who me?* look.

"Come on, then," Jezza said. "This is no time for false modesty. I want to see the fire-breathing rebel who shook the foundations of traditional ballet."

David stood in the shaft of light where Jezza placed him and crossed his arms over his chest. He tilted his head back and gazed directly into the lens with a cool, challenging stare.

At half past seven, David called a halt to practice for the day. "Get some rest and be back here at ten tomorrow. I'd have you here earlier, but there's a belly dancing class at nine." He smiled. "And I need the morning to work out a few things. Jezza, you'll join us?"

"I will, thank you. I'd also like to talk a bit about the possibility of some outdoor photography."

"We'll see what we have time for," David said. "Au revoir, mes enfants." He paused. "Does everyone have a ride? Yes? Good. Good."

Lucas sat on the floor beside Jule to remove his practice shoes. He ignored the fact that Bram was sitting a couple of feet away. "Are you busy later?"

"Jezza asked to speak with me, but I don't have plans."

"Want to hang out?" Lucas paused. "No drama. I promise not to make any moves."

"I'd like that actually. Did you have something in mind?"

"Watch a movie. Eat some popcorn. Paint each other's toenails."

Jule smiled. "That does sound like fun."

"What does?" Bram asked.

"Watching a movie," Jule answered.

"That does sound like fun."

Lucas dithered for a moment before inviting Bram, because he didn't *want* to invite Bram, but if he didn't, Jule would think he was trying to get him alone, which he was. Despite his feeling that they were at least friends again after the scene atop the Empire State Building, he didn't want to jeopardize the truce by moving too fast. "No big whoop," Lucas said. "We're going to pick out a movie and pop some corn. Want to come over?"

"I'd love to, but I have a dinner date," Bram said. "Next time."

Lucas felt like he was being rewarded for not being a dick when, one by one, the others opted out for previous engagements. "I guess it's just us," he said to Jule.

"Probably better that way. We'll actually be able to hear the movie."

Lucas chuckled. "True that." He stood and offered Jule his hand.

After an almost imperceptible hesitation, Jule let Lucas pull him to his feet. After pulling a pair of sweats on over his warmups, Jule put on his coat and hat and headed outside with Lucas. They only had to walk a couple of blocks before they found a cab that didn't already have a fare.

Lucas unlocked his apartment door and stood aside to let Jule in. He picked up the remote from the table by the door and turned on the lights.

"Do you really want popcorn?" he asked. "I'm in the mood for something more substantial."

"Mate, I'm famished."

"Pick out a movie while I put something together, okay?" Lucas raised his eyebrows. "Do you dare have a beer, or should I open a bottle of wine?"

"Yes," Jule said before he went over to the couch.

Lucas smiled and hummed a little to himself as he made a snack tray out of his cutting board. After loading it with slices of roast beef, cheese, onion, and garlic pickles, he sliced a whole-grain loaf. He managed to fit a jar of mustard on a corner before carrying it over to the coffee table.

"Bloody hell," Jule exclaimed.

"Too much?"

"No way."

"I tried to make it as low cal as possible." Lucas smiled as he watched Jule pile roast beef on a piece of bread. "I'll be right back with drinks."

"Water for me, thanks."

Lucas returned with water, a Harp lager, and a bottle of pinot noir. "What are we watching?" he asked as he sat on the couch.

Jule looked away from the screen displaying Lucas's to-be-watched list. "Have you seen *Bohemian Rhapsody*?"

"Nope. Hit Play."

Lucas and Jule made their way through a couple of big-league sandwiches as they watched Freddie Mercury's life story. Jule refused a beer but accepted a glass of wine.

Lucas sat back, edging subtly closer to Jule as he did. "Good pick," he said when the movie ended. "I like Queen, but I didn't know all that stuff."

"It makes me sad how hard it was for him to be him."

"Yeah."

"Imagine if being gay wasn't treated like a, um, stigma. Just imagine."

"That would be nice, but at least things are better now than they were in Freddie's day."

"I suppose."

"This is nice," Lucas said. "Sitting here with you just chilling."

"I missed you," Jule said candidly. "A lot."

"You could have come to see me anytime."

"No, I couldn't."

"Why not?"

"This is going to sound so stupid, but I couldn't be with you because of how much I wanted to be with you."

"Yeah, that makes no sense."

"It's just too much, okay? I like you too much, and I'm not sure I can deal with that along with everything else."

"I really wish I hadn't fucked it up." Lucas sighed. "How are you coping?"

"Dance is where I've kept my head since… you know."

"Since someone made you believe I was playing you."

"You did play me."

Lucas swallowed. "I'd take it back if I could."

"You've said that before."

"I meant it then, and I mean it now. Do you know how annoying it is to have your life wrecked and to know it's your fault?"

"It sucks."

"Sure does." Lucas smiled wistfully. "It kills me to know I used to have the liberty of touching you whenever I wanted. Sometimes I want to hug you so bad…."

"I miss that."

"They're still available whenever you want. Free of charge."

"Thanks." Jule stood up. "I'm going to try to get in before curfew."

Lucas got to his feet. "Try not," he quoted. "Do or do not. There is no try."

Jule smiled. "If you look at the Dark Side, careful you must be. For the Dark Side looks back."

"And on that note…." Lucas walked with Jule to the door. "I enjoyed the evening."

"Yeah, let's do it again," Jule said quite naturally. As he walked down the hall, he didn't see the look of quiet joy on Lucas's face.

WHEN JULE got out of the elevator on the ground floor, he took out his phone and made a call.

Sasha answered Kelly's phone. "Hi, Jule!"

"Hi, Sasha."

"If you wanted to talk to Kelly, he's at a council meeting. Something about rezoning the area where the school is."

"Sounds boring. Do you have a minute?"

"Of course I have time for you. Just let me turn down the heat under the stew. Thanks for the links to the articles about you."

"I felt a bit conceited sending them, but since I was sending them to Mum anyway, I thought you'd like to see them too."

"Kelly is so proud. He cried when he saw the photo in the *New York Times*."

"I won't tell him you told me." Jule cleared his throat. "We have kind of a problem here. The Downtown Ballet has lost its funding. I'll tell you the whole story later, but right now I need your advice."

"Of course."

"We've come up with several ways of getting the money we need to stage the ballet, and I'd like to get your opinion."

"Don't stall. Just say it."

"One of things we can do is sell merchandise. Do you think that's too low-class?"

"Send me a T-shirt with your face on it."

Jule chuckled. "One of things we might sell is a calendar. With pictures of dancers."

Sasha laughed. "Listen, Jule, if you're *worried* about being disrespectful to ballet, then you probably aren't."

"That weirdly makes sense. So, you think I should pose for the calendar?"

"Why not? As long as it's tasteful."

"Okay, that's one down. The other thing is, there's this journalist who wants to make me famous. The more famous I am, the more money we'll make, or so he says."

"Do you want to be famous?"

"Not particularly, but if being famous makes more people come to the ballet, I'd go along with it."

"Then that's your answer."

"Yes, but... is it right?"

"Does it feel right?"

"Yes and no, but it's probably nerves."

"You don't have any."

Jule chuckled again. "I wish you and Kelly were here so I could talk to you."

"We're talking right now."

"You know what I mean."

"Yes, I do."

"I'd like to talk about Lucas again."

"How is it going with him?"

"I'm still his friend, but I can't forget what he did."

"Of course you can't. No one forgets the first time they realize their loved one is only human."

"I don't know what to do. He wants to get back with me, and I miss him horribly, but I don't want to make a mistake."

Sasha snorted. "You will make many mistakes. Tell me, does being with him make you happy?"

"Yes." Jule paused. "It's so hard to be around him, though."

"So, you can't forget. Maybe you can forgive?"

"But doesn't that make me a fool?"

"To some, you will look like a fool, but if you're happy, what does it matter?"

"You're still happy, aren't you?"

"I am. Listen, *fiu*. When you find love, you hold on to it with both hands, but not too tightly. You hold it like a bird, understand? But you hold it and take care of it."

"You wouldn't think I was an idiot to take him back?"

"I could never think that."

"I miss you and Kelly so much."

"We miss you as well. Your mother was here yesterday. We had tea and talked about you. You should call her more often."

"I know." Jule sighed. "There's just never enough time, is there?"

"That is a central truth of life."

"Well then, I'll just have to make the best of the time I have."

"You make me so proud." Sasha held the phone away from his mouth for a moment. "I love you, Jule," he said when he could speak again.

"I love you too." Jule hung up. Talking with Sasha made him feel lighter, but it wasn't long before he remembered his responsibilities again. He promised himself he wouldn't let it overwhelm him again and kept walking.

Chapter Twenty-Three

JULE SHOWED up early at the studio and found Bram already there.

"Hey," Bram said. "I was just warming up."

"Give me a few minutes, and we can practice the third act variation."

Bram nodded and sat on the floor to watch Jule stretch. "Mighty tempting tushie," he remarked when Jule bent from the waist to touch his palms to the floor.

Jule gave him a vague smile and continued his routine.

Bram set down his water and went over to Jule. He came up behind him and put his arms around his waist. "When are we getting together?" he said in Jule's ear.

Jule grasped Bram's wrists and moved his hands before he turned to face him. "I don't know, but this is inappropriate."

"Are you kidding?"

Jule shook his head. "It's time to work, not play."

"I was thinking we could combine the two. No one else will be here for another hour."

"Thank you but no."

"I'm not offering you pie."

"I didn't think you were. You've made it clear that what you're offering is sex."

"You like sex. I like sex. Works out great."

Jule sighed. "Can we please just do what we came here to do?"

"Okay. It's work time. I get it." Bram smiled. "So, when *can* we play?"

"I'm not over Lucas."

"I can help with that."

"He should be first to hear this, but I'm thinking of taking him back."

"And if you don't get back together?"

"You're going to have to take *I don't know* for an answer." Jule moved his feet into third position, forward leg *tendu*. He gave Bram a significant glance.

"Okay. Okay." Bram took his place next to Jule. His left hand rested on the small of Jule's back and his right was raised, echoing Jule's gesture.

They ran through the passage twice without missteps. At the end of the second run, Bram wrapped his arms around Jule's hips and lifted him up. Jule gazed down at Bram in one of the key moments of the ballet. Bram looked up into Jule's eyes with the expression of a man witnessing a miracle.

"IT'S NONE of my business, boy," Charlotte said to Lucas as they entered the studio. "But if I were you, and I still wanted to get Jule back, I'd lock that down fast."

Lucas watched Bram lower Jule to his feet. "Girl, what would you suggest I do?"

"Get in there and get up on it. Remind Jule—and Bram—who's supposed to be dancing with him."

"David wants me to wait a couple more days."

"Luc, you're ready." Charlotte made a face. "You don't think David wants to trade you for Bram, do you?"

"Nah, I believe him when he says he wants me to dance *Fireheart* on stage. Bram's good and all, but—"

"But you and Jule really sell it," Charlotte finished for him. "I'm glad you and I have a dance together." She smiled. "When the love goddess puts the fire in your heart."

"Me too." Lucas looked over at Bram and Jule again. "If you'll excuse me?"

"Go get him, killer," she said.

"Roger that."

Lucas walked over to Bram and Jule. "It's time to change partners," he said.

Jule smiled at Lucas. "Ready when you are."

Bram didn't argue. "I'll spot you," he offered.

"Appreciate it, but not necessary. Give us some room?"

Lucas waited for Bram to walk several feet away. "Hey, hot stuff," he said to Jule, going for a breezy tone.

Jule rolled his eyes.

Lucas sighed and pretended to wipe away a tear. "I remember when I taught you that, and now look at you. Rolling your eyes like a real teenager."

"Are you here to talk?"

"Nope. I'm here to take my place back."

"Fantastic." Jule lowered his voice. "Nothing against Bram, but he *is* a stand-in, after all."

"You're damn skippy." Lucas held out a hand. "Let's dance."

"Love to." Jule took his position en pointe, back straight, working leg extended behind him at ninety degrees to the floor. His arms were stretched in front of him, elbows slightly bent, hands crossed at the wrists, palms up.

Lucas curved an arm around Jule's waist and lifted his other hand over his head. He nodded slightly and Charlotte pressed play. Jamison's recording of the main piano theme poured from the speakers, and Jule and Lucas began to dance. Despite the weeks Lucas had been limited from practicing, he partnered Jule perfectly through the dramatic steps.

DAVID ENTERED the studio and came over to watch with Charlotte and Bram. "Be still my heart," he murmured. "*Exquisite.*"

"It's like they were made to dance together," Charlotte said. "You see that?" She poked Bram.

"Yeah, I sure do," Bram said somewhat wistfully.

"It's not your fault," she said. "You're a great dancer. They've just got mad chemistry."

"As much as it pains me to admit it, you're right." Bram watched Jule and Lucas perform the same moves he'd just practiced with Jule. "They're not just good, they bring the heat like a solar flare."

"*C'est vrai,*" David said before he walked over to talk to Jule and Lucas. "That looked very good," he said. "Beautiful."

"It felt good," Lucas said. "I can bring more power to it, but I didn't want to go all out until I was sure I was one hundred percent."

"Go again?" Jule asked.

"I should think," David said. "Show me the fire this time. *Impressione-moi!*"

Jezza and more members of the cast came in and stopped to watch Jule and Lucas dance the scene of a man dying of AIDS with his devoted lover supporting him until the end.

"Fuck, that was beautiful," Jezza said. "I didn't even think to take a photo."

"You'll have more than one chance," David said. "Okay, now, Charlotte, let's go through your entrance. And when you bend over Lucas to comfort him as he cradles Jule's body, I'd like it to look a little more, um, Pieta-ish, if you know what I mean."

Bram brought up a page on his phone and handed it to Charlotte. She looked at the picture of Michelangelo's statue and nodded.

"I get it," she said. "*So* much mood."

The rest of the practice went so well that David forgot his financial problems for several hours. However, he couldn't keep them at bay forever, and he couldn't expect Marilee, Jamison, and the dancers to continue working without pay. Something had to be done soon; the owners of the venue wouldn't hold the dates open without a payment in the near future. He was worried, but he didn't let it show on his face. He had a baseless belief that everything would work out because this ballet was too important to let it wither and blow away. One way or another, he'd get the money.

"Good job, kids," David said. "Now scamper and have some fun before you have to come back here. I'll be cracking the whip again, same time tomorrow."

Jule waited for David to finish talking to Charlotte before he caught his eye.

"Yes, what can I do for you?" David asked expansively. "*Mon étoile.*"

"I've been locked out of the dorm."

"Shit. I didn't think she'd stoop that low." David chewed his bottom lip. "Who else is homeless?"

"Just me for the moment."

"I'll speak to Catherine. Meanwhile, you can stay with me. I promise to behave."

"Thanks. I'm going to hang out with Lucas for a couple of hours. I'll see you later."

"YOU FEEL like doing something?" Lucas asked Jule.

Jule, who was practically vibrating from all the physical contact with Lucas, didn't answer for a few moments. He was weighing his wants against his doubts.

"Hey, if you don't want to, I under—"

"No, I'd like to do something."

"I'm not talking big plans, pretty much the same deal as last time. Chilling with a movie. Ridiculous number of snacks. Heavy sexual tension."

Jule chuckled. "Perfect. Your place?"

"Outstanding."

A little less than fifteen minutes later, they arrived at Lucas's building.

"The place is kind of a mess," Lucas said as he opened the door to his loft apartment.

Jule looked around as the lights came on. "Looks normal to me, mate."

"Great. Have a seat and find us something to watch. I'll throw some snacks together."

Jule found the remote and looked through the guide on the big TV. He looked away from the screen when Lucas came out of the kitchen. Jule got up and took the bottles of sparkling water from Lucas, who looked in imminent danger of dropping the platter he carried.

"I made sandwiches," Lucas said unnecessarily. "I think I remembered how you like yours."

"Mate, roast beef and bread are all I need, but this is perfect." Jule clinked his bottle against Lucas's. "Thanks."

"It's my genuine pleasure." Lucas paused and then spoke again. "Making you smile makes me feel good."

"So, it's a completely selfish thing on your part."

"Precisely." Lucas put down his beer. "What are we watching?"

"I couldn't decide. I'm too tired to watch something complicated, but I don't want to watch something I've already seen, which is what I'd usually do."

Lucas carefully considered his next words and then said them anyway. "You ever watch porn?"

"Porn?" Jule said in surprise.

"Yeah, you know, fuck films."

"Well... I've seen some porn. Not a video or anything, just a magazine Sasha didn't hide very well. Those photos gave me my first clue that I was different. Or at least gave me a name for it."

"So, you haven't watched any?"

"I sense you're leading up to something." Jule smiled.

"I'm just saying that if you were curious, I could guide you through it."

"Let's see it, then."

Lucas took the remote and found his subscription channel. "I think you might like this one. It's one of my favorites called *Nasty and Curious*. It's kind of a parody of *Fast and Furious*. The acting is so-so, but the actors are hot, and the production values are high."

"Twenty-First Century Cox?" Jule laughed as the first title came onscreen. "That's hilarious."

Lucas moved a little closer on the couch under the pretense of reaching for some chips.

Jule didn't notice Lucas's maneuver. He was enthralled by his first taste of modern pornography. There was nothing cheesy about the sets, and everyone on screen was attractive. It didn't take long for the clothes to come off, and Jule couldn't take his eyes off the action. He was absolutely riveted by the graphic moving images of hard cocks sliding between rosy lips, hands gripping hard muscles, a scatter of glistening come on rock-hard abs.

"WELL?" LUCAS said when the first sex scene ended. "What do you think?"

"That bloke looks just like Paul Walker. The other one doesn't look so much like Vin Diesel, but he's just as large. Large down there, as well!" Jule stopped talking for a moment, took a breath, and started again. "Bloody hell, that was *brilliant*!"

"So... you liked it?"

"I'd say so. I don't think I've ever been this horny." Jule looked over at Lucas. "Except for when we... you know."

"I remember."

"I miss it."

"I don't know how deep you want to go with this, but I gotta know. Do you miss *me*, or is it just the sex?"

"Sex isn't hard to come by, not that I'm getting any," Jule said. "I miss sex *with you*."

"Good enough." Lucas took a nervous sip of the now-flat water. "Want to keep talking about it?"

"I'd rather kiss you, but I'm not sure it's a good idea."

"Take all the time you need. I'll wait. Not being sarcastic."

Jule smiled. "This would be easier if I wasn't so hard."

"True that." Lucas paused. "Oh, you meant—" He laughed. "Well, that is the purpose of porn."

"It's doing its job, then." Jule shifted his weight and his thigh ended up pressed against Lucas's. "Sorry," he said as he moved away.

"Jule—" Lucas caught the hazardous words before they could tumble from his mouth. True, Jule was behaving as though he didn't hate his guts, but it would be foolish to abandon his policy of taking it slow. He had to show Jule that whatever might happen between them was up to Jule. It had to be Jule's choice. It wasn't easy to back off, but Lucas was willing to endure any hardship if it brought Jule back to him. And that included keeping his hands to himself.

Lucas held his breath when Jule shifted again as though he was going to stand up, and then Jule was in his face, and Jule's lips brushed his. The rush of relief was so great it brought tears to Lucas's eyes, and it was a moment before he thought to embrace Jule. Jule came easily into his arms, and the kiss went from warm to white-hot in seconds. Lucas was pressed against the cushions with Jule's knees on either side of his hips and Jule's tongue dueling with his. He moved his hands down to cup Jule's round ass and squish their crotches together.

"That's nice," Jule sighed as Lucas trailed little sucking kisses down his neck.

"It sure is." Lucas's lips moved against the notch between Jule's collarbones. He licked the small hollow and savored Jule's moan. "I'm really into this, but I feel like I should ask how far you want to go."

Jule leaned his forehead against Lucas's, breathing hard.

"If it helps," Lucas said, "there are no strings on this. If you just want to get off, I'm your man. It doesn't have to mean anything."

"Every time you touch me, it means something."

Lucas had no reply for this statement, so he kissed Jule again and did the things he'd been longing to do every day since Jule had left. With mouth, fingers, and every other part of him, Lucas strove to bring Jule as much pleasure as possible. His efforts were not in vain.

Lucas swallowed Jule's cry of release like a mouthful of fine wine. "I love you," he murmured as Jule pushed a hand under his waistband.

If Jule heard, he didn't react. He seemed intent on getting hold of Lucas's cock. His hand had little room to maneuver in Lucas's trousers, however, Lucas was set to go off like a bomb with a motion sensor. As his orgasm bloomed, he wrapped his arms tightly around Jule and held him close. It was awkward with the trapped hand, but Jule didn't complain.

"Good?" Jule asked softly.

Lucas nodded, his hair tickling Jule's ear. "So good," he sighed. "You mind if we stay like this for a few minutes?"

Jule reclaimed his hand and settled more comfortably on Lucas's thighs. "No, this is lovely," he said as he bent his head to kiss Lucas.

They made out for a while with none of the urgency of three minutes ago. Long, languid kisses and desultory caresses made a dreamlike thing of the afterglow.

"I don't want to move," Jule said several minutes later. "But I really need to use the toilet."

"Stupid bladder." Lucas chuckled as Jule got up and wandered, sleepy-eyed, toward the bathroom.

Currently, his campaign to win Jule back was going insanely well, but it would be stupid to get cocky now. Especially now that he'd realized he didn't want this boy for a night or a week or even a season. He wanted him for the rest of his life, and he'd spend every minute of it making sure he was worthy. When Jule returned and said he had to go, Lucas didn't make a fuss.

DAVID OPENED the townhouse door and let Jule in. "I'll give you a key tomorrow, or as soon as I can find one," he said. "Are you hungry?"

Jule nodded. "I am. Anything is fine, really."

David took Jule into the kitchen and opened the refrigerator. "What's mine is yours," he said grandly. He stood back to let Jule peruse the contents.

"It's hard to choose," Jule said.

It hadn't escaped David's attention that his muse looked extremely well-laid. "Why don't you let me fix you something? I know just the thing for your condition."

Jule frowned. "My condition?"

"Trust me. I was your age once. Had a pet stegosaurus."

Jule's frown smoothed out. "It wasn't *that* long ago."

David smiled as he cut slices of ham. "Always charming," he said.

"I'm not doing it on purpose."

"Yeah, that's probably the most annoying thing about you." David cut boiled eggs in half and put them on the plate with the ham. He added a handful of raw mushrooms and some almonds and set the plate in front of Jule. "You don't know how good you are."

Jule made a rude noise. "What rubbish." He looked at the plate. "So, couldn't you find any more protein?"

"Eat," David ordered.

Jule complied.

David cleared his throat. "I know we've discussed this briefly, but I'm bringing it up again."

Jule stopped chewing and looked at David.

"Swallow that," David said. "You look like a chipmunk. Okay, I'm not going to try to tell you who you can... date, but I'd like to be kept in the loop."

"What does that mean?"

"I just want to know who you're... dating, okay?"

"You keep saying dating, but I think you want to say fucking."

"That *is* more to the point."

"I still don't think it's any of your business who I shag."

"It kind of is right now." David thought for a moment before he spoke again. "*Fireheart* is a good ballet, but when it's danced by you and Lucas, it becomes a *great* ballet, transcendent even. You make it great because the heat between you comes through in the steps."

"Are you saying you *want* me to sleep with Lucas?"

"Kid, I don't know what he's doing to you, but after you've been with him you *glow*."

"It's just the usual things, I imagine," Jule said. "I'm not that experienced, so I can't really say."

"Then I guess he's just gotten really, really good at it."

"I couldn't say, but I do enjoy it quite a lot."

"Good. Good. So, do we have an understanding?"

"I understand that this is the oddest conversation I've ever had."

"I just want the ballet to succeed. I *need* it to succeed."

"I'll do everything I can to make that happen. Short of *dating* Lucas onstage."

David smiled fondly at Jule. "You've changed a bit since you've been with us, or are you just showing a little more of the real you?"

"I'm always the real me." Jule stood and took his plate to the dishwasher. "Thank you for the snack."

"Go to bed. It's after eleven."

"Good night."

"Sleep well and have good dreams."

Chapter Twenty-Four

JULE WAS in the kitchen when David came downstairs the next morning. "Good morning. I didn't think you'd mind if I made myself breakfast."

"Of course not. How long have you been up?"

"Since six. I did my stretches and went for a run. Do you want eggs?"

"God, no. But is that coffee I smell?"

"Sit," Jule said. "I'm going to make you breakfast."

"Bossy." David grumbled, but he looked pleased as he sat down at the table.

Jule brought David a mug of black coffee and went back to work. In a few minutes, he put a plate of scrambled eggs and sausage in front of David. In another minute, half a grapefruit in a bowl was set at David's elbow, and Jule sat to eat.

"Is this pretty typical for you?" David asked as he dug into the grapefruit.

Jule shook his head. "I usually have a smoothie first thing, then, around ten, Sasha usually puts out a heap of food: eggs, bacon, sausage, tomato…." He stopped speaking and a wistful look stole over his face like mist softening a familiar landscape.

"I'm sensing a bit of homesickness."

"I miss it horribly." Jule paused. "But this is where I want to be."

"Good. Good. I need you to make my ballet a success, so no running off to England, okay?"

"I won't."

"I know you won't. You're not the type that runs."

"I ran from Lucas and look what happened."

"Lucas's accident was not your fault."

"I feel as though it was, and you can't deny that I ran away like a spoiled brat who didn't get his way."

"You ran away like someone who'd been stabbed in the back." David paused. "If I haven't apologized before, I'm doing it now. Jule, I'm genuinely sorry I caused you pain."

"Thank you. Can we never talk about it again?"

"As you wish." David sipped his coffee. "I could get used to having you around. Aside from the way you improve the scenery, you make a good cup of coffee." He raised the mug in salute.

"Thanks. I appreciate you letting me stay here."

"You're welcome for as long as you please." David smiled faintly. "Though it won't please Lucas, I can tell you that."

Jule shrugged. "I think he trusts me."

"I *know* he doesn't trust me." David's dark eyes glittered in the shadow of his heavy bangs.

"That's not really relevant."

"Excuse me?"

"He's not dating you. He's dating me."

"You don't think he worries about me making a move on you?"

Jule shrugged again. "I'm not sure worried is the right word. He's pretty sure you're going to *come on to me*, as he puts it, which I find funny."

"Why funny? Is it so ridiculous that I'd flirt with you? Am I too ancient?"

"God, no. You're terribly sexy. It's just the words, you know? When I hear that phrase, it gives me a mental image, and it's funny."

"Ah, I see." David grinned.

"Are you picturing a money shot?"

"A *money shot*?" David chuckled. "Why do I think that wasn't in your vocab before you hooked up with Lucas?"

"You'd be right." Jule put his fork down on his empty plate. "But it isn't a hookup."

"If you say so," David said neutrally. "I've known Lucas since he was your age, and I've never seen him serious about anyone."

"Then it's time, isn't it?"

"Maybe, but are you sure *you're* ready for that?"

"All I know is Lucas makes me happy. He makes me feel like I have a home."

David nodded. "All good things, but correct me if I'm wrong, isn't he your first?"

"He's my first lover, if that's what you're getting at."

"You aren't curious? About what it would be like with someone else?"

"Of course, but not enough to do something about it. I'm more than satisfied." Jule frowned. "Why are you talking like this? I thought you were happy that we're together."

"Just idle chit-chat."

"No, it isn't."

"Then I obviously suck as a mentor, and I withdraw the question." David rose from the table. "Thanks for feeding me. I'm going to have a shower and get dressed. Will you be ready to go to the studio with me?"

Jule nodded.

"Excellent. I'll see you back down here in a half hour?"

Jule nodded again, and David walked away. After David had gone upstairs, Jule cleared the table. He thought about David's words as he put the dishes in the dishwasher. Maybe it was too early to settle on one person, but Lucas was the one he wanted, now and forever. He'd never been so sure about anything besides dancing. Now, he just had to figure out how and when to let Lucas know.

PRACTICE BEGAN as soon as Lucas arrived, about five minutes behind David and Jule. They were working on the second act when they were interrupted. David turned as the door to the studio banged open. Lucas and Jule remained in position as Catherine stalked toward them.

"Cath," David called out. "It's about time. It's been over a week since your latest drive-by disapproval."

"Is this really the best you could do?" she asked as she glanced around the shabby space.

"The price was right," David said. "What are you doing in such a dump?"

"I didn't want to discuss this on the phone." Catherine glanced at Jule and Lucas. "Can you... dismiss them or something?"

"I could." David made no move to do so.

Catherine's frown deepened. "Very well." She pulled something from her messenger bag purse. "How could you?" She held up a calendar as though it were a piece of evidence.

"I forgot those went on sale today. Man, Jezza wasn't kidding about that fast track. Thanks for your donation, by the way."

"I know you're desperate." She looked around the studio again. "But a cheesecake calendar? Really?"

"I think it's very tasteful," David said. He turned to look at Lucas and Jule. "At ease."

"Can I see it?" Lucas asked.

Catherine glared at him. "*Your* photo is particularly suggestive."

"Can *I* see it?" Jule asked immediately.

Catherine sniffed. "Your acolytes have as little regard for tradition as you," she told David. "Well done. Another giant step on the path of self-destruction. What were you thinking?"

"I needed to raise money, and my advisors recommended the calendar."

"Enjoy it while you can. The novelty will soon wear off, and the stalwarts of ballet will reject you."

"Stalwarts?" David repeated. "That's an archaic word, *Doudou*, like your mindset." He took a deep breath. "Did you really come here just to raise hell about a few photos?"

"I thought I might make one last appeal to your more sensible side. Don't commit career suicide, David. You have too much to offer."

"*You have so much to offer, David. So much potential. Don't waste your talent.*" David smiled bitterly. "I've heard that all my life. Well, I'm not wasting anything. I wish you could see that this is the best expression of my talent, but apparently, you lost that ability."

"I'm trying to save you from yourself."

"You should take a day off," David said. "Or even longer. You cut me out of your life, and I don't appreciate you popping in to disrupt whatever I'm doing with some rant."

"This will be your ruin." Catherine threw the calendar at David.

The calendar had very poor aerodynamics and fell to the floor between them. David took a few steps, bent, and picked it up. He handed it off to Jule as he held Catherine's gaze.

"Are you actually trying to intimidate me?" she asked.

"I'm waiting for you to leave so we can go back to work. Since I've realized I don't know what you're capable of, I'd rather keep an eye on you until you're gone."

Catherine ran her gaze over Lucas and Jule before she walked out.

"I feel like I was just marked for death," Lucas said. He put his arm around Jule's shoulders. Jule continued looking through the calendar.

Bram walked in looking back over his shoulder. "Man, she is *steamin'*," he said. "Who stepped on her tail?"

"She didn't care for our vulgar little calendar," David said in an effete tone. "And she dropped by to express her displeasure. She is *not* amused."

"Is that it?" Bram pointed to Jule. "I haven't seen it."

"Mate, your picture is so sexy." Jule held the calendar up.

Rather than perfectly posed attitudes from famous solos, Jezza had chosen to show the dancers at practice. Instead of elaborate costumes, they wore their warmup clothes, leotards, tights, and leg warmers of every style. Instead of color, the pictures were in soft, sooty black and luminous, silvery white. In Bram's photo, he was resting on his side on the hardwood floor supported on one elbow. One long leg was stretched out and the other was bent at the knee bringing his calf muscles into high relief. He was laughing at something someone had said off camera, flashing a bright white smile. There was nothing overtly sexual about the image, and yet, it radiated eroticism.

"I'd go out with me," Bram said. "Let's see yours."

Jezza had caught Jule in a spin. He was en pointe, arms curved in a circle, hands almost meeting, one knee bent, as he accelerated in a revolution. His face was a serene mask of perfect concentration.

"I like the way your hair is flying out like a figure skater's," Lucas said. He ran his fingers through Jule's hair.

"It's getting pretty long," Jule said. "For me, I mean."

"You are *not* to get a haircut," David said in a tone that brooked no dissent.

"I know," Jule said. "You've told me a million times." For a moment, he imagined he heard Kelly answer that he'd told him a million and one. A wave of homesickness struck him, and his smile faded.

"Hey, it's not that bad," David said. "You're cute with longer hair. You don't look so much like a junior banker anymore."

"You take that back," Lucas said. "My boy Jule never looked like any kind of banker."

"More like a junior partner at a Manhattan law firm," Bram said.

"Do I have to come over there and talk to you?" Lucas replied.

Bram laughed. "Admit it, Jule was pretty square."

"Not square, *classic*," David said. "There's a difference, but then again, you're from Cali, so...."

Bram laughed again, clearly taking no offense. "Dude, only posers say Cali. How are the calendars selling, by the way?"

"I haven't checked since they went on sale," David said. "But I don't expect much until word gets around, assuming it does."

"Jezza seems confident," Jule said.

"He *does* have a lot of contacts in the media," David said. "Mostly pop culture media, but any publicity is good publicity, right?" He drew himself up. "Okay, back to business. Bram, I'm sorry to throw this at you now, but I've written a new solo—a dance that embodies undying love. I want you to dance it at the very end. After Alex dies and the curtain comes down on our heartbroken Philip and the angels, it will rise again on a dark stage. There will be one spotlight, and it will be on you."

"I'm excited," Bram said. "What inspired you?"

David smiled at Jule. "Someone once asked me if the ballet could have a happy ending. Sadly, that wouldn't have the same impact, considering I'm trying to illustrate how badly LGBT folks have been treated, but there's no reason it can't have a hopeful ending. Therefore, you shall be my phoenix, the spirit of love rising from the ashes."

"That's lovely," Jule said.

David smiled at Jule again before turning back to Bram. "Of course, I'm assuming you care to stick around and dance for a share of the profits, if there are any."

"I'm in," Bram said. "Us West Coast boys are quirky like that."

"Aw, look at this." Jule held up a photo of Bram, Lucas, and himself working out the blocking for an intricate step. "I like this picture best… though the one of Charlotte is lovely."

Charlotte was pictured sitting on a folding chair, bent over at the waist, winding the ribbon straps of her toe shoe around her right ankle. Her shining hair was gathered at her nape and several tendrils had escaped to fall softly on the graceful lines of her neck and shoulders.

"Damn," Bram said under his breath.

"Right?" Lucas agreed. "How can someone look so innocent and sensuous at the same time?" He turned his gaze on Jule. "Care to give us some insight?"

Jule snorted. "I don't think you can call me innocent any longer."

"Yeah, but you *look* fresh," Bram said.

"You look like you'll be sweet sixteen on your next birthday," David added.

"You can all shut up now," Jule said.

"That is a gorgeous calendar, though," Bram said. "I need to order a copy now." He got his phone out.

"You can," David said. "But you'll all be getting a free one."

"Sweet," Bram said. "But I'm going to order a few for friends."

"Lucas, Jule, you can go," David said. "I'm going to work with Bram on the phoenix solo."

"Okay, see you tomorrow, then," Lucas said as he put his arm around Jule.

"WE'VE GOT the entire evening free," Lucas said as they walked away. "What do you want to do?"

"Practice?"

"No," David called after Lucas and Jule. "No practicing until tomorrow."

"Then I'd like to see more of the city," Jule said.

"Done." Lucas took out his phone and punched in a number one-handed. "It's Luc the Lucky," he said. "Can you set me up?" He listened for a moment and then said, "As soon as possible." He listened again and hung up. "We're all set."

"For what?"

"You'll see. Let's walk across to Starbucks. They'll pick us up there."

"Who?" Jule smacked Lucas's shoulder when he didn't answer. "Who? Who?"

"Patience, my little owl."

"Evil man."

"I'm not being evil, but I do have an ulterior motive."

"Which is?"

"My continuing campaign to show you why you should be with me."

"I *am* with you."

"I'm going to keep reminding you just the same."

"Then I suppose I'll just have to put up with being spoiled." Jule squeezed Lucas's hand and then let go as they entered Starbucks.

Chapter Twenty-Five

JULE AND Lucas got coffee and waited under the awning. About twenty minutes went by before a long hot-pink car pulled over to the curb. The driver rolled down the passenger side window.

"Hop in before I get a ticket."

Lucas opened the back door and Jule got in behind him. Jule stared in surprise at the driver. The very large man was wearing a Dolly Parton wig, full makeup, and a strapless, sequined dress.

"Welcome to Drag Me Through New York," he said. "I'm Sister Barbarian of the Everlasting Latex, and I'll be your guide to all the lame touristy bullshit New York has to offer. Are you ready to ride?"

"Say yes." Lucas poked Jule.

"Stop poking me."

"No poking until the end of the tour," Sister said.

"Thank you," Jule replied. "Yes, I'm ready. I hope."

Sister laughed heartily. "Relax, my good twink. I haven't lost anyone yet."

For two hours, Sister "Call Me Barb" Barbarian drove Jule and Lucas around. She stopped at Radio City Music Hall, the Metropolitan Museum of Art, Central Park, the Rockefeller Center, and more so she could snap photos—"Pictures or it didn't happen!"—of Lucas and Jule in front of the landmarks.

"You want to do the Statue of Liberty?" she asked as they got back in the car at Times Square.

"No," Jule said. He was thoroughly enjoying the tour and Sister's sense of humor.

"Why not?"

"First, because she's a lady. Also, she's three hundred feet tall and made of copper. I doubt my willie would make a dent."

Sister laughed uproariously. "You should do drag," she said. "You've got good timing."

"He's already a performer," Lucas said. "And not too shabby."

"Good. The world needs entertainers. More now than ever before."

"True that," Lucas said.

"But let's forget all that for now. We're here to have fun!" Sister said. "Next stop, the Empire State Building. I have tickets for you for the observation deck, but I'll be waiting in the car." She shuddered dramatically. "I get dizzy when I wear heels, so you won't catch me a hundred stories up."

Jule and Lucas rode the elevator to the top and walked out onto the observation deck. The wind played with the hems of their jackets and tugged at their hair like a mischievous lover. Jule hurried to the edge to look down. Lucas followed and wrapped his arms around Jule from behind. It was cold, but neither felt it just then.

Lucas lips were warm on Jule's ear. "I'll never forget this moment," he said softly.

Jule turned his head and kissed Lucas. "Neither will I."

"I love you, you know."

"I do know." Jule sighed happily.

"Is there something you want to say to me?"

"I'm famished."

Lucas smiled. "Brat." He hugged Jule tightly for a moment before letting go. "Come on, then. Let's find you a trough."

Jule laughed, as he took Lucas's hand. "Now that you've got me, you might regret it."

"I've got you?" Lucas stopped short of the elevator. "What does that mean to you?"

"I mean, I'm yours. Exclusively."

"So… we're going steady?"

"What?"

"We're a couple. Is that what you're saying?"

"Of course. What else would we be?"

"Fuck buddies?"

"I hadn't heard that term before, but I can figure it out." Jule paused. "I'm your friend, for sure, but we're definitely *not* fuck buddies."

"So, you'd say it's a bit more serious than that?"

"What are you on about? We're lovers. We're a couple. I don't want anyone but you. Is that clear enough?"

"In other words, if Bram put some moves on you, you'd tell him to fuck off."

"For sure."

Lucas smiled. "You know, I really thought he'd have tried something by now, but maybe he's serious about being a heterosexual." He studied Jule's face for a moment. "What is it?"

"I don't think he's all that serious about it."

"The fucker came on to you."

"You can't be surprised."

"No, not really. His ego would compel him to at least take a run at you, once he knew I was interested too."

"He's not a bad guy, you know. He's just such a… *guy*."

Lucas smiled again. "Okay then, let's get back down to the ground and have some dinner."

"Aren't you going to make a lame double entendre about dessert?"

"I would, but aren't we beyond that now? Can't I just say I'm going to take you home and love you up until you beg me to stop?"

"You could, but I've grown fond of your idea of humor."

"My *idea* of humor?" he repeated in a tone of disbelief. "Look, you can call me out for my foolish face, my horrible dancing, and my lack of taste, but don't ever malign my sense of humor."

"What will happen if I do?"

"I suppose I'd have to punish you somehow." Lucas gave him a wicked grin.

"Really? And what form would this punishment take?"

"I wouldn't rule out an old-school spanking, young man."

"That's good to know," Jule said thoughtfully. He looked around. "I think I'm going to think of this as our place."

"That's sweet," Lucas said. "Now we need our song."

The elevator doors opened on an empty car, and Lucas playfully shoved Jule inside. Heedless of security cameras, they made out all the way to the bottom floor.

Jule and Lucas got back in the car, and Lucas asked Sister the name of the best Italian place she knew. He found the number and called ahead. Sister parked out front, while Lucas ran in for his order.

Sister glanced at Jule in the rearview mirror. "If you don't mind me saying, and even if you do, that's one fine hunk of man you've got there."

"Isn't he beautiful?" Jule said.

"Honey, he's all that. And he is *clearly* head over heels for you, you lucky thing."

"Do you really think so?"

"You should see the way he looks at you when you aren't looking at him. I nearly swooned. God as my waitress." She put a hand over her heart.

Jule smiled. "I like him a lot too."

"Does he know that?"

"I suppose. I try to show him how I feel. I'm a very physical person."

"Some things need to be said out loud once in a while." Sister met Jule's eyes in the rearview mirror. "Even if you are the finest twink this old queen has seen since the eighties. Don't let him slip away because you're so sure you've got him. Tell him how you feel. Understand?"

"I don't—" Jule stopped in midsentence to think about her words. Maybe he did take it for granted that Lucas loved him. Maybe he did assume Lucas would always be there. To be fair, these were things Lucas had said to him, but was he properly grateful for Lucas's devotion, or did he feel entitled to it? "All right," he said. "I'll be more mindful."

"You know what, cutie? I believe you." Sister picked up a gift bag from the seat beside her and handed it back. "I'm supposed to make a big sassy deal out of giving you this when I drop you off, but I want you to take that man home and—"

"I get the idea," Jule said quickly. "Thank you."

"Not for nothin', honey, but there's a bottle of nice wine in there." Sister winked at Jule. "And a few party favors."

"How does Lucas know you?"

"He doesn't know me. He knows my boss. She's his ex."

Jule went numb with shock. "Really."

"Oops. I thought you knew." Sister paused. "It's nothing to make a fuss about. Tish said the marriage lasted literally a month before she got him to agree to an annulment. Now that I've seen him, I think I would've given it a little longer."

"Do you know why they divorced?"

"Are you kidding? He's gay."

"Oh. Right."

"Look, I can tell you're not happy about hearing this, but don't let it come between you. That would break my heart."

Jule looked out the window and saw Lucas coming out of the restaurant with a carryout bag and a pizza box.

"I'm only half joking," Sister said. "Give him the benefit of the doubt."

"I will. I promise," Jule said, and Sister turned to face forward again.

"We are set for the evening," Lucas said as he got in the car. "This place has an amazing menu. I picked out a few things from the display case while they were boxing the pie."

"Ready to go home?" Sister asked.

"Yes, we are," Jule said.

"YOU SHOULD just move in with me," Lucas said as Jule moved one of his sweatshirts off the couch. "Half your clothes live here already."

"Do you think it's a good idea?" Jule opened the pizza box as soon as Lucas set it down.

"Yes, I do. We could spend more time together."

"That's true."

"And you'd be away from David's sphere of influence for longer."

Jule hit Lucas with a throw pillow.

"What was that for?"

"For insulting me. Do you really think I can't resist David?"

"Many have tried and failed. Believe me, *I* know. You haven't seen him really turn it on."

"Like the first time I met him?"

"That wasn't full throttle. He was courting you for his company, not himself."

"And that's all the faith you have in my willpower, is it?"

Lucas opened his mouth and closed it again without speaking.

"Were you about to say something about how young I am?"

"Yes, I was, but I thought better of it."

"Why don't we eat this pizza and watch something?" Jule paused. "My eating habits have really gotten bad since I met you."

"You're welcome. What should we watch?"

"There's this old movie that always makes me feel good. Have you seen *Strictly Ballroom*?"

"No, but I know it has dancing in it."

"You'll like it. I promise. It's old, but you can't tell."

"Fine with me. Fire it up. I'll be right back." Lucas took a slice of pizza with him to the kitchen. "You want a beer?"

"No. I've been bad enough for now. Sister Barbarian gave us wine. Fewer calories. Bring the corkscrew?"

Lucas came back with a beer and the corkscrew. "Why would she give us wine?"

"It's actually a gift from the owner of the company."

Lucas froze with the beer bottle at his lips and then slowly lowered it. "Did I mention I was able to get a tour on such short notice because my ex-wife owns the company?" he said as lightly as he could manage.

"No, you didn't. I would have remembered that." Jule looked up at Lucas. "Sit down, please, so I don't break my neck looking at you."

Lucas came around the couch and sat next to Jule. "I wasn't trying to hide anything. It just didn't occur to me to mention it."

"I know you had a life before we met, but you really didn't think you should mention it?"

"Not really."

"I'd like to hear it."

"Sure. It was a mistake anyway. When I met Tish we were both seventeen, and I had just moved here from Tuxedo Park for classes. Because of who my family was, I was into proving I was normal, and Tish was happy to help. Eventually, we both realized that the homo outweighed the straight in me and didn't see any point in staying married. Honestly, it just wasn't fair to her."

"You still know each other, though."

"We're what you'd call casual friends. I know I can count on her for certain things, and she knows the same about me."

"Like fuck buddies?"

"No! Christ, no!" Lucas exclaimed before he got a grip. He lowered his voice. "Like she'd call me if she was moving and needed help packing up."

"Oh." Jule bit his lip. "I'm sorry if I'm acting like a complete knob. It's just that—I'd just made up my mind to take you back and then—"

"I'm truly sorry." Lucas sighed. "I'll be more thoughtful, I promise."

"Thanks for being honest with me."

"Wait. Hold on a minute. Are you telling me all I have to do is tell you everything?"

"Um." Jule took a bite of pizza. "Maybe not *every*thing."

"Maybe I'm exaggerating," Lucas said. "But I'm not great at deciding what I should tell people. Usually, it's too much or not enough, never just right."

"I'm going to tell you what Sasha told me when I was twelve."

"This sounds serious."

"Just listen. The trick is to put yourself in the other person's place."

"That's it?"

"It's not that easy, no. You have to know me well enough to decide whether you should tell me you have an ex-wife, instead of letting me find out by accident."

"Yeah." Lucas took another drink of beer. "I guess that's not something you want to find out by surprise, huh?"

"Would you like it if someone told you I used to date Bram?"

"You couldn't have."

"Work with me, Madding."

"No, I wouldn't like it. I would hate it." Lucas paused. "And it would hurt a lot that you hadn't told me first." He smiled. "Are we done, Yoda?"

"Help you, I can."

"Are you trying to turn me on?"

"Trying?" Jule smiled impishly. "I can't believe we aren't snogging already."

Lucas set down his beer and pulled Jule into his arms. "Is this more like it?" he growled.

"Actually—" Jule gasped when Lucas squeezed him. "It's very—"

Lucas claimed Jule's mouth in a kiss that left no doubt about his intentions.

Jule responded eagerly, catching fire like dry grass ignited by a careless ember on a warm and windy day. He knocked over an empty bottle as he climbed onto Lucas's lap.

"You like it this way?" Lucas asked as Jule settled on his thighs facing him.

Jule laced his fingers behind Lucas's neck and pulled him into another passionate kiss. "I love it this way," he said breathlessly.

"I'm partial to it myself."

Lucas left Jule's mouth to kiss his way down his neck, fingers busy with the buttons of Jule's shirt. He pulled the shirt open, and Jule obligingly moved his arms so Lucas could remove it. Lucas took a pink nipple between his teeth and Jule moaned loudly.

As Lucas kissed, sucked, and nibbled, Jule dug the fingers of one hand into Lucas's hair and cupped Lucas's crotch with the other. He squeezed and rubbed Lucas's cock through his trousers until it wasn't enough anymore.

"Too many clothes," Jule mumbled.

Lucas lifted his head and met Jule's heavy-lidded gaze. "What was that?"

"I want to touch you," Jule said. He gave Lucas's cock another squeeze.

"Okay, I see the problem. Can you move for a minute?"

"I don't think so."

Lucas chuckled as he physically moved Jule from his lap to the couch. "Stay," he said drolly.

Jule watched as Lucas pulled his shirt over his head and pushed his trousers and underwear to the floor before stepping out of them. "Bloody hell, you're gorgeous all over."

"Take off those pants."

"You take them off."

Lucas didn't wait to be told twice. He unzipped Jule's trousers and pulled them off. Instead of pulling the boxers down right away, he slipped his hand through the fly and took hold of Jule's hard cock. Slowly, he shuttled his hand up and down as he took possession of Jule's lips again. After a kiss that had both of them aching for more, Lucas moved down.

Jule shivered as Lucas drew his boxers down far enough to take him in his mouth. The hot, wet suede of Lucas's tongue caressing the head of his cock felt almost too good to bear. And then Lucas pinched his nipple while taking him deep down his throat and Jule came abruptly. He clutched at Lucas's hair at the overwhelming sensation of Lucas swallowing his come.

"I was kind of hoping for a sixty-nine," Lucas said, after relinquishing Jule's spent dick.

"I couldn't stop. Everything you were doing just kind of came together at once and boom!"

Lucas chuckled. "It did seem pretty intense."

"Mate, you swallowing with me so deep—" Jule took a breath. "That was amazing." He took another breath. "Can you teach me that?"

"Sure, kid. Whenever you're ready."

"You like calling me kid, don't you?"

"I don't mean anything by it. It just comes out of my mouth." Lucas watched Jule stretch and kick off his boxers. "It doesn't bother me that you're young, but it doesn't particularly turn me on either. I love *you*, not your age."

"That's cool. I've never liked being treated like a child."

"That's because you aren't one." Lucas stroked a hand down Jule's chest and abs to his crotch. "In any way, shape, or form."

"Not according to my mum."

"I find your lack of faith disturbing." Lucas said and then gasped when Jule grabbed his dick. "Rebel scum!"

"Don't get cocky… kid."

"I love you," Lucas growled.

"I know." Jule bent his head and took Lucas's cock in his mouth. It was exactly his fifth time giving head, but he already knew this was his favorite part. He loved the way Lucas reacted to his caresses as he learned what pleased him best. What he currently lacked in technique, he made up for with earnest enthusiasm, and he was determined to get better.

Lucas pushed his fingers into Jule's hair, cradling his skull.

Jule reached up with his free hand to toy with Lucas's nipples as he went down on him. He gripped Lucas's shaft at the base with his other hand and stroked the pad of his thumb along the thick vein on the underside. He felt the slight pressure of Lucas's fingertips on his scalp and knew he was about to come. He ran his tongue around the blunt head of Lucas's shaft before taking him deeper, bobbing his head faster.

Lucas's deep groan signaled his orgasm. He held Jule's head gently but firmly, urging him to stillness.

"God damn!" Lucas said, as he eased back. "What's my name again?"

Jule laughed and sprayed Lucas's belly with the come he hadn't swallowed yet. Lucas looked down and cracked up.

"Sorry," Jule said. He wiped his mouth with a takeout napkin.

"Don't be." Lucas grinned. "Sex is supposed to be fun."

Jule took another napkin and wiped Lucas's stomach. "Blow jobs *are* fun," he said. He dropped the napkin and picked up a slice of pizza.

"What? No cuddling?" Lucas gave Jule a comically reproachful look.

"You get cuddles when you *deserve* cuddles."

Lucas laughed. "This is what it would be like all the time if you lived here."

"Surely not *all* the time."

"I mean the way we feel right now. It just feels... right. Doesn't it?"

Jule poured wine into a plastic goblet he found in the basket. He took a sip and looked at Lucas over the rim. "Mate," he said. "It feels amazing."

"Awesome." Lucas pulled Jule closer and put an arm around him.

"Are we really going to sit here naked and eat pizza?"

"*And* watch the rest of this fine film."

"Yeah but... naked?"

"If you get anything on you, I promise to lick it off."

"Fair enough." Jule settled happily against Lucas's chest.

THE MOVIE ended without Jule or Lucas noticing. They were curled around each other, lazily making out. Not until Jule's phone alarm chirped did they raise their heads.

Jule sighed heavily. "I ought to go. David forgot to give me a key again."

"He stays up late." Lucas kissed Jule's bare shoulder.

"Where is my shirt?"

"I seem to recall throwing it in that direction." Lucas grabbed his cock and used it as a pointer.

Jule laughed. "Grow up."

"Come closer and I'll grow for you."

Jule chuckled. "You're the worst." He found his shirt over a floor lamp and pulled it on. His pants and boxers were at the foot of the couch, but he was wary of approaching Lucas in this mood. He could find himself facedown over the arm of the sofa with Lucas wrapped around him. That would normally make him happy, but he didn't want to wake David up to let him in. "Could you toss me my trousers?"

"I could, but I don't really want you to have them."

"You know I love playtime, but I really need to go now."

Lucas sobered instantly. He handed Jule the trousers and boxers and watched him get dressed. "I'll see you tomorrow, then?" he said a bit plaintively as Jule pulled his boots on.

Jule jumped on Lucas and kissed him thoroughly. "You just try and avoid me," he said as he left.

As he left Lucas's building, he was satisfied that he'd made the right decision in taking Lucas back. Even without the mind-blowing sex, he'd still want to be with Lucas, but the sex was definitely an attraction. It was just his phenomenal luck that he and Lucas shared a sense of humor and enjoyed doing the same things. If only the rest of his life was so easy.

Chapter Twenty-Six

THE NEXT day, David called the core members of his diminished company to assemble at the discount studio at 10:00 a.m. By 10:10, those who had remained loyal during the shake-up had gathered. They sat on folding chairs or on the floor and waited for David to speak.

David glanced at each person in turn. "Why so serious?" he cracked in his best Joker impression. "I have good news today." He waited for the cheers and applause to die. "As you know, the calendar is doing very well, and the other *merch*, as Jezza calls it, is catching on too.

"While this is encouraging, it won't be nearly enough to rent the kind of venue *Fireheart* deserves. However, the really good news is, we now have the funding we need."

"What?" Charlotte gave David a sharp look. "Are you saying you managed to get a couple of million dollars together yesterday?"

"I did. Five in fact."

"How?" Bram said. "I'd like to give it a try, whatever it is."

"The details aren't important," David said. "You can believe I borrowed from the Mob or sold a kidney to the highest bidder. I don't care. What's important is that we can start rehearsing tomorrow at Lincoln Center."

"What?" Lucas exclaimed. "And just how did you swing that?"

"You may not be aware that I'm an expert at swinging," David said drolly, wagging his eyebrows.

"Who cares?" Marilee said. "Let's get to work."

"I'm not quite fin—" David began before he was interrupted.

"Look at this!" Jezza came in waving a magazine triumphantly over his head. As David and the rest gathered around, Jezza opened the thick magazine to a page near the middle. Jezza's photo of Bram, Lucas, and Jule arm-in-arm took up a two-page spread and was captioned "Ballet's Three Musketeers."

"First the calendar, and now we're in *Vanity Fair*." David smiled. "You said you'd do it, and you did it." He tousled Jezza's long hair.

"This isn't the end of it," Jezza said, producing a few sheets of printer paper. "I saw this online today and printed it out. It's a very popular vlog with young dancers and dance fans. Jule is being called ballet's teen idol."

"I hope you're taking the piss." Jule turned red.

"This is good," Jezza said. "*Very* good. The next thing we have to do is put you on a T-shirt."

"It just keeps getting worse, huh?" Lucas poked Jule.

"Get stuffed!" Jule poked him back.

"Actually, it gets better," Jezza said. "As the current clearinghouse for Downtown's public relations, I've been on the phone all day. Everyone wants to talk to you."

"This is all great," David said. "Why don't you take a seat, and as soon as this meeting is over, we'll talk strategy. Good?"

"*Eh bien*," Jezza said with a wink. He sat down next to Jule. "We need to talk," he said softly before giving his attention to David.

"Now, I know what you're thinking," David said. "No way will they give us the Koch theater."

"Did you trade a firstborn we don't know about?" Lucas said.

"No, but we *will* have the stage at the Koch for at least a week, maybe two. They're willing to cancel one of their own programs if we draw a crowd. Butts on seats make the world go 'round, mes enfants."

"That's awesome," Jule said. "You did it."

David looked extremely pleased. "Sometimes I manage to pull one out of my derrière," he said. "I have a meeting in half an hour to discuss details with Mr. Jacobs. I want you to practice here as usual, but when you leave today, be sure and take everything you brought with you. We won't be back here anytime soon, I hope." He looked at Jezza. "I'll call you."

"As soon as possible, please," Jezza said. "Meanwhile, I'll get started on Jule."

"I don't like the sound of this," Jule said.

"Ditto," Lucas said.

David shook his head. "Wish me luck."

"*Bon courage*," Jezza called after him.

AFTER DAVID was gone, Jezza turned to Jule, "I know you aren't going to like this, but—"

"Just say it," Jule said.

"We need to do a photoshoot. I've lined up a couple of friends to help with the clothes and location, but we can't do it without you obviously."

"Why are we doing this?"

"It will generate a megaton of publicity. All we have to do is attach the *Fireheart* name and the performance dates to your image and get the photos into the right publications. *Vanity Fair* is happy to publish more photos, and thanks to friends, I've lined up *Interview*, *Rolling Stone*, *Advocate*, and *Entertainment Weekly*, for a start."

Jule's brows drew together. "Why don't we have Lucas and Charlotte in the photos as well?"

"There will be plenty of photos of all the cast members, but we have to take advantage of the fact that you're an item of interest at the moment."

"It makes me seem a bit up myself, though."

"You're worried that people will think you're conceited?"

Jule nodded.

"Darling, you can't worry about whether people think you're conceited or weird or gay. You need to craft an image. Look at it as just another part of the job, which is getting attention for the ballet. Try and see it as a tool."

"I just know it's going to be horribly embarrassing," Jule said.

"Can I tag along?" Lucas asked.

"No way!" and "Please do," came out of Jule's and Jezza's mouths simultaneously.

After a brief silence, Jezza spoke. "We need to do it yesterday, if the publicity is to be of any use. We have slightly more than a week to get this snowball rolling. If we work our bums off, I'm confident we can build a blizzard of interest by the time *Fireheart* debuts."

Lucas nudged Jule's shoulder. "Go on," he said and winked. "I'll guide you through it."

Jule chuckled. "All right. I'll do it. Just promise not to make me look too ridiculous."

"Now how would I manage that?" Jezza patted Jule's cheek. "Are you available later today? I'd like to take some shots in natural lighting. How about tonight? Tomorrow?"

Jule glanced at Lucas. "Tomorrow?" he said hesitantly.

Lucas sighed. "If we must."

"I know tomorrow is supposed to be a rest day," Jezza said apologetically. "We can get the photography done in a few hours, and then you can take off while my team does the rest."

"That sounds so cool," Jule said. "*My team.*"

"You'll meet a couple of them tomorrow. It *will* be fun. I promise."

"Are they doing this as a favor to you?" Jule asked.

"No, my darling." Jezza showed his teeth in a smile. "I pay them. I consider it an investment. Don't fret for me. I'll end up with a tidy sum. As will you. The company, I mean, but also you personally."

"I wouldn't turn it down," Jule said. "What time do you want to do this?"

"As early as possible. First light and last light are the best lights."

"So sixish. Where?"

"I will text you the address after I speak with my cohorts." Jezza smiled again. "It won't be awful. It will be somewhat tedious and probably embarrassing for you, but we always make a party of it. So, there's that."

"I won't let him back out," Lucas told Jezza. "If we're done here, we should get to work."

"Right." Jule followed Lucas over to where Bram was talking with Charlotte.

"Ready to practice David's phoenix coda?" Lucas said brightly.

"Yes, I'm ready to lie on the floor and pretend I'm dead," Jule replied.

"And I'm ready to hold you in my arms while you pretend to be dead and Bram prances around us." Lucas winked at Bram.

"I guess I'm ready to prance, then," Bram said. "I might even flounce a little."

Charlotte laughed. "And I am ready to be the backdrop for the tragic tableau making sure to frame Lucas's head with my boobs."

"Splendiferous!" Lucas exclaimed. "Let's get at it."

Dominic Jacobs walked into the chic Aviary cocktail lounge at the Mandarin Oriental and spotted David across the room.

"Dom! Good to see you." David rose to shake his hand. "I hope you don't mind meeting here. I thought it was convenient for both of us."

Dom looked around as he sat opposite David. "I love the Aviary. They have those cute ice cubes that come in different shapes."

"Good. Good. I'm excited to talk about the details of our agreement."

The server arrived and took Dom's order.

"I'm excited as well," Dom said. "I miss your company, to be honest. You could turn any occasion into a party by walking in the room."

David made a self-deprecating gesture. "I miss the old days too… sometimes. But mostly, I'm too excited by the present to dwell on it."

Dom's cucumber lemongrass martini arrived, and he took a sip before he spoke again. "I can see how excited you are about this ballet. I'm excited about hosting it at the Koch. But, of course, there are always fiddly details to iron out."

"I have the money."

An expression of mild distaste warped Dom's aquiline features briefly. "Good, but that's not what we're here to talk about today."

"I'm all ears." David sat back and took a sip of his bourbon sidecar.

"As I said, I'm very excited to bring your ballet to an audience. The board has just a few concerns that they want me to put in front of you."

"I thought they might." David gave him a slight smile.

"They aren't concerned about the content. There are no bigots on the board. The issue is a much more practical one. Your principal danseur recently injured himself."

David nodded.

"We aren't certain he's ready to perform yet. If he were to reinjure himself on our stage, we'd not only be held liable, but our reputation would suffer. Our judgment would surely be called into question, if lawyers were involved."

"You're afraid we'll sue you?" David's lip curled. "So, it is about money after all."

"There's no need for that tone."

"Isn't there? Does it occur to you that you just called *my* judgment into question?"

Dom cleared his throat. "Well… you aren't known for your cool-headed decision-making abilities, are you?"

David took a deep breath. "No, I'm not. I'm known for being a brilliant dancer, choreographer, and lover."

Dom nodded. "Indeed. Here is where we stand. You will have access to the stage, dressing rooms, and studios. You're guaranteed a run of no less than seven days. The board may decide to offer you a second week. You are expected to deliver a complete ballet to be called *Fireheart*. The principal roles will be danced by Julian Parry and Abraham Silber or other danseurs of their caliber. Do you agree to our terms?"

"Not just no but hell no." David stood up. "I will sign anything you like saying I won't hold you liable, but this is bullshit, and you know it, Dom."

"This wasn't my decision. Would you sit, please? People will think I'm breaking up with you."

David sank into his chair as if he was deflating. "Why?" he asked simply.

"I don't pretend to understand how the board makes decisions."

"Lucas is ready. I swear to you. If you need to hear it, I swear no one associated with me will sue you."

"I believe you, but those are the terms."

"I wrote this ballet to be danced by Lucas Madding and Julian Parry. No one else is going to dance it for the first time. I don't care if I have to put this show on in the middle of the street. It's Lucas and Jule, or it doesn't happen."

"Then it doesn't happen." Dom's eyes were sad when he met David's gaze. "If there were something I could do, I'd do it. From what you've shown me, it's a wonderful ballet."

"I happen to agree, but it's not just *my* ballet. It belongs to Jule and Lucas too."

"Please reconsider."

"There's nothing to consider. If you had any balls, you'd admit you never intended to let us use the space."

"That's an outrageous accusation."

"It's the truth. I can see what's happening, and I know who's behind it, but if you go along with it, you're just as bad."

"Surely, you don't think I—"

"No, I don't think you're part of it. You're just a tool to her."

"I've no idea what you mean by that, but I can see how passionate you are about the matter. Perhaps a bit too passionate?"

David leaned forward. "I sold my house to finance this, that's how committed I am, and I'm absolutely sure I don't want this ballet performed by anyone else. Final word." He stood. "I'll take care of the bill."

"David, be reasonable," Dom called out as David went to the bar to settle his tab.

"Boyfriend trouble?" the server said.

"Yeah." David signed the bill. "You think you could manage to spill something on him?"

"What's my reward?"

"Name your price."

"Just put your phone number next to your name and we'll call it square."

David wrote down his number. "*Merci*," he said as he walked away. The door hadn't quite closed behind him when he heard Dom shout in surprise and the clatter of a tray hitting the floor. Despite the recent setback, he was smiling as he joined the moving crowds on the sidewalk.

Chapter Twenty-Seven

LUCAS CROWDED Jule through the apartment doorway ahead of him and wrapped his arms around him from behind as soon as they were inside. "I've been thinking about this for the last hour," he purred in Jule's ear.

Jule let some of his weight rest on Lucas, relaxing as Lucas's lips traversed the sensitive skin of his earlobe, the hollow at the hinge of his jaw, the nape of his neck. "You're really good at this," he said.

"I'm sorry. Could you repeat that? I didn't quite catch it."

Jule laughed softly. "You're a sex-master, Lucas Madding, in case no one told you."

Lucas let Jule feel his teeth. "As long as *you* like what I'm doing…."

Jule shivered in reaction. "Mate, are you joking? If you let go of me, I'll fall down. It's insane."

Lucas paused. He turned Jule in his arms to face him. "Insane? As in insanely good?"

"More like scary."

"I don't want it to be scary. I want it to be mind-blowing."

"It's definitely that. Do we have to talk about it now?"

Lucas took Jule's mouth in a sweet kiss. "We don't have to talk at all," he said when he drew back. "But I feel like I have to mention that you took to it like a duck to water."

"It's like you have this weird power over my body. I've told you this more than once."

"Nah, it's just that you were so inexperienced, but please, tell me again."

"You're truly an evil man, you know that."

Lucas gave Jule a wicked grin. "I know you love it."

"I do. I really do." Jule went up on his toes to kiss Lucas.

"I love you so much right now." Abruptly, Lucas lifted Jule off his feet and hugged him tightly.

Jule braced a hand on Lucas's forearm and hooked the other around his neck. He bent his head and covered Lucas's lips with his in a slow, deep kiss that went on for some time.

"You're getting really good at that," Lucas said. "So, what's your pleasure this evening? Want to try something new?"

"There is no try. Do or do not," Jule quoted.

Lucas faked an orgasmic groan.

"Trouble with your droid?" Jule flexed his buttcheeks, thrusting his crotch against Lucas.

"You get me so hot," Lucas said as he kneaded the firm muscles of Jule's ass. "I want to fuck you through the mattress."

"Is it that good?"

Lucas frowned when Jule lowered himself to his feet. "I don't follow. I thought we were done talking and well on our way to another night of incredible sex."

"Sorry."

"Hey, no, don't be sorry. You should speak up if you aren't comfortable with something."

Jule looked at the floor. "You're a good boyfriend."

"Good to know, because that's what I'm trying to be and feedback is always welcome, but what's going on?"

"I really ruined the mood."

"I don't care, and let's be real. We're talking about you and me. One kiss and we'll be back where we were. Spontaneous combustion is not a myth."

"Well, that's true enough."

"So, what was the question?"

"Was it really that good for you when you, you know, put your willie in me?"

"Jeez, I thought it would be obvious from my reactions and the way I came like a freight train with no brakes." Lucas paused. "Wait a second. You've never done it, have you? Of course, you haven't. What am I saying? You were the virginest virgin that ever virgined when I met you."

Jule shrugged. "I can hardly deny it."

"And it's no longer true. You've changed a lot since you came to New York."

"Not really."

"Come on. You're way sassier."

"That's because I know you now."

"Makes sense. Why don't we get out of the foyer?" Lucas led Jule to the bedroom. "You want a drink or something?"

Jule smiled. "What does the *or something* include?"

"Everything from chocolate cake to my dick with a ribbon on it."

"Could I have both those things at the same time?"

"And I thought I couldn't love you any more than I already did." Lucas smiled at Jule. "But back to the main subject. We've done a lot of stuff sexwise, but there's still a lot more to explore."

"Like what?"

Lucas reached out and cupped his hand around the back of Jule's neck. "How would you like to fuck me?"

"I don't know if I'd like it, but I want to try it."

"Man, you are hands down the most honest person I've ever met."

"Does it turn you on, baby? Does it make you horny?"

Lucas laughed. "Never do Austin Powers impressions when we're getting busy. It gives me such a soft-on."

Jule cracked up.

"And now we're having fun again. Yay," Lucas said. "Why don't you get undressed and I'll be right back?" Without waiting for an answer, he went to the bathroom.

When Lucas returned sans clothing, Jule was sitting on the bed looking at his phone. "Porn?" Lucas said.

Jule put the phone away quickly. "Research," he said.

"Why aren't you naked?" Lucas asked.

"I don't know."

Lucas sat next to Jule and put his arms around him. "What's up, pup?"

"It's so stupid, but I'm really nervous about this."

"Wow, that *is* stupid."

Jule turned to stare at Lucas and saw the glint of humor in his eyes. "Sorry. I really am nervous."

"Believe me, kid, you're not going fuck it up."

"How do you know that?"

"I've seen you move on a dance floor. Anyone who can do *that* with his hips is going to be a natural at fucking." Lucas smiled. "But you really are going to have to take some clothes off."

Jule framed Lucas's face with his hands on Lucas's cheeks. He looked into Lucas's eyes. "I want to do this," he said before he claimed Lucas's mouth in a fierce kiss.

Lucas let himself fall onto the mattress and took Jule with him. He rolled onto his back and wrapped his legs around Jule's legs. As he ran his hands down Jule's back, he looked up to meet Jule's gaze. For a couple of heartbeats, Jule lay atop Lucas, crotch to crotch.

"Seriously," Lucas said. "Take the pants off."

An unforced laugh bubbled up in Jule's throat. He rose to his knees, unzipped his jeans, and shoved them down as far as they would go.

"Now you're talkin'," Lucas said.

"You're sure you want to do this?"

"Pretty sure it was my idea, rookie. Now, are we gonna talk, or are we gonna rock?"

"I—" Jule paused. "What should I do first?"

"Well, I thought about getting ready for you while I was in the bathroom, but then I thought, you being you, you'd want to do everything."

Jule nodded.

Lucas handed him the lube. "It's okay to ask questions," he said.

"I've got it now. After all, I was paying attention when you did this to me."

"Well, all right, then. I'll just lie back and enjoy it." Lucas smiled warmly.

"Would you? That would be awesome."

Jule remembered everything Lucas had done to prepare him for penetration, and he followed each step with scrupulous care.

"Jeez," Lucas said breathlessly. "If you keep that up, I'm gonna come any second."

Jule slowly slipped two fingers out of Lucas's sheath and left off stroking his cock. "Sorry. I got a little lost there."

"Nothing to be sorry about. I'd just rather come with you inside me."

Jule closed his eyes for a second and then opened them again. "I feel so—" He swallowed. "I love you, you know?"

"Same."

Jule chuckled. "You always know what to say."

"Thanks, but less talking, okay?"

Jule chuckled again to cover his nervousness. He was about to do something he'd never done but had thought about often enough. What if he did it wrong? What if he got too excited and shot off too soon? What if it wasn't everything he'd imagined?

"I'm cooling off here," Lucas broke into Jule's thoughts.

Jule shifted to a better position and took hold of his condom-sheathed cock. He was so focused on the target that he flinched when Lucas raised a leg to rest on his shoulder. He quickly realized how much easier it made things for him and smiled at his lover before his gaze returned to Lucas's glistening port. The head of his shaft bumped the small opening and warmth flooded his body. Of their own volition, his hips snapped forward and the tip of his cock popped through the tight ring of muscle. He froze.

"Sorry, I didn't mean to be so—"

"It's fine. Less talking, more fucking, okay?"

Jule eased into Lucas as slowly as possible. "God," he said in a shaky voice. "I didn't know—" He took a breath. "I didn't know anything could feel this good."

"It's been a while since I bottomed." Lucas tightened his interior muscles, relaxed, and then clamped down again. "But it's all coming back to me."

Jule gasped at the delicious sensation. "Bloody hell" was the last coherent thing he said for several moments.

He found a rhythm timed to the clenching of the channel that hugged his cock so sweetly. He'd been moving to a beat most of his life and had no trouble maintaining a steady stroke, at least for as long as he lasted. The physical sensations were overwhelming, and the visuals ratcheted his excitement up another notch each time he watched his shaft slide into Lucas. He felt connected in more than a physical way; he felt as though he was touching Lucas's essence and it elevated his excitement. Jule reached the point where he knew he couldn't hold off his orgasm another second. He looked up and met Lucas's gaze, melting in the heat of his need.

"I can't—" Jule managed to say before he came like Christmas morning. He clutched at Lucas's thighs, fingertips dimpling hard muscles as his release exploded at his core, filling him with warmth as he filled Lucas's sheath in three strong bursts. He could hear the panting sounds of his breath over the thunder of his heart as the wonderful feeling spread throughout his body.

"C'mere," Lucas murmured as he held out his arms.

"Wait," Jule said weakly. "Just a second."

By centimeters, Jule withdrew and crawled into Lucas's embrace. He rested there, completely enervated for the moment, listening to the steady-as-the-surf sound of Lucas's heartbeat.

"You can keep wearing it if you want, but most people get rid of the rubber at this point," Lucas said softly.

"What do I do with it?"

"Wrap it in a tissue and toss it in the trash."

After getting rid of the condom, Jule let his hand drift down to Lucas's crotch. He drank in the small sounds of Lucas's pleasure as he shuttled his fist on Lucas's cock. He felt like a silver bell struck by a golden hammer, reverberating with bliss that echoed throughout his body and soul. Never again would he doubt that this man was his mate. No matter what else happened, he would not give Lucas up for fame or money, and no, not for family either.

Jule felt Lucas's shaft swell in his hand and pushed his tongue into Lucas's mouth. He swallowed Lucas's groan of release as his heart swelled with love and pride.

"Kill me now," Lucas said as he broke the marathon kiss. "It doesn't get much better than this."

"Hold my beer," Jule murmured.

Lucas's startled laugh was loud in the tranquil aftermath of sex. "Who taught you that?"

"You taught me to jerk a guy off. Charlotte taught me 'hold my beer.'"

Lucas wrapped his arms around Jule and held him close. "I'm not sure I deserve you, but I'm grateful that you're mine."

Jule met Lucas's gaze. "I *am* yours," he said. "I hope you never regret it."

Lucas shook his head. "I can't see the future, but one thing I'm sure of, you're my kryptonite."

Jule smiled as he remembered thinking the same thing about Lucas. "But am I red or green kryptonite?"

"You're both, obviously. The source of my greatest strength *and* my greatest weakness."

"Wouldn't they cancel each—?"

"Shhh...." Lucas's covered Jule's lips with his and there was no more talking for a while.

"We have to stop," Jule said a few minutes later. "You know I live for two things: dancing and snogging you, but I should get going."

"Why don't you sleep here?"

"Because I need some actual sleep." Jule kissed Lucas's forehead. "Being on a bed, or any horizontal surface, with you is not conducive to rest."

"That's true." Lucas gave Jule a hug. "See you tomorrow."

Having remembered to ask for a key, Jule let himself into David's townhouse a little before midnight. He walked soft footed to the stairs, but the sound of someone clearing their throat stopped him.

"Hello, *mon etoile*. Have a drink with me?"

Jule had never heard David sound so weary. He dropped his shoes where they wouldn't be tripped over and joined him in the living room.

David was sitting on the floor in front of the fire with a scrapbook on his knees. He wore one of his silk dressing gowns, and a bottle of Remy Martin sat close to hand.

"Grab a glass." David lifted the bottle and drank from it.

Jule poured sparkling water into a glass and returned to the fire.

"I assume you were out with Lucas."

"More like I was in with Lucas. We just watched a movie at his place."

"How much of it did you see?"

"How much have you had to drink?"

"Oh, was I ina—inappro—inapprociate?"

"Definitely inapprociate."

David smiled wistfully. "You sound so much like him sometimes."

"I'm sorry?"

"Kelly. You sound just like him."

"Oh. Well, I suppose that's to be expected, since he trained me."

"He certainly did."

"I don't understand your tone."

"It's probably this brandy." David took another drink straight from the bottle. "But... it might also be my incompatible feelings about him."

Jule sipped his water and stayed quiet, hoping David would say more about Kelly's past.

David turned his gaze on Jule. "Look at you," he said softly. "As perfect as anything I've ever seen, sitting there on my chair drinking from my glass, completely indifferent to me. This must be my punishment visited upon me."

"I'm hardly indifferent." Jule paused. "What are you being punished for?"

"What?" David blinked. "Oh, I was just being dramatic. You know me."

"I'd like to," Jule said candidly. "But you don't make it easy. You seem so open, but…."

"Mr. Pot meet Mr. Kettle," David replied.

"Am I like that?"

David nodded. "At first glance, you're a shy, naïve boy, but you have a lot of… compartments." He paused. "Just like Kelly. He showed up on the first day of tryouts looking like every queen's dream of a strapping, corn-fed country boy in the big city. He had the bluest eyes."

"He still does."

"Yeah." David sighed. "So strange to see him again, to talk to him like nothing ever happened." His voice trailed off.

Jule waited for a few minutes, but David didn't speak. He started to stand up and say he was going to bed. He was exhausted and wanted to be alone to relive the night with Lucas as he fell asleep.

"We're fucked," David said abruptly.

"Excuse me?" Jule dropped back into the chair.

"We lost the venue."

"What? How? When?"

"The board wanted me to replace Lucas with Bram. I said no. They said take a hike."

"No."

"It's true, though, and I see Catherine's not-so-subtle hand in it. Director Halvorsen is an old friend of her family." David raised the bottle "Sure you don't want a drink?"

"I'm sure. It's time to think, not drink."

"Oh, well then, don't I feel like a fool."

"You're not a fool. You're foolish sometimes, but you're mostly brilliant."

"You really think so?"

"If I didn't, I'd join another company."

"Your honesty is breathtaking sometimes." David sat up. "I was just having a glory days moment." He tapped a photograph with his forefinger. "That's me and Marjorie Langham dancing Romeo and Juliet."

Jule knelt to look over David's shoulder. "Gorgeous," he said.

"She was my perfect partner, but she retired young. She really wanted kids. Married a Frenchman and lives happily in Bordeaux."

"How many kids?"

"I don't know. I sort of... deleted her from my life when she retired."

Jule sipped his water while he tried to think of a reply. He was trying to imagine shutting out someone he'd loved and abruptly realized he'd been doing that to Lucas when they broke up. He was so used to blocking out his father, but he didn't have to keep doing it.

"I'm probably boring you," David said.

"No, of course not. It's just that I have to be somewhere at six."

"Then you should go to sleep."

"Will you be okay if I go to bed?"

"I'll be fine. I'm a grown-ass man."

"No falling into the fireplace, right?"

"Not even a little bit." David looked up. "You're right. I should go to bed. Give me a hand?"

Jule pulled David to his feet, put David's arm around his shoulders and helped him navigate the stairs.

"I can take it from here," David said at his bedroom door. "Get some sleep."

"You sure?"

"*Je suis sûr*. We'll talk in the morning."

"Don't forget I'm meeting Mr. Belanger at six."

"Barbaric. I'll see you...." David looked confused for a moment and then his eyes went liquid. "I don't know when or where I'll see you. I gave up that rat-trap studio, and I lost the venue, plus I sold this place, so in two weeks, we'll have to find somewhere else to live. I'll help you, of course."

Jule didn't let his dismay show when he answered. "I can probably stay with Lucas."

"How did I know you were going to say that?"

"Because you're brilliant."

"Oh, am I?" David said archly. He fluttered his extravagant lashes as he leaned against the door in a provocative pose.

Jule caught David's wrist and kept him from falling on his ass.

David threw an arm around Jule, and Jule walked him to his bed.

"Thank you for the assist. Much appreciated. Now seriously, go to bed. That's what I'm going to do." David got under the covers. "Please turn off the light."

Jule turned off the light and went down the hall to the guest room. After looking at his modest wardrobe, he decided to wear his most comfortable warmup clothes to meet Jezza. While he was brushing his teeth, he remembered a moment from his evening with Lucas and a smile spread over his face. He caught sight of himself in the mirror with foam dripping from his mouth. He spat into the sink.

"Oh yes, you're a real sex symbol, you are," he said before rinsing his mouth.

He was still smiling when he got into bed. He wondered if making love was this good for everybody or if Lucas was simply an amazing lover. Jerking off made him feel good, but it wasn't the explosion of all-consuming pleasure that Lucas triggered in him. That was beyond—

Jule stopped his train of thought. If he kept thinking about Lucas, he'd get aroused again. He supposed it was normal, but it was irritating that he couldn't control himself better. He tried thinking about other things he enjoyed doing with Lucas. Clearing his mind was harder than it used to be, but he managed it. He fell asleep and didn't wake until his alarm went off.

JULE HAD just finished getting into his warmup clothes when his phone chimed. "Hi, Lucas."

"Get your fine ass out here. It's fucking cold."

"You could come in."

"Negative. Let's go, rookie."

Jule shoved his arms into his parka and jammed his feet into his snow boots in the front hall. He pulled his hat and gloves from his pockets and put them on as he joined Lucas at the curb. One cab, one subway ride, and another cab later, they arrived at their destination.

Four hours later, Jezza declared he had enough photos and dismissed the small staff. Jule changed back into his own clothes while Lucas watched with undisguised interest.

"Can I have one more moment of your time, Jule?" Jezza called out.

"Of course," Jule said reluctantly.

"Thanks for being such a good subject," Jezza said. "I'll have some proofs to look at tomorrow."

"Cool," Jule said.

"I thought you might like to see this one. I took it during one of the breaks at our photoshoot."

Lucas and Jule gazed at a photo of Lucas tucking a red carnation into Jule's hair.

"That's… beautiful," Lucas said. "I definitely want to see more, but I need to get this boy some food before he starts gnawing on my leg."

"I suppose I should be thankful he didn't say third leg," Jule said. He put his parka on over the hoodie and went with Lucas to the elevator. It was cold but clear when they walked out onto the sidewalk, so they walked for a while for the pure pleasure of it.

"How much farther to Times Square?" Jule asked as they waited for a light to change.

"About nine blocks, I think."

"I really like walking, but I'm also hungry."

"Let's grab a cab, then."

The taxi let them out one street over from Junior's restaurant. After they ate, they went out and made a right and a left into Times Square. It was cold, but the sun was out, so the area teemed with people, both local and tourist. At the edges, vendors had set up carts that offered everything from food to pashmina shawls to caricatures drawn in three minutes.

"I know I just ate, but those nuts smell great," Jule said.

"You can't possibly smell them through my pants and underwear." Lucas paused with a thoughtful expression on his face. "Unless you have superpowers." He gave Jules a sharp look. "*Do* you have superpowers?"

"Only one."

"I must know what it is."

"Being the adult in our relationship."

Lucas laughed and then hooked his arm through Jule's. "Come on. Let's go across the street to one of those cheesy souvenir stores."

"Why?"

"So, I can buy you a suitably cheesy memento."

Several minutes later, Jule and Lucas made their way out of the store through the sets of luggage near the door that seemed designed to slow down invaders. His protests ignored, Jule carried a plastic shopping bag that contained a pair of boxers with the words Big Apple superimposed on a graphic of a bright red apple silk-screened across the butt.

"I'll not wear them," Jule said. He sniffed the air and then shoved the bag at Lucas. "I'm going to get some of those roasted nuts."

"These are fantastic!" Jule said when he returned to Lucas.

"I've had them once or twice before, and you're right, they are fantastic. But honestly? I'd rather watch you eat them."

"That makes no sense." Jule took the shopping bag back from Lucas.

Lucas assumed a look of patent sincerity as he gazed into Jule's eyes. "Love means never having to make sense."

Jule shook his head. "I'm in love with a loon," he said under his breath.

"Excuse me?" Lucas cupped his hands behind his ears. "I didn't quite hear that."

"It's just an expression."

"Yeah, it sure is." Lucas grinned and pulled Jule into hug, unmindful of the fact that they were on a crowded street. "I don't care if you were being sarcastic, I'll take it."

"Hey, douchebags," someone said loudly. "You're blocking the sidewalk."

Lucas let go of Jule but took his hand as they started walking again. "At least he didn't call us faggots," Lucas said. "So, not a hater."

"No, he seemed mainly concerned with the safety of other pedestrians."

Lucas and Jule looked at one another and burst into laughter.

"I love you so much right now," Lucas said.

"I'd love it if we weren't in public right now."

"Home?"

"Yes, please. I'm in the mood to suck you off."

Lucas's hand shot up and a cab pulled to the curb like a bright yellow deus ex machina.

Chapter Twenty-Eight

JULE WOKE from a delicious post-orgasm nap and his hand went out for the phone on the night table. He looked at the time, put the phone down, and stretched thoroughly and methodically.

"I could watch you do that all day," Lucas said.

"It's nearly eight."

"And you're, let me guess, famished?"

"Mate, I'm close to passing out."

"Of course you are." Lucas sat up. "Okay. Go get a snack while I get dressed, and we'll go out."

Jule gathered his clothing and dressed while walking to the kitchen area.

"Pure talent," Lucas marveled as he got out of bed. "Hey," he called out. "Want to shower with me?"

Jule turned toward Lucas with an apple in his mouth.

Lucas grinned. "Okay then. You know where to find me."

Lucas was rinsing off when the glass door of the large shower slid open. He moved aside as Jule stepped in and then turned on the second showerhead. He squirted liquid soap on the loofah and drew it across Jule's chest.

Jule grabbed the loofah from Lucas's hand. "Not now," he said firmly. "If you want to take another shower after dinner, we can play all the water sports you like."

"Uh, don't say that to anyone but me, okay? It has a pretty specific sexual meaning."

Jule raised an eyebrow at Lucas.

"It involves pissing, get it?"

"Really?" Jule finished soaping up and moved under spray to rinse off.

"'Fraid so."

"Whatever, I guess. I'm finished here," Jule said. "Are you staying in the shower?"

"Uh, no." Lucas turned off the water and stepped out of the glass-walled booth behind Jule.

Jule went to the shelving where he kept most of his small wardrobe. He pulled on a clean pair of dark jeans and a white T-shirt. He got out the tweed sport coat his mother had given him and which he loved for the leather patches on the elbows. He put it on, and then he sat to lace up his shoes.

"I wonder what David's doing," he said.

"Probably searching madly for another venue."

"Why don't we invite him to dinner?"

"Because I don't want him there?"

Jule's mouth fell open. "Come on. He probably feels awful right now."

"I doubt being with us would cheer him up."

"Are you about to say something outrageous?"

Lucas slid his arms into a leather jacket. "I'm about to tell you something unpleasant. Do you want to hear it or not?"

"If you're going to tell me again how David has designs on me—"

"No, it's much worse than that." Lucas shook his head.

"Tell me."

"It's me. I don't think I can control my jealousy for an entire evening."

"Rubbish."

"No, it's true. As much as I love David, I know who he is. The man has many, many fine qualities, but sometimes his ego gets the best of him."

Jule took his parka off the coatrack by the door. "Did you sleep with him?"

"No. He asked. I said no. That was that."

"Good."

"So, you get my point?"

"If your point is that David likes having sex with attractive people younger than him, then I don't know what to say, other than the sky is blue."

"But you understand that it's not right, right?"

"Is it just because he's older? He doesn't, you know, force himself on anyone, does he? Isn't that, I don't know, ageism or something?"

"Not when he's the boss. Get it?"

Jule frowned.

"When I think about how conditioned you are to follow instructions…."

"What?"

"You know, it just makes it easy for someone older or more experienced to take advantage of you."

"Okay, I understand what you're saying, but I already let David know how very not interested I am. And I believe him when he says he'll behave himself." Jule paused. "I wouldn't want you to be uncomfortable at dinner, though."

Lucas rolled his eyes. "You're getting pretty darned good at manipulating me. Okay, then. Call him and see if he wants to ruin my dinner."

Jule smiled. "You're a good man, Madding. I'll make it up to you." He took out his phone and called David.

A half hour later, David met Jule and Lucas at the LeGrande Lounge on the mezzanine at the Time hotel. The lights were dim, but that didn't detract from the sleek, modern décor.

"Cozy," David said as he sat. He looked at the glass in front of him. "A martini? For me?"

"I took the liberty." Lucas raised his martini. "Cheers," he said before he drank.

Jule picked up his water and took a sip.

"Thanks for inviting me," David said after their server had taken their orders. "I was having a bad day and a worse evening."

"We don't have to talk business if you don't want to," Jule said, though he was anxious to hear any news.

"I don't have a venue yet, which is a real problem." David sighed. "At least I don't have to be out of my house for another week. You know, with the money I made, I could almost build my own theater."

"Surely you can rent one," Lucas said.

"I've been talking to people all day. I don't know how Catherine does it. It's inexpressibly tedious." David finger-combed his hair back from his face. "Everything is booked."

"*Everything*? That's hard to believe."

"Here's the thing," David said. "Everyone is *telling* me their space is booked, whether it is or not. A lot of people owe Catherine favors, and she's made it her mission to block this ballet."

"Why is she being so mean to you?" Jule asked. "I thought she liked you."

"Oh, she does," Lucas said. "But she wants something David can't give her."

"That's quite enough of that," David said. "Let's talk about something fun."

"Jule learned how to deep throat yesterday," Lucas said. "I'm so proud."

Jule punched him on the arm—hard.

"Ow!" Lucas gave Jule a reproachful look. "Was I lying?"

David snorted. "Luc, could you try being a decent human for five minutes?"

"Sounds like a lot of work," Lucas said. He turned to Jule. "And you should be proud too. Not just anybody can handle what I've got to work with."

David snorted again. "I almost begged off when you called, but I'm glad I came. I wasn't sure I was ever going to laugh again."

"Drama queen," Lucas said.

"It's in my job description," David retorted. He gazed at Lucas and Jule for a few moments. "You look like a real couple," he said. "Does this mean you've got past my ill-advised machinations?"

"I thought we were talking about fun stuff," Jule said as the food arrived.

"Well, I'm apologizing, if it means anything to you," David said after the waiter had gone.

"It does," Jule said.

"Sorry, but I gotta say this." Lucas met David's gaze. "I'm not going to say anything stupid like 'act your age.' I just want to know if you know what you did wrong."

"I was deceitful," David answered. "As were you."

"We're not keeping score, but you're right. I lied to Jule. But I owned up and I won't do it again. But we're talking about your problem now."

"Please tell me we're not about to bring up my libido."

"We could talk about you and Catherine instead."

David frowned. "Did you invite me here for an intervention?"

"No, it was a spur-of-the-moment thing, but now that you mention it, why do you feel compelled to seduce every hot young dancer that comes along?"

"I believe I'm a bit more selective than you portray me."

"We're not bantering, David."

"Well," Jule said. "You were right about being uncomfortable."

David immediately turned to Jule. "Did I make you uncomfortable?"

"Um, I feel like you said some things that made it seem like you wanted to sleep with me. Like you were flirting. It was weird because I thought of you like Kelly or someone my dad's age. You know… an adult. Someone I could look to for guidance."

"Do you get it now, David?" Lucas asked.

"I'm David Dulac Downes, Mr. 3-D. People expect me to be larger than life." David's lips twisted as though he'd tasted something bitter. "Christ! Am I a caricature?"

No one answered. After a moment, David began to eat. Not until the meal was over did anyone speak again.

"I'm not happy that I seem to have a reputation as a dirty old man," David said. "I was thrilled when I had a reputation as a cocksman, but the other… not so much. I'll be giving it some deep thought, believe me. Jule, I apologize if I behaved inappropriately."

"Thank you," Jule said softly.

"I mean it," David said. "I think it's actually going to be a relief knowing I don't have to seduce every attractive dancer I see."

"Excuse me for being a little skeptical of your abrupt one-eighty," Lucas said. "Plus, it's a hard habit to break… or so I hear."

"Sad but true." David looked down at his empty plate. "I wasn't planning on it, but now that I'm centered, I think I'll drop in on Charlotte's party. Are you guys going?"

Lucas looked at Jule. Jule shrugged.

"Oh, you're *totally* a couple," David remarked. "Come on. Go with me. We can share a cab. I'll keep my hands to myself. Sorry, bad joke."

"Yeah, it was," Lucas said. "Wow, you sure bounce back fast."

"Oh, sorry, am I supposed to be devastated?"

"God, you're maddening." Lucas gritted his teeth. "Do you take anything seriously?"

David sobered instantly. "Look, you broadsided me. Actually, it was more of an ambush. I've always thought that you and I were on the same page about this."

"How?"

"Well, you know, the whole being a man thing."

"Being a man doesn't mean sleeping with everyone."

"It used to," David said a bit plaintively.

"Times change."

"And I should change with them?"

Lucas sounded weary when he answered. "Just promise you'll try to do better, okay?"

"I'd like to go to Charlotte's party," Jule said, clearly uncomfortable. David glanced at Lucas.

Lucas shrugged. "He's the boss," he said, nodding toward Jule.

"I hope you didn't think that was a secret," David replied.

"Stop talking rubbish, both of you," Jule said. "We should be thinking of ways to get a theater."

"Yes, we should," David said. "But right now, we're going to a party."

"Yes, we are," Lucas said. "But this discussion is only tabled for now."

"HI, GUYS! Come on in." Charlotte stood aside to let David, Lucas, and Jule in the door. "Welcome to my humble commode. Sorry about the music, but it's Amani's turn to deejay."

David kissed Charlotte's cheek and plowed into the crowd. In another second, he was dancing with several people.

"It hurts to see him so depressed." Charlotte raised a perfect eyebrow.

Jule smiled.

Lucas cleared his throat. "I was kind of hard on him at dinner."

"Tell me everything."

"It was just a few things he needed to hear."

"You could have picked a better time, boy."

"Girl, I had one hundred percent had enough of his sleaze."

"Sleaze?" Charlotte looked shocked.

"You know what I'm talking about."

"David's a hound, for sure," she answered. "But I don't think he's a bad person. Different generation, you know?"

"Hey, if I can change, so can he," Lucas said.

"Easy, I'm on your side," she said. "That whole notches on the bedpost thing should just die."

"You cut your hair," Lucas said to change the subject.

Charlotte patted the tumbled, shoulder-length tresses. "I'll still have to put it up when I practice, but it's a lot easier to take care of." She smiled and ran a hand over Jule's tufted hair. "You've done something different too."

"I styled it," Lucas said. "You like it? I call it JBF."

Charlotte chuckled and gave Lucas a mock-slap on the cheek.

"I don't get it," Jule said.

"I'm sure you will, though." Charlotte winked, and Lucas laughed.

"I'm going to get a drink." Jule walked away from them.

"Hey, boy," Charlotte said softly to Lucas. "I've been missing you."

"Same, girl."

"Think we could get together for a boozy brunch soon?"

Lucas's gaze went automatically to Jule on the other side of the room.

"You can bring your skank," Charlotte said. She paused at his change of expression. "Oopsie. I meant to say that Jule is welcome to come too."

"Nice save. You always land on your feet. It's one of the things I've always loved about you." Lucas cocked his head. "I think of you as a sister, you know."

"We're definitely from the same family."

"Bingo." Lucas smiled, his eyes going to Jule again. "He's something else, isn't he?"

"Bingo," Charlotte said in the same matter-of-fact tone Lucas had used. "I had my doubts at first."

"About?"

"About Mr. Frozen Fire."

"He thawed out just fine."

"I wasn't sure he had the stuff. He dances like a dream, but I wasn't sure he was tough enough."

Lucas watched Jule sip from a tumbler of clear liquid on ice and wanted to run his tongue up the sweet curve of his throat. "He was a naïve kid when he showed up here, but he learns fast, scary fast. I'm not sure I understand him, but I want to."

"What's to understand?"

"He's not quite what he appears to be on the surface."

"Well, duh. Who is? Anyway, no one could be as perfect as he seems."

"Right. Anyway, it doesn't matter. I'm crazy about all of him."

Charlotte looked up at Lucas. "You're well and truly hooked."

"Girl, please."

"Boy, hush. I've never seen you look at anyone the way you look at him. Jesus, you'd think you gave birth to him."

"When I meet his mama, I'm gonna thank her," Lucas replied.

"You do that, but right now, come with me. We need to have a serious talk."

"Right now?" Lucas cast another glance at Jule just as Amani engaged Jule in conversation.

"Yes, now." Charlotte waved a beckoning hand at David and then drew Lucas into her small home office. She waited for David before closing the door and sitting on her desk chair.

Lucas and David sat on the bar stools she'd brought in.

"This isn't awkward at all," Lucas said as he looked down at Charlotte from his perch.

"Just listen for a minute, okay?" Charlotte moistened her lips before she spoke again. "You're going to be mad and that's okay. You should be mad, but honestly, I only did it to get ahead. There was nothing personal in it."

"In what?" David asked.

Charlotte didn't drag it out. "I spied on you for Catherine, and you know, kept her informed."

"Fuck!" David exclaimed. "That explains how she kept showing up at dramatic moments."

"I'm sorry. All I really did was feed her information, but it turns out she used it to hurt you. Not to mention she didn't keep her promise to me."

"Why are you confessing now?" Lucas asked. "No one would ever have known. Hell, I didn't even suspect."

"I'm telling you because I'm sick of feeling like a piece of shit," Charlotte rolled her eyes. "I was jealous of Jule because it felt like he was getting all of David's attention. And I'm sick of *her* shit. She walks around like the Queen of Goddam Everything and fucks people over for fun. She needs to learn she can't have her way every time."

Lucas hesitated for a moment and then held out his fist for Charlotte to bump. "I'm in, girl," he said. "And I understand why you did it."

David opened his mouth, closed it, and then opened it again. "So, what do you have in mind?"

"Just a second." Charlotte went to the door and called out, "Bram, you can come in now."

JULE FROWNED as he watched Bram walk through the door Lucas had disappeared behind.

"Uh-oh," Amani said. "What happened to your smile?"

"Nothing." Jule smiled at her. "See? Still working."

"I'll say." She winked at him. "Tell you what. If you ever get curious enough about girls to do something about it, come see me."

"I *know* I'm blushing now."

"It's adorable."

"I'd rather be a hottie, but I get so flustered when anyone flirts."

"Speaking of that, Lucas is so heckin' hot!" Amani said. "Are you really hittin' that?"

"Is it so hard to believe?"

Amani laughed. "Yeah, a little, but I think it's awesome. He's so funny and so smokin' hot, and you're so serious and cute."

"Lucas thinks I'm hot," Jule said, thinking he was getting pretty good at banter.

"Duh." She sipped her grapefruit juice. "That look he gave you before he left with Char...." She shook her head, tossing her cloud of hair. "I'd say you're in for a very good night 'cause that man is ready to love you up right here and now."

"Am I blushing again?"

"Just a little." Amani smiled.

"By the way, what's JBF?"

Amani laughed. "The letters stand for *just been fucked*." She took his hand. "Come on. Let's go see what Jezza and Jamison are talking about."

Jule let her lead him over to a small group standing by a sliding glass door. Through the glass, he could see the ever-burning lights of the city.

"Hello, my darlings!" Jezza said as Jule and Amani joined the group. He kissed Jule's cheek. "I'm not playing favorites. I kissed Amani earlier." He grinned. "Wait until you see the photos! I even impressed myself."

"You have photos?" Amani said. "Are they here?"

"Well... yes. Would you like to see a sample?"

"Are you high?"

"That's a yes, then," Jezza said. "Follow me, darlings."

"Where you headed?" Lucas asked as he joined the group.

"Jezza has something to show us." Amani grinned wickedly at Lucas.

"I'm all kinds of intrigued," Lucas said.

Jezza set a large portfolio on Charlotte's dining table and unzipped the case. "Stand back, please. I'd rather you see only the photos I choose. This is my favorite." He placed an eight-by-eleven print on the table.

"Have mercy!" Amani pretended to fan herself.

"I didn't know I could look like that," Jule said.

"I did," Lucas whispered in Jule's ear.

"Do you remember?" Jezza said. "This is the photo where I asked you to pretend you were alone with Luc."

The palette of the photo was black and white except for the suggestion of warm skin tones and the bright splash of red from the carnation tucked into Jule's hair. He was looking straight into the lens, eyes drowsy, lips softly parted, a comma of dark red hair falling over his forehead.

"The camera really likes you," Jamison told Jule.

"The camera wants to have his babies," Amani said. "Oops, was that out loud?"

"You're all daft," Jule said, leaning back against Lucas. "I look like a dozy cow."

Bram came over to see what everyone was looking at. "Whoa!" He picked the photo up, batting away Jezza's hand as he held it up. "*This* is the poster for *Fireheart*," he declared.

"I concur," David said from behind Charlotte. "I wanted a piece of art of two men dancing, but this… yeah. This is the face of my ballet. Longing, desire, and—"

"Needing a nap," Jule said. He was pleased when the group laughed. He was getting more personal attention than he was comfortable with, but he was determined to *get* comfortable with it. He was thankful for Lucas's solid presence at his back, though.

"You can laugh, but it's perfect," David said. "The face of a young man in love."

Lucas kissed the top of Jule's head and received a collective "awwwww" from the group. "Suck it," Lucas said. "He's coming home with me."

"Evil man," Jule said, but he was smiling. "I'm ready to go if you are." Once again, he was gratified when his friends laughed. He supposed he dared call them friends now.

After saying their goodnights, Lucas and Jule left. Before the door closed, they heard David say, "How soon can we get the poster in circulation?"

A FEW hours later, Lucas woke from a brief sleep lying on the fake fur rug in the loft, legs entangled with Jule's. His chest was Jule's pillow; the weight across his midsection was Jule's left arm. *His* left arm was under Jule and still asleep. He didn't care about the pins-and-needles to come. He was so happy that he had the urge to call someone and tell them about it. However, he couldn't think of a single person. He felt sorry for himself for about two seconds.

Gingerly, Lucas pulled his arm from under Jule and propped himself on his side. Oh so gently, he ran the palm of his hand down Jule's back to the perfect hemispheres of his ass. He loved the sweet curve at the small of his lover's back where his hand fit perfectly, whether they were dancing or making love.

"What's the time?" Jule mumbled.

"It's no time at all. Go back to sleep."

Jule snuggled in a little closer. "Love the way you smell."

Lucas continued to stroke Jule's back. "Same," he said.

"Tell me what you're thinking about, and then I'll go to sleep."

Lucas was startled. There *was* something he needed to tell Jule, but he'd decided to wait until morning. No point in ruining great sex.

"What did you and David and Charlotte and Bram talk about?" Jule asked.

"I was going to tell you tomorrow anyway." Lucas shifted. "Why don't we move this to the bed? The floor's getting kind of hard."

Jule got to his feet, took a wobbly step, and stopped. "Mate, I think you might have shagged me silly," he joked.

Lucas laughed and swept him up in a fireman's carry. He walked across the loft and dropped him on the bed like a basket of laundry. He looked down at Jule sprawled across the sheets. "I guess I'll just have to fuck you back to your senses, then."

"In a minute." Jule sat up and patted the mattress beside him.

"Oh, right." Lucas looked down at his lap. "Sorry, big fella."

"Just get it over with."

"Isn't that what you said the first time we had sex?"

"No." Jule stared at Lucas. "Stop stalling."

"Okay, here it is. Charlotte confessed that she was spying for Catherine in return for advancement. She was mostly eavesdropping and passing along information. She said after Catherine screwed her over, she realized who her real friends were."

"Good."

"Good? That's all you have to say? You don't want to call her a bitch just once?"

"Not if she's sorry."

"I believe she is."

"Good."

"You know...." Lucas paused.

"What?"

"I just expected you to be a little more, you know, upset."

"Why? It's over, and you forgave her."

"True, but, seriously, I thought there'd be more of a reaction. It's like when you found out I had an ex-wife. You were surprised and hurt, but you were so calm. Almost like you didn't really care."

"I care."

"Okay. I mean, it's good that you aren't overly emotional, but keeping feelings bottled up isn't. That's what leads to panic attacks."

"I feel as though I've said this before, but my entire life is discipline. I've never acted out or been impulsive. Not until you anyway."

"But that's a good thing, right? God knows, you needed to loosen up."

"Is it a good thing, though? I sort of feel as though I lost my way. On the other hand, I feel like this is exactly where I belong."

Lucas took a deep breath "I love you just the way you are."

"I love you too," Jule said in a voice squeezed tight by large emotions.

Lucas pulled Jule to his chest and hugged him tightly. "Man, I thought it couldn't get any better, but hearing you say that...."

"I just thought you should know."

"Hey, you know, it's okay to be serious."

"I don't understand."

"Just don't feel like you have to keep up with me in the banter department. That's all."

Jule chuckled. "You really do fancy yourself, Madding."

Lucas hugged Jule and held him all through the night and woke happier than he'd been in years.

Chapter Twenty-Nine

"GOOD MORNING," Lucas said when Jule opened his eyes.

Jule smiled when Lucas leaned in to kiss his nose.

"Stay right there and keep looking cute as fuck," Lucas said. "I'm going to make you breakfast."

"Awesome, but I have to pee." Jule swung his legs over the side of the bed.

"Hey, by the way, I didn't mean to leave you out of things last night at Char's."

Jule didn't speak until after he flushed the toilet. "Understood," he said. It reminded him of Kelly, of home, of Mum. Abruptly, his eyes filled with tears.

Lucas pulled Jule into his arms and held him gently. "I am so sorry," he said sincerely. "I promise you, I will never keep anything from—"

"I'm not upset about last night," Jule interrupted. "I just suddenly missed home."

Lucas smoothed Jule's hair. "I tend to forget you had a family before me."

"You have a very short memory," Jule replied before his tears broke free and chased one another down his cheeks.

"Hey now." Lucas held him a little closer and stroked his back soothingly. "You'll see them again. It's all just a plane ride away. Meanwhile, you have me."

Jule snuffled. "I can't believe what a baby I am."

Lucas made a scoffing noise. "Give yourself a break. How many teenagers could deal with what you've been dealing with for weeks? For years. You've been under a ridiculous amount of stress, you just discovered sex, and David keeps making it clear the ballet is riding on you."

"On us," Jule corrected. "We're a team."

Lucas swallowed before he spoke again. "Yes, we are, and I'm not going to let you down."

"You'll have to eventually." Jule smiled. "You can't carry me forever."

"Watch me."

Jule's smile grew wider, and he gave Lucas a squeeze before letting him go.

"Better?" Lucas asked.

Jule nodded.

Lucas kissed Jule's forehead. "Now get back into bed so I can bring you breakfast."

Lucas's idea of "making breakfast" consisted of opening a box of bakery croissants and placing them on a tray with butter and jam. In his defense, he made a very good cup of coffee with his french press. His phone rang as he was setting the tray in front of Jule, and he nearly spilled the pitcher of cream on him.

"'Scuse me." Lucas went over to the coffee table and scooped up his phone. "Yeah? Oh, hey, David." He listened for a minute. "Sweet! Yeah, I'll tell him. See you soon." Lucas put the phone down and went back to the bed.

Jule looked away from the croissants and plum preserves. "What?" Lucas's smile was so infectious, he couldn't help smiling back. "Tell me!"

"We have a venue."

"Where is it?"

"The New Jersey Ballet Company."

"How far away is that?"

"Not too far. I can't believe we didn't think of them before."

Jule's phone rang and he reached for it. "Hi, Jezza," he said. "Rubbish!" He listened for a while. "All right," he said in a defeated tone. "Yeah, see you later."

"What was that about?" Lucas asked as he spread butter on a croissant.

"I have a fan club," Jule said the way another person might say, "I have a migraine."

Lucas cracked up.

"Jezza says I have to sign something so they can be an *official* fan club."

"I'm sorry." Lucas stopped laughing. "It's not really funny."

"It's humiliating."

"What? No! No, it's not. That's the exact wrong attitude." Lucas met Jule's eyes. "These people in the fan club like you. They're your fans, get it? Your attitude should be nothing but gratitude that they like you enough to band together in your name."

Jule thought about it and then nodded. "You're right, of course."

"I'm all kinds of happy for you, babe."

"Don't call me babe." Jule kept a straight face for almost a second before he started laughing at Lucas's expression.

"You got me." Lucas chuckled. "I shouldn't be surprised. You learned from a master."

"Would that be you?"

"Finish your breakfast, rock star. We have things to meet and people to do."

Jule laughed. "I can't keep eating like this. I'll get something on the way. Right now, I'm going to have a shower."

"You need help?" Lucas asked.

"Actually, I wouldn't mind."

After the best shower ever, Jule and Lucas got dressed and left the apartment.

"How are you feeling now?" Lucas asked as they reached the curb.

"I feel like having a look at where we'll be dancing."

"Right. We should do that." A laugh bubbled out of Lucas's throat.

"Loon," Jule commented.

"It's weird. I'm ridiculously happy this morning. Today, I feel like nothing bad can happen." Lucas looked down at Jule. "And it's all because of you."

Jule rolled his eyes. "Also, the fact that we have a venue."

"Nope. All you." Lucas grinned. "Though it was nice to hear David sounding enthusiastic again."

"That's great."

"It sure is. Okay. We can take the subway or get a cab. Takes about an hour and a half on the train. Cab would be faster but expensive."

"Subway."

"As you wish."

Several stops and almost two hours later, they reached Microlab Street and gazed up at the New Jersey School of Ballet. Inside, a receptionist had them sign in and replied to their question in the affirmative. They would find Mr. Downes in practice room four.

"Hey, kids!" David said cheerily as Lucas and Jule came through the door. "What do you think?" He made a sweeping gesture.

Jule and Lucas looked around as they shed their outerwear, leaving them in tights and leotards.

"It's almost exactly like the large practice room we used to have," Lucas said.

"It's perfect," Jule said.

"Good. Good." David put a hand on Lucas's shoulder and one on Jule's. "Listen, only a few people know about this deal, okay? Don't tell anyone else."

"Got it," Lucas said.

"Is this to do with Miss Dahlman?" Jule asked.

"*Exactement*! I don't know how much influence she has in Jersey, but I don't want to find out, *comprenez?*"

Jule frowned.

"Babe, we don't want her to find out because she'll try to fuck us," Lucas said. "*Again.*"

"Yes, I get that, but she'll find out anyway as soon the dates are announced."

"I'm assuming once we're on the schedule, the New Jersey Ballet Company will be reluctant to kick us off. It wouldn't make them look good at all." David glanced at the door as Charlotte and Bram arrived.

"What are you three conspiring about?" Charlotte asked. "No, wait, let me guess. The Ice Queen."

David recapped the conversation for Charlotte and Bram.

Charlotte tapped a manicured nail against her full lips as she thought. "What if someone leaked the location to Catherine? Naturally, she'd get on her broom and fly over to intimidate the director of the NJBC. Suppose someone warned the director ahead of time what to expect?"

"Sounds like a trap," Bram said.

"Clever boy." Charlotte patted his cheek. "Of course, it's a trap. Don't you all think it's high time someone put a stop to her shenanigans?"

"Yes, but not by playing her way," Jule said.

David sighed as he patted Jule's shoulder. "Thanks for putting it into words. I wouldn't be comfortable doing something like that to Cath."

"But *she's* allowed to use every dirty trick in the book?" Charlotte asked sarcastically.

"You don't know her like I do," David said.

"Explain it to me," Lucas retorted. "Because I swear I can't understand why you put up with her. It can't be just for the money."

"Don't be so quick to downplay the money, but you're right. I put up with her because she's my oldest friend. She stuck by me when no one else did. Without her, I wouldn't be the man you see before you today."

Lucas snorted. "Not exactly a ringing endorsement."

"Why do you have such a hard-on for me lately?" David said sharply.

"Because you're better than—" Lucas struggled for words. "You know what I mean. I like you, and I want to keep liking you, so just stop acting like it's okay to act like that."

"You don't know her," David repeated.

"I know she's a hater," Lucas responded. "How can you, you know, overlook how she feels about queer people? I mean, since you're a homo and all. Doesn't it bother you?"

"It's not as bad as you're making out." David frowned. "Cath doesn't hate gay people."

"No, she's just disgusted by them."

Bram spoke up. "Look, I have no idea why Catherine's determined to destroy The Downtown Ballet Company, but if we're going to fight back, let's do it right."

Everyone looked at him.

Bram smiled. "It's easy. Go ahead and announce the dates, put out the posters, do whatever we're doing to promote the ballet. Don't tell Catherine anything ahead of time but warn the director. It'll be the same result, just a day or so later."

Charlotte pouted a little. "It just makes me sick that she gets away with her shit."

"It makes me sad that she feels like she has to do shitty things," Jule said.

"Whatever, Saint Julian," Charlotte said.

"Come on now," Lucas said. "Let's all take a deep breath."

"I could just go talk to her," David said. "Do a little calculated ass-kissing."

"Fuck a duck! No!" Lucas exclaimed.

"Fuck a whole flock," Charlotte added. "We won't let you lower yourself."

"Well, I guess that's settled then," David said. He cleared his throat. "Marilee will be here soon with costumes. I'm sorry I didn't notify you, but things are moving fast now. She'll do fittings today, and I'm hoping for a dress rehearsal day after tomorrow." He looked at each of the group in turn. "This thing is about to go into hyperdrive. Are you ready?"

"Check," Lucas said instantly.

"Born ready," Charlotte said.

"If I'm not, I will be," Jule said. He caught Lucas's caring glance and gave him a reassuring nod.

Bram chuckled. "I've just got the one solo. Don't worry about me."

"I feel like we should cut our fingers and take a blood oath," Lucas said. "Anyone else feel that? No? Just me, then?"

David laughed, and his good humor spread through the group. "I feel unreasonably optimistic right now."

"So does Lucas," Jule said.

David turned to look at Lucas. "He does have that look."

Charlotte snorted. "That well-laid look."

"Don't be hatin'," Lucas replied.

"Not me," Charlotte said with a sly glance at Bram. "No jealousy here." She gave Lucas a teasing smile. "Though, I have to say, if Jule was curious about...."

"Cool your jets, girl," Lucas said.

"I'm not poaching, boy, just putting it out there. And you wouldn't be left out."

"I know you're fucking with me," Lucas told her. "But it's not going to work. No one can shake me up today."

"Hold on a minute," Jule said. "I'd like to hear more about Charlotte's offer."

Charlotte, Bram, and David burst into laughter. Jule smiled sweetly at Lucas.

"*Now* you've been fucked with, mate."

"Is it just me?" David said. "Or does *every*one have a potty mouth now?"

"I'm just trying to keep up," Jule said.

"Stop sassing me and show me some magic." David made a swatting gesture.

Lucas and Jule walked across the expanse of polished hardwood until they had enough room to work. Jule rose into an arabesque. A few feet away, Lucas took a stance with one foot forward and his arms in fourth position. David clapped a beat and Lucas glided over to Jule. He took Jule's hand and spun him like a top before letting go. Jule twirled away from him in a series of small leaps. Lucas elegantly pursued and caught him by the wrist.

"*Ça suffit*!" David called out.

Lucas reeled Jule in and gave him a hug before letting him go. "I love dancing with you."

"Me too." Jule smiled at the floor.

"That was beautiful," David said. "You don't need to work on that bit anymore. *Parfait*!"

"I need to work on my variation in the second act," Jule said.

"You do that," David said. "I'll borrow Luc so he and Charlotte can practice their pas de deux." He looked around. "Bram!"

"Yes, boss?"

"Marilee just pinged me. Would you go to the front lobby and give her a hand, please?"

"*Please*?" Bram bugged his eyes in exaggerated shock. "Who are you, and what did you do with David?"

"Just go, *putain*." David flapped a hand at him.

MANY MINUTES later, Bram returned with Marilee, a handcart, and several containers. She immediately began opening and unpacking the clear plastic tubs. As she removed the garments, she shook them vigorously before laying them over the backs of folding chairs behind a screen.

Jule walked over and watched for a minute before he spoke. "Is there more?"

Marilee looked up at him. "More what?"

"Are those the costumes? All of them?"

She nodded. "Skimpy, huh?"

"That—That's a thong," Jule said.

"Not just any thong." Marilee winked. "*Your* thong."

Jule turned to look at David. The expression on his face made David walk away from Charlotte and Lucas.

"What's going on?" David asked.

"When were you going to tell me I'd be dancing with a bare bottom?"

David pursed his lips and stroked his mustache. "It's only for the first act," he said.

"I'm not comfortable with this."

"You could wear flesh-colored tights," Marilee said as Charlotte and Lucas joined them.

"That's not my vision," David said.

"It's not your arse either," Jule retorted.

"I love it when you're feisty," Lucas said. "It makes my naughty parts tingle."

Marilee laughed. "Okay, I can see we have some sort of misunderstanding here. Jule, come with me. I think, once you see the costume on you, you'll understand why it's appropriate."

"In what world is that appropriate?" Jule pointed at the scrap of material.

Marilee beckoned to Jule. "Come on."

Jule followed her behind a set of folding screens. "Don't you think it's, you know, indecent?"

Marilee shook her head. "No, I surely don't, or I wouldn't ask you to wear it."

"Sorry."

"It's okay. I understand. I really do. It's a very brief costume." She smiled impishly. "But you'll be wearing more than Lucas will."

"All right, then. Let's try it on."

With Marilee's help, Jule got into the costume, which consisted of a faux suede thong, a loincloth, and strings of suede-like fabric crisscrossing his torso. She turned him toward the full-length three-panel folding mirror and began adjusting the network of twisted, rolled fabric. After a lot of tweaks, she stepped back.

"Perfect."

Jule turned one hundred eighty degrees to look at the rear view. The string of the thong was visible where it attached to a small triangle of leather and then it disappeared into his crack. He shifted his weight several times trying to get comfortable.

"It feels so weird," he said.

"You'll get used to it."

Lucas stuck his head around the screen. "Holy shit!" he exclaimed.

"You like?" Marilee asked.

"Lady, you're about to be a one-woman ringside audience to a live sex show."

Marilee chuckled. "I should be so lucky. Seriously, what do you think?"

"It's perfect for the character in the first act," Lucas said. "Primitive man through the Roman Empire." He licked his lips. "But I gotta tell you, that outfit is incendiary."

"Wait until you see yours."

"Yeah? Where is it?"

Marilee grinned. "I'm wearing it as a headband."

Lucas and Jule laughed along with her.

"If you're ready, Luc, come on over here," Marilee said.

Lucas put on the leather pouch she handed him, and she threaded it onto the leather and fur belt she fastened low around his waist. A cord at the tip of the pouch passed between Lucas's legs and up his crack to loop over the belt. A harness of thin leather strips was fastened around his torso, with soft suede pauldrons overhanging his shoulders.

Marilee stood back and looked at both of them with a critical eye. "Dancer butts," she sighed.

"None finer." Lucas preened comically.

"I'm going to add some more rolled strips around your arms, Jule, and some sort of vambraces around your forearms, Lucas. You dance the first act mostly barefoot, but I have some slippers that look like boots for the end of the first and the beginning of the second act. I don't have them here, because I'm dyeing them and they're drying."

"Are you really sure our bums should be hanging out?" Jule said.

"Your butt doesn't hang," Marilee said. "It's perky."

"It sure is," Lucas said. "Why didn't I think of perky?"

Jule groaned. "I'll not hear the end of this," he predicted.

"Whatever," Marilee said. "If my butt looked like yours, I'd move to Rio."

"I don't know what that means," Jule said.

Lucas cupped one of Jule's asscheeks. "It's a compliment."

Jule swatted Lucas's hand. "Stop that."

"It *is* pretty inappropriate," Marilee told Lucas. "Honestly, I don't know how or why a nice boy like Jule puts up with your tomfoolery."

Lucas leaned toward her and whispered loudly. "It's my huge cock."

Marilee exchanged a glance with Jule.

Jule shrugged. "It *is* pretty big," he said.

Marilee laughed. "You're a real sport," she said. "I like that. I also like your sculpted glutes. Believe me, you've got nothing to be ashamed or embarrassed about. You'll be like a Greek statue brought to life. There's nothing obscene about that, is there?"

"I suppose not." Jule glanced into the mirror again, and Lucas came to stand beside him.

Marilee came over to run her fingers through their hair until it was in wild disarray. "There," she said as she gazed at their reflections. "Alex and Philip, the tragic lovers brought to life."

Chapter Thirty

JULE AND Lucas were up early again the next morning, keenly aware of how little time was left before opening night. Despite their hurry, Lucas stopped to embrace Jule before they left the apartment. He slid his hands into Jule's unzipped parka and hugged him tenderly. His heart swelled when Jule hugged him back fiercely, pressing as close as possible. It was with great reluctance that they broke apart.

"Doing good?" Lucas inquired.

"Yes. Why?"

"Just checking."

"I'm fine, really. I'm not going to freak out again."

"Well, if you do, I'm here for you, and you can take that to the bank."

"What?"

"It's a saying. It means you can bet on it. It's a sure thing, you know?"

"I'm really glad we're back together," Jule said.

"Me too, because I can't live without you."

"Don't exaggerate," Jule teased as he opened the door to the street.

As had become their habit, they stopped for coffee to go at the corner and went to the curb to hail a cab. All the taxis in sight had fares, but they knew it wouldn't be long before the light would change, and another selection would roll slowly by.

"Want to hear something weird?" Lucas said as he looked up the street. "I think I enjoyed cuddling on the couch last night as much as having full-blown sex."

When Jule didn't answer, Lucas turned to see what had his attention. Lucas's jaw dropped when he looked across the street. Jule's giant face stared back at him. Jezza's luminous photo had been reproduced on a banner and plastered on the side of a bus. The word *Fireheart* was superimposed over Jule's head like a halo of flame.

"I guess David's spending some of that money," Lucas said.

"It's unreal."

"It's gorgeous, and it's going to sell tickets." Lucas smiled at Jule. "Ready to go to work?"

"Yeah." Jule glanced at the bus again as it pulled into traffic to a fanfare of horns. "It's just so… huge," he said.

"About 27,000 wisecracks just popped into my head," Lucas said. He put up his hand and a cab pulled over.

"Thanks for keeping them to yourself," Jule said as he got into the back seat.

Lucas gave the driver the address and sat back. After a moment, a big grin spread over his face.

"What?" Jule asked.

"I was just picturing Catherine's reaction when she sees it."

Jule frowned.

"What are you thinking about?" Lucas asked.

"Miss Dahlman."

"Thank God. You had the most annoyed look on your face. I was afraid it was something serious."

"She *is* something serious." Jule sighed. "You think it was David who broke us up, but it wasn't. It was her. She's the one who told me. She deliberately drove a wedge between us."

"Fuck," Lucas said under his breath. "I didn't think she was still playing those games. Back when David thought he wanted me, she was a real bitch to me."

"Why is she like that? Is it just because she's jealous?"

"Mostly. At least, I think so. What I can't understand is why she seems happy to keep running into the brick wall. David is never going to be what she wants him to be. She's known him long enough to realize that."

"It doesn't matter now." Jule laced his fingers with Lucas's. "I can't hate her. After all, we made up, and it's even better than it was before."

"I'm not as forgiving as you."

"Look at it this way. I have you and *Fireheart*, and back in London, I have Mum and Dad and Kelly and Sasha. Who does Catherine have? I feel a bit sorry for her."

Lucas squeezed Jule's hand. "If you say so, but you're probably going to have to put up with me getting mad when someone hurts you."

"I will, because it's one of the reasons I love you, but you'll have to do the same for me."

Lucas looked into Jule's eyes. "Stop being so perfect for me. It's kind of spooky."

"Hey, lovebirds," the driver said. "The eagle has landed. You want I should leave the meter running while you decide if you want a big wedding?"

Lucas and Jule chuckled as they got out of the cab at the station.

A LITTLE after nine, they arrived at the NJBC and went to the practice room. Marilee was already there and had her costuming booth set up. She turned from her conversation with Jamison and smiled at Lucas and Jule.

"You're the first," she said cheerfully. "Let's get you into your costumes."

By the time Marilee was finished with Lucas and Jule, David, Charlotte, Amani, Samira, and Bram had arrived. Jule and Lucas walked over to David as Marilee got started on Charlotte.

"Bram," David said. "You realize you don't need to be here for another hour, right?"

"I shared a cab with Charlotte."

"So, you're here because you wanted to save a few bucks?" David said.

"Not exactly. I had nothing better to do, and honestly, there's nowhere I'd rather be right now."

"Good enough," David said. He turned as the door opened and Jezza came in carrying his large case.

"Excellent! You're in costume!" Jezza said. "Davo, my darling, may I borrow Jule and Lucas for a tick?"

"Take them," David said.

"Lucas first," Jezza said. He beckoned to Lucas with a curled forefinger.

Jezza maneuvered Lucas into the best light in the room and snapped pictures while Lucas ran through part of his solo in slow motion. Jule watched, admiring how his lover morphed from wisecracking player to noble warrior preparing for battle.

"He's a fucking god in tights," Bram said.

Jule replied without looking at Bram. "I know."

Bram mimed a shudder. "Do I feel a chill?"

Jule shrugged.

"It's just, I thought we were becoming friends, but since you got back with Luc, I never see you," Bram said.

"Is that what you were doing? Being my friend?"

"You don't sound mad, but I get the feeling you're not happy with me."

"Because I realize now what you were actually doing."

"What was I doing?"

"It'll just sound silly if I say it out loud, but you were seducing me."

"Well, maybe a little." Bram smirked.

Jule finally turned his head to look at Bram. "I thought you were nice, but you were gaming me."

"That's a little harsh." Bram coughed. "Would I like to get with you? Yes, I would. But I wouldn't take advantage of you."

"I'm not debating it. You asked, so I'm explaining why we aren't mates." Jule turned his gaze on Lucas again. "Do you have anything else to say about it?"

"I'm sorry."

"No, you're not. You were about to try it on again not two minutes ago."

Bram spread his hands in a self-deprecating gesture. "A wolf's gotta hunt."

"I'd never deny the truth of that," Jule said as he met Bram's gaze again. "But a smart wolf hunts deer and rabbit. I like you well enough, Bram, but I don't trust you."

"I can live with that."

"Jule darling," Jezza called out. "Get your sublime arse over here."

"What was Bram saying to you?" Lucas asked as soon as Jule was close enough to hear.

"Nothing that would interest you."

"Do I need to talk to him?"

"Don't be stupid," Jule said.

"Don't worry. I know you like being the stupid one in the relationship," Lucas retorted.

Jule shook his head and then gave his attention to Jezza.

DAVID HAD noticed the air of tension between his dancers and approached Bram. "*Comment allez-vous?*"

Bram shrugged. "Lucas is bent about who-knows-what. I probably looked at Jule's ass too long or something. You know how he is."

"Yes." David stroked his elegant beard. "I know how he is. I don't think you do, though. My advice to you would be, don't push him too far."

"I can handle myself."

"I'm sure you can, but if either of you is injured before the end of *Fireheart*'s run, I'll personally see to it that you never dance in this town again."

Bram wore a faint smirk as he answered. "That would be quite a threat, if you could back it up. But hey, why are we getting so stressed? We should be focused on the ballet."

David pursed his lips as he studied Bram's face. "I can't argue with that." He walked away.

Four hours later, David dismissed the troupe. "Dress rehearsal here tomorrow," he said. "Dinner afterward. Day after tomorrow, full-dress rehearsal at the hall. Make sure all your *canards* are in a row."

As people were packing up and walking out, David walked over to Jule and Lucas.

"I know," Lucas said resignedly. "You need to have a talk with me."

David shook his head. "No, I thought about it, and talking to you would be futile. However, I *would* like a few minutes of Jule's time."

"Sure," Jule said.

"Okay," Lucas said. "That means I get to pick the restaurant."

"Why don't you go change?" David told him.

"Right." Lucas went over to Marilee.

"Jule," David began and then paused. "This isn't the first time I've dealt with a similar situation, but it's different enough this time to put me off-balance a little."

"Are you talking about Miss Dahlman?"

"No, mon tresor, I'm talking about you." David grimaced. "We open in three days, and at least two of my principal dancers are bent out of shape. You might wonder why I'm talking to you instead of Bram and Lucas."

"Because you're brilliant?"

"Good guess. Talking to Lucas and Bram would be ineffectual at best. You, however, can still be guilted in into behaving."

"I'm not misbehaving."

"Fair point." David put his hands on Jule's shoulders. "Do you think you can keep them apart until the end of the run?"

"Any ideas on how I should do that?"

"Lucas takes emotional cues from you, in case you hadn't noticed. If you're upset...." David took in the stubborn set of Jule's features and spoke again. "Look, I can see you've cooled toward Bram. I'm not stupid. I can probably even guess why." He paused. "Though I heard he swore off boys."

Jule sighed. "Not that I've noticed."

"Now you see what I meant by entanglements?"

"I just want this conversation to end."

"What's done is done, but we can try to keep further damage from occurring."

Jule nodded.

"Good. Good." David smiled at Jule. "Go have a great dinner and then get some sleep. Big day tomorrow."

"Big day the day after that," Jule answered.

"Even bigger day after that one." David grinned. "Go on now."

"What did David want?' Lucas asked when Jule joined him.

"Should I tart it up or just say it?"

"Tell me."

"He wanted to know if I could keep a muzzle on you until after *Fireheart*'s run."

"What did you say?"

"That I'd do my best, what else?"

Lucas's eyebrows drew down in an incipient frown, but he smiled at Jule instead. "What else indeed? Hurry and change. I booked a table at a new sushi place."

Jule made a face. "I don't fancy raw fish."

"Yet you'll go down on me?"

"That's different."

"How?"

"I'm not in love with seafood."

Lucas smiled warmly. "It's healthy. Now, go change and make it quick, or I'll come help and we'll never make the rez."

Jule managed to have a good time at the restaurant because Lucas kept him entertained. He ate the selection Lucas ordered for him and enjoyed it. In fact, wasabi might be his new favorite thing. It was fun, and the food was pretty, but when they left, he was still hungry and said so.

"What do you want?" Lucas asked.

Jule sniffed the air. "Whatever that is."

"You smell the bahn mi cart over there. Come on. It's tasty."

Lucas bought Jule one of the Vietnamese baguettes spread with pâté, chili, and mayonnaise and loaded with chicken, pickled cucumber, carrots, and daikon garnished with cilantro.

Jule took a big bite, chewed, and swallowed. "Mate," he said. "*This* is food."

Lucas smiled fondly at Jule. "You couldn't be any cuter if you had kittens glued all over you."

"Cute, am I?"

"It's a fact."

"Jezza says I have a natural sensuality."

"He's not wrong." Lucas wiped a smear of chili paste from the corner of Jule's mouth with his thumb. "You're still cute as fuck, though."

"I suppose I should be thankful that you like kittens."

"I don't actually. Cute usually makes me want to vomit, but you…." Lucas gave Jule a wicked smile. "You make me want to lick the cute right off you."

Jule took another bite of the sandwich and then rewrapped the remainder. "A good time isn't a threat, but now I want ice cream. I'm never allowed to have it at home."

"It's like twenty-eight degrees out here."

"Yeah, that's when ice cream tastes best, and it doesn't melt."

"You do have a point. Come on, I'll buy you ice cream, but you better put out."

Jule laughed. "Mate, I'm a sure thing where you're concerned. And I'll have to burn those calories off somehow."

Chapter Thirty-One

WHEN JULE and Lucas arrived at the hall for the dress rehearsal, David was sitting at the edge of the stage talking with Charlotte and Bram.

"Hey, kids," David called out. "Join us."

Jule and Lucas didn't notice Jamison until he started playing Wagner's "Bridal Chorus" as they came down the aisle.

"That's hilarious," Lucas called out. "Lame, but still funny."

"I happen to have a certificate that allows me to perform weddings," David said. "Just in case."

Jule rolled his eyes. "Really, David, you know I'm saving myself for you."

Charlotte made an invisible mark on the air with a slim forefinger. "That's one point to Parry."

"Are we keeping score now?" David asked.

"When did we stop?" Charlotte retorted. "Hey! I think that's a point to me."

Bram chuckled. "You guys. After all you've been through in the last two weeks, you're still crackin' jokes."

"Something wrong with that?" Lucas said immediately.

"Easy," Bram said. "It was a compliment. I admire your spirit. Okay?"

"Kelly used to ask me if I'd rather laugh or cry," Jule said.

"I'm no Kelly Holloway," Bram said. "But that's my philosophy. No point sitting around moaning. Get up and do something. If you do the wrong thing, fix it."

Jule nodded. "Sounds just like him."

"Yes, yes," David said. "I think we can all agree that Kelly Holloway is a combination of a saint and Superman, and we could extol his virtues all day long in a series of rounds, but what do you say we get to work?" He turned his gaze on Jule and Lucas. "You two get backstage and see Marilee. Come back when you're in costume."

"You got it, boss," Lucas said.

Marilee greeted them cheerfully. "Ready to put the socks on, boys?" She gestured to an area where she'd set up a couple of space heaters and folding chairs. A few scraps of fabric hung over the chair backs. "You need help or…?"

"We got this," Lucas said.

He and Jule stripped naked while Marilee turned her back and fussed with a crown of woven grapevine she had covered with silver leaf.

"It's such a rush, isn't it?" she said. "Even though I haven't slept in almost thirty-six hours, I wouldn't trade this experience for anything."

Jule walked over to her. "I *think* I've got this on right," he said as Lucas joined them.

"Yep." Marilee reached out to untuck an edge of the thong but drew her hand back. "Maybe you should do that yourself," she said. "Now we're ready to wax."

Jule looked startled. "What?"

"We need to get rid of any stray hair," Marilee explained. She glanced down at Jule's crotch. "You're fairly tidy already, so it won't be too bad."

"I remember the first time I had to wax." Lucas made a face. "Ouch!"

"Don't let him scare you," Marilee told Jule. "I'm pretty good at this. It stings, for sure, but it goes away fast."

"Okay," Jule said. He sighed. "There's a lot more to ballet than Kelly taught me."

"Word," Lucas said. "Want me to go first?"

Jule made a scoffing noise as he turned to Marilee. "Do we do it right here?"

She nodded. "I need you lie down on the table there, and we'll get it done."

Jule looked suspiciously at the pot of hot liquid, small wooden paddles, and strips of gauze as he hopped up and stretched out. A few minutes later, he climbed gingerly down and gratefully took the ice packs Marilee handed him.

"Just hold them over the area for a few minutes." She crooked her finger at Lucas. "Come on, Sasquatch," she said.

"I'll kiss your boo-boos later," Lucas said as he walked past Jule.

By the time Marilee was finished with Lucas, Jule had set aside the cold packs and was examining the rest of his costume. She came over to take the long rope of rolled fabric out of his hands. As he stood motionless, arms at shoulder height, she wound the vivid red ribbon around his arms and torso, leaving the ends to dangle several inches from his wrists.

"Luc, when it's time, you just hold on to this end here," Marilee said. "When you spin Jule away from you, it will unwind smoothly. Jule, you hold on to this end."

"Got it," Lucas said. "I have to admit, I'm a little nervous about this. I expected David to throw in a few surprises, but this new bit is a fairly complicated series of steps."

"I'm not worried." Jule smiled at Lucas. "As long as I'm dancing the steps with you."

Lucas smiled and then grimaced. "Damn, that burns." He adjusted his ice pack. "If we pull it off, it will look mega-cool, but if we don't, one or both of us will end up on our ass." He paused. "Our asses?"

"Don't worry about the fabric," Marilee said. "The tensile strength is way beyond what you need."

"It will look cool," Jule said firmly.

"You've got the hard part. I just have to hold on to the rope," Lucas said.

"Then I should go practice," Jule said. "Ready?"

"Almost." Lucas took Jule's wrist and pulled him over to stand in front of the full-length mirror. "Alex and Phillip," he said. "We look perfect. All we have to do now is what we do best."

"Better than mortals deserve" was Marilee's judgment.

David concurred when Jule and Lucas joined him on the big stage. He left off his conversation with Jamison to look over the costumes. He walked once around Jule and Lucas admiring the sculpted muscles artfully displayed. "Perfection," he said. "Let's give them a test drive."

Jamison provided accompaniment as Lucas and Jule danced their first pas de deux of the ballet. They'd practiced the first nine-tenths several times and performed the steps faultlessly, despite the change in Jule's costume. As they reached the showy sequence that ended this section, both sharpened their focus as they prepared to execute the new steps.

Lucas grasped the end of the fabric rope and appeared to fling Jule away like a spinning top. True to Marilee's word, the ribbon of cloth unreeled as Jule pirouetted away from Lucas. When Jule reached the end of the rope, he and Lucas leaned back at the same time, perfectly balanced, connected by a cord of bloodred. They held the pose for a beat and then spun toward each other, wrapping themselves in the ribbon until they met, Jule's back against Lucas's chest. Lucas bowed his head and curved his arms around Jule like folding wings. Jule lifted his chin and froze with his arms overhead in a soft, crossed fourth position, one hand cupping Lucas's cheek.

"Bravo," David said. "Do it just like that tomorrow night."

"That felt good," Jule said as he started untangling himself.

Lucas surreptitiously ran a hand over Jule's smooth bare buttcheek. "*That* felt amazing."

"Awkward."

Jule turned at the sound of that familiar, beloved voice, his mouth falling open in surprise. A big smile spread over his face and he started eagerly forward.

"Whoa!" Lucas said in warning, but it was too late.

A loop of cloth pulled tight around Jule's ankle and Jule went down.

Lucas knelt beside him and unwrapped the cloth as he looked Jule over for injuries. "You okay?"

Jule turned bright pink as Kelly and Sasha joined them on the floor.

"Smooth move," Sasha murmured.

Jule pushed away from Lucas and threw his arms around Sasha. Sasha hugged him back, and then Kelly wrapped his arms around both of them. It was several moments before the group hug broke apart.

"I missed you so much," Jule said in a choked voice as he got to his feet.

"Of course, you did," Sasha said. "Looking at you, it's obvious you have no one to keep you on task. Have you been running wild since we left?" He pinched Jule's side. "What have you been eating? Everything?"

Jule chuckled. "I still have a routine," he said. "And I do my own laundry."

"Liar," Lucas said loudly.

"Usually, I do my own laundry," Jule amended.

"Try again," Lucas said.

"Sometimes?"

Lucas gave him a stern look.

Jule sighed. "Lucas does my laundry."

"And now it's too much information," Kelly said. "When can you break for lunch? Or can you?"

"I'll be the judge of that," David said. He looked at his watch. "Let's say one half hour from now. Assuming these two do another perfect run-through and change fast."

"I CAN'T imagine it takes long to get out of *those* costumes," Kelly said. His eyes bugged out when Jule turned to go to the dressing room. "Jesus Christ in Cleveland!"

Sasha smiled at his partner's scandalized expression. "It's a nice bottom, yes?"

Kelly shook his head. "He might as well be naked." He watched Lucas follow Jule off the stage, his demeanor decidedly disapproving.

"Try to remember that we're here to support our boy," Sasha said gently.

David cleared his throat. "I'm so grateful you could come."

"I was surprised to hear from you," Kelly said. "The plan was to let Jule make his way on his own, but if he needs us, of course we're here for him."

"Great. I need you to learn a few steps by tomorrow. And if you think those costumes are indecent, wait until you see yours."

"Hold on a minute," Kelly said. "I was thinking more along the lines of moral support."

"Actually, morale is good," David said. "I need you on stage."

"Why?" Sasha interjected.

"Are you kidding? If I can advertise the return of Kelly Holloway and Alexandru Vasile for a once-in-a-lifetime appearance in my ballet, there won't be an empty seat."

"This is exciting," Sasha said.

"It's more like emotional blackmail," Kelly said. "But I have to say, I *am* a little excited."

"So... you'll do it?" David asked.

"We'll do it," Sasha answered. "But if you lied to us about anything, I wouldn't want to be you."

"Would I drag you across an ocean if it wasn't dire?"

"I think you'd drag me across an ocean just to prove you could do it," Kelly said. "But that's not the point. We're here for Jule. Everything else is water under a burned bridge." He glanced in the direction Jule had disappeared in. "I just hope we're not too late."

Sasha frowned at Kelly. "So dramatic. Did you see him? Maybe he gains a few extra ounces, but he looks healthy as a bull and just as strong."

"I saw most of him," Kelly countered.

"And he looks beautiful," Sasha said. "You can't tell me he doesn't."

Kelly sighed. "No, I can't."

"Jule is fine," David said. "He had a good teacher."

"Don't try to grease me up, Downes. I know Jule's a good kid."

"Then trust him to make a few decisions about his own life. If you're worried about me corrupting him, you can relax. As far as I can see, he's immune to any charm I might have." David smiled. "Honestly, he's rubbed off on me far more than I've rubbed off on him."

"Unfortunate choice of words," Kelly said. "But I hear you." He looked down at his feet. "You got shoes to fit these canoes?"

"A dozen pair at least. You and Bram wear the same size." David gestured. "Come on backstage."

Kelly and Sasha followed David past the dressing rooms to wardrobe.

"Your characters change from act to act," David said as they walked. "You'll be fathers, soldiers, priests, whatever I need you to be. And I was kidding about the costumes. I don't want to fill the stage with half-naked dancers."

"Nine-tenths," Kelly said.

"What?" David turned his head toward Kelly.

"They're more like nine-tenths naked."

"You're really fixated on that, aren't you?" David observed. "I understand. Here's what I do these days. I pretend I'm in a museum looking at a work of art. It helps."

"That's not the—" Kelly broke off as they entered the wardrobe department.

"I'm so excited to work with you," Marilee said, after introductions. She took two hangers off a rack. "This is you, Kelly." She shook the dark blue tunic, light blue tights combo. "And this is you." She held out the red tunic with black tights to Sasha.

"Seems as though you were pretty confident we'd show up," Kelly said as he took the costume from Marilee.

"No harm in being prepared." David smiled sheepishly.

"What sort of steps will we be doing?" Sasha asked.

"That's kind of up to you. Mostly, you'll be standing around, but I think it would be great if you did a few steps. While we're rehearsing today, I'll point out to you the spots where I need you. I'm sure the two of you can come up with something."

"Should we go ahead and change?" Kelly asked.

"*Absolutement*," David said. "I'll get some shoes for you."

"I'm on that," Marilee said.

"Great, I'll get back to the stage," David said. "You can't leave Charlotte and Bram alone for too long."

"I wouldn't mind being alone with her."

David raised an eyebrow at Marilee. "Well, all right, then," he said before he left.

Kelly and Sasha returned to the stage area as Jule and Lucas were practicing their pas de deux again. Neither spoke until the dance was over.

"That's a breathtaking run of steps," Kelly told David.

"This dance makes my heart feel the way ballet should make it feel," Sasha added.

"That means a lot coming from you." David smiled. "But it wouldn't look half that good without Lucas and Jule."

"You're probably right," Kelly said. "But you deserve the praise. If the rest of it is as good as that piece, ballet has a new classic."

"I'm not sure I'd go that far," David said. "But if you want to, I won't stop you."

Jule and Lucas came over, pulling on robes as they walked.

"What did you think?" Jule asked eagerly.

"Son," Kelly said sternly. He paused for a beat before breaking into a huge grin. "I've never seen a better performance."

Jule grinned. "I can't believe I impressed you."

"I've always been impressed with you."

"But this is something completely separate from you."

"I understand," Sasha said. "I'll explain it to Kelly later."

"Why are you in dance clothes?" Jule asked.

"Why do you think?" David rapped Jule's forehead with his knuckles.

"We've agreed to fill a couple of parts for David," Kelly said.

"Really?" Jule bounced on his toes a couple of times. "This just keeps getting better!"

"We'll see," Sasha said. "But whatever happens, it will be a cherished memory for me."

"Isn't this amazing?" Jule said to Lucas.

"I'm beside myself at the thought of your pseudo-parents watching me like a hawk."

Jule laughed. "I can hardly believe this is real."

"Okay, I get that it's a joyous occasion," David said. "But we've got work to do." He looked at his watch. "I'm going to order in lunch." He took a head count. "Okay, great. Work on anything you feel needs work until I get back. After lunch, we'll do a run-through."

A MOUNTAIN of Chinese takeout cartons was delivered, and the company sat in the rows of theater seats to eat. Jule sat sideways in his seat so he could talk to Sasha and Kelly in the row behind him. Lucas used his chopsticks to methodically convey food swiftly to his mouth in hopes of avoiding saying anything stupid. Up until Kelly and Sasha arrived, Lucas had hardly given a thought to the age difference between him and Jule. Now, he couldn't stop thinking about how he must look in Kelly's and Sasha's eyes. He sank a little lower in his seat next to Jule and concentrated on his food. He jumped when Sasha touched his shoulder.

"I was wondering," Sasha said.

Lucas cringed a little as he half-turned to look at Sasha. "Yeah?"

"Can I ask a personal question?"

Lucas swallowed. "Sure."

"Who cuts your hair?"

"What?"

"Your hair." Sasha pointed. "I really like it."

"Uh, thanks."

"Wait." Kelly broke off his conversation with Jule. "What are we talking about?"

"*I* am talking about getting a haircut," Sasha said.

"Why?"

"I'm ready for one." Sasha finger-combed his shoulder-length hair.

Lucas smirked at Kelly's dismayed expression. "I don't think Kelly is ready."

"Kelly should get a new style," Sasha said. "Jule's hair is getting very long too."

"It's for the ballet," Lucas said quickly. "He can't cut it."

"Sounds like you're not ready either," Kelly said smugly.

"You got me." Lucas smiled. Without thinking, he stirred the fringe of hair at Jule's nape with his fingertips. "I love these curls."

Kelly cleared his throat and caught a dark look from Sasha. "What?" Kelly said.

"Nothing," Sasha said. "See that it stays that way."

"I don't know what you're talking about," Kelly said.

"Neither do I," Jule added. "I haven't understood half of what you've all been saying."

"Good," Kelly said. "I'm having a hard enough time coming to grips with the fact that you have a boyfriend... or so I assume. Please don't rub it in my face."

"Fine," Lucas said. "Same goes for you."

Sasha laughed. "He's got you there, Kelly."

Kelly looked at Jule. "Sorry, kid. I guess I was being a little hypocritical there."

"Don't be sorry," Jule said. "I know why you act like that, and I'm happy you care that much about me." He paused. "Just don't be a pain in the arse about it, okay?"

"I'll do my best," Kelly said.

Jule smiled at him. "Compared to how my dad would be reacting, you're the definition of calm acceptance." He leaned closer to Kelly and spoke softly. "Honestly, I can hardly believe I have a boyfriend, especially such a pretty one."

"He *is* pretty. You're being... careful, right?"

"Hey," Lucas said. "I can hear you."

"Good." Kelly turned and focused his gaze on Lucas. "Well?"

"We're being careful," Lucas said meekly.

"Good," Kelly said again. "You can't be too careful. Nureyev died of AIDS."

Sasha shook his head. "Could you be more depressing?"

"I don't think so," Lucas said under his breath.

"Before we were interrupted." Sasha shot a look at Kelly. "You were going to tell me the name of your salon, Lucas."

"Sure, no problem," Lucas said to Sasha. "But if you want, I could arrange for him to cut your hair at my place."

"No one is cutting their hair until after the run," David said from behind them. "I can't stress this enough. It's bad enough Charlotte chopped hers off."

"You didn't say anything to me about not cutting my hair," Charlotte said in the tone of someone who has said the same words many times before.

"*Bordel de merde*," David cursed. "No one respects me anymore."

"I respect you," Jule said around a mouthful of shrimp roll. "Mostly."

"I'll take it," David said. "Hurry up and finish eating. Fifteen minutes rest, and then we hit it again. Kelly, Sasha, can we talk for a minute?"

"Stay," Lucas said. "We can go."

JULE GOT up and followed Lucas down the row of seats to the aisle. "What do you think they're talking about?" Jule asked as they walked down the incline.

"I don't." Lucas looked over at Jule. "I'm trying to keep my head in the dance. Lunch with your dads was a little stressful."

"Why?" Jule was genuinely puzzled.

"You seriously didn't notice the way Kelly was looking at me?"

"Come on, you can't let his teacher face scare you." Jule put a hand on Lucas's forearm.

"Cut it out. I can feel him looking at us."

"You must be joking. Mate, relax. Kelly isn't going to smack you for touching me."

"You sure about that?"

Jule nodded. "I'm sure… he'd let Sasha smack you."

"That's not funny, Parry."

"It was funny to me."

"What? His face?" Bram said as they passed him.

"Everyone is a comedian," Lucas said darkly.

"Get off it," Jule said. "Why are you pretending to be grumpy?"

"Hold that thought," Lucas said. "I need the toilet." He walked briskly away.

"I can tell you why," Bram said.

Jule turned a wary gaze on him. "Let's hear it, then."

"Lucas is going into asshole mode. According to Char, it's what he does when he wants to break up with someone but doesn't want to do the dirty work. He just keeps stepping up the nonsense until his lover leaves him, and he doesn't look like the bad guy. Clever, yeah?"

"I don't believe you."

Bram shrugged. "Okay."

Chapter Thirty-Two

LUCAS WAS tucking himself away when Jule walked into the bathroom. He looked over his shoulder, saw Jule, and turned around. "You miss me?"

"I want to know what's wrong."

"I told you, I'm just a little stressed."

"Are you sure?"

"Yes."

"You're not mad at me?"

"No. Why would you think that?"

"Bram said you were acting like this so I'd break up with you."

"That's because Bram is an asshole." Lucas met Jule's eyes. "I would kill or die for you, so there's no question of breaking up. Okay?"

"So, what's really bothering you, then?"

"If I tell you, you'll just say I'm being stupid."

"*Are* you being stupid?"

"Maybe, but I still feel bad, and I don't like feeling bad."

"I don't want you to feel bad." Jule looked up into Lucas's eyes. "Just tell me. I won't laugh or tell you you're being stupid."

"Can we go somewhere other than the men's room?" Lucas led Jule to an empty dressing room and sat on one of the swiveling chairs.

Jule faced Lucas and leaned a hip against a table. "Tell me. No matter how silly you think it is."

"It's Holloway, okay? I can feel him judging me, and I can tell he thinks I'm not good enough for you."

"I think you're good enough for me."

Lucas smiled. "I'm honored, but I know you look up to him. You care what he thinks."

"Kelly won't try to poison me against you. And even if he was that kind of person, which he's not, Sasha wouldn't allow it."

"He seems really nice. Sasha, I mean."

"He's amazing. And so are you."

"Come here." Lucas reached out and Jule moved closer. Lucas slipped a hand through the front of Jule's robe and stroked his thigh. "Okay, I feel better now."

"Really, Madding?" Jule said in a weary tone.

Lucas nodded as he slid his hand farther up.

Jule grabbed Lucas's wrist and held it immobile.

"I forget how strong you are," Lucas said and then added, "Ow."

Jule let go. "Are you insane? I can't go back out there with a chubby."

"Good thinking." Lucas grinned. "I tend to lose track when I'm alone with you. You're always saying I have some kind of magic power over your body. Well, I'm here to tell you that it works both ways. Most of the time, I can barely restrain myself from touching you."

"You'll not hear me complain about your perpetual horniness, not in private anyway. I *adore* being petted by you. But we're only *sort of* alone right now."

Lucas stood and gave Jule a quick kiss. "Okay, let's get back out there before someone looks for us, but tonight, I'm going to make you come so hard, you'll forget your name."

"That's fine with me. My mum wrote it on the inside of my underwear."

"God, I love you," Lucas said. "How the hell did that happen?"

"I have no idea how it happened or any idea how to make it stop."

"Wait." Lucas frowned. "Why would you want to?"

"Well, you know, if it became too hard to juggle my career and a love life...." Jule let his voice trail off. He tried to keep a straight face, but a smile escaped.

"You had me going for a second." Lucas grinned.

"Just you wait until I get you home." Jule opened the door and went into the hall before Lucas could retort. "I believe that's a point to me," he said under his breath. He was starting to the see the charm in this game of verbal sparring. And then he smiled as Lucas caught up and put an arm around him. Despite recent difficulties, things were working out, and now Kelly and Sasha were here. The future was something to look forward to again.

DAVID, KELLY, and Sasha were still seated in the audience, though they'd finished their lunch. Down on the stage, Charlotte, Amani, and Astra practiced. David kept half an eye on them as he spoke to Kelly and Sasha.

"Really," David said. "Thanks again for coming. When I decided to call you, it was on Jule's behalf. I was sticking my nose in, but on the other hand, I felt like you left him in my care, as it were. He's a sharp cookie, but he's a kid, and I was worried that this thing with Lucas would warp his focus."

Kelly nodded. "I can understand why you'd feel that way, as I said on the phone."

"Yeah, but the thing is, once I decided to call you, I realized it would be good for everyone if you were here. I don't want you to just fill out a scene. I want you to be my second-in-command for this production. You know how to stage a ballet. You had such a knack for it in the old days."

Kelly glanced at Sasha. Whatever he saw in Sasha's eyes seemed to make up his mind. "You're willing to give *me* some control over *your* ballet, which I barely glanced at on the plane on my iPad, and which is scheduled for its debut day after tomorrow?"

"Yes, I am."

"The age of miracles has returned," Kelly said. "David Dulac Downes gave up his complete control over something."

"Hallelujah," Sasha said.

"Same goes for you," David said. "You and Kelly are my co-directors. It's just a title for now, but you're in for a share of any profits."

"As you wish," Sasha said. "I'm happy to be a part of the ballet you wrote for our Jule."

"Well… it's more the idea of him than the real him," David said.

"I don't need to hear an explanation," Sasha said quickly. "We have one day to create steps and integrate them. We should get started."

"Whoa," David said. "Take a minute." He looked down at the stage where Amani, Astra, and Charlotte had formed a tableau that might have been the Three Graces, the Fates, or the Crone, the Mother, and the Maiden. "You must understand, I have everything riding on this. My reputation. My livelihood. My *home*. I believe in this ballet. I believe in Jule's and Lucas's ability to make it accessible to the audience, relatable. I believe the story will touch anyone with a heart." He paused. "I need *Fireheart* to be a success, critically, creatively, and financially. To that end, I am not too proud to beg."

"We already said yes," Kelly pointed out.

"You're still a bite in the ass, Holloway," David said. "You just had to step all over my noble sacrifice speech."

"Sorry," Kelly said.

"Now I've lost my momentum," David said. "Forget it. Just know I'm grateful. I couldn't ask for better help."

"I'm doing this for Jule," Kelly said.

"Of course. Of course." David looked up as the sound of the piano died away. "Okay, let's get down to the stage. We'll call the cast together. Make introductions." He sent out a group text as they descended to the stage.

In a short time, Charlotte, Bram, Jule, Lucas, Amani, Astra, Dylan, Marilee, and Jamison stood in a semicircle on the stage in from of David, Kelly, and Sasha.

"Okay, people," David said. "I have exciting news."

"Wait," Jezza called out as he came down the aisle. "Whatever you're about to say, I want to hear it too."

David waited until Jezza reached the stage. "As some of you know, the gentlemen standing beside me are Kelly Holloway and Alexandru Vasile. They've graciously accepted small roles in *Fireheart*, and they've agreed to co-direct. So, listen to them. They know what they're talking about.

"Also, the set builders will be here in a few hours, so we need to get in as much rehearsal as we can before then. Tomorrow will be a full-dress rehearsal with sets." David turned Jezza as the others moved away with purpose. "*Quoi de neuf?*"

Jezza handed David a large plastic folder. "The program," he said.

David opened the folder and gazed at the black and white image of the so-called "Pieta Plus" tableaux that ended the third act. Lucas knelt on one knee, his arms around Jule, who lay on his side with his head propped on Lucas's thigh. Behind Lucas, Charlotte hovered, arms in second position, framing them with gossamer wings. To either side, Amani and Astra, in diaphanous gowns and veils, stood en pointe with bowed heads, hands outstretched in graceful gestures of solace. The stage was dark except for a silvery light that illuminated the dancers.

"It's perfect," David said.

"That's the back cover." Jezza reached out and flipped the top photo to the other side of the folder. "This is the image I think should represent the ballet."

David nodded as he took in the picture of Jule in the brief first-act costume. Jezza had photographed him in an arabesque, arms in crossed fourth position, one raised, one curved softly along his torso. He stood with the working leg extended behind him at a perfect right angle.

Every contour and hollow of his exquisitely toned physique stood out in stark relief. His hair was an unruly mop of deep red that shadowed his doe-eyed gaze. His expression was a complicated mélange of sorrow, courage, determination, and hope. The word *Fireheart* floated above his head in letters of flame.

"It's even more perfect," David said.

"So, if I have your approval, I'll get these to the printer."

"Excellent. Send me the bill."

"One more matter. It would be lovely if you could convince Director Moses or whomever to set aside a block of seats for Jule's fan club."

"*Excusez-moi?*"

"Not for free, of course. They'll pay full ticket price, but they'd like to sit together."

Bemused, David said, "How many people are we talking about?"

"In the club? Oh, of course, how many seats. One section would be great."

"I'll see what I can do."

"Wonderful, darling. Would you get back to me as soon as you know? The president of the fan club is hounding me as only a besotted schoolgirl can, bless them."

David smiled. "Thanks for taking one for the team. See you this evening?"

"Absolutely." Jezza left in a swirl of scarves.

David looked around the cavernous space, the rows of seats, the chandeliers, the lit stage, and felt a rare sense of peace. He felt as though he'd been running at full speed for days through a landscape filled with sharp stones and freezing wind that cut like a knife, but now he'd reached a resting place, a sunny spot on the leeward side. He wasn't even nervous about Catherine's inevitable stormy entrance.

For once in his life, he'd reached out for help, and to his amazement, though he hardly felt he deserved it, help had appeared. He reflected on words Lucas had said, flippant, of course, but still valid. *He wasn't dead yet.*

SHORTLY BEFORE seven, David declared that they had reached the point of diminishing returns. He told everyone to go home, rest, and be back in twelve hours.

Jule changed quickly and went to join Kelly and Sasha while Lucas and Marilee dealt with a minor costume malfunction.

"Hey, kid." Kelly smiled warmly as he spotted Jule coming toward him. "Ready to eat?" His smiled broadened to a grin. "What am I saying? You can't have changed that much in a few weeks."

"I definitely *feel* like I've changed. A lot has happened since you left."

Sasha ruffled Jule's hair. "I love this," he said. "You always keep it so short."

"It's more aerodynamic when it's short," Jule said.

Sasha smacked the back of Jule's head. "Don't be so practical all the time."

"I'm working on it," Jule said. "But too be fair, I was trained to be practical."

"So, let's go find some food," Kelly said.

"Lucas is still getting changed," Jule said and then reacted to Kelly's grimace. "What?"

"I know this is rude, but does he have to come with us?"

"No, but I want him to," Jule replied. He paused and then spoke again. "Do you really think he isn't good enough for me?"

"Of course, he isn't," Kelly said. "He's too slick and too handsome, and he's too old for you. But you chose him, so *you* must think he's good enough. End of story."

"Really?" Jule said.

Kelly sighed. "Would I like to choose the people in your life? Yes, I would, but I can't. And because I want to stay in your life, I'm not going to bitch about the people you choose to love."

"I'm proud of you, my heart," Sasha said.

"I still think he's too old," Kelly groused.

Jule laughed. "Have you met him? He might have been around for more years, but he's not older than me."

"That's called being immature."

"That's why he needs to be around you and Sasha. He needs good role models."

Sasha shook his head. "Did you really think we'd buy that?"

"Worth a try." Jule looked sheepish. "Sorry, I just want you to like him. You're the most important people in my life, next to Mum, so it's going to be awkward if you hate him."

"I don't hate him. I just don't… respect him, I guess," Kelly said. "Of course, I don't know him well," he amended.

"You can start getting to know him at dinner."

"You walked right into that one," Sasha said.

"And you let me," Kelly said reproachfully.

"God, it's good to have you here," Jule said. "Now tell me how the Christmas pageant went."

For a few minutes, Kelly and Sasha spoke of the triumphs and tragedies inherent in putting on a holiday ballet with a dozen or so poppets ranging in age from seven to twelve. From high drama to low comedy, Jule enjoyed every second of the story.

"Luc!" Jule called out when he spotted him. "Do you fancy French tonight?" He was disappointed when his lover didn't make a joke about oral sex.

"Whatever sounds good to everyone."

"I want to go to one of those chophouses," Sasha said.

"Like a steak house?" Lucas asked.

"Yes, one of those where they bring meat until you ask them to stop."

"A churrascaria," Lucas said. "There are a few in the city. Let me see what I can do." He took out his phone and turned his back to the group.

"You have new clothes," Sasha commented to Jule while they waited for Lucas.

"Um, yeah. I didn't have anything chic enough for the city, so I did a little shopping so I wouldn't look too shabby."

"You look good," Kelly said. "You always have."

"Says the fashion expert." Sasha smiled at Kelly.

"Okay!" Lucas turned around to face the group. "I hope you don't mind that I went ahead and made a reservation. If we leave now, we'll get there in time for a cocktail before dinner."

Kelly looked at his watch. "At home, dinner's over by seven. It's now seven-forty-five and we're still *talking* about eating. I guess you eat late in the city."

"Did you forget you used to live here?" Lucas retorted.

"I guess I did," Kelly said. "Then again, I wasn't part of the social scene when I lived here."

"My Kelly is a good boy who eats his vegetables and goes to bed early," Sasha said.

"Is that how he got so big?" Lucas swept a hand at Kelly indicating his six-foot-two, broad-shouldered frame.

"You're practically the same size," Sasha told Lucas. "Kelly has broader shoulders, but—"

"Can we talk about this later?" Jule said. "I'm famished."

Kelly and Sasha exchanged a fond smile as they followed him toward the exit.

In seven minutes, by Kelly's watch, they got into the SUV that pulled to the curb outside the NJBC. Many more minutes later, they got out of the Uber at Fogo de Chão. Their table was ready, and they were seated right away. Lucas said something quietly to the host, and the man nodded genially before he went back to his station. They were looking at menus when their server arrived with a carafe of sangria and bowls of feijoada.

By the end of the meal, even Jule and Sasha admitted they'd had enough to eat. It was Lucas's opinion that consuming half a cow was probably not a good idea, but he saluted their stamina and capacity. Kelly actually laughed at the remark. The only discord came when Kelly realized Lucas had paid for dinner on the sly.

"I can't let you do that," Kelly said. "I can only imagine how much all this cost."

"A little over five hundred with the tip," Lucas said coolly. "Probably should have stopped at two bottles of wine."

"Now I *really* can't let you do that," Kelly said.

"It's done." Lucas finished his wine. "Ready to go?"

"Hold on," Kelly said, as the others rose to their feet. "We haven't settled this."

"I understand," Lucas said as they walked to the front. "I'd feel the same if I was you, but it's really okay." He held the door open for Jule, Sasha, and Kelly.

"How is it okay?" Kelly said as he stepped onto the sidewalk.

"Because I'm stinking rich," Lucas said.

"What?" Jule turned to look him.

Lucas shrugged. "It's true."

"No, you're not," Jule said. "I'd know if you were." He paused. "If you were rich, you'd have lent David money."

"I did." Lucas smiled. "In a way. Tell you about it later. Come on. The hotel is close enough to walk to from here."

While walking to Kelly and Sasha's hotel, Sasha engaged Lucas in a conversation about his hair. Kelly and Jule trailed them slightly as they made their way to Times Square.

"Hey," Kelly said softly. "Is this how he treats you all the time, or is he trying to impress me?"

"This is him," Jule said. "He really just wants me to be happy, but it's true that he desperately wants you to like him, though he'd never say it."

"All right, then."

"To be completely honest, it gets annoying sometimes," Jule complained. "I have to remind him I'm capable of taking care of myself."

"You do, huh?"

"Yes. He's as big a mother hen as Sasha."

Kelly smiled broadly. "How awful for you."

"Sasha's right. You aren't funny."

"Sasha is always right. What's your point?"

Jule laughed. "I wish you could stay here forever."

"You could always come home."

Jule was silent for several long moments. "I didn't realize until just now that I've started thinking of this as home."

"And that's how you know you're not a kid anymore," Kelly said. "When you stop thinking of your parents' house as home and make a home of your own."

"I might cry."

"Yeah." Kelly put his arm around Jule's shoulders. "That sounds like you, you big baby."

Jule laughed so hard that Lucas turned to see what was going on. Jule laughed even harder when Sasha gently smacked the back of Lucas's head to get his attention back. Clearly, Sasha had decided to treat Lucas like one of the ballet students. Jule smiled; it was going to be all right.

They said good night under the Marquis' porte-cochere, and then Jule and Lucas walked toward Fifth. It would be easier to find an unoccupied cab a little farther from Broadway.

"Are you really rich?" Jule asked.

"Yep."

"How rich?"

"I put up five million as a half payment on David's brownstone."

"Five million *dollars*?"

"It wasn't all my money," Lucas said. "I was just the front man."

"Whose money was it then?"

"Well… it was mostly my mom's money, if you have to know."

"I'm gobsmacked. Why didn't you tell me?"

Lucas shrugged. "I didn't want anyone to know. As far as people here are concerned, I'm a farm boy from upstate." He put his arm around Jule. "I'm sorry I didn't tell you, but I learned early on that some people treat you different when they find out you have money." He gave Jule a squeeze. "Not you, of course, but honestly, how did you think I afforded that loft?"

"Is it expensive to rent?"

"No, I own it."

"Shite!"

"Yeah. You won't tell anyone, right?"

Jule hid a smile. "What's it worth to you?"

"Brat."

"But I'm your brat."

"You know, Parry, it's possible to be too smart."

"How would you know?"

"You are definitely not the same guy I asked to dance in the bar at the Marriott."

"Bloody hell! You had me so wound up, I'm amazed I could speak. I was practically paralyzed."

"Is that so?" Lucas flagged down a cab. "Tell me more."

"You know, Madding, it's possible to be too conceited."

Lucas laughed as he got into the cab. "Come on, let's go home."

Jule got in, but his playful mood faded as he remembered Kelly's words. If he wanted to, he could go back to London. It wasn't something he'd considered before. It smacked too much of crawling back because he couldn't hack it in the real world. But it was a very attractive notion. His life would be much less complicated if he returned to England.

"Everything okay?" Lucas asked when the silent cab ride ended.

Jule looked up at the sky. There was no snow tonight, and the stars shone with a hard, cold light. He shivered and felt Lucas's arms go around him. It was terribly comforting, and he leaned into the embrace. This was definitely something he'd miss if he left New York.

"It's nothing," Jule said. "Seeing Kelly and Sasha made me homesick again, that's all."

Lucas shivered and held Jule closer. "It's so cool that they're here for the debut," he said. "But I hope they don't think they're taking you back to England. I just got you back, and I'm not letting anyone take you away."

Chapter Thirty-Three

"JULE, WAKE up."

Jule opened his eyes and saw Lucas leaning over him. "What? Why?"

"Sorry," Lucas said. "David called a few minutes ago. He needs us *now*."

Jule sat up and swung his legs over the side of the bed. "I'm glad I took a shower last night."

"You needed it," Lucas said emphatically.

"What?" Jule looked over at Lucas.

"You had so much jizz on you, you looked like a glazed donut."

"Gross." Jule found a pair of clean underwear and pulled them on.

"Hey, totally your fault for making me come twice." Lucas brought Jule's boots over and set them down. He ran a hand through Jule's hair. "Better do something with that."

"JBF again?"

Lucas grinned. "The very definition of JBF hair." He handed Jule a small insulated bag. "You can eat this on the way."

Jule dressed, tamed his hair, and by the time they got to the street, he'd finished the breakfast sandwich Lucas had packed. He folded the bag and stowed it in one of the parka's pockets.

"So, what's going on?" Jule asked as they waited for a cab.

"The Ice Queen is stirring the shit again. Apparently, she manipulated Director Halvorsen and several board members of the NYCB into lodging a complaint with the NJBC. David demanded an immediate hearing. We're moral support."

When Lucas and Jule walked into the NJBC's main building, they saw Kelly, Sasha, and the rest of the small cast of *Fireheart* in the lobby. Greetings were somber. No one really knew what was going on. And then David came down the hall.

"Thanks for coming," he said. "Follow me. We're meeting in Director Moses's office."

"I'm surprised," Kelly said. "People come to Halvorsen, not the other way around."

"Director Moses didn't see why he should waste his time traveling to Manhattan to settle a matter he regards as frivolous, and I quote."

"Sassy," Charlotte commented.

"He seems to be on our side," David said. "Then again, I'm not sure he's on any side, except that of the New Jersey Ballet."

"I'll take impartial any day," Kelly said. "What's the complaint?"

"We're peddling pornography."

Kelly frowned. He started to speak, but they'd arrived at their destination.

The door stood open, and Director Moses motioned to them to enter; Director Halvorsen and Miss Dahlman were already present. "I wasn't expecting such a crowd," he said drolly. "I'm afraid some of you will have to stand."

"We all stand with David," Kelly said. He ignored the look of cold scorn from Catherine.

"Mr. Holloway," Director Moses said. "And Mr. Vasile. I heard you were back, but I didn't quite believe it. Welcome, gentlemen. It's a genuine pleasure to see you." He glanced at Director Halvorsen over the top of his glasses. "Though I regret the circumstances."

"If we could get to business," Halvorsen said. "I'm a busy man."

"You took the words right out of my mouth," Moses said. "So, make your case, and it had better be good. The New Jersey Ballet is not in the habit of going back on its word."

Halvorsen turned to Catherine.

Catherine got to her feet. "Where do I begin?" she said, spreading her hands in a graceful little gesture of hopelessness. It was easy to see what a great ballerina she might have been.

"Try stating your complaint," Moses said dryly.

"Very well." Catherine held up a copy of the *Fireheart* program before she placed it on Moses's desk.

"I've seen it," he said. "I did have to approve it, after all."

"You approve of bare derrières on ballet programs?"

"If the buttocks are attached to a person performing a dance, then yes, I do. If you've taken me for a prude, let me disabuse you of your misconception. I would not care if the dancers were naked if the nudity were essential to the story of the ballet."

Catherine folded her lips into a thin line. "It appears we have different definitions of what constitutes art and what is a vulgar display."

"If you say so. I'm waiting for you to present me with a creditable reason to deny Mr. Downes a venue for his ballet."

"There's a much larger issue here," she said. "Giving approval to this work will lower the tone of our entire community. What's next? Stripper poles in *Swan Lake*?"

Lucas was startled into a laugh but turned it into a cough.

"Don't you think you're exaggerating somewhat?" Moses said.

"Have you seen the content of this *soi-disant* work of art?"

"I've not seen all of it."

"Perhaps you weren't aware that two men will be simulating gay sex on your stage."

Moses stared at her for a moment before he spoke. "And where in the ballet does this occur?" He turned to David.

"Well… there's a kiss," David said. "And it's clear through the dancing that the protagonists are in love. However, no one is simulating anything beyond a passionate embrace. And the simulated part is debatable."

"So you say," Catherine said. "I've seen it."

"Impossible," Lucas said. "You're seeing what you want to—"

David put a hand on Lucas's arm. "There's nothing obscene in my ballet," he said firmly.

Catherine smiled. "What about him?" She pointed to Jule.

Kelly bristled as though she'd leveled a gun on his protégé. Only Sasha's hand on his wrist kept him from responding.

"What the actual—?" David cut himself off. When he spoke again, his voice was even. "Please go on. I can't wait to hear what you've fabricated."

"Until recently, Julian Parry was a resident in the dorms at The Downtown Ballet Company. The rules are the same as the rules for dorms at the NYBC, aren't they, David?"

"You know they are. You insisted on it."

"And what's the punishment for breaking those rules?"

"It depends on which rule is broken."

"Fraternizing in a dorm room after curfew," Catherine said triumphantly.

"Suspension of activities," Halvorsen spoke up when David took too long to answer.

"Then I think we can assume Mr. Parry won't be dancing for you tomorrow night," Catherine said. She turned her gaze on Lucas. "And what about the seducer? Should he get off scot-free?"

"I'm assuming all parties being accused of… unbecoming behavior are of the age of consent," Moses said. "If not, it certainly doesn't negate the fact that a rule was broken but would in fact make it more serious."

"I'm not accusing anyone of molesting a minor," Catherine said.

"Good. As to the accusation, what proof do you have?"

"I have a witness."

Mr. Moses waited for the murmuring to stop before he spoke again. "When might we expect to hear from your witness?"

Catherine fixed her gaze on Bram. "Mr. Silber can corroborate," she said.

Moses turned his attention to Bram. "Do you have anything to say about this?"

"As a matter of fact, I do, sir." Bram cleared his throat. "Here's what I know." He glanced at Catherine. "The lady making all the claims has a long history with Mr. Downes. They were friends, but lately, things have been rocky between them. More than once, I've heard her say she was going to 'fix him.' I didn't know what she meant until today."

Catherine frowned. "Just tell Director Moses what you saw without editorializing."

"Look, Miss Dahlman, I know what you want me to say, but I'm not going to lie for you."

"I'm not asking you to lie, just tell him what you told me."

"Okay. A few weeks ago, I saw Lucas, Mr. Madding, showing Mr. Parry around the Downtown facilities. I stopped to say hi, and I got the idea they were friends already." Bram shrugged and shot Jule a sheepish glance.

"And you saw them engage in lewd behavior," Catherine prompted.

Bram stared at Catherine in surprise. "Lewd? Ma'am, and sir, I did not see anything *lewd*."

"You're a liar," she said.

"I don't know what to tell you," Bram said. "You've clearly got an ax to grind, but I'm not going to make up stories of wild orgies in the dorms so you can get some weird revenge on David."

"How dare you!" Catherine said through clenched teeth.

"Miss Dahlman," Director Moses said. "Do you have any other evidence to back up your claim of *lewdness*?"

"They're queer!" Catherine burst out. "Of course, they were being obscene. Taking any opportunity to be disgusting. It's what they do." She pointed a quivering finger at Jule. "Oh, they look like innocent boys, but they're filthy. Filthy inside and out, and they spread their filth."

Halvorsen finally spoke. "Catherine," he said calmly. "I came here with you out of respect for your family, but if this all you have to offer in—"

"Be quiet," she told him impatiently. "Just keep your mouth shut and do as you're told. It's not as though you haven't done it before, and this is no different than the last time. We got rid of the filth once, but it always comes back." She glanced at Kelly before she continued. "Now it's time to root it out again."

"Hold on," Kelly said before Halvorsen could retort. "What are you talking about?"

"Please, Mr. Holloway," Director Moses said. "I have the greatest respect for you, but this meeting has already lost all structure."

"I'm sorry, sir. May I speak?"

"I'd rather you wait until Ms. Dahlman is finished bringing her complaint."

"I don't mind answering," she said, a note of smugness creeping into her voice. "Degenerates don't belong here if they can't keep it to themselves. Mr. Holloway was another one who thought he could flaunt his perversion, but he learned it wouldn't be tolerated."

Kelly looked over at David and shook his head. "All this time," he said.

"What?" David gave Kelly a puzzled look in return.

"Please," Director Moses said. "Let's have a little decorum." He looked at Halvorsen. "Do you know what they're talking about, Rickard?"

"Ten years ago, I was forced to dismiss Mr. Holloway from the New York City Ballet."

"No one held a gun to your head," Kelly said.

"Mr. Holloway." Director Moses looked sympathetic but impatient. "Pretend we're in school and wait until I call on you."

"Sorry, sir."

"Go on," Moses told Halvorsen.

"I was informed by someone I trusted that one of our principal dancers was engaged in a flagrant homosexual affair under our roof. His lover was a dancer who'd been let go from the Romanian National Ballet for being a deviant. I didn't believe this of Mr. Holloway, but in good conscience, I had to look into it. When I found out it was true, I had no choice. The good name of the NYCB was at stake."

"How did you determine that it was true?"

"Mr. Holloway told me, in no uncertain terms, that he was in love with Mr. Vasile and that it was no one's business but theirs. He was wrong, of course. Once it was in the open, it became my business. For the good of the company, I had to dismiss him."

"I see," Moses said, as he turned his gaze on Kelly. "I always wondered why you walked away from such a promising career. What a pity bigotry and short-sightedness robbed ballet of a great talent. You're owed an apology, I think, Mr. Holloway."

Catherine laughed harshly. "Can we get back to the matter at hand?"

"Which is?"

Catherine opened her mouth and then shut it again.

"If I may recap." Director Moses laced his fingers together and gazed solemnly at her. "Your first complaint concerned what you perceived as inappropriate imagery. You then accused Mr. Downes of scheming to present pornography from the stage of NJBC. Your third complaint appears to concern inappropriate sexual behavior under the aegis of The Downtown Ballet."

"Yes."

"All of these *charges* have been handily refuted, wouldn't you say?" Moses glanced at Halvorsen.

Halvorsen nodded. "I'm sorry to have wasted your time and mine." He shook Moses's hand before he left without a word to Catherine.

"Was there anything else, Ms. Dahlman?" Director Moses said.

Catherine ignored him. It was as if there were no one in the room but David and her. "This isn't the end of it," she said to him before she followed Halvorsen out of the office.

"Well," Director Moses said. "That was certainly… distasteful." He smiled at the people standing around his office. "I'm sorry you had to get up so early for this."

"Are you kidding?" Lucas said. "I would have paid money to watch her fall on her face."

Jule put a hand over Lucas's mouth.

"Well," David said. "If that's all, we've got work to do."

"Please, get out of my office." Director Moses rose to shake David's hand. "I'm joking. Glad it turned out well for you. I'm really looking forward to seeing this ballet."

"We're having a full-dress rehearsal today. Drop in."

Moses smiled. "I want to eat the cake, not watch you bake it."

David chuckled. "We'll be on our way, then."

THE GROUP left the administrative wing and walked to the auditorium with David out front like a drum major in his velvet blazer. Halfway there, Kelly caught up and kept pace with him.

"I owe you an apology," Kelly said.

"For what, exactly?"

"It was Catherine," Kelly said. "She told Halvorsen about me and Sasha."

"It sure looks that way."

"I thought it was you."

David stopped and Jule ran into him. Lucas ran into Jule. Everyone else managed to avoid the pileup, and David waved them on.

"You thought I ratted you out to the authorities?" David said reproachfully. "Me? A narc?"

"You said you were going to make me sorry."

"Of course, I did. You hurt me, so I lashed out." David met Kelly's gaze. "It killed me that you chose him over me. I had so much to offer you, but you couldn't see anyone but him. Sure, I was sore, but I would *never* have turned you and Sasha in."

"I hated you so much," Kelly said. "I hated Halvorsen, too, but not as much as I hated you."

"I can't believe you left Jule with me."

"Me either." Kelly looked over at Sasha and then back at David. "Man, I feel so much better."

"Come here," David said.

"Why?"

David waved him closer. "Bring it in, big guy." He put his arms around Kelly and hugged him.

After a moment, Kelly returned the hug.

"I don't understand," Jule said. "Why would Miss Dahlman do that?"

"It's complicated," David said.

"But she sounded like she hates gay people," Jule persisted. "It doesn't make sense. I mean, she likes you so much."

"She did." David nodded. "And for a long time, I think she was able to ignore or pretend she didn't know about my lovers. Then Kelly came along. That's when she started to crack."

"You two?" Jule looked from David to Kelly and back again.

David shook his head. "My lust was unrequited. Kelly had already been smitten by a smoldering beauty from Eastern Europe."

"Me," Sasha said helpfully.

"I've never taken rejection well," David said. "And Catherine was happy to commiserate. If I'd known she was going to do something like that, I would have cheerfully strangled her."

"It kind of sucks that she gets to walk away without so much as a slap on the wrist," Lucas said.

"She lost a lot today, believe me," David said. "She lost credibility in the eyes of two powerful people in her sphere. I wouldn't be surprised if she's shunned, at least for a while. If you want her to suffer, rest assured, she'll suffer."

"This has all been very sad," Jule said.

"But it's over," Lucas said. "Let's move on." He squeezed Jule's shoulder.

"Hey," Bram called out from the end of hall. "You guys working today?"

"Yes, and I want everyone in costume by the time I get there," David said sternly.

Bram quickly ducked back in the stage door.

"Thanks," Lucas said as he passed by Bram.

"For what?"

"You lied for us."

Bram shook his head. "You're cute, but I didn't exactly lie. I saw a kiss, but I didn't see anything lewd... dammit."

Lucas smiled. "Thanks anyway."

KELLY, SASHA, Jule, and Lucas were the last members of the company lingering in the auditorium after the rehearsal. Kelly and Sasha were sitting in the front row watching Jule and Lucas practice.

"They work well together," Sasha murmured.

"I've got eyes," Kelly answered.

Sasha grinned. "You sound annoyed. Are you jealous?"

"No. What a ridiculous idea."

"Is it, though?"

"Of course, it is. I'm not interested in Jule that way."

"Not everything is about sex." Sasha raised an eyebrow. "For a long time, you've been a father figure to Jule. You loom large in his life."

"I loom large?" Kelly shook his head, but he was smiling.

"Yes, you do. Also, you and Jule spent a significant part of each and every day together. Now, he'd rather spend his time with Lucas... and who can blame him?"

"Should I be worried about you?"

Sasha laughed. "Always."

Abruptly, Kelly stood up. "Jule!" he called out. "Can you guys take a break? I'd like to talk to you about something."

"Of course." Jule came to the edge of the stage and sat, swinging his legs.

Lucas sat, rested his aching ankle on his knee, and started massaging it. He was surprised when Sasha came to take over, but he didn't protest.

"Damn, you're good at that," Lucas groaned a few moments later.

Kelly ignored the byplay. "Remember watching the Winter Olympics and how much you liked the figure skating?" he asked Jule.

Jule nodded.

"While I was watching Lucas lift you, I had an idea. David said we could add new steps, and I think we can come up with one that no one's seen before."

"I'm intrigued," Lucas said.

"So am I," Jule said. "It sounds... unconventional."

"What has gotten into you?" Sasha asked Kelly. "Never mind. I like it."

Kelly got up on the stage as Jule got to his feet. "The basic idea is that I launch Jule and Lucas catches him."

"That would certainly be different," Lucas said. "I like it."

"During the first act, when the goddess lights the fire in your hearts would be the perfect moment for something like that," Sasha said.

"It's great metaphor," Kelly said.

"How would we do it?" Jule asked Kelly. "I'm assuming I'll be doing a jump with some extra power from you."

"Exactly." Kelly nodded. "The way I'm picturing it, I'll be kneeling, and you'll be climbing me like a flight of lumpy stairs. One foot on my thigh, one on my hand as I lift, and the last step is off my shoulder."

"Let's try it." Jule said. He glanced at Lucas. "If you're up for it."

Lucas stood and put some weight on his ankle. "I'm good."

"I agree," Sasha said. "Ankle is warm and flexible."

"I've got other parts that are warm and flexible." Lucas smirked.

"That'll be enough of that," Kelly said. He paced off a few steps and pointed. "I want you right there, pretty boy."

"I've heard that one before." Lucas smirked again as he stopped on the spot Kelly indicated. "What's my move?"

"You just be ready to catch Jule. If you drop him, I'll drop you. Got it?"

"Noted." Lucas set himself and waited.

Kelly positioned himself on one knee and nodded to Jule. Jule took three accelerating steps, put one foot on Kelly's bent leg and the other on Kelly's palm, as Kelly rose to his feet. Jule pushed off Kelly's shoulder with his left foot as Kelly gave added impetus to the right. And then Jule was flying, legs extended front and back in a grand jeté, in complete trust that his partner would catch him. Lucas caught him around the waist and one thigh and lowered him into an arabesque. They stood for a moment looking into each other's eyes.

"That was awesome," Jule murmured.

"Okay," Kelly called out. "Not bad for a first try."

Jule spun around to face Kelly. "I think we should add something. While I'm in the air, I could do a twist, like a diver."

"Let's give it another go," Kelly said. "You felt solid with your foot placement. Is there anything I can do to make it easier?"

"You could push a little harder on my right to help start a spin."

Kelly nodded. "Sasha, give us a beat?"

Sasha began a rhythmic clapping and Jule began his run. This time the launch went more smoothly as Kelly timed his rise with Jule's first jump. Kelly flung Jule toward Lucas. Jule extended an arm as he drew the other in and did a roll in midair with his legs together. Lucas caught him and used his momentum to swing him up and onto his feet.

"Beautiful!" Sasha exclaimed.

"Again!" Jule said as he hurried back to Kelly.

They performed the maneuver three more times before Lucas reluctantly admitted his ankle was bothering him. Jule reckoned that meant Lucas had been in pain for a while and became quite authoritarian in ordering everyone to stop immediately. Lucas sat as commanded and let Sasha work his ankle again.

"I'm fine," Lucas said a minute later, pulling his foot from Sasha's grasp.

"I tell you when you're fine," Sasha said, taking the foot back. "This belongs to me now."

Jule knelt next to Lucas. "Mate, let Sasha do his magic. Then you're going to rest until the performance. We're not taking any chances."

Chapter Thirty-Four

A FEW hours later, Jule looked away from the mirror when David walked into the men's dressing room. Bram, Lucas, Kelly, and Sasha also stopped what they were doing to give David their attention.

"You look like shit." Lucas said.

"Wow, thanks," David said. "But I've got a good reason. I just talked to the ladies, and now I'm telling you, because I don't want you to be surprised when you go on stage."

"Is it the sets?" Kelly asked.

"I wish." David tugged at his hair. "The hall is half-empty, even though the performance is sold out. There's no one in the subscription seats. I know Catherine did this, but knowing that doesn't fix it."

Sasha put a hand on David's shoulder. "Put it out of your mind," he said. "Concentrate on your ballet."

"Good. Good." David nodded. "Good advice for sure. Is everyone set here?"

"Absolutely," Bram said. "Don't worry about us."

"We're going to do you proud," Jule added.

David nodded again and then left.

"Well that sucks," Lucas said. "I should have known she'd have at least one more dirty trick up her lacy sleeve."

"It doesn't matter," Jule said firmly. "Even if the theater was completely empty, I'd go out there and dance my best."

"That's my boy," Kelly said. "The dance is the thing. The performance, not the applause." He looked at the clock. "Fifteen minutes."

"I'm gonna hit the john one more time," Lucas said.

"Hey, Jule," Bram said after Lucas left. "If you're completely honest with me, is Luc one hundred percent?"

"I don't know anyone who is," Jule said. "But if you're asking if he can finish this ballet, the answer is yes. He won't let us down."

"I'm only asking because a performance is different from practice or rehearsal. There's a different tension."

"I know." Jule met Bram's gaze. "I also know that Lucas will finish this performance even if he breaks a leg."

Bram held up his hands. "Just checking. Believe it or not, I want this show to be a success as much as you do."

"Impossible," Jule said flatly.

"Bram," Kelly said. "Since you don't have anything to do until the very end, why don't you find David and make yourself useful until you have to get into costume?"

"I—"

"It wasn't a suggestion," Sasha said, scowling at Bram.

"I'm on it," Bram said as he left the dressing room.

"Why don't I like him?" Sasha asked of no one in particular.

"He's all right," Jule said carefully. "Beautiful dancer."

Sasha narrowed his eyes at Jule. "I think that tone in your voice is good enough reason to dislike him."

"What? No?" Jule stood up and smoothed the belt that held his costume together. "Bram was really nice to me when Lucas got hurt."

Sasha snorted. "You mean, once your boyfriend was out of the picture, Bram started hitting on you."

Jule shrugged. "He flirted. I flirted back. It was stupid. End of story."

"No." Sasha shook his head. "That story ended when you forgave Lucas."

"How do I look?" Jule changed the subject.

"Perfect," Sasha said without hesitation.

"You look great," Kelly said. "Maybe you should do a *Peter Pan* ballet before you get any older."

Jule rolled his eyes, but he was secretly delighted by the idea. "I suppose you want me to take Tinkerbell's role."

Kelly grinned. "You stole my joke."

"Joke was obvious," Jule said in a spot-on impression of Sasha's faded East-European accent.

Sasha smacked the back of Jule's head. "For disrespect," he said solemnly.

"Ten minutes," Kelly said.

Jule wiggled his toes. "How glad am I that you made me learn to dance barefoot?"

"A dancer must be prepared for any surface," Kelly said.

"A dancer must have calluses," Jule replied.

"And not just on the feet," Sasha said.

"Five minutes," Kelly said. "Let's go."

Lucas returned and fell into step with Jule as they went down the hall. "We should do it," he said.

"What?" Jule looked startled.

"The new jump."

"But no one will be prepared for it," Jule objected.

"It doesn't matter. It takes up the same amount of time as the original steps."

Jule glanced back at Kelly. "Lucas wants to do the new move," he said.

"I agree with him," Kelly answered, shocking Jule.

"So do I," Sasha said. "People will talk about it, and tomorrow, you will have a proper audience."

"That's what I'm saying." Lucas nudged Jule's shoulder. "What do you say?"

Jule's heart beat a little faster at the thought of performing a maneuver they'd practiced exactly five times. He glanced over at Lucas, and Lucas smiled at him. A profound sense of calm draped itself over Jule like the reassuring warmth of one of Sasha's hugs. Taking chances was risky and made him uncomfortable, but he'd learned that breaking routine wasn't lethal, and sometimes the reward was massive. If he hadn't taken a chance, he wouldn't have Lucas.

"I'm game," Jule said.

The group of four walked to the wings where David was waiting. Jule went to stand next to Lucas and waited to hear David's last instructions before the curtain went up. Kelly and Sasha went to take their places in the wings at stage right.

David put a hand on the back of Jule's neck and one on Lucas's forearm. "You know I believe in you," he said softly. "I know that you have the skills, the talent, and the fire to bring my vision to life. You're both amazing performers in your own right, but when you dance together, it's pure magic. No one who sees you tonight will ever forget it."

"So... we should just go out there and be perfect?" Lucas said.

"That's all I ask," David said.

"We got this," Jule said.

Out front in the orchestra pit, Jamison raised his baton.

"This is it," David said. "*Allez, mes enfants. Voler.*"
He commanded them to fly, and fly they did.

NEAR THE end of the first act, at the point where Lucas and Jule were meant to meet in the middle of the stage, David sensed something off. As he watched along with everyone else in the auditorium, Jule danced toward Kelly as Lucas moved to center stage. Jule leaped and Kelly was there to launch him. Jule soared in a *grand jeté,* leaving out the twist, toward the spot where Lucas waited. Lucas was poised and perfectly positioned to catch his costar. It was a tricky maneuver that could send both of them crashing to the floor if not performed correctly. However, Lucas fielded Jule's rapidly moving mass deftly and used the momentum to swing Jule to his feet and send them both into a decelerating spin. It happened so smoothly that it was a moment before anyone recovered enough to clap. When they did recover, the applause was loud and continued until the curtain dropped on the first act.

"Are you insane?" David shouted as the dancers left the stage.

Kelly took David's arm and pulled him aside. "If you want to be mad at someone, be mad at me. I told them to do it."

"It was magnificent," David said. "But damn. It could have been tragic."

"If you're worried about me," Lucas said loudly, "I admit, I felt some strain in the ankle when I caught Jule, but I'm fine."

"It *was* magnificent, wasn't it?" Kelly smiled.

David returned the smile. "It was unprecedented."

"Not for long," Kelly predicted. "Jule's going to be watching figure skating videos."

"Why?"

"I suggested it."

David groaned, but then he brightened. "Well, after all, why not? It's basically ballet on ice." He went to praise Lucas and Jule, and then it was time for the second act.

AFTER THE second, and sold-out, performance, Lucas invited everyone to his loft for an after-party. Champagne was poured, and the host made a toast. Holding his glass up, Lucas read an excerpt from the *New York Times'* review of the first performance.

"The debut performance of *Fireheart* was not only flawless but unique. The chemistry between Julian Parry and Lucas Madding is palpable and incandescent. David Dulac Downes has once again proven himself a visionary, if unconventional, genius. All those involved in the production are deserving of the highest praise."

Everyone drank and then broke into groups. Lucas did not let Jule get far away from him, though. He had an arm around Jule's shoulders as he talked with Jezza and Charlotte.

"Your photos are a viral sensation," Charlotte told Jezza.

Jezza took a bow. "We really ought to thank Jule's fan club. They took it upon themselves to conduct their own social media campaign. It was a veritable blitz twenty-four seven."

"I have more gossip," Charlotte said. "Apparently, all of Catherine's powerful friends heard about her outburst in Director Moses's office, and they weren't thrilled."

"Which explains why the seasonal seats were full tonight," Lucas said.

"A triumph," Jezza declared before wandering off.

At the end of the evening, Jule kissed Charlotte's cheek and accepted a kiss on the cheek from David before he closed the front door. He was fairly certain they were the last guests, other than Kelly and Sasha, who weren't really guests but family. As he passed the alcove set up for reading or listening to music, Sasha called to him. Jule stopped and sat on the shelf bench opposite the super-comfy Eames chair Sasha was ensconced in.

"We haven't had a chance to really talk," Sasha said as he set aside the headphones.

"We *have* been a bit busy."

"Everything is okay with you now?"

Jule nodded. "It was rough for a while. I didn't like what I was feeling, and it was—I was feeling everything so intensely. It was hard to stay focused. I had trouble falling asleep a few times." Almost, he mentioned the anxiety attack he'd had, but he was too tired for that conversation right now.

"Yes, you told me on the phone. I was worried about you." Sasha smiled. "But you got through it, and now you're happy."

"I am." Jule smiled.

"I like that smile," Sasha said. "He's a good lover, your man?"

Jule felt his cheeks grow warm, but he answered honestly, as he always did. "Well, he's the only lover I've ever had, so I can't compare him to anyone else, but I have to say, if the sex was any hotter, I'd be a pile of ash."

"Good. It's more important than you think."

"It's actually *very* important to me."

"I understand." Sasha grinned. "So, tell me, is that why you decided to forgive him?"

"It was certainly an incentive." Jule chuckled and then sobered. "I don't really know why I took him back. It just sort of happened naturally." He bit his lip. "I mean, I love him, obviously, but there wasn't some moment of clarity or anything like that. He was just around, you know? He was teaching classes while he was healing and just hanging out. Aside from letting me know he felt awful and wanted a second chance, he never pestered me. It was kind of scary how much I missed being with him. When he touches me, I get this rush of feelings so strong, it's like I'm going to pass out. That can't be normal." He looked hopefully at Sasha.

"Kelly can make my heart race just by looking at me across a room."

Jule smiled. "I guess I just remembered how much I loved being with him. I believe he's a good person who did a stupid thing, so I forgave him."

"And other than the bedroom, you get along well?"

Jule nodded. "I can't believe how good it is. He can be a bit laddish sometimes, but I like it, so it isn't a problem."

"He likes playing with you?"

Jule smiled again.

"Good." Sasha returned the smile. "Try not to lose that. It's also more important than you might think."

"You've never given me bad advice before."

"I never will. When I speak to you, I weigh each word. Since we met, I've been constantly aware that your mind is a hungry one, so I've always been careful what I say around you. I'm always telling Kelly to watch his words."

"I'm not sure how to feel about that."

"It wasn't hardship. It made me a better person."

"Oh... then, you're welcome?"

Sasha chuckled. "All right. Now, I believe you are fine, and I can see you are happy."

"So, you're satisfied Lucas isn't going to sell me to sex traffickers?"

Sasha nodded. "I can't speak for Kelly, though."

WHILE SASHA and Jule were talking about Kelly, the subject of the conversation was helping himself to a beer. He brought it back to the living room area and joined Lucas.

"How old are you again?" Kelly said as he dropped into an easy chair opposite Lucas. "You're not thirty yet, right?"

"Right," Lucas said firmly. "I'm twenty-seven."

"I wasn't much younger than you when I met Sasha."

"Nice catch, bro."

Kelly frowned slightly and then smiled. "True."

"I mean, he's a looker and that body…." Lucas mimed fanning himself.

"I can't argue with that." Kelly took a sip of his beer.

"I can sense you aren't comfortable with me drooling over your boo." Lucas cleared his throat. "So… are we about to have a talk with a capital T?"

"Yes, we are."

"About Jule."

"You're two for two."

"Why do you want to bust my balls?"

Kelly met Lucas's eyes. "You're kidding, right?"

"No. I'm not. I mean, I know you're protective of Jule. I get that loud and clear." Lucas took a deep breath before he continued. "I just don't see why I have to answer to you."

"Because it would be courteous and respectful for one thing, but mainly because you want me to know you love him as much as I do."

"Maybe a little more."

"You've known him for a season. I watched him grow up."

"Then how about admitting he's grown up?"

"Jule is mature for his age… in some ways."

"Then why don't you want me to have him?"

Kelly shook his head. "It's not him I'm worried about. Jule will be fine. Even if you break his heart, *again*, he'll bounce back. You, on the other hand... I don't like your chances."

"'Cause what? You'll fuck me up?"

"Do you really think I'd need to?"

Lucas sat back. "I'm confused. At first, I thought this was going to be a straightforward threat to kick my ass if I hurt Jule and yada yada, but now I'm not sure."

"You love Jule," Kelly stated.

"Roger that. To my complete and utter amazement, I'm one hundred percent in love with that kid. Can you believe it?"

"Yes, I can. He's very lovable." Kelly smiled. "And he loves you. My advice is be good to him, so good that he'll never want to leave you. Because if he does leave you, all he's going to leave behind is a big hole where your life used to be, understand?"

"I do." Lucas nodded. "Whew. I thought you were going to ream me."

"I could, but it would be redundant, and I wouldn't dream of depriving Sasha of the pleasure of threatening you."

"I'm starting to see what Jule likes about you."

"I wish I could say the same." Kelly winked.

"Ah, come on. *Every*body likes me."

"And that's exactly what I don't like about you." Kelly paused. "Sorry. I guess I *am* having a little fun with you. It's just that you were so clearly trying not to piss me off and losing the battle."

"Was I supposed to be feisty?"

Kelly shook his head. "I was prepared to hate you," he said. "But honestly, I'm pretty impressed with what I've seen of you this time. Either you were just acting like a jerk when I met you, or you've undergone a profound change."

"Blame Jule. He won't let me get away with shit." Lucas met Kelly's gaze. "When he walked away from me—" He swallowed and started over. "When he left, he took all the bright with him. My life literally turned gray. No color. No flavor. No joy. So, I get what you're saying, and I won't fuck it up."

"Okay, then." Kelly nodded. "Thanks for talking to me."

"Hey, now, where you going? I was just starting to enjoy it." Lucas stood. "Let me get a couple more beers. Be right back. Don't go anywhere."

Kelly settled back. When Lucas returned, he accepted the bottle offered to him. "So... are you really well-off?" He looked around. "I know this space didn't come cheap."

"I own it," Lucas said. "I don't have a lot of personal wealth... *yet*, but my family is loaded, and my mom really likes me, so in essence, I'm well-off." He met Kelly's gaze. "Jule will never have to worry about money, if that's what you're getting at."

"God, I really do sound like an overprotective dad with a teenage daughter, don't I?"

"Don't worry about it," Lucas said. "I think it's pretty awesome that he has people like you in his life. I don't know what he did to me, but I know I'll never be the same, and I'm glad." He took a drink of his beer. "Just a few months ago, I was depressed, not that I let it show. It was all because my birthday was coming up. I saw thirty getting closer and closer. I know some dancers continue to perform into their forties and even fifties, but when I think of how hard it would be fifteen years from now to push my body to the same standards—" He looked down. "It made me feel so tired. And then you came to town with your prize student, and I...." Lucas took another drink as he thought about the circumstances under which he'd met Jule.

"Hey, it's okay," Kelly said. "And by that, I mean, it's okay if you don't want to talk about it. I understand if it makes you feel lower than a snake's belly."

"Oh, for fuck's sake, he told you about that?" Lucas looked stricken.

"He tells us everything," Kelly said. "Fair warning."

"Let's skip over that part and just say that while I was supposed to be seducing Jule for David, I fell in love. I don't know how or why. He just smiled at me this one time, and it was like some god of love flipped a golden switch somewhere, and suddenly, I couldn't see anyone but him."

"Yeah, that's what it's like," Kelly said. "Now, imagine him gone, and remember what I said about being good to him."

"Be good to him? Mister, you ain't gonna believe how good I can be when I'm motivated. It's going to be off the dial."

"Then I guess he'll be staying here." Kelly sighed. "Don't laugh, but I've always had this dream that he'd take over the school some day when he retired from a hugely successful career."

"I wouldn't give up on it." Lucas finished his beer and set the bottle down. "Now... there's something I'd like to talk to you about."

"Fair enough."

"One of the reasons it was hard for me to warm up to you—" Lucas paused. "Man, I've thought about this a lot, but I still don't know how to phrase it." He cleared his throat. "Jule once said to me that he was used to ignoring pain, and it made me feel so bad that I can't describe it. I could only assume he was referring to his training with you. So… what's that about?"

"Becoming an excellent athlete involves a certain amount of pain. You should know that."

"Of course, I do, but—it was the way he said it. Like it was an everyday thing like brushing his teeth."

Kelly sighed. "The last thing I want to do is talk about this, but if Jule hasn't told you…. His father is… less than accepting of Jule's choices. Sadly, for him, his loud disapproval just made Jule work harder to be a great dancer. Jule can be very… determined." He paused. "I did my best, and so did Sasha, to keep a close eye on him, but I know there were times he sneaked into the studio for extra practice, and it wasn't easy to keep him inactive after an injury. If I wouldn't let him dance, he'd go out running." Kelly met Lucas's eyes. "I wish we could have been with him twenty-four seven, but it just wasn't possible."

"Ohhh-kay." Lucas thought for a minute. "I was so close to hating you for pushing Jule too hard, but he was pushing himself."

"Does that really surprise you?"

"I guess it shouldn't. Hey, look, I'm sorry."

Kelly shook his head. "No apology necessary. In fact, you just convinced me you're good enough for our boy."

Before Lucas could answer, Jule and Sasha came in, and Kelly saw how Jule's gaze went to Lucas first and the way they both lit up. As long as Jule was happy, Kelly was going to be happy for him.

Sasha smiled at Jule and Lucas. "What a beautiful couple."

Kelly nodded. "Lucas thinks you're pretty too," he told Sasha.

"He said this?"

"Well, yeah," Lucas said. "I'd have to be blind not to notice."

"You're right. Sasha is gorgeous." Jule paused. "Not as pretty as you, of course."

"I have to agree," Sasha said. "Lucas is prettier… for now. Wait until you see me with my new hairstyle, though."

Kelly groaned. "You aren't serious about that."

"Wait and see," Sasha said with a devilish smile. "And now, it's time to go."

Kelly looked at his watch. "How did it get to be two o'clock? Let's go and let Jule and Lucas get some sleep."

"WHEW." LUCAS mimed wiping his brow as he closed the front door behind Kelly and Sasha. "I think I finally passed the boyfriend test."

Jule put his arms around Lucas. "Kelly will be calling you son in no time," he predicted.

"Gee, you really think so?" Lucas said with exaggerated enthusiasm. "Because I would hate that."

"You're absolutely insane, aren't you?"

"Not according to my last psychological evaluation. They're tedious, but it's just once a year, and it keeps Mom happy."

"You're still joking, right?"

"Of course I am." Lucas smirked. "Or am I?"

"I swear to God, I can't tell." Jule let go of Lucas. "We should probably get some sleep."

"True that. And we should take a little time to practice the throw before the next performance." Lucas grinned. "I wish I could have seen David's face when Kelly launched you at me."

Jule nodded. "That would have been something. I hope he's all right. I mean, he has to be, right? The performance was a success."

"I think you're right. Whatever problems he might have, I believe he's happy right now. So you just relax and be happy too."

DAVID TURNED up the collar of his overcoat as he stared at the front of his former home. He'd declined the offer of Jamison's couch and had somehow wound up here at three in the morning. It was freezing, but he hardly noticed.

The ballet was a triumph. His labor of love had been embraced by critics and audience members alike. Reviews were of the kind referred to as raves. Despite all the odds and Catherine stacking the deck against him, he'd pulled it off. He'd created a ballet that was destined to be a classic. He was here now proving to himself that it had been worth it while saying goodbye to the Duchess, as his grandfather had called the building.

"Somehow, I knew you'd be here." Catherine stepped out of the shadow of the covered entrance and came down the front steps to stand in front of David. She wore an ankle-length coat with a cowl collar of snow fox and looked as though she'd stepped straight off a page of *Town and Country* magazine.

"I've never been able to hide from you." David's tone was far from playful, and he refused to meet her gaze. He continued to look at the house. "Adieu, old girl," he said softly.

"I tried to buy it," Catherine said.

"Of course you did. It represents a mountain of leverage. You'd have had me on a leash again in no time."

"Don't be unpleasant."

"Unpleasant?" David lowered his voice when he spoke again. "Honestly, Cath, why would you expect me to be pleasant to you?"

"Because you're civilized?"

"I guess one of us has to be."

"May I buy you breakfast?"

David finally looked at her.

After a few moments of his steady stare, Catherine spoke again. "Too soon?"

"You're acting like this is just another of our little teapot tempests."

"We both know that in a few days or a week you'll call me, and we'll have brunch or dinner, and we'll both remember how well we complement one another."

"Not this time."

Catherine laughed. "All right, then. I'll give you a few more days before I call."

"Don't call me."

"There's no reason to be rude."

David took a deep breath. "Did you really think there wouldn't be consequences?"

"All right." Catherine sighed. "You won. There. I said it. You put your little gay fantasy on stage. You must be thrilled by those bare bums bouncing around. Enjoy it."

"I will."

"A pity you didn't get the one prize you really wanted."

"And what was that?"

"Your muse, of course. He eluded your bed, I understand."

"You understand nothing," David said sharply. When he spoke again, his tone was softer. "I accept my share of the blame. I should have seen how my affairs affected you, but was I supposed to be celibate for you?"

"You were supposed to be mine."

"If I ever gave you a reason to think I loved you romantically, it wasn't intentional."

"But you were happy to take my money."

"*Pardonne-moi* for being blunt, but I don't want you to call, text, email, fax, sky-write, smoke signal, yodel, or otherwise contact me ever again. You're toxic, and I want you out of my life. I'm willing to leave New York to be rid of you."

"No need to be so dramatic. It was a game. I lost. Director Halvorsen won't return my messages, and my so-called friends are conspicuously silent. I'm all but shunned."

"I have no sympathy for you. You hurt people, Catherine. People I care about."

"That's a good one." She laughed her brittle laugh. "You. Caring about people."

"Surprise! Somewhere along the way, I grew some compassion. You should try it."

Catherine's lip curled. "I see you're going with the self-righteous stance. Fine. You call *me*, then, when you get down from your high horse." She walked away but stopped after a few steps. She looked back.

David was gazing at the brownstone. Not once did he glance in Catherine's direction. He could no longer pretend her attitude was an inside joke. He saw her clearly, and he did not like what he saw, in himself as well as her. However, he had truly changed, and they could no longer fit together. He would never be able to give her what she wanted from him, and she would never be what he wanted. It was better for both of them that their dance ended here.

Epilogue

Two years later....

KELLY HOLLOWAY stood alone in the dance studio where he'd trained ballet's newest international star. He couldn't be prouder of Jule and what his student had accomplished in such a short time. It appeared that hardly anyone was immune to his protégé's unaffected charm. All around the world, record numbers of people were attending ballet performances.

Tonight, Kelly and Sasha were attending a special showcase at the Royal Opera House in Covent Garden. It had been nearly six months since Jule's last whirlwind visit, and they were looking forward to seeing him.

"Ready?" Sasha asked from the doorway.

Kelly turned and smiled at his partner. He held out his arms. "Do I look ready?"

"You know I love the way you look in formalwear. I know it isn't required for the performance, so thank you."

"Thank you for growing your hair out again."

"Such a child," Sasha said fondly. He took Kelly's hand. "Come on. Let's go see our boy."

When they arrived at the Opera House, Kelly and Sasha were passed backstage and directed to the dressing rooms. As they started down the hall, they saw Lucas coming toward them.

Lucas smiled. "Hey! Good to see you. Come with me."

Sasha took in Lucas's costume. "Tarzan?"

Lucas chuckled. "This is Marilee's new design for *Fireheart*'s first act. We're dancing the so-called Love Spark pas de deux. It's always a big hit. People love that big jump when Jule flies into my arms. Tonight, none other than Bram Silber, formerly of the San Francisco ballet, will be doing the Jule-tossing." He opened a door and gestured to Kelly and Sasha to precede him.

"Where's Jule?" Kelly asked after he looked around the room.

"I'll take you to him, but I'd like to talk to you first," Lucas said. "Please sit."

"Is something wrong?" Sasha asked.

"No." Lucas smiled. "At least, I hope not. That depends on what you say."

Kelly and Sasha sat and looked expectantly at Lucas.

"Okay." Lucas smiled again. "You know, maybe I should wait until I'm dressed more appropriately."

"Just spit it out," Kelly said.

"Okay." Lucas cleared his throat. "I love Jule with all my heart. I love him for all he is and will be. I love him for making me want to be a better person. I could go on all day about him, but I actually have a point." He cleared his throat again. "I want to ask Jule to marry me. So, I'm asking for your permission. Before you tell me to talk to his parents, I'm telling you that I think of you as his parents. That's probably disrespectful to Mr. and Mrs. Parry, but it's how I feel."

Kelly and Sasha exchanged a long look.

"I think I might cry," Sasha said.

"Do I have your blessing, though?" Lucas looked anxious. "If it makes a difference, I turn thirty next year, and I'll inherit a buttload of cash. No lie."

Kelly chuckled, and Lucas relaxed a little. "I'm honored you felt it was necessary to consult us," Kelly said. "Even if we aren't Jule's real dads."

"To him you are… and to me," Lucas said. "So?"

Kelly stood. "Where's Jule?"

"Uh, just down the hall." Lucas now looked confused.

Kelly took one of Lucas's arms. "Sasha?"

Sasha took Lucas's other arm. "It's okay," he said softly to Lucas. "This is Kelly's idea of gentle teasing."

"Are you sure?"

"It's how you can tell he likes you," Sasha confided. "Like a little boy, he teases you."

"Great." Lucas sighed. "It's the next dressing room."

KELLY KNOCKED and then opened the door. He grinned as Jule turned from a full-length mirror to face him. "Admiring ourselves, are we?" he joked.

Jule jumped into Kelly's arms and hugged him. "It's so good to see you," he said.

"Likewise." Kelly let go so Sasha could hug Jule. "If we're all reacquainted, Lucas has a question for you, Jule."

"Stop!" Lucas begged.

"Why?" Kelly shrugged. "No time like the present right?"

"Please! Let me do it my way."

"What's all this?" Jule looked from Lucas to Kelly and back again.

"We have to go on stage in half an hour," Lucas said. "This is *not* a good time."

Jule looked to Sasha.

Sasha shrugged, but he had a twinkle in his eyes.

Lucas sighed and then went down on one knee in front of Jule.

"What are you doing?" Jule asked, looking amused.

Lucas pulled the new ring off his little finger and proffered it on his palm. "Julian Richard Parry, will you do me the honor of wearing my ring as a token that you want to spend your life with me?"

"Well, sure," Jule said. "But I don't need a ring."

"Take the damn ring," Sasha said impatiently.

Jule glanced at his chosen fathers and the gravity of the situation finally impinged on him. He looked down into Lucas's eyes and saw the love that made them glow like sunlit honey. Gracefully, Jule lowered himself to kneel with Lucas.

"I'd be proud to be your partner until the end," Jule said.

Lucas took Jule's hand and slid the ring onto his finger. He pulled Jule into his arms and held him for several moments before letting go.

Jule gave Lucas a kiss and then got to his feet.

"It wasn't quite the romantic scene I had planned," Lucas said as he rose. "But the important thing is that you're mine." He gave Jule a wicked grin. "And soon, you'll be mine in a very real and legally binding way."

"You're absolutely mad, and I love it." Jule laughed. "But that was *Monty Python* not *Star Wars*."

"Is it too soon to lobby for an English wedding?" Kelly asked.

"Yes," Lucas said instantly.

Jule laughed. "I think Lucas has had enough for now. After the performance, we'll talk about it."

"Argh," Lucas groaned. "I just hope I can remember the steps."

"Just don't drop me." Jule winked and then took Lucas's hand. "Let's go show them how it's done."

Keep reading for an excerpt from
Table for One
by Connie Bailey!

Chapter One

COPELAND SHORE'S phone chimed and jarred his concentration. He glanced from his laptop screen to his wristwatch. He wore the atrociously expensive timepiece because it was a gift from his best friend and because it was a damned good watch. He registered the fact that it was now six minutes past seven just as his phone reminded him he'd received a text message.

"It is now xactly 7:05, Cope. Where the hell r u?"

A smile formed on Cope's full lips as he read the message from his boss, William Donnelly. Will was as subtle as a chili sauce colonic and always assumed he was in charge, but they'd been friends since college, and besides, Cope genuinely liked him. William played the sophisticated alpha male to perfection, but Cope knew it was just an act, and the competition kept him on his toes.

He took his charcoal-gray silk suit jacket out of the closet, slipped it on, and gathered his long, espresso-dark hair into a neat ponytail. Being chic wasn't just a personal choice; it was a prerequisite of his job at Collezione di Gio. The New York–based clothing company he worked for sold stylish sportswear for affluent young adults and expected its executives to dress with flair, but Copeland was more than just a sharp-dressed man. He was one of CdG's top troubleshooters, spending most of his time getting new store locations up and running. His reputation was that of a no-nonsense organizer with a crushing work ethic, and he used that well-crafted image to do half his work for him.

Cope's phone chimed again, and he automatically switched it to Vibrate. A new text message from Will informed Cope that it was now eight minutes after seven and that Cope was demonstrably not in the lobby. Cope considered begging off with the excuse that he was worn out from the transatlantic flight and the half day at the office.

It had been four months since he'd slept in his own bed. Milan had been nice, but he longed to reacquaint himself with his king-size mattress. He veered away from the thought that he had no one waiting for him at home. At one time, he'd been a romantic who hoped for true love, but now he settled for a warm body with a modicum of good manners. He hadn't given up on love completely, but he'd stopped waiting for his prince to come. He had a fairly steady stream of good-looking strangers to satisfy his sex drive, and he had Will for company.

Cope's phone vibrated, and he looked at the screen again.

"Do I have your attention? If this phone isn't up your butt, get down here now!"

Cope pocketed the phone and walked out of his eleventh-floor office to the elevator.

"What the hell?" Will greeted Cope as the elevator doors opened on the lobby of CdG's flagship store on Fifth Avenue. "I got us reservations at Bento Hadaka. If we aren't there on time, we'll be shunned." He looked for confirmation from the two men standing with him.

"Let me guess," Cope drawled. "It's the most exclusive restaurant in town."

"Too right!" said Drew Cooper, an Australian import known affectionately as Drooper. "Harder to get into than a nun's knickers. I've been desperate for a rez, but so far, they've not yielded to my manly charms. Welcome back by the way."

"Good to see you too," Cope said as he shook Drew's hand. "How are things Down Under?"

"That sounds like a double entendre," Will said with a laugh.

"Everything sounds like a double entendre to you," Cope said.

"Don't be jealous." Will grinned at Cope before he introduced the fourth member of the party. "This is Thompson Wells—Tom to you—straight out of Hotlanta, Gee Ay. He came on board as my assistant about two weeks after you left. I emailed you about him."

Cope nodded. "I remember. The whiz kid. Good to meet you," he said. He and Tom shook hands, and there were a few moments of silence before Cope spoke again. "Why are we standing around? I thought you were in a hurry."

"Asshole." Will grinned as he punched Cope's shoulder. "If you weren't a fucking genius *and* a world-class fuck, I'd—"

"Come on. Let's go," Drew interrupted. "I worked through lunch, and I could eat the ass end of a dead dingo, no lie."

"Yeah, let's go," Tom said. "I can't wait to see this place."

Will started for the door before Tom finished speaking, leaving the others to follow at their own pace. Tom fell into step with Drew as they crossed the lobby, and Cope strolled along in their wake, unabashedly eavesdropping.

"What did Will mean by that last remark?" Tom asked.

"About Cope being a world-class fuck?"

"Yeah."

Drew shrugged. "He probably means that Cope makes him come like a freight train with no brakes. The way Will tells it makes *me* want to give Cope a root."

"They're gay?" Tom's shock goosed his voice up a half octave.

"Mate, if you have a problem with poofters, let me suggest another line of work."

"I'm not a homophobe," Tom said quickly. "I just haven't been around very many gay people."

"You have now," Drew said. "When it comes to shagging, I'm equal opportunity."

"Good one," Tom said. "But this isn't really my kind of humor."

Cope stopped listening in on the conversation, and a lazy smile dimpled the corners of his lips when his gaze fell on Will, who was striding along as though he owned everything under his feet. As always, Will was impeccably put together, and his tall, long-limbed frame was the perfect rack for his suit. As Cope assessed Will's clothes with an expert's eye, he noticed little touches that showed how much he'd influenced Will's taste since they'd met. The boy Cope had met at freshman orientation would never have worn that shirt with a suit, no matter how well the black turtleneck flattered his fair hair and skin. The pearl-gray jacket was anything but conventional either; it ended at Will's waistline, displaying his toned buttocks and long legs in black silk serge trousers.

"So I'm a great fuck, am I?" Cope said as he caught up with Will at the curb.

"I believe the term I used was 'world-class.'" Will smiled. "Best I've had anyway." He cleared his throat. "Hey, listen, Tom isn't into the whole man-on-man thing."

"What was your first clue?" Cope fell easily back into the teasing, brotherly relationship as though he'd seen Will yesterday, instead of four months ago. "So what's the deal? You usually hire based on the applicant's looks and how quickly they can get on all fours with their cheeks spread. Tom's a looker, but I don't think he meets your second criterion."

"He *is* a good-looking kid, and you know I like the lanky ones." Will winked at Cope. "But he's as straight as the straightest thing you can think of. He's immune to innuendo, and gayness is so far out of his worldview that he assumes any mention of it is meant as a joke."

"That could make for an interesting evening." Cope shook off his jet lag and made up his mind to enjoy the night. "What are you doing later?"

"You." Will laughed at Cope's blank expression. "Isn't that what you were asking?"

"Not really, but I could use a little quality time between the sheets."

"You know I'm happy to get busy with you anytime. I wasn't kidding about you being a great fuck."

"You're not so bad either." Cope gave Will the sideways smile that he knew never failed to jump-start Will's libido.

Though they weren't a couple, they slept together from time to time. What had started out as curiosity in college had become a comfortable habit when each was between lovers. There was no question of them falling in love, but they knew each other's likes and dislikes, and in the bedroom, all trappings and façades were set aside, allowing them to simply be themselves, to take what they needed without strings.

Cope couldn't place a high enough value on the energetic sessions that left him drained, glowing, and content to just *be* for a little while. That didn't happen often in his world, and more and more, he found that what he really craved was peace—not wealth, not success or status, but peace and the time to enjoy it. Lately the words of poems he'd never got around to writing had been beating in his brain like the wings of moths around a lamp. Maybe he'd outgrown his ambition to be a force in the fashion industry. Maybe he should take a long, hard look at his life and ask some tough questions about where he was headed and whether it made him happy. And maybe he was just creating a little drama because this was his thirtieth birthday, the big Three-Oh, a supposed milestone in a person's life.

"What are you brooding about?" Will asked as he poked Cope in the ribs. "The car's here. Get in."

"A limo?" Cope stared at the long shiny car that came to a stop in front of them.

"Thirty is a significant age in a man's life and should not pass without proper notice being taken. Tonight is my present to you. We will celebrate in appropriately Roman style."

"Now I'm scared," Cope said in the joking manner he knew Will was expecting.

"Don't be silly. What's there to be afraid of?"

"The name, for one thing. *Bento Hadaka*? *Naked Lunch Box*? Really?"

Will grinned. "You're going to love it. I know what you like, and you'll love it, trust me. Now get in the damn car. I'm paying by the hour."

Cope smiled at Will's bluster. He climbed into the back of the limo, and the others followed. Will sat next to Cope, while Drew and Tom took seats on either side.

"The restaurant sounds really cool," Tom said. "Atlanta's a big city, but I bet you won't find anything like Bento Hadaka there."

"That Tokyo sales rep who had that luscious antique slubbed silk told me this place does sashimi and all kinds of sushi," Drew said. "He said if I went there I *had* to do the body shots."

"Sounds like we have no choice." Will smirked and nudged Cope.

Cope knew Will was waiting for him to ask, so he did. "So what's so special about this sushi bar anyway?"

"You'll see." Will's eyes gleamed gleefully. He was almost vibrating with happiness, overjoyed at having a chance to give his friend something truly special, and that was one of the reasons Cope loved him so much and indulged his less attractive qualities. "But let's just say, you can take something out of the dream box and add it to the scrapbook."

"I'm in your hands," Cope said. He sat back against the leather upholstery, prepared to enjoy the ride. He idly wondered which dream box wish would come true tonight, but he was content to wait and see.

BY SIX o'clock, the evening staff of the fashionable Bento Hadaka restaurant had arrived to get ready for work. In the employee locker room, two men were talking over the sound of a shower in the background as one dressed and the other undressed.

"Harlooooow?" Daimaru Tanaka crooned as he set his running shoes in the locker. He turned a winning gaze on friend and coworker

Masahiro "Call me Harlow" Nakamura, big doe eyes melting under jet-black bangs.

"What?" Harlow asked suspiciously. Whenever Dai gave him the puppy-dog eyes like the little prick-tease from his favorite movie *Carrie*, he tensed a little, wondering what outrageous thing his roommate might ask for. He was pretty sure Dai wasn't going to ask him to humiliate Carrie White at the prom, but you never knew with this guy. "What do you want?"

"We were going to play rock, paper, scissors for the shift tonight. Remember?"

Harlow stopping fussing with his tie and left it draped around his neck. The black silk was the color of his eyes and contrasted sharply with his platinum-blond hair. He paid dearly to touch up the dark roots once a week, but the hair was part of his signature look, and he was convinced that a signature look was essential to an aspiring dance star. He'd only left Tokyo two years ago, but he'd assimilated the local culture so quickly that strangers took him for a native New Yorker. "Why are we even talking about this? It's your turn."

"Come on, Harl. Be a sport."

Harlow narrowed his eyes. "Why do I let you get away with stuff like this? You got to wait tables last night. By rights, I should get my turn tonight. Plus, I'm already dressed."

"I gave you a ride home last night, remember? I asked if we could trade places tonight, and you said we'd play rock, paper, scissors for it."

"I must have been delirious with exhaustion. You give me a ride home every night."

"Yeah, because it's really tiring lying around for hours."

Harlow stuck out his lower lip. "You know it's not the work that tires me. It's the…." His voice trailed off as he searched for the right word.

Dai waited silently for Harlow to start talking again. Idly, he admired Harlow's compact gymnast's body in the crisp white shirt and black trousers. A toned physique was a requirement where they worked, and though neither Harlow nor Dai was planning on making a career of this job, they took pride in looking their best. Being gym partners was just another perk of their friendship.

"It's a strain," Harlow said. "You know?"

Dai nodded his understanding. "Yeah, it *looks* like all we do is just lie there, but it *is* a real strain having all those eyes on you. And the way they talk about you like you're not there."

Harlow nodded. "Sometimes I want to jump up and yell at them to have some common courtesy."

"But you grit your teeth and wait for it to be over."

Harlow nodded again. "Yeah."

Dai put an arm around Harlow and gave him a squeeze. "It won't be for much longer, man. The way you save money, you'll be able to quit soon."

"I hope so. I'm never going to get anywhere if I have to work full-time. I came to New York to dance on Broadway not to literally be furniture."

"I know that, and you'll get there."

"I need to practice, and I need to go to every audition. I need enough money in the bank to pay my bills for at least a year so I can concentrate on getting into a show."

"That's why you should switch places with me tonight. You'll make better tips."

"Let's settle it now." Harlow held up a hand and made a fist.

Dai brought his hand up at the same time, fore and middle fingers extended in a V.

"Ha!" Harlow shouted gleefully. "I win!"

"Fine," Dai said, opening his locker. "I'll just give you my tips."

"Don't be ridiculous. I'm not taking your hard-earned money."

"It's not as hard for me as it is for you." Dai's grin disappeared for a moment as he pulled his shirt over his head. "Honestly, I don't mind it so much."

"Exhibitionist."

Dai's grin reappeared. "I'm not a show-off," he said. "I'm just not as self-conscious as some people."

"Not now, but I remember your first night. You blushed so much the customers thought you were sunburned."

Dai chuckled. "You'd only been here two weeks when I signed on."

"Well, you know, when you've danced naked in front of an audience…." Harlow shrugged.

"Are you considering that stripper job again?"

"Very funny. You know it was an avant-garde ballet."

"I know I enjoyed it, but honestly, any time there are a half-dozen naked men I can stare at, I'm going to enjoy it."

Harlow shook his head. "Even when you're saying something like that, you have this air of… innocence, I guess is the word. You could be giving someone a blow job under the table and still look virginal."

"Yes, but we know differently, don't we?" Dai shucked his underwear and stepped out of them, leaving him completely naked. Even in the wan lighting, his skin glowed like satin draped over sculpted marble.

"You really are gorgeous," Harlow said.

"Come on. You see me naked almost every night. I'd think you'd be bored by now."

"No way. I'm knocked out every time."

Dai threw a towel at Harlow. "Knock it off, you big tease. You always compliment me, but you never do anything about it."

Harlow shrugged. "You're not my type."

"Bullshit," said Kei Ito as he came out of the shower room. "Dai is everyone's type." With a sly smile, Kei sidled up to Dai and nuzzled at his shoulder. "You have skin like a baby's butt," he said. "And you smell like cherry blossoms."

"Cherry blossoms don't have a scent." Dai brushed Kei off. "Quit screwing around. You just got clean."

Kei shrugged. "If I'm not sanitary enough for work, I'll take another shower. Want to join me?"

Dai rolled his eyes. Kei was a hottie, but he was a kid, and Dai wasn't interested in him at all. He wanted someone more sophisticated, which was the main reason he'd taken this job. Bento Hadaka's clientele was mainly wealthy businessmen who were much more refined than the guys Dai was used to. He wasn't a gold digger; he just wanted someone who'd take him somewhere besides arcades and cheap bars, someone whose conversation didn't revolve around the latest pop star or sports champion, someone who wanted a relationship that was more than a series of one-night stands. Maybe it was because he'd just turned twenty-four and being a quarter of a century old made him think about how he was spending his time. He was still young, but he didn't want to waste a single minute he had coming to him.

"Why won't you go out with me?" Kei persisted. "Harlow had no complaints."

"But no repeat performance," Dai retorted.

"Not after I realized Kei was systematically sleeping his way through the staff," Harlow said.

"But I'm doing the hottest ones first," Kei said, completely unrepentant.

"I'm going to take my shower," Dai said as he walked away. "See you guys up front."

"Come on," Harlow said, pulling Kei away. "Let's get to work."

Kei took one last look at Dai's heart-shaped ass and went with Harlow to get ready for opening time. There was always more side work to do.

CONNIE BAILEY is a Luddite who can't live without her computer. She's an acrophobic who loves to fly, a faultfinding pessimist who, nonetheless, is always surprised when something bad happens, and an antisocialite who loves her friends like family. She's held a number of jobs in many disparate arenas to put food on the table, but writing is the occupation that feeds her soul.

Connie lives with her ultralight-designer husband and Ickle Thelma the Wonder Whippet at a small grass-strip airfield halfway between Disney World and Busch Gardens. Connie enjoys painting, photography, and yard work. Logic and reality have had little to do with her life, and she likes it that way.

Blog: baileymoyes.livejournal.com

DREAMSPUN
BEYOND

SONG
AND KEY

Bekins & Bailey

So-called monsters won't
hold these spies back!

A Men from GLEN Mission

So-called monsters won't hold these spies back!

For two secret agents on a mission to a secluded Romanian village, the toughest fight they face may not be against the folktale monsters lurking in the foggy mountains and old ruins, but against their unlikely attraction to each other.

Keller Key is the top operative at the covert Global Law Enforcement Network—and boy does he know it. Sexy half-Ukrainian, half-Korean Sevastyan Song is a close second. When the agents go undercover to investigate an old friend's suspicious death, it soon becomes clear something sinister is afoot in the ancient forest and decrepit abbey. If an evil organization doesn't spell the end of them, the angry locals might. But if they're going to conquer their enemies, they need to keep their hands off each other and their minds on the case, in a rivals-to-lovers paranormal mash-up that gives new meaning to spy-on-spy action.

www.dreamspinnerpress.com

CONNIE BAILEY

TABLE FOR ONE

Exposing his body for work is no problem, but after his heart's been broken, putting it out there again won't be so easy.

Up-and-coming young executives Copeland Shore and William Donnelly have been friends and sometimes more for years. For Cope's birthday, Will plans a very special dinner—at a nantaimori restaurant where the most enticing thing is the table. Dai—the naked man beneath their sushi—has both their mouths watering, but when it comes to Dai's heart, there's only room at the table for one, and Will gets there first.

Will's everything Dai thinks he wants in a man... until he's betrayed. The betrayal also ends the friendship between Will and Cope and leaves Dai shaken and unsure if he can put his trust in another man— not even when a second chance for love and happiness rises from the ashes of the broken relationship. Cope wants to tempt Dai to take a risk with him, but the pain of the past is hard for Dai to shake off... and Cope has obstacles of his own to overcome.

www.dreamspinnerpress.com

DREAMSPUN
DESIRES

FINDING
FAMILY

Connie Bailey

When you find your family,
you'll do anything to keep it.

When you find your family, you'll do anything to keep it.

When Charles Macquarrie inherits a fortune and an international clothing company, he also inherits three young cousins he desperately needs help raising. By a stroke of luck, he discovers and hires Jonathan Lamb, who spent his life in a children's home due to chronic illness, to be his nanny.

If Jon thought a budding romance with his wealthy boss complicated his life, he has no idea of the hardships awaiting him when he's charged with embezzlement and kidnapping. But even when threatened by accounting discrepancies and mob connections, Jon and Charles won't let go of the family they've built together without a fight.

www.dreamspinnerpress.com